Journee & Juelz 2
A Dope Hood Love
Written By: Nikki Nicole

True Love Will Never Die, We Were Made For Each other, It's in the cards for us…

Acknowledgements

Hey you guys. I'm Authoress Nikki Nicole some of you may know me and some of you don't. I'm introducing myself. This is my seventh book. Journee & Juelz 2 is finally here.

I was in a really good writing space while writing this. Journee Leigh Armstrong and Juelz Thomas have been a pleasure to pen again. They have their own stance, they've grown a bit.

I want to thank God for giving me this gift to share with you, without him there is no me. I want to thank my supporters, I appreciate each, and every one of you guys. I always say, "If it's something that you want to do in life please do it. Step out on faith you have nothing to lose and everything to gain. I'll support you because you supported me and I'll help you because you helped me."

It's time for my **S/O Samantha, Tatina, Asha, Shanden (PinkDiva), Padrica, Chamyka, Darletha, Trecie, Valentina, Troy, Pat, Crystal, Reneshia, Toi, Ella, Ava, Snowie, Bacia, Sherelle, Shawn, Danetta, Blany, Karen.** The list goes on S/O to every member in my reading group, I love y'all to the moon and back. These ladies right here are a hot mess, I love them to death. They go so hard about these books it doesn't make any sense. Sometimes, I feel like I should run and hide sometimes.

If you're looking for us meet us in Nikki Nicole's Readers Trap on Facebook we are live and indirect all day.

S/O to My Pen Bae's **Ash ley, Chyna L, Ashley Robinson, Quanna Lashae, T. Miles, Brittany Pitteard**, I love them to the moon and back head over to Amazon and grab a book by them also.

To my new readers I have two complete series available

Baby I Play for Keeps Series 1-3

For My Savage, I Will Ride or Die Series

He's My Savage, I'm His Ridah

Join my readers group **Nikki Nicole's Readers Trap on Facebook**

Follow me on **Facebook Nikki Taylor**

Like my Facebook Page **AuthoressNikkiNicole**

Instagram **@WatchNikkiwrite**

email me *authoressnikkinicole@gmail.com*

Join my email contact list for exclusive sneak peaks.
http://eepurl.com/czCbKL

Contents

Chapter 1-Juelz

"Nikki your cries ain't gone fucking save her. Get your wife Skeet. Journee answer my fucking question, before you end up seeing your mother sooner than you would like. Ms. Julissa, I'm sending your oldest child home today to join you. Get her spot ready right next to you. I promise you, I will kill your lying ass right here, right now in front of your child.

You don't fucking know me like you think you do. Do you know how bad I want another child? Jueleez looks just like me, you better tell me something right fucking now!"

"She ain't yours Juelz get the fuck up out of here," she argued and cried.

"Oh, so your actually about to sit up here in my face and lie to me, like she didn't come up of my nut sack. Nikki take my child up out of here so I can handle my business. I hate bitches that lie and steal. Keep it real with me." I pounded my fist in my hands and paced back and forth, pulled out my extended clip and loaded my Draco back up. I'm pushing Journee's shit back fuck that, if she wanted me to make an example out of her I would.

"Journee, please stop lying and just tell him truth. damn Juelz this your daughter." Skeet's wife Nikki cried.

"I want to hear it from Journee's mouth, I didn't fucking ask you, Nikki I asked her. Tell me what the fuck I need to here, before I make this Draco clap."

"Yes, she's yours Juelz, now get the fuck up out of my place of business," she argued, cursed, and cried, and then took my daughter to the back.

"Watch your mouth you ain't off the hook, I should be the one crying. I haven't done shit to you Journee, but love you and you weren't worthy of that. You kept my daughter from me, how could you? Never play God with a nigga like me." I argued back, I followed right behind her.

Journee took everything from me, she took my heart, and never gave it back that's why I'm heartless. I'm a ruthless ass nigga, I kill for fun fuck our past. To make matters worse, you had my first born and you kept her away from me. What more do you want from me? I don't deserve this shit, yeah, I fucked up a few times, but I'm sorry. I cheated once, name a nigga or a bitch who hasn't.

Journee

My secret is out. Yes, Jueleez is Juelz daughter but hold up before y'all start talking shit and judging me. I don't have to deal with Juelz if I don't want too, that was my choice. I can raise my child without him I've been doing just fine.

No, she doesn't call Kairo her dad, she knows he's not her father. I should've listen to Nikki a long time ago, but I didn't, that's what happens when niggas go looking for shit they need to leave alone.

I don't have to deal with the shit that comes with him. Kairo and I discussed this plenty of times, and my answer remains the same. Do I care that Juelz feelings is hurt? Fuck no! I'm pissed that he did this is front of Jueleez.

I understand that you're mad at me, but don't act this way in front of my child. You can lash at me behind closed doors, and do what the fuck you need to do. My child should've never saw any of this.

I picked Jueleez up and carried her to my office she was crying hysterically, she's not use to this type of shit.

I finally calmed Jueleez down. Our breakfast was ruined and my restaurant was a fucking mess. I can only imagine the fucking tab to get this shit fixed, so I can open back up tomorrow for business. My window needs to be repaired. Juelz was standing in the door looking at us, and grilling the fuck out of me. I knelt in front of Jueleez so I could speak with her and explain to her what's going on.

"Jueleez, I'm so sorry about all of this ok, please forgive me? I will never put you in harm's way, or your life in jeopardy. Juelz Thomas, is your father I made a mistake, I was young and dumb, hard-headed and going through a lot. I shouldn't have kept him from you, I made permanent decisions on temporary emotions. Give him a chance please." I cried.

"I forgive you mommy," my daughter stated and hugged me.

"Thank you."

Thank God Jueleez forgave me, I couldn't take her being mad at me. She is everything to me, I love my little princess to death. She turned around, and looked at Juelz they just stared at each other.

"Hi Jueleez, I'm Juelz your father, I'm so sorry that I over reacted, I'm sorry for using foul language. A man should never speak to a woman that way. I'm asking for your forgiveness. I WAS in love with your mother, she took my HEART, and never gave it back. I love you, and to know that she kept you from me, for eight years is a tough pill to swallow.

I will never hurt you, BUT I will hurt anybody that think they can come between you and me. I want to get to know you. I want you to meet your grandmother, grandfather, uncle, and sister. Can I have a hug?" he asked and was looking more at me than his child.

"I forgive you. Don't hurt my mother please, she said she was sorry. Mommy, can you apologize to my father? Can I call you daddy or Juelz?" My daughter stated as she hugged her father.

"You can call me daddy I'd prefer that, but if you need time to adjust you can call me Juelz," he stated.

I swear to God I should beat Jueleez ass she's too damn grown. What do I need to apologize to him for?

"I'm sorry Juelz." I looked him in his eye so he could know that it's real.

"I'm keeping my daughter for a week or so, she needs to meet my family. Does she have a phone? If not, I'll get her one and we'll see you later," he argued.

"She has a phone. All I ask is that you keep Giselle away from my daughter that's it, and you can do you. Give me a kiss Jueleez I'll see you later FaceTime me before you go to bed and be on your best behavior."

"Jueleez, grab your stuff, and let me speak with your mother in private please," he stated.

"What is it now?" I argued and rolled my eyes.

"Journee you're not in the business to have any attitude with me. You fucking disgust me. To think I loved you. I still want a DNA test, get me a spoon and put your fucking mouth on it," he argued and picked me up by my neck and slammed me against the wall. He smashed my face up against my desk.

"I almost killed your dumb ass out there, I hate liars you know that. I should've killed you," he yelled in my ear.

"It's not too late."

"You ready to die, because I can make that shit happen in less than a minute," he argued.

"Get your fucking hands off me." I yelled and attempted to catch my breath.

"Shut the fuck up before my daughter hears you," he yelled and put his hands over my mouth.

I bit his fingers so hard until I could feel his bones crack, I could taste his blood in my mouth. He let me go, and I pushed him so hard he almost fell.

"Stay away from me, I don't even put my hands-on women, but I'll fuck you up every chance I get. Since you thought it was cool to play with me," he argued.

"In case you forgot, I have been staying away from you, BUT if you ever put your hands on me again; I put it on my mother, and God can take me right now, you will not be able to use them." I spat his blood up out of my mouth.

"Mommy what's wrong what happened to your hair? Daddy what happened to your hand you're bleeding? You need a band aid mommy clean his hand up," my daughter asked.

"Nothing is wrong Jueleez. My hair is itching I need to wash it so I scratched it."

"Clean up my daddy's hand mommy please," my daughter asked.

"Ok Jueleez I'll do it."

I swear Jueleez is getting on my last fucking nerves since he popped up. I know my mother is laughing at me. Gosh I wish she was here right now.

"Come here Juelz so I can clean your hand please?" I couldn't even look at him. I pulled out my first aid kid and cleaned the wound and blood off his hand.

He was staring at me. I poured alcohol all over his bite. I heard him cuss under his breath, but I didn't have the energy to even go back and forth with him. I need to fix my window and start my day over. I have money to make.

"Thank you Journee we're about to head up out of here, she'll call you later," he stated.

I waived bye to Jueleez she was so happy to go with her father.

<u>Nikki</u>

Oh Lawd. I told Journee this shit would happen the other day. Did she listen? Hell no, I knew he was going to find out. For the record, I didn't agree to any of this shit. I can't make anybody do nothing that they don't want to do.

I feel so bad for Juelz he wants another baby so bad. Giselle has had so many abortions the bitch can't give him anymore kids. He has Giselle's daughter, but I know she isn't his and he's too dumb to see it. Jueleez looks exactly like him there's no comparison.

"Nikki, did you know about this?" my husband asked.

"Yes, Skeet but I told her to tell him, I can't make nobody do shit they don't want to do."

"Miss me with that shit she's almost eight years old. You foul for that one. I can't believe I've been laying next to your lying ass, and you keeping secrets from me. Loyalty don't even matter right now. If he would've killed her I wasn't about to stop him because she's dead wrong.

Y'all playing God and dictating this man relationship with his daughter," he argued and gritted his teeth.

"Skeet calm down it's not our business. Let Journee and Juelz handle their stuff."

"I understand what you're saying, but do you know how this shit looks to my nigga? It's our business when you know about the shit. I lay down with you every night, and didn't even know that Journee had a kid by my nigga. She's the same age as Lil Skeet that shit is not cool at all," he argued.

"I'm sorry Skeet, please forgive me. It wasn't my business to tell."

"Nikki, the shit is wrong on all levels. Nothing is right about this situation at all. Loyalty is priceless, but damn the line has to be drawn somewhere," he argued.

"I understand where you're coming from Skeet I made a mistake, but that's some shit that Journee and Juelz need to deal with, not you and me our shit is solid. Trust me I was in Journee's ear on a numerous occasions about this situation but she didn't listen."

"Nikki, I don't give a fuck. You should've opened your fucking mouth. She would've been mad, but she would've gotten over that shit. He had the right to know," he argued.

"Skeet, I know I'm sorry." I pouted.

"Nikki, don't try to guilt trip me, I'm not the one you need to apologize too. I'm mad at you. I can't even look at you right now. I'm so disappointed in you," he explained.

"Tell me what I have to do for you to forgive me?"

"It's nothing that you can do right now, we'll talk about this shit at home," he argued.

"I love you Skeet, I'm not coming home, I'm staying at my mother's house. I'm sorry your being too hard on me." I pouted.

"No, the fuck you ain't, take your ass home now! I love you too, but don't guilt trip me. I'll see you at home," he stated.

"I'm not trying to do that. I promise you. I'm sorry and this is the reason that I wanted her to say something a long time ago, because I didn't want any issues between me and you because of this. I already knew how you would act." I cried.

"Come here, don't cry man. I love you. I'm not trying to be hard on you. Don't ever in your life pull a fucking stunt like this again. It's not even about being loyal, think about how your husband would feel if he found out," he stated as he wiped my tears and kissed my lips.

Thank God, my tears get my husband every time. I already knew how he would act. Don't get me wrong my husband isn't a sucker, but he's crazy, and when he's mad at you he'll be mad for a long time.

I wasn't going out like that behind Journee. I love her to death, and I wouldn't trade her for nothing in the world. My husband would punish me just because Juelz was still in his feelings, and that's his best friend. I see now exactly what Skeet was saying about staying out of people's business. It's different for females versus males. I've learned my lesson she almost got killed.

Journee

Tears cascaded down my face as Jueleez and Juelz left my office. My eyes were puffy and red. My hair was in shambles from Juelz roughing me up. Scratches adorned my neck, and traces of his blood were on the corners of my lips.

I fucked up good, and I'm woman enough to admit that. I own up to all my shit. I know I hurt Juelz I wanted him to feel my pain. I'll apologize to Juelz again. I'm sure he doesn't want that from me. I should've never denied him from Jueleez looks so much like her father it's crazy. I can't change the past. I can only mold the future.

"Damn bitch that nigga fucked you up good. You deserve that shit. I told you to tell him BUT nooooo you just had to do shit your way. If he would've killed you then what? We've been friends more like sisters all our lives.

I would never steer you wrong. You know my loyalty lies with you. I'm riding with you right or wrong," she stated as she stood in the door way of my office with her hands on her hips.

"I fucked up Nikki, and you were right. I can't take back nothing I did. I don't regret any of it. Given the chance, would I do some shit different absolutely. I would've told Juelz sooner but I was a bitch, THAT bitch.

I never knew that he would catch me. I feel like shit he did all of that in front of Jueleez, but she loves him already. Her eyes lit up looking at him. I couldn't even smile, he was grilling the shit out of me. He tried to kill me. He choked slammed me. He wants a DNA test. He took his daughter."

"I hate to say, I told you so, but I knew how he would react. Juelz is crazy that nigga loved your dirty panties up until today. That's why I came by the other day. I felt that shit coming. I didn't know that it would be so soon.

Girl, a bitch was in tears when that nigga started shooting. Did you see the snot threatened to escape my nose? I almost had a heart attack. Bitch you know my face was beat to the gawds, and it was ruined because I thought he was about to kill you.

What the fuck were you thinking when you told him she wasn't his? I picked your casket out as soon as you let that shit roll off your tongue. I wouldn't trip off a DNA test because she's his, he can't deny that one. I wonder did he get DNA test for Kassence? Ain't no way she's his child, I'm taking bets on this one.

I'm happy he finally got to meet his daughter and laid hands on her mammy. Now my God-daughter doesn't have to be a secret any more. Her Godmother can take her to Bankhead and play with the black kids and do ghetto shit," she laughed.

"Nikki, you a gawd damn fool. He wasn't about to kill me, he was hurt, and that's how he responded. Look at my restaurant it's a fucking mess. I must get my window fixed and some new wall and light fixtures replaced. Thank God Kairo left me with his Black Card. How are we supposed to co-parent?"

"No bitch, that nigga was going to kill you, make no mistake, and never let that shit slip your mind even for a minute. Jueleez would've been motherless real shit. Juelz isn't pulling out a gun just because, and he gave you the opportunity to tell the truth.

How are you going to fix this? My husband is mad at me. Fuck Kairo, he's gone again? Damn he just came back. Journee that nigga got some shit going on, and you're too dumb too not see that," she explained.

"I don't know. I need to speak with Skeet first, I can't have y'all two at odds because of me. Juelz and I need to have a sit down. My heart hurts Nikki."

"Good, it should hurt you'll be all right. You need to wake up and realize what the fuck Kairo has going on. All he does is flood you with money, cars, clothes, diamonds, gold, and trips to Islands you can't even pronounce, and he buys you a new house every year. Why hasn't he married you after all the years you guys have been together. If y'all two are so in love?

What's the hold up? Let me say this Journee you're the strongest female I know besides my mother, don't be nobody's fool. Wake up and ask that motherfucker what the deal is? Don't let what he does for you cloud your mind, because last I checked you didn't need a nigga for shit not even no hard dick.

I know something is going on between the two of y'all because you only drive that Benz truck to piss him off, when the two of you are having a disagreement. The Benz truck got you fucked up today. God don't make any mistakes it was time for you and Juelz to reconnect," she voiced her opinion in many ways.

"Nikki, I hear you and I'm listening. If Kairo ever played me I put it on Julissa Armstrong he wouldn't live to tell about it. I will pull the fucking skin off him it'll be nothing but blood and flesh. You thought what I did to Juelz was hell. I have a beast lying inside of me ready to explode, and begging to be freed.

I'm grown ass woman. I'm real about my shit. Kairo is my everything. I love him, but I'm not in love with him. We made a bond that we'll never cheat on each other because of what we went through.

If he broke that shit Nikki I will fuck him up, probably kill him. We had a disagreement the other night when I came home. He has somebody following every move I make, and they had pictures of me getting in the car with Juelz the night we met up at Kapture.

As soon as I was about to lay down. He shoved his phone in my face with an attitude. We argued for hours he accused me of cheating and he left. We never argue and he knows I will never cheat on him. I'll walk away first." I argued and clapped my hands together.

"Calm down. I'm going to be honest with you, I think that motherfucka cheating. I could be wrong, but he has some shit going on. I'm not just saying this because

Juelz is back on the scene. Pay attention to how he moves," she stated.

"I'm as calm as can be."

"Sit back and observe," she stated.

"Kairo is one man that I would never have to question. He's perfect in every aspect. We've been together for so long we balance each other out."

"I hear what you are saying, think about what the fuck I said," she stated.

"Nikki do you know something that I don't know?"

"If I did I would've exposed him all ready, for your sake and not mine. He better be everything you claim he is. I just don't trust him, I have a good judge of character," she revealed.

Chapter 2-Juelz

Love is motherfucker. Journee is the one female I can honestly say, I loved besides my mother. I refused to love another female that's not my daughter's. My heart ain't up for grabs no more. I took that shit back from Journee today. How could you do that to me? I thought I was heartless, she broke me with that revelation.

I don't love Giselle. I just tolerate her because she's the mother of my child. If Journee thought she hated me before, and was mad about the little petty shit. She hasn't seen anything yet. I could give two fucks about her.

Journee could do no wrong in my eyes, she was everything to me. I haven't met a woman yet that could compare to her. I know I cheated yeah, I stuffed my dick inside of Giselle on numerous occasions. Real niggas do real shit.

I was young and dumb. I'm man enough to admit I was wrong and I fucked up. I don't know how many times I apologized, and said I was sorry. The fact remains the same you kept my daughter from me for eight years for that reason alone I could never fuck with a bitch like you.

Every time I see you I will put my fucking hands on you if my daughter ain't around. When I pulled my gun out and let that bitch rip, the devil was on my back telling me to push that bitches shit back for playing with a nigga like me.

It's not too many times that I spared a motherfucker that has been deceitful to me. She had better thank God for Jueleez, because I could feel her eyes staring a hole in me begging me not to hurt her mother.

After I choked slammed Journee and attempted snatch her hair from her scalp. I had to rough her up so she could feel me. I have never man handled a female the way I handled her. I was in love with this bitch. To physically put my hands on her and hurt her. I knew the love was gone. I couldn't stand the site of her.

She dictated my life, she made choices for me that I didn't agree with. It'll never be the same no more. If it's not about Jueleez it's not about nothing. Truth be told Journee wouldn't ask me for anything she has too much pride.

I gave her the opportunity to tell me the truth and she still wanted to lie.

My daughter and I walked out of Journee's office with my hand wrapped up from her biting me like she was a fucking dog. She ruined my fit for today. I can't believe I had to fuck her up. Jueleez is so smart she paid attention to detail.

She knew something happened between her mother and me. She made sure her mother fixed the wound that she inflicted on me. We walked toward the entrance of the restaurant. Journee's employees were cleaning up my mess.

They waived at Jueleez. I walked toward Skeet I needed my nigga to drive. I was fucked up and my finger felt like it was broken.

"Skeet, ride with me. Jueleez this is your uncle Skeet." I threw him my keys.

"Are you Lil Skeet's and Nyla 's daddy?" my daughter asked.

"Yes, I am," he stated.

"I'm Jueleez Monroe Armstrong. Those are my cousins. We went to Disney World with our Grandmother Valerie last month. We had fun," my daughter stated.

"Oh, for real. I bet y'all did. We'll have to go back one day soon so your father and I can have fun too," he stated.

Jueleez Monroe Armstrong. She has my whole fucking name expect my last name. If this bitch could piss me off anymore. You cared enough about me to name my daughter after me, but you denied me to know her. I need to get this DNA test done asap.

Jueleez needs my last name and I need to sign her birth certificate. My mom is going to go ape shit when she sees my mini me. My mom will have a few words for Journee. It's not going to be anything nice.

Skeet

I'm not believing this shit. I didn't know what the fuck was going on when Juelz called me. I wasn't expecting this shit right here. I'm pissed with my wife never in a million years, would I think that she would help Journee pull this shit off.

I know it's not our business, but Juelz is my nigga, and you don't get a nigga back like that. I can't even look at Journee the same no more, she almost lost her life behind this shit. Yeah Juelz fucked up years ago they both were young, get over that shit and move on. He could've known his daughter despite what y'all went through.

"You good."

"Hell nah," he stated.

"I didn't know about this shit."

"I know I saw you grilling the fuck out of Nikki. If I wouldn't have come here today I still wouldn't know. I hate I lost my composure in front of my baby girl. I took one look at her, and I knew she was mine. I still love Journee that's why I'm so mad.

I wasn't even going to trip until she told me to leave. She still didn't want me to know her after I saw

Jueleez. I put my hands on Journee. I don't even get down like that, I lost it," he explained.

"I understand where you're coming from. I don't agree with you putting your hands on her, you need to apologize. Y'all must co-exist because a child is involved. I'm pissed too, she knows Lil Skeet and Nyla and don't know me."

"I peeped that, take me over Smoke's house. Journee said she didn't want Jueleez around Giselle. What the fuck am I supposed to do? Kassence and Jueleez don't look shit a like do they?" he asked.

"Okay, Hell no, Kassence doesn't even look like Giselle. I swear when I looked at Jueleez I was like damn Journee you foul as fuck. Tell Giselle the truth. You can't really blame Journee for not wanting her around her. The whole situation was messy, but that was years ago. Giselle would probably feel some type of way about you and Journee sharing a child together."

<u>Khadijah</u>

I can't believe Journee did that foul as shit. I had no clue that Juelz was Jueleez father. Me and Smoke have been chilling heavy since we met back up two weeks ago. I'm chilling at Smoke's house and Juelz and Skeet walk in with my niece Jueleez.

He ran up on me going off talking about why didn't I tell him about Jueleez. I was confused I didn't know what the fuck he was talking about. He said that Jueleez was his daughter. I knew Kairo wasn't her daddy. I thought Journee had sneaky pussy, and didn't know who fathered Jueleez.

Now that I think about it Jueleez looks exactly like Juelz and Smoke. Jueleez ran up to me and hugged me and told me that Juelz is her daddy. She's going to be staying with him for a few weeks, and her mommy and daddy were fussing. Smoke looked at me like he was disgusted. I introduced Jueleez to her uncle Smoke.

She shook his hand and she said, I'm Jueleez Monroe Armstrong she's so proper it doesn't make any sense. Smoke fell out laughing. I wanted to know what was so funny? He said that Juelz name was Juelz Monroe Thomas.

The joke was on me. I told Smoke that I'll talk to him later I had to get up with Journee's lying ass. It makes since now, she was fucking Juelz the whole time, that's why that girl came to the house and they fought.

We moved because she was pregnant and she was running from him. Why couldn't you just say that. I must talk to Journee face to face. The conversation couldn't even be done over the phone. I was so pissed at Journee. I called Nikki and she didn't even answer. I know why now, she's not slick. I made it to Journee's restaurant in about thirty minutes it was a mess.

The window was broken and shattered, I didn't care. I walked to the back of the restaurant like I owned this motherfucka. I walked toward Journee's office, it was a mess. She was crying, I don't give a shit about her tears.

"Damn Journee I'm your sister and you weren't woman enough to tell me that Juelz was Jueleez father. I should've found out from the horse's mouth, and not his."

"Khadijah I'm sorry, let me explain," she cried.

"What are you crying for? Did he put his hands on you?"

"We fought Khadijah but I'm fine. Look Juelz is Jueleez father she's named after him. I wanted to tell you a few days ago when Nikki wanted you to meet us but you didn't come. I never said anything before because I was ashamed and embarrassed, and I felt like I was disgrace. The first time I had sex I got pregnant.

Mother told me before she died that I should never give myself to a man if he wasn't worth it. Juelz was my first love. He was everything to me, the day that Giselle came to our house, and revealed that he was cheating on me with her, it was a wrap.

To make matters worse a few weeks after we moved when your dad took you guys to Disney World. I went back to the West Side to see what was up with him. He was with another bitch oh it got worse. Nikki called me later that day and told me some more stuff about him and Giselle that same day. I was done.

I passed out that nigga broke me, I found out that I was pregnant a few weeks later. I chose not to deal with him. I probably shouldn't have taken that route, but I did what I had to do," she explained.

"Journee, you're wrong for that. You're my sister and I love you no matter what, and I'm riding with you right or wrong. I'm woman enough to tell you that you fucked up. You're the strongest female I know besides my mother, and he didn't break you that bad for you to do that.

No matter what he did to you, and how you felt about him he should've been in Jueleez life from day one. You were selfish as fuck, and instead of you facing your problems you ran from them. You moved us way across town because of him."

"Khadijah, let me clarify some shit for you. Don't judge me, you couldn't walk a mile in my shoes. I've been raising you for as long as I can remember. I've made so many sacrifices for you, and I wouldn't trade any of it.

I never had a childhood, but guess what I made sure you had the best of every fucking thing. I took penitentiary chances to make sure you and Khadir were good clothes and shoes wise. Yeah, I did move us across town to get away from him, that was the best decision I ever made despite the circumstances.

I changed our surroundings so you wouldn't be the fast ass thirteen-year-old girl who was ready to fuck because her friends were. We moved not because of Juelz, we moved because I wanted the best for you and Khadir. If I didn't do anything right in my life I raised you how my mother would've wanted me too. I don't give a fuck about nothing you're saying or how you may feel about me I'll take it," she argued.

"Journee, don't flip this shit on me. I appreciate everything that you do and have done for me. You were wrong bottom-line, I wanted you to know that. I'm your blood and you couldn't even tell me. Juelz thought I knew and he approached me on some rah-rah shit, I'm in the blind.

I tell you everything, you're my personal diary. I'm just hurt that you didn't tell me. I trust you with my life but you don't trust me at all." I cried

"Khadijah, don't cry come here. I love you and I'm sorry I kept that from you. I didn't tell you because you look up to me and I didn't want you to follow me. I felt like I failed you. It's nothing wrong with having sex, but I had to be your mother and not your sister in that situation. I prayed every night that you didn't have sex early, and get pregnant because you were curious," she explained.

"Journee, I understand I really do. So where do y'all go from here with co-parenting and Kairo?"

"I don't know Khadijah, everything happened so fast. I haven't even called Kairo. I must get this window and light fixtures fixed, he tore up my restaurant," she stated.

"I see, are you ok? Jueleez looks exactly like him. If Juelz wants his family what are you going to do?"

"Juelz made it clear that I disgust him, and it could never be us and I'm cool with that," she stated.

"He's just upset eventually he'll get over it. Y'all love each other I knew it was a reason when we went out y'all were acting different toward each-other. Journee, you had to know that he would find out. The day I ran into him his face lit up like a kid on Christmas. I should've known. I'm about to leave, let me know how your visit with Ms. Simone goes." I smirked.

Chapter 3-Journee

Juelz, really put his hands on me. I'm livid. I need to call my protector where is he when I need him.

"Yeah," he answered with an attitude.

"Where are you, I need you." I cried.

"What's wrong? I'm not in the states right now. Do I need to come home, or I can send Free or security," he asked?

"I need you to come home now. Juelz found out about Jueleez. He came to the restaurant this morning, and busted the window, and shot at me. He took Jueleez." I cried.

"Journee, did he put his fucking hands on you," he argued and asked?

"No."

"Alright FaceTime me so I can see the damage," he asked?

I did as I was told. He hit his FaceTime button before I did. I answered.

"Journee, look at me," he stated.

I hesitated a little bit because I knew he was about to trip. I didn't want him to do anything crazy. I looked at him. Kairo knows me like a book?

"I'm going to ask you again, did he put his hands on you? Journee don't lie because the way you look right now I'm guessing that motherfucka did," he asked.

"Yes, Kairo we had a scuffle that's it." I cried.

"Journee, I told you to tell him years ago, but no you were to stubborn. I can't blame him for being mad, BUT I can fuck him up for putting his hands on you. I'm on my way. I'll be home tonight. I love you go ahead, and get whatever you need fixed," he stated.

"I know."

"Next time you need to listen, when somebody's trying to tell you something. It's for your own good. I got you no matter what. You got the black card get everything you need. I need to talk to him too. He could've did shit differently," he stated.

I placed my phone down on my desk, and started cleaning up my office. It was a mess papers scattered everywhere, and specs of Juelz blood stained the hardwood floors. The company that was fixing the light fixtures were out installing new ones.

The window was getting replaced as we speak. I couldn't even open today with the mess Juelz has caused. My phone alerted me that I had text from an unknown number.

404-286-3209- I'm sorry for putting my hands on you. You don't have to forgive me, but I want you to know that I'm sorry.

I wasn't even about to respond because I didn't have anything to say. My only focus was putting my restaurant back together so I could open back up tomorrow.

***

Three hours later and my restaurant was back to normal. I locked up, and headed to my truck and prepared my drive home. I need to get rid of this truck for good. It's practically brand new. I guess God has a funny way of doing things.

I haven't drove this truck in about three years. The first time in three years, I drive this truck and he pops up, and gets ahold of my secret. My heart dropped when he banged on the window and saw Jueleez. I knew it was over.

Jueleez, asked me was that her dad she looked at him and she automatically knew it was him. Thank God, she wasn't traumatized by his actions. Hopefully we can move on from this soon.

I miss my baby, but thank God for this break. I'm about to let my hair down. Kairo said he was coming home tonight. We'll see, if he doesn't he's not ready for my wrath. Let me call Alexis Nicole to see what she's up too.

Alexis is like the sister I never had. I met her through Kairo eight years ago, she's Free's fiancé we hardly ever get to hang out because she's a Marine and she's been stationed overseas for seven years.

We talk everyday via Skype or FaceTime. She's served her time and she's not re-enlisting. She likes to cook too, so we are going in business together to open an upscale restaurant in Midtown. Let me call my best bae and see what she's up too?

"Umm I was waiting on you to call me. I heard about you," she laughed.

"Oh, you did, well damn why didn't you pull up to come and see about me."

"Girl, Nikki said Juelz showed his ass, I can't wait to meet him. I don't do baby daddy drama, and street niggas with guns. Where's my niece? Does he have any cousins for me? I like my men crazy like a loose cannon," she asked and laughed.

"Y'all hoes ain't shit, so y'all been laughing at my expense behind my back today? Call Nikki's ass on three-way right now. I bet she didn't tell you that snot was running down her nose when she was crying because she thought he was about to shoot me." I laughed.

"Oh she told me, she didn't leave shit out. Journee why did you tell that man Jueleez wasn't his? I just knew you was a dead bitch when Nikki said that," she laughed.

"Alexis, bitch I was scared, this lunatic banged on my fucking window like a madman. I jumped out of my fucking skin. I told him to leave, he got a big ass brick and busted the window open, and climbed in that motherfucka, and Jueleez is laughing while he's doing it. She said mommy my daddy crazy. You know she's a good actress, but girl when that nigga pulled out a gun she started crying."

"Journee, stop lying all of this couldn't have happened today? I'm taking Jueleez to audition for Disney.

I like Juelz and haven't even met him yet. So, Jueleez is calling him daddy already? Momma will be calling daddy too pretty soon," she laughed.

"No, the fuck I won't. Trust me that nigga said I disgust him he choked me out, then he had the nerve to apologize via text. I'm in love with Kairo."

"So, the kiss y'all shared, and him playing in your pussy a few weeks ago didn't mean shit? Fuck Kairo and Free. Free up to some shit, he's been moving funny. I'll tell you this Journee, whatever you do in the darks comes to the light. I'm not going to go look for anything, but if Free has been cheating on me and it lands in my lap. I'm bodying that nigga right where the fuck he stands," she stated.

"Calm down. The kiss, and him playing in my pussy didn't mean anything to me. Girl if Kairo cheated on me. I would pull the skin off him and carve his fucking eyes and lips off him and send his body back to Africa. Kairo has been doing some strange shit too. I'm not going to go looking for anything either. I don't have time, let's go eat and get something to drink. Fuck talking about niggas and beating ass."

"Ok that's cool. Call Nikki and Khadijah too. Let's go to Kapture, maybe I can meet some potential. Let me tell you this right quick before I hang up. I went by Farrah's this morning and guess who was sitting up in that bitch sipping tea?" she stated.

"Who."

"Kairo's ex-wife Tyra," she revealed.

"What the fuck is she doing at Farrah's, she swore up and down she hated and despised that bitch."

"Girl, your guess is as good as mine, but you know I can't hold water I was spilling that shit. Farrah was smiling all up in her face. My loyalty lies with you, I never liked Tyra or Farrah and those bitches never liked me. I was giving you the heads up," she explained.

"I appreciate you. Kairo is supposed to come home today. If he doesn't come home like he's supposed too, then I'll know that something's up. I'm going to get off this phone. I want some Mexican and margaritas pick a spot and shoot out a group text I'll meet you there. No Kapture hot ass."

I love Alexis. I swear I'm blessed to have her and Nikki in my life. I wouldn't trade them for shit, they keep it real no matter what. My mother always told me, never go looking for anything, and don't run to no fights. What's in the dark will always come to the light. I have too much shit going on to be focused on what a nigga ain't doing.

I must call my brother Skeet and apologize. I can't have him being mad at his wife because of me.

"Yeah," he answered with an attitude.

"Skeet, brother, what's up don't be mad at me? I'm sorry. Nikki didn't have anything to do with my decisions. It was all on me. I'm sorry I dragged y'all in my mess."

"Journee, you know that you're my sister no matter what, I'm mad at you real shit. I wouldn't expect you to do that shit right there. I can't stay mad at you forever, but I feel like you should've came to me. I don't agree with you keeping her from him, you kept her from me too. My kids know her, but I don't.

It was selfish. He should've been there from day one. You live and you learn. I'll accept your apology, but I'm still mad at yo ass and Nikki too, she's still in the doghouse. I don't want to see you until my birthday. You need to apologize to Juelz too, you hurt him, put your pride aside and handle your business." He explained.

"I am. Trust me thank you for listening I'm sorry. I'm going to let you go. I hope Juelz can be as forgiving as you, but that's too much like right."

"He'll come around just apologize, I'll talk to you later," he stated.

Apologizing to Juelz is easier said than done. I will never forget the way he looked at me. He was pissed, he had no business sneaking over here anyway. He loves to buy somebody some flowers and jewelry that shit doesn't impress me anymore.

I'm twenty-five not seventeen. I'm not trying to rekindle an old flame. He was my past and he can he stay there. Of course, things are going to be different now because Jueleez is in the picture. Eventually, I was going to tell him about her since Khadijah and Smoke are dating. It was bound to come out. He just had to pop up and find me.

Juelz

Jueleez and me had a busy day today. She met her uncle Smoke, and Skeet for the first time today. We dropped Skeet off at home, and Jueleez begged me to go inside so she could see Nyla and Lil Skeet.

I didn't want to go in because I was liable to cuss Nikki out. Lil Skeet was grilling me because I told him Jueleez was my daughter. Nikki apologized I didn't even say shit to her, I ignored her ass.

I had to make a final stop before we went home. I had to take her by my mother's house so she could meet my aunties and my father of course. My mother called a niggas phone one hundred times already.

She wanted to see a picture of Jueleez, but I wanted her to see my daughter in the

flesh. I had another issue, how was I supposed to tell Giselle that me and Journee had a child together, and she was seven years old the same age as Kassence. Journee made it clear that she didn't want Jueleez around Giselle.

**

We finally made it my mother's house and it was full. She invited everybody over. I parked my car and unlocked the door for Jueleez we walked to my mother's house hand in hand. As soon as I opened the door the food aroma hit my nose. Jueleez grabbed my hand as we made our way through the house looking for my mother and father. I found my mother she was running her mouth.

"Ma." She turned around and looked at me.

"Juelz, is that her," my mother asked, she dropped her cellphone and cried.

"Yes."

"What the fuck did you do to her mother, for her to keep your child away from you," she asked.

"Cheat."

"I should beat your cheating ass," she argued and smacked me in the back of my head.

Simone Marie Thomas

Let me introduce myself I'm Simone Marie Thomas. I'm Juelz and Myshir (Smoke) mother. Let me cut the bullshit and get straight to it. The moment I laid eyes on Jueleez Monroe Thomas. I knew she was my blood. None of that shit matters right now. I have an issue with her trifling ass mother and I won't to be good until that shit solved.

Tears flooded my eyes just looking at her she looked just like my son and to know that her mother hid this shit from him for eight years doesn't sit well with me. I needed to have a sit down with her asap. Juelz said that Jueleez's mother was Khadijah's sister. I liked Khadijah for, Smoke she was sweet and respectful but I'm not giving her sister a fucking pass.

Juelz made Jueleez by his damn self, her mammy just laid on her back and took the dick. I hate to even address this bitch, but she's going to hear from me and feel me. It ain't no way that Kassence is Juelz child. I put it on my mother, if Giselle put a baby on my son I'm masking up and I'm knocking that bitches head off. I need both kids tested.

"Ma, what's wrong," my son asked.

"A lot I need to speak with Jueleez mother give me her phone number."

"Ma, chill out I already straightened her out," he stated.

"Juelz, what the fuck does that have to do with me? I raised you to never hit women, but my hands ain't excluded."

"Ma, chill out I got this," he insisted.

"Juelz, let me do me and you do you. Give me that little whores phone number so we can have a sit down."

"Ma, she's not a whore don't call her that," he stated attempting to assure me.

"You said the same thing about Giselle so why should I believe you?'

"Trust me ma just take my word for it," he argued.

Journee

My phone rang again and it was Juelz the Bluetooth was on automatic answer.

"Hello."

"What's up, did you get my text?" he asked.

"I got it. I wasn't ignoring you, but I haven't had time to respond because I'm trying to clean up my restaurant, that you fucked up, so I can open backup for business tomorrow. I forgive you. You good."

"I'll pay for it, how much do I owe you? My mother asked for your number she wants to sit down with you and talk," he stated.

"I got it Juelz you don't have too, it's cool you can give her my number. Is that all?"

"I need you to meet us tomorrow, we need to get the DNA test done. I need Jueleez Monroe's last name changed set that up for me," he stated

"All right, let me speak to Jueleez."

"Hey mommy," she stated.

"Hi, I miss you. I just wanted to say hey and I'll see you tomorrow. I love you and be good ok."

"I will mommy, I saw auntie Khadijah, Lil Skeet and Nyla earlier. My daddy took me to the mall and brought me everything. I'm at my granny's house now eating dinner," she stated.

"It's Glama," Juelz mom yelled in the background.

"All right Jueleez go have some fun and mommy will see you soon."

The sound of Juelz voice sent chills through my body. Jueleez sounds like she's having fun. I'm so happy for her.

Chapter 4- Giselle

Juelz, didn't come home tonight that was strange. Something was going on. I could feel it. I called him to see what was up. He answered on the first ring.

"Juelz, where you at? What time are you coming home?"

"Giselle, I'm not coming home for a few weeks," he stated

"What the fuck do you mean that you're not coming home for a few weeks? Where are you staying at? Give me the address so me and Kassence can come too."

"Look, Giselle, I found out today that I have another daughter, she's seven years old and her mother doesn't want her around you. I have to respect her wishes," he explained.

"Juelz, whose her mother? I've been with you for eight years, so you mean to tell me that this baby pops up out of nowhere and you claiming it? I can't be around the child. I know I'm a threat, but damn I would never hurt somebody's child. I'm low but I'm not that low."

"Who her mother is don't matter. I know she's mine I'm getting a DNA test done for her tomorrow. Can you schedule one for me, you and Kassence also? I need to make sure all of my children are mine," he asked.

"Juelz, are you fucking serious right now? After these years, you want a DNA test for Kassence you got to be fucking kidding me? I can't believe you. You're questioning me, but a bitch you just met today pops up with your daughter and now we need a DNA test."

"She didn't pop up on me. I popped up on her, and when I looked at her child it was like looking at myself. Set the DNA test up or I will. You don't have shit to hide, do you? You were fucking another nigga too. I just want to be sure after this," he explained.

"Why are you out cheating on me and popping up on women?" I cried.

"Giselle, I'm not cheating on you, stop crying man. If it makes you feel better she fucking disgusts me. I'm not cheating on you with a bitch that kept my child from me. I'm going to bed," he argued

"Daddy, who are you talking too," his daughter asked, I could hear her in the background.

"Is that her Juelz, Let me see her, she sounds so cute."

This little bitch is already calling him daddy.

"You'll meet her soon. Good night Giselle," he stated.

"Where's her mother if she's over there with you?"

"Giselle, her mother is at home. She has somebody she ain't checking for me. Goodnight," he argued.

"Juelz, why can't I see you and her on FaceTime?" I cried.

"Giselle, because I know you? You're still childish. I can FaceTime you right now and you're going to screenshot a picture of my daughter and try find out who her mother is. I don't care, if you want to see her that bad go ahead, and hit that FaceTime button, so you can get your feelings hurt," he argued.

"Juelz, it's not that serious. I'm hurt that you had a baby on me by another woman. Once again, your actions and cheating, has slapped me in my face. Her feelings are put before mine. It's only one bitch that had you gone, and that was Journee. Is it her?

Why do you always put females before me? Do you love me because you have a funny way of showing it? I'm just saying, don't I have some say so? You've been lying next to me for eight years, and all a sudden a baby pops up, and you're going to be gone for some weeks? I'm not ok with that?" I cried.

"Giselle, stop crying. You know I love you, but I'm not in love with you. Yes, we are in a relationship. I'm not trying to hurt you, and I'm not putting anybody before you. It's a respect thing, her mother doesn't want her around you. Put yourself in her mother's shoes. Her mother knows that you're still in the picture. The three of us will talk soon about whatever issues she has with you," he explained.

"Good night Juelz. I love you."

"I love you too," he stated I could feel that it wasn't sincere.

Juelz got me fucked up. He has the nerve to ask for a DNA test for Kassence seven years later. True enough Kassence wasn't his child but he didn't need to know that. I don't even like this whole situation.

Who is her mother and why couldn't I know who she was, and what's the reason I can't meet your daughter. I don't like females having one up on me with Juelz. To be honest I wouldn't be able to look at Juelz's daughter because I didn't have her. I've had so many abortions because Free knocks me up on purpose.

I couldn't give Juelz a child if I wanted too. I can't have any more kids. Juelz's has asked me to give him another child plenty of times. Lord knows I can't let him do a DNA on Kassence because that would prove that she's not his daughter.

Free had a DNA test done on her three weeks after she was born. Let me call Tyra my nerves are bad. I could go to stay at my other house and call Free over. Fuck Alexis, daddy's coming home tonight to play house with his favorite girls.

"What Giselle, daddy isn't home so you're on my phone," she asked.

"Tyra, can you talk is Kairo over there?'

"Yes, I can talk he's here. What's up?" she asked.

"Girl, Juelz has a daughter and he won't tell me her name, or whose her mother. To make matters worse, the nigga said he's not going to be home for a few weeks. His baby mammy doesn't won't her child around me. He asked for a DNA test for Kassence. You know I can't give him one." I cried.

"Giselle, stop crying. I'm here for you. I got your back no matter what. I know you don't want to hear it, but it might be time to let Juelz go. If he finds out that Kassence isn't his, he'll never forgive you.

You and Free deserve a real shot out in the open with your child. Ugh and I hate Alexis too, he wants to marry you and give you everything but you're still holding on to Juelz. Let him go," she explained.

"Damn, who are you Iyanla fix my life? You're giving out such good advice tonight, are you going to let Kairo go home so he can be with Journee?"

"Hell no, I told him I'll follow his ass home, and tell that bitch everything. I fucked him and sucked him to sleep, and cut his phone off. I'm ready to do it. I don't have to shit to lose, but he does.

Listen Giselle, Kairo is my husband and I fucked up. We were in love with each other. He was my first everything, and I'm woman enough to admit that I fucked up because I was curious to see what was out there.

To be honest, yes, I fucked a couple of niggas to test the waters but nobody could compare to him. The day my husband caught me fucking another nigga my world was over. He left me the same day he caught me, and I watched him love another bitch for seven years that's not me.

I'm your big sister listen to me, don't make the same mistakes that I did. Free isn't going to wait around forever. Don't miss a good thing chasing Juelz. Don't watch Free love another woman, and he's ready to give you and his child everything. I had it all and fucked up and now I'm trying to get it back," she explained.

"Ugh, I love you but I hate you right now. Let me let you go so I can call Free and fuck him to sleep."

Don't get me wrong I love Tyra she's cool, and she gives great advice, but bitch you know Kairo don't want you. He makes that shit very clear. The only reason he's even doing this shit with you, he doesn't want you to tell Journee it's a business relationship. The both of y'all are making money in the process.

My relationship with Juelz is different. I love Free, but I've never thought of him as being my main nigga always a plan B, and Kassence's father that's it. Tyra hasn't even taken her own advice, and let her husband go.

Chapter 5-Journee

Today has been crazy as fuck. Never in a million years, I would've thought Juelz and me would lay hands on each other. My heart is hurting so bad, because I hurt him. I still had feelings for him. I still cared about Juelz today was conformation. If he was a guy I didn't care about, it wouldn't hurt. I got drunk tonight to mask the pain and guilt.

I had so much fun out with the crew I needed that. I'm a sucker for fajita's and margaritas. I headed back to the North. Jueleez Face Timed me before she went to bed. Juelz was walking around in the background with his shirt off wanting me to see him. He was still sexy as fuck and easy on the eyes. I couldn't deny that.

We had fun. I needed a lady's night. I was surprised at Alexis, Free called her phone at least thirty times, and she didn't answer. He called me my phone and I put him on block. I'm not getting in their business.

I'm drunk and full and the only thing that I want to do is fuck Kairo, and go to sleep. I rode the bull so many times tonight, it's time to ride some dick. I can't wait to get home he should be there by the time I get there.

***

I finally made it home thirty minutes later. I hit the garage button to open the garage and guess who's not home, and it's 3:00 am. I'm putting a stop to this shit. I called you, and ask you to do one thing because I needed you.

You can't even come through. I dialed his number and placed my phone on speaker the voicemail came on the first ring. What are we together for because clearly, it's not the sex, we're not fucking that much because you're always gone. I was leaving a message. I wanted him to understand why shit was about to go left with us.

"Kairo, I don't ask you for much, but when I need you I expect you come. Wherever you are stay there. Don't come home. Your phone is never cut off. Clearly, it's somebody else you're always gone. You ain't fucking me so it's must be somebody else. I'm not the type of female that's looks for anything. It always falls in my lap.

Real niggas do real shit, be a man the one that you claim to be and let me go. You're doing you and I'm about to do me. I'm tired of it. Your shit will be packed, and I'll take it to Free's or your mother's house. I'm changing the locks."

Fuck my life. Fuck everything, if it's not about Jueleez it's not about nothing. She's my greatest creation. My phone rung it was Alexis.

"Hey, I made it home safe, but Kairo isn't home. I called his phone and it's going to straight to voicemail. I left him a nice nasty message."

"Really, I didn't even go home. Fuck Free. I got me a room at the W. Pack your bags, and get an Uber down here. I'm sure he'll be bye in the morning to explain."

"Alexis, he will die. I'm down, I see you're on some good bullshit, but I want that nigga to look me in face and tell me he's not cheating on me."

"I hear you Journee, but come on, he'll think that you're with another man. Fuck Kairo get his blood pressure high. Make him trip the same way you're tripping right now."

Don't get me wrong I'm all for get back shit, but tonight I wanted to be alone. I wanted Kairo, but he's somewhere else.

"Fuck it I'll go ahead and come. I'm too drunk to be driving downtown. Uber, it is. I pulled up my Uber app to schedule a ride. My ride will be here in thirty minutes. I thumbed through my closet to find something to wear. I forgot that I scheduled the DNA test with LabCorp tomorrow at 11:00 am. I sent Juelz a text to the location of the DNA test and time. He sent a text back

Juelz- Why are you texting my phone this late?

Me- I'm sorry, I'm drunk, I forgot to send it earlier, so before I close my eyes and forget

here you go.

Juelz- You forget a lot of shit huh?

I don't even have time to argue with Juelz. It's pointless he told me to set it up so I did. Here he goes calling my phone. I'm not trying to argue with him.

"Hello."

"You can text my phone at 3:30 am, but if I text you back you can't respond," he asked?

"It's not that Juelz, it seemed like you wanted to argue, and I'm not trying to do that. I forgot to send you that information earlier, and I know once I close my eyes I'll forget. I just didn't want to do that." I continued to look through my closet for something to wear.

"Whatever Journee, stop assuming shit where you at?" he asked.

"I'm at home now looking for something to wear."

"Damn where are you going this time of night," he asked.

"I'm about to go downtown to the W. I'm waiting on my Uber."

"Ole boy let you leave the house this time of night," he asked?

"I'm grown I do what I want. He didn't come home last night like he said he was. So tomorrow I'm changing the locks, and packing his shit. Wherever he's lying his head he can continue to."

"You're not about to do shit," he laughed.

"I wasn't going to leave, but my friend Alexis she's on some good bullshit and she booked a room at the W and she asked me to come."

"Come over here," he asked?

"For what so you can kill me?"

"You crazy, and drunk you coming or what?" he laughed.

"Juelz, what is Jueleez going to say if she wakes up and I'm there?"

"What can she say? You said I'm her father and you're her mother. It is what it is," he explained.

"Do you think this is a good idea what about Giselle?"

"Stop making excuses, why are you worried about Giselle? She ain't worried about you, if you don't want to come just say so. If you do, you got an hour to get here. I'm sending you the address." He stated and hung up.

Who am I kidding I was coming. Let me call Alexis and see what she thinks?

"Are you on your way?" she asked.

"Change of plans, Juelz wants me to come over, do you think I should go?"

"Hold up bitch, what are you doing talking to Juelz after hours," she asked?

"Alexis, it wasn't like that. I sent him the text of the DNA test information, and he sent a text back going off about me texting him late. I ignored him and he called me, and he listened to me rant, and he told me to come over."

"You know I like dancing with devil. If I was you I would go. Does he have any cousins, homeboys or somebody for me shit," she laughed.

"Are you sure? I'm not going to go, but I want too, but I'm going to fight temptation, because I know where this would lead too."

"Look Journee for once in your life, let your hair down and let whatever happen, happens stop fighting you and Juelz damn. Take your ass over there. Fuck Giselle or whoever else. Stop sparing these hoes feelings because a bitch ain't spared yours. Gosh you are so hard-headed it doesn't make any sense. Just go, has Kairo made it home yet? You don't have to sleep with him," she argued.

"Nope he hasn't come home."

"That's clarification on why you need to go. I'll pick you up tomorrow from the restaurant and I'll take you home," she stated.

"Ok Alexis, I'm going, he said I have an hour to get there. Wish me luck, because he's crazy."

"You don't need luck you got it. I'll talk to you later. I love you, put that pussy on that nigga, show him how you are doing shit now," she laughed.

"Girl that's why I don't want to go. I'm not trying to go there."

"Bye Journee," she laughed.

***

I made it to Juelz house. I was tired and sleepy. Wish me luck let's see how this goes. I called his phone he answered on the first ring.

"What Journee, you ain't coming, you didn't have to call me back to tell me that?" he stated.

"I'm outside open the door."

He hung up in my face. I sat on the step and placed my face in my hands. I'm tired the only thing I want to do sleep. I heard the door open, he tapped me on my shoulder and grabbed my bag.

I walked in, I remember this house I cleaned it a few times. It looks like he redecorated the house.

"Follow me," he stated and slapped me on my ass.

"Stop."

"You got it out there, I had to see if it was real or not," he laughed.

"Whatever, you know ain't nothing fake about me. Everything's natural, where's my room so I can go to sleep."

"Oh, you in my room for tonight. I don't like people roaming through my house."

"Juelz, you have five rooms here, why do I have to go in your room?"

"You remembered?"

"Of course."

"Journee, I'm not going to do nothing, that you don't want me too." he laughed.

"Where's Jueleez?"

"She's asleep." he laughed.

"Whatever. I hope you changed the sheets, I don't want to be laying my head where you and somebody else laid theirs."

"Shut up, go take shower and do what you got to do," he said.

Chapter 6-Juelz

Some shit never changes. I couldn't sleep, I've been tossing and turning all night. I couldn't stop thinking about her. I was caught off guard when she sent me a text about the DNA information it was 3:45 am. I had to make sure I wasn't dreaming. It was her.

I called her and listened to her vent about her whack as nigga not coming home. I'm not hating Nikki told me that nigga was never at home, and she didn't trust him. Nikki was still my sister despite this petty shit that happened earlier, she called me and apologized. If I had Journee I would be at home every night, he was stupid if you asked me. Skeet had Journee on speaker phone when she called him.

I couldn't do anything but shake my head and smile. I had to check Skeet too because he lied about not seeing Journee, he hit me with, he wasn't hooking anybody's woman up with another man.

The fuck did that mean, she was mine before she was that niggas. He didn't want anybody hooking Nikki up with another nigga, his wife ain't crazy she ain't going nowhere. He didn't have shit to worry about it.

I wanted to see if she really meant what she said. I asked her to come over to see if she would come and she came. She was taking a shower. I started to go in there, but I decided not to. I heard the shower cut off.

I sat on my side of the bed and rolled my blunt. I was taking this one to the head. She walked out of the bathroom and commanded attention, her legs were still thick as fuck and toned. I didn't pay her no mind. She was trying to tease a nigga. Her ass swallowed the boy shorts she slid on.

I kept doing what I was doing. She climbed in the bed and pulled the covers over her head. Her scent lingered through the room. I just licked my cigar and sparked it. I had to get high before I laid down next to her. I just wanted to go to sleep that's it. I've been awake long enough and I'm tired as fuck.

***

I smoked my blunt to the head, and pulled the covers back and climbed in the bed. I had my back turned the opposite way. I knew she wasn't sleep I felt her squirming in the bed. I haven't laid next to Journee in forever this was our daily routine after her mom passed.

I would come home to her mother's house from trapping all day, and she would do the same thing. If she wanted to play dead I would let her.

"Juelz," she pouted.

"Journee."

"I'm sorry," she sated.

I ignored her, I didn't even say shit because I really didn't even want to talk about this shit right now. I closed my eyes praying that sleep would take me over because if we talked about this shit right now. I'm liable to act ignorant again, and I don't want to do that shit.

I felt Journee get out of the bed. I rose up to see where she was going.

"Where are you going?"

"Oh, you can talk now?" she asked.

"Look Journee, I'm and tired and I don't want to talk about this shit right now. I'll be mad all over again, and I don't want to be mad. Get in the bed and go to sleep please."

She did as she was told and snatched the covers back and got in the bed.

I shouldn't even have told her stubborn ass to come over here, she should've stayed at home and waited on ole boy. I busted out laughing.

"What's so funny?" she asked.

"You, come here, and let daddy put you to sleep."

"No, my daddy dead," she argued.

"Ok." I picked her up and laid her on my chest and smacked her on her ass, and whispered in ear to shut the fuck up and go to sleep, before I put this dick up in you.

"Whatever, good night, I'm sorry," she whispered in my ear.

We went to sleep after that. I wrapped my arms around her waist and her arms were around my neck.

<u>Giselle</u>

Y'all can call me crazy or insane it doesn't even fucking matter to me pick one. I've had enough, and I'm sick of all this shit. I couldn't even fuck Free like I wanted to because my mind was consumed with Juelz, and who he was with. I had a premonition that he was with Journee.

I jumped off Free dick, so quick my pussy was soaking and wet, I threw on my clothes, and told him to watch his daughter I'll be back.

"Giselle, where in the fuck are you going this time of morning," he yelled and jumped up behind me.

"I don't feel good Free, I feel sick. I'm going to the emergency room."

"I'll go with you, are you pregnant again?" he asked.

"No, I'll go by myself Northside Hospital is right around the corner, and Kassence doesn't need to be out this time of morning." I lied I didn't want him going with me.

I had some wipes in the car, and a nice outfit in my hoe bag I could change into, guess what I don't give a fuck. I tracked Juelz phone to house in Roswell, GA.

I've never been there before, but guess what a bitch was on her way. I don't trust this nigga, and shit he said on the phone. The only female that could ever keep Juelz away from me was Journee, and I got a feeling I'm right. I wish a bitch would think they can come in between what we have.

Don't get me wrong I love Free, but I'm not in love with him. I'm in love with Juelz he's the only man that I've ever loved. I just couldn't get him to love me how I wanted him too. He loves me, but it's not enough. It would take me forty-five minutes to get there.

***

I made my way over there to see what the fuck was going on. I felt like Carmen San Diego again. I called Juelz phone and he didn't answer. The funny thing about this GPS it didn't show the exact address but it showed the street. Juelz would never park his car outside.

All our cars are garage kept. I would have to peek inside of these garages to see which one was the house.

I called his phone repeatedly, and he didn't answer. He finally answered.

"What Giselle, what you want?" he answered, I could tell he was asleep.

"What's the address to the house I'm outside?"

"Outside of where Giselle. You're hard-headed take your ass back home. Why are tracking my phone? Where's my fucking daughter at? I'll come outside to get her, but you can take your ass home," he argued.

"My mom has her."

"When did you drop her off, let me call your mom and see what time you dropped her off, you should be in bed," he argued.

"I couldn't sleep Juelz. I had a dream you were laid up with Journee, that shit was real."

"Giselle, you are crazy get off my fucking phone, take your ass home and I'll see you later. "he argued.

"Why Juelz?" I cried.

"Giselle, you didn't even stay at home last night. You set the alarm as soon as we hung up with each other, so the real question is where did you lay your head?" he asked.

"I did stay at home Juelz, I went to get some food from the Mexican, my mom called me and asked could

Kassence come over. I dropped her off after that I went home and went to bed.

"You are questioning me about what I'm doing, but you're doing something. See the difference between me and you I'm real about my shit. I'll never lead you on. I'll leave you before I cheat.

If I ever catch you cheating on me and you can't speak up. I'm going to fuck you up. Your mother sent a text and said Kassence isn't over there, where the fuck is my daughter? I'm on my way outside?" he threatened.

I pulled out of the neighborhood so quick, you could hear my tires burn rubber. I didn't have time for Juelz and his bullshit. All I wanted to do was show him that I cared, but no he wanted to flip shit around on me. Why was he checking the surveillance and alarm anyway?

Oh, he wanted to call my phone back now.

"What Juelz, clearly you don't want me wherever you are. I know you have someone in there."

"Come back Giselle, so you can take me to get my daughter. Where is she if your over here. She better not be at home by herself. Turn around now," he yelled.

"Goodbye Juelz, if Kassence and I meant anything to you we would be there despite what your new baby mammy has to say." I hung up in his face and cut my phone off. My child was with her real father. Fuck him and his new child.

Chapter 7-Juelz

"Who was that Juelz? I knew I shouldn't have come here. I don't have time for this shit. Thank you for letting me come over, and use your chest as a body pillow. I appreciate you," she yawned, and attempted to raise up off me.

"It was Giselle, lay down you're not going anywhere." I secured my arms around her waist so she wouldn't get up.

Giselle think a nigga stupid, she was clocking my moves, and shit she was right I was with somebody, but it wasn't like that at all. She ruined my sleep, I'm tired as fuck.

"Juelz, go to sleep," she stated and kissed me on my neck.

"I'm trying, keep your lips to yourself before you get yourself in some trouble you can't get out of."

She ignored me and got off me.

"Where are you going?"

"I can't sleep, I'm going to brush my teeth, and cook some breakfast, go to sleep. I'm not going anywhere yet."

"Yet."

"I shouldn't be here. The two of you are in a relationship, and I'm not coming in between that. The bitch is crazy, and I'm crazy, but this time I won't hesitate to kill a bitch, so for that reason alone I'm going to cook you and my daughter breakfast, and I'm going to get an Uber and I'll meet y'all at LabCorp later," she explained.

"You're here because I wanted you here. If I wanted her here, and she knew where I laid my head, she would've knocked on the door. If that's your excuse to leave, then you don't have to cook shit. You can put your clothes on, and bounce and I'll have my driver to take you home."

"Ok," she stated under her breath.

"I didn't hear you Journee, do I need to call my driver, what's it going to be?"

"I'm staying," she sassed.

"Good, I like my eggs scrambled with cheese, and my bacon well done. The rest is on you."

Damn she get on my nerves. She's still stubborn and hard-headed, just shut the fuck up, and go with the flow. She's always running from some shit grow up, talking all that tough as shit. I know you beat Giselle's ass before. I don't care about none of that shit, that's still the mother of my child, and I refuse to have y'all two at odds, and y'all need to respect each other.

***

Journee, fixed me and Jueleez breakfast. I could smell the food aroma from my room. She had an attitude the whole morning. I don't care, she should've took her bitter ass back to sleep, or she could've went home. I guess she was still mad about Giselle earlier.

Oh well I'm not about to pacify her or Giselle, we're not together, her choice and not mine. I'm not pressed on feelings. I couldn't wait to take this DNA test, and she can go ahead about her business and I can go ahead about mine.

I couldn't wait to see Giselle's sneaky ass, she got me fucked up. Putting trackers on my phone and shit. I haven't cheated on her in years. I haven't come across anybody that was worth cheating with. She pulled up like a boss. She had every right to be mad because I haven't done this before. If she would've knocked on the door I'm sure her and Journee would've had some issues.

Journee

My mind was all over the place, and I'm sure it showed. Yes, I was pissed that Giselle is still up to the same shit, but I couldn't dwell on that because Juelz is her man and not mine. Kairo was blowing up my phone asking a shit load of questions that he couldn't answer last night. I blocked him, I wasn't fucking talking to him. It was over, and I didn't want to hear any excuses.

I got Jueleez dressed. I braided her hair in two French braids. She was so happy to see me this morning. She talked my head off. I missed her too, she asked a shit load of questions that I didn't have the answers for.

I took my shower and put my clothes on. Juelz was still arguing with Giselle. I brushed my hair up into a knot bun. I coated my lips with NYX nude lipstick. I slid on my white distressed Balmain jeans, with a white crop top that showed my stomach. I placed my big gold hoop earrings in my ear and threw on my big face white Chanel shades with the dark tint. Gucci flip flops adorned my feet.

"Mommy, you look pretty," my daughter said.

"Thank you baby, you look pretty too."

We were finished getting dressed, we were waiting on Juelz now. Jueleez was on her IPAD looking at YouTube videos. I was checking my emails, sales reports from last month and exchanging text with Alexis and Nikki's nosey ass. Alexis couldn't hold water.

When I woke up Nikki sent me at least ten text messages asking me what that dick do? I don't know, what that dick do, because I didn't ride that big motherfucka last night. Juelz old ass didn't even have WIFI, Jueleez was pissed and using my hotspot.

I'll have to tell him get Comcast or AT&T over here soon she can't live without WIFI. That's the first thing he needs to get if he plans to keep her for a few weeks.

"Are y'all ready?" he asked.

"Yep," we said.

I can't believe he dressed like me. I can't deal. He looked good though, he always cleaned up nice. He smelled good too. I wanted to lick my lips, but I decided not to. No wonder Giselle was pulling up at 5:00 am ditsy bitch. I couldn't wait to roll that bitch like some dice. If she ever tried me again. I grabbed my bag and followed him to his garage.

Juelz was pushing a 2017 black Range Rover I wanted one of these. He still had a custom plates fetish. I just shook my head and placed my bag in the back seat. He walked up behind me and started breathing down my neck. My body was covered in chills.

Last night his dick was hard as fuck. I kept trying to get off him and lay next to him, because his dick kept tapping my pussy the way we were laying. He refused to let me lay beside him, he wanted me on top of him.

I heard everything that bitch said she had a premonition he was with me. Damn right he was. I wanted to bust out laughing. He was pissed, I'm so glad that I'm grown and not messy. If I was I would've been sucking on all over him. She would've known I was over there because he would've said my name, Journee Leigh Armstrong is a name that she'll never forget.

***

We finally made it to LabCorp it took us about thirty minutes to get over there. Juelz and I didn't speak much the whole ride. I noticed he kept catching glances at me. Jueleez kept the both of us entertained. I had my iPad opened doing some work for the new restaurant that Alexis and I have in the works. I signed us in and filled out the paperwork.

The medical assistant escorted us to the back to get our mouths swabbed. She swabbed my mouth first, then Jueleez and Juelz. The results only took about forty-five minutes to comeback. I sent a text to Alexis, and told her to head over this way. She said her Nikki, and Khadijah where on their way.

See this is the shit I'm talking about. Juelz went outside to talk on his phone. It kept ringing. The nurse finally came out, and said that the results were back. I went outside to get Juelz so we could get the results and be on our way. I tapped him on his shoulder and whispered that she's ready, and he ended his call and followed behind me.

We made it back inside the nurse read the results and Jueleez Monroe Armstrong was 99.999 % his. He gave me a hug and he grabbed Jueleez. I told Jueleez and Juelz that I would see them soon Auntie Nikki, Alexis and Khadijah was outside waiting for me. Juelz was pissed I could tell by his facial expression. I walked to his truck and got my bag out. I gave Jueleez a hug and kiss. I thanked him again for letting me stay at his house and call me if he needs anything.

I gave Juelz a hug. I had to give these bitches something to talk about they were already talking anyway. The scent of his cologne invaded my nostrils. I was mesmerized. I walked off with the biggest smile plastered on my face, and jumped in the backseat and slammed the door.

"Drive bitch." I laughed.

"Fuck that Journee, how did you end up with Juelz last night," my sister asked.

"A drunk text."

"What that dick do, you are giving hugs and shit," my best friend Nikki asked.

"We didn't make love, I'm a lady and he's a gentleman."

"Bitch please," my best friend Alexis laughed.

"I'm serious I laid on his chest all night, and that third leg between his legs, good Lawd it kept tapping my pussy all night. I wanted to slide these panties to the side and ride that motherfucka. The mood was ruined when

Giselle called his phone and said she had a premonition about me and him being together.

To make matters worse the bitch pulled up in the neighborhood at 5:00 am looking for the house. He asked where his daughter was and she wasn't with her. He told her he was coming outside take him to his daughter. I heard her tires screech. I wanted to laugh so bad." I blushed.

"You want that old thing back?" my sister asked.

"Journee, stop fucking lying that's some powerful dick. If a bitch having dreams about another bitch on it. Gawd damn y'all sure Skeet and Juelz don't have anybody for me? I need some powerful dick in my life," my best bae Alexis laughed.

"Alexis, chill out I think I might have someone for you. Journee, do you remember Alonzo? He's back in Atlanta from New Orleans, he's good friends with them. He came by the house the other night. Kassence was probably with her real daddy.

Giselle is slick as fuck. I told Juelz a long time ago to leave that dirty South hoe alone, he should've left her ass in Jonesboro. Y'all two are going to have some problems again Journee once she finds out that it's you that has the baby by Juelz," my best friend Nikki stated.

"I already know."

The rest of the ride we just rode and talked shit. The vibe was good. I loved hanging out with them. I was missing Juelz like crazy. I couldn't stop thinking about him. It's crazy we haven't seen each other in eight years. Despite the little bullshit yesterday, he put that aside if only for a minute. I missed everything about him. I missed the way he smelled. I missed the way he held me.

"You miss him huh," my sister asked.

"I do." I whispered.

Alexis took me home to get my car. I went to the restaurant to finish working. I had work to do tons of it. I couldn't afford to sit around and not do shit, because I'll mad later because I would be extremely pissed at myself for getting this backed up. I like to stay busy with work and inventory. If not, I would be at the mall blowing some cash on some bullshit, and sitting around day dreaming about Juelz.

Juelz

We took the DNA test and the results came back that Jueleez Monroe Armstrong was mine. I knew she was. She looked exactly like me. Her mother pulled a fast one on a nigga. I wanted to take them both to lunch, but imagine my surprise when we walked outside and her girls were outside waiting on her. I spent the entire time arguing with Giselle.

"Daddy, what's wrong?" my daughter asked.

"Nothing."

"Are you sure?" she asked.

"I'm sure, what do you want to do today?"

"I want to go back over Glama house. Can you get the internet at your house? My iPad won't work without it. Is mommy coming back over when we get home?" she asked.

"We can go over there. I don't think she is, but you can ask her though. I'll call Comcast over to see if they can come out and hook the internet up."

My daughter was smart as hell. It didn't make any sense. She knew I was pissed because her mother left. Of course, I wanted my family. The few hours that we spent together was everything. It's not on me this time. It's on Journee, I've done all the pursing and chasing last time. I'm not doing it again. I refuse too.

If she wants us then she better speak-up. At this point I'm over it. If it's not about Jueleez or Kassence it's not about nothing. My daughters are the only thing that matter to me. Giselle was still on that bullshit this morning, and my daughter was nowhere to be found.

I told her to bring Kassence to my mother's house. I wanted her and Jueleez to meet today. It's crazy because they were two weeks apart. Kassence birthday was April 19th and Jueleez birthday was April 6th.

Giselle

Fuck Juelz, we argued all morning he wanted to see his daughter. He wasn't thinking about me or Kassence when he was playing house with his new child. He wanted me to bring her over his mother's house, for what so she can size, my child and say that she looks nothing like him?

Simone is so fucking crazy, she probably has a DNA kit at her house already waiting to swab Kassence mouth, nope my child will not be going over there. He couldn't wait to call me back and let me know that she was indeed his, and the test came back 99.999% his.

Kudos to you I don't give a fuck about that. Who is her mother and what's the big fucking secret? He refused to answer that question. Juelz hasn't kept any secrets from me in a very long time. We're open about everything except this small piece of information.

I didn't need to know that. It's like a slap in my face another woman carried his first child and it wasn't me. That's a big blow to my ego. I should've stop seeing Free years ago, but I couldn't. He was my daughters father and a great provider. I couldn't just cut him off because we had a child together.

If Juelz ever found out that Kassence wasn't his. He would probably kill me. Kassence knew that Juelz wasn't her real father. Free is very active in her life. His fiancé didn't know about her, but his family did. Her grandparents love her dearly she's their first grandchild. Gosh it seems like my past is coming back to bite me in the ass.

Juelz said he'll be home tomorrow, good because I was driving myself crazy trying to figure out what the fuck he was doing, and with who. I've known for- a- fact he'll continue to pressure me about a DNA that I refuse to give him.

Maybe I'll stay gone for a few weeks for this shit to blow over, at least until he forgets about it. I'll play mad with him and stay away.

Chapter 8-Kairo

Tyra drugged me and fucked me to sleep. I knew I shouldn't came by here. She knew I was supposed to go home. I didn't give a fuck about her threats. I would've silenced her if she ever told Journee about us.

To make matters worse you cut my phone off. I rolled over and cut my phone on Journee left me a nice nasty message at 3:00 am. Tyra over stepped her boundaries, we fucked but don't touch my fucking phone. It's off limits I don't even touch yours.

I couldn't explain this shit. I couldn't look Journee in the face and tell her I'm out here living foul, and I broke our bond. I couldn't do that. Yes, Tyra and I are still married and I have obligations to her, but Journee comes before her. I looked at Tyra and pimped slapped the fuck out of her.

"Kairo, what did you do that for," she cried.

"You cut my fucking phone off and you drugged me. You knew I had to go home. Spending the night here isn't the fucking agreement. I'm divorcing you rather you like it or your family likes it."

"Kairo, I deserve another chance I fucked up, and I'm sorry, can't you see that I've changed. We never even tried to work past our differences. Can we at least try please?" she asked.

"What do we need try for? When we were married did I ever cheat on?"

"No," she said under her breath.

"That's your answer no we can't work it out."

"Why does it have to be this way," she asked.

"I'm in love with Journee, and you know that. I made a few mistakes along the way, but I love her. You ruined us, she wouldn't even be in the picture if you weren't curious to see what it was like to fuck another man."

"Do you actually think that she'll be with you after she finds out about us," she asked.

Journee

My restaurant was back to normal after the drama that popped off yesterday. I made it to the restaurant a little after 12:00 pm. It was lunch time, and business was booming. I walked straight to the kitchen to greet my staff. I love them and I'm hungry I need food. Next stop was to speak with my General Manager she was the best. I wouldn't trade her for nothing.

I finished making my rounds and walked back to my office it was covered with red and white roses and an I'm sorry card. He wasted his money because I was trashing this shit. Fuck Kairo you need more than an I'm sorry card to get back in my good graces. My phone rang breaking me out of my thoughts.

"Hello."

"Hi, is Journee available," she asked with an attitude.

"This is she, may I ask who am I speaking with?"

"I'm Simone Marie, Juelz's mother."

"Hi, how are you?"

"I would say good, but I'm not. Normally I don't even talk shit over the phone, but I'm making and exception for you," she argued.

"I'm sorry to hear that, but how can I help you?"

"We need to have a sit down. I'm upset that you kept my granddaughter from us. I don't appreciate that, it was very distasteful, foul and trifling. I've had to school young hoes like you about fucking with my sons, she argued.

"Excuse me, no disrespect I understand that your mad and upset. I apologize, your son isn't a saint, and you can call him a hoe because I never been a hoe. I refuse to let anybody call me one."

"You'll be whatever I want you to be," she argued.

"No offense Simon, I meant Simone. I'm too grown and classy to argue with my elders over the phone. I don't do that, and I refuse to go back and forth with you about what I did and why. When you're ready to sit down and talk like adults send me the location. I'll beat you there, I don't argue over the phone about bullshit. You have a good day." I hung up in her face.

I don't know who she thought I was, but I'm not Giselle. I'm Journee Leigh I don't give a fuck about her being Juelz mother or Jueleez grandmother. Nobody is going to talk to me crazy and think that I'm going to be cool with it. This bitch had the nerve to send me a text with an address on it, and a location. I called my Godmother Valerie.

"Umm huh, I was waiting on you to call me. I heard about you, I had a dream about your mother the other night and she was laughing at you. I know why now," she laughed.

"Umm huh, why didn't you call to check on me, if you heard about me?"

"I knew you would be calling me soon, You're ok, what's up?" She asked.

"Juelz mammy called me talking shit and popping off at the mouth, and she wants us to meet tomorrow. I need you to come with me, you raised me not to disrespect my elders but this lady is pushing it."

"Who is his mother? I make house calls. I don't play that shit, ain't nan bitch gone disrespect my kids. I don't give a fuck how she may feel," she argued.

"I know that's why I called you, in case she got ignorant."

"I'm definitely coming, pick me up. Make sure you have my bond money ready because I'll bust a bitch face wide open coming at you sideways," she stated.

"I already know hopefully it won't lead to that. I love you and I'll see you tomorrow."

Juelz mother rubbed me the wrong way. I thought we was better than that. I know we haven't moved passed our issues, because we haven't officially talked about it. Damn you ever throw no salt on my fucking name.

Even though you didn't know Jueleez I never spoke foul about him. I always spoke good about him despite what we went through. Our good days outweighed our bad days. I don't hate Juelz. I just don't fuck with him like that, because he was sneaky and he played me. I'm over that now. I sent him a text.

Juelz- I don't care how you may feel about me. I've never been a hoe. Tell your mother the truth. You were the hoe not me.

Journee- What are you talking about?

I wasn't even about to respond because obviously he was discussing me with his mother for her to call me that. I don't have time for any of this shit. I've never been a hoe or even thought about doing hoe shit. My mother didn't raise any hoes. It took Kairo a year and three months to get the pussy. He wanted to call my phone now.

"What Juelz? You should be calling your mother, and clearing up what the fuck you told her instead of calling me.

"Journee, what are you talking about and lose your attitude. I haven't done shit to you," he argued and yelled through the phone.

"Your mother called me getting fly at the mouth, talking about she has to check hoes like me. I was raised to respect my elders, but she almost got it."

"Calm down, you know me better than that. I told her you weren't a hoe. She's just fucking with you," he laughed.

"I don't like being fucked with." I laughed.

"My mom is wild as fuck. She thinks that she's still young. I'm sorry that she offended you," he laughed.

"Umm huh ok. I had something for her ass tomorrow if her mouth got to slick." I laughed.

"You have something for my mother," he asked and laughed.

"Hell yeah, my Godmother Valerie, you didn't know." I laughed.

"You should be good, she just wants to meet you that's it. I like how you pulled that slick move earlier, and had Nikki, and Khadijah pick you up earlier. I could've took you home or to work. I do need to know where you lay your head at, since you have my daughter," he stated.

"Juelz, it wasn't like that. I tried to tell you earlier, but you were on the phone and I didn't want to interrupt you. I don't have a problem with you knowing where I lay my head at."

"Yeah ok. Jueleez wanted to know if you were coming back tonight," he asked.

"Probably not, I need to get some sleep."

"Oh, so you didn't get no sleep last night? I couldn't tell the way you were slobbering on my chest. You sounded like a grizzly bear all of that snoring you was doing last night," he laughed.

"You're a lie, you know I was drunk. I may have had a little slobber, but I wasn't snoring."

"Ok blame it on the alcohol. Are you coming or what you know you want me to rub on your ass and put you to sleep," he asked?

"I don't know yet, it's too early to tell."

"Be here by eight, I'm texting you the address," he stated and hung up the phone.

Juelz is funny. If he wanted me to spend the night that's all he had to say. He didn't have to use Jueleez. I think I will go back over there. I did enjoy his company and his chest as a body pillow.

I wouldn't tell him that I was coming over, because he thinks he's running shit with his times that I better be there. I'll be there after 9:00 pm.

I couldn't resist him. I laid across my bed at home thinking about his ass. I had my bag already packed. I had to look presentable because I was meeting his mother. I was still debating if I wanted to go over there. My mind was saying yes, and my heart was saying yes also, but I was saying no.

For some reason, I was still drawn to him. After our first encounter at Kapture, and when we went back to his house. I couldn't stop thinking about him. The way he kissed me that night. His tongue hypnotized me, and him pinning me to the wall I was mesmerized.

When he dug his fingers inside of my pretty snatch I came instantly. All the feelings that I had for him, that were tucked and hidden resurfaced.

I guess because it's been so long and everything felt so right with him. He put a spell on me again, and I hate it. What was it about him, was it his cologne or the way held me. His touch alone did something to me.

I couldn't shake him right now, the way that I shook him in the past. I was being submissive, and I didn't want to do that. For that reason alone, I'm still sitting here trying to figure this thing out. I decided to drive my Benz truck. It was after 8:30 pm now. I knew Juelz was tripping. Jueleez sent me a text and asked me was I coming over and if so bring her some snacks.

I didn't respond because I wasn't sure if I was coming or not. My phone rang it was Juelz.

"Hello."

"You hard headed ain't you," he asked.

"What I do?"

"You are playing dumb now," he asked.

"Never that."

"I told you to do something, and you didn't do it. You are waiting on that sucker come back home that's why you can't come," he asked.

"Nope I was just thinking about some stuff, and I lost track of time. It's after 8:00 pm, so I figured the offer wasn't on the table anymore."

"Journee, you know I know you. I know you better than you know yourself. You have never been good at telling a lie. I know you feeling daddy it's ok. I want you in my presence," he laughed.

"Whatever Juelz you're so full of shit. It might not be a good idea for me to come over, if daddy thinks I'm feeling him. You know daddy has a situation and somebody might die if they have another a dream about me being over there."

"Yeah whatever Journee. You're the one that fighting us. Keep fighting it though, and let me know how that's works out for you. I'm not going to chase you this time though. I've put myself out there more than enough.

If you want us, you're gone have to show me, put your big girl panties on, and do work. Until then keep wasting your time with a nigga you ain't supposed to be with," he argued.

"How am I fighting us? It is what it is Juelz. You have a situation. I'm not going to pursue you, and I know that y'all have something going on."

"You haven't come over here yet. You worried about the wrong shit. Have we crossed that line yet? Trust me I'm not going to take your pussy. When it's time you're going to be willing to give it up. Giselle ain't nothing to me. I don't feel like I'm doing anything wrong. I don't even talk on the phone. Bring your ass on, you are pissing me off.," he argued and hung up the phone.

Lord what I have gotten myself into? Let me call Khadijah and see what she thinks. I should confide more in my sister than what I have been. My heart was hurting so bad because she was in tears because she thought I didn't trust her. My mother would kill me treating her baby like the step-child.

"Hey, Khadijah, what are you doing, can you talk?"

"Of course, what's up. I'm cooking me and Smoke some dinner, but I can rap with you for a few," she stated.

"Awe look at my baby growing up on me? Why don't you ever invite me over for a dinner? I'm confused right now, and I'm coming to you because I need some advice."

"Whatever Journee every time I do cook for you, you insist on cooking everything like you didn't teach me how to cook. I'm listening what type of advice do you need I'm all ears," she asked.

"Girl Juelz wants me to come over again tonight, but I don't know."

"Journee, damn you hard-headed. Why are you not going? Are you sitting at home waiting on Kairo to come through? What you got to lose? You scared, he's gone bust that pussy wide open again huh," she laughed.

"Excuse me Khadijah. He has a situation, and no I'm not waiting on Kairo to come through. I don't have anything to lose, and I'm not scared that he's going to bust this pussy open your mouth is too foul."

"Go Journee let your hair down, stop worrying about the wrong shit. Just go with the flow fuck Giselle she said fuck you a long time ago. Why do you even care about her anyway," she asked.

"Ugh why do you have to say the right shit, at the wrong time?"

"What's that supposed to mean? It needs to be said, are you happy? I just want you to be happy no matter who you're with. I want to see you smile. I want to witness you being in love. I never got that from you and Kairo," she explained.

"No, I'm not happy Khadijah."

"How come, I thought you said that you missed him earlier," she asked.

"I do, my hearts wants it, but I'm not ready for it."

"Girl get your stubborn ass off my phone playing ghetto games. Take your ass over there right now. Stop prolonging shit you've done that enough and you're still missing him when you don't have too," she stated.

"I am Khadijah, come by tomorrow I'm meeting with Simone."

"I heard, she's going to tear you a new ass," she laughed.

Chapter 9-Juelz

Journee likes playing a with fire. I meant what I said. I'm not going to chase her this time around. I refuse to I'm not playing games with her no more. I'm not even mad at her ass no more. I should be, but I'm not.

Smoke called me, and told me that she called Khadijah for advice about coming over here. It doesn't make no sense how stubborn she is. She wants too, but she's trying to fight it. She's not hurting me she's hurting herself.

***

It was a little after 9:00 pm. Jueleez was already asleep my mother wore her out. My doorbell rang. I shouldn't even answer it, but I'm not that type of nigga. I know what I want and I don't hold back. I opened the door and we looked at each other. I just shook my head.

"Bring your ass on in here, don't act shy now."

"Whatever Juelz, where's my child? Somethings never change, a different house huh" she asked.

"Yep you know I have a few. She's asleep, come here give me a hug?"

About time she didn't fight me on this shit. I picked her up, and she wrapped her legs around my waist. I bit the crook of her neck.

"Ouch," she pouted.

"Don't let these legs around my waist get you in trouble. You'll be all right stop playing with me."

"What I do," she asked.

"You know, you smell good. You had to stop by, and see that nigga before you came over here?"

"Whatever Juelz, you play too much put me down. You told me to come at 8:00 pm because old girl was coming through here, and you put Jueleez to sleep so she wouldn't tell me," she laughed.

"Whatever you miss me?"

"Maybe, maybe not," she blushed and laughed.

"I know you did, come on follow me."

"How you know," she asked.

"I just do, but unlike you I'm real about my shit. I miss the fuck out of you. I'm not going to hold back about how I feel about you. I'll leave that up to you."

"If you know that I miss you, why would you ask," she asked.

"Why does everything have to be twenty-one questions with you? What's wrong with me wanting to hear that you missed a nigga? I don't have a problem telling you how I feel about you. You still acting like that same feisty mean ass seventeen-year-old little girl." We made it to my room I cut the TV on for her. I threw the remote on the bed, and headed to the bathroom. She's the only person that can piss me off, and get up under my skin.

I have never had a problem with a female telling me about how she feels about nigga, but Journee she won't tell me shit. It's like it kills her. She has her guard up. I understand that, but I'm not trying to hurt you.

I filled the tub up with bubble bath and candles. Jueleez picked out some bubble bath for her mother, that she likes at the mall and candles. Nikki told me what kind of wine she likes. I have never done this shit for a female before not even Giselle. She's the only person I want to do this shit for.

I'm jumping through hoops for her. Shit she should be jumping through hoops for me after that stunt she pulled. I love my baby girl to death, it's only been two days and Jueleez got me wrapped around her finger like her mother. She told me she loved me today a tear crept in my eye.

She looks nothing like Journee she looks exactly like me, that's why I flipped out. How would you feel if you see a child that look exactly like you and somebody you use to be in love with has the child, but you knew nothing about it? Jueleez said I knew you was my daddy because of how you acted. She's so smart.

The tub was filled with bubbles, the candles were lit. Let's see if her mean ass is going to get in.

"Journee, come here." I yelled.

"What's up," she asked.

"You, are you getting in?"

"Of course, you did this for me Juelz? Thank you I really appreciate it, can I hook my phone up and play my playlist," she stated.

"Who else is here?"

Journee and I undressed, she hooked her phone up to my Beats pill speaker, and got in the tub. I should've known when I saw her at the club she had a child or something, she had child baring hips. She bared my child. She got in the tub and headed toward the other end. I motioned with my hands for to join me on my end. She made her way to my end of the tub and sat between my legs. I filled her wine glass with Pinot Grigio.

"You're not drinking with me," she asked.

"Nope."

I don't drink. I smoke, I had a blunt rolled. I lit the blunt, puffed a few times blew out smoke inhaled again. I let the warm smoke marinate in my lungs. Journee laid her head on my chest. I've been looking high and low for this motherfucka right here. I had some shit on my mind, but I wasn't ready to speak on it just yet.

"I missed you," she stated.

I didn't respond I wanted to know what else did she miss.

"Juelz," she pouted.

"Journee Leigh."

"I said I miss you," she pouted.

"I heard you, what you miss about me?"

Journee

"I miss everything about you. I miss the way you hold me. I miss your touch. I'm not going to lie, these past two days you haven't left my mind at all. I find myself thinking about you and reminiscing about us.

Despite everything, I still have to put my feelings in my pocket, I'm not in the business to get hurt again. My heart can't take it."

I put it out there, that's what he wanted to hear, but I can't dwell on the past. I refused for a nigga to play me again. I be damn. I don't know why he wanted me to say it so bad, just for him to not respond.

I couldn't sit here with him in this tub. I stood up and prepared to get out of the tub and he grabbed me and pushed me back down in the tub. I folded my arms up I across my stomach. Yeah, I was mad I don't care.

"What you mad for," he asked.

"Because you wanted to know how I felt, and I told you, and you didn't say anything."

He still didn't say anything I attempted to get up from his embrace. He insisted on pinning me down with his arms.

"Let me go."

"It's not that simple, you mad because I didn't say shit? What do you want me say? Journee I'm sorry I've said that enough. I don't want to break your heart again. I'm tired of telling you. I have to show," he argued.

That's all he had to say to begin with. I knew it was a bad idea coming over here. For this reason alone, that's why I didn't want to come. I should've kept my ass at home it's too early to be putting my feelings out there, knowing damn well me and Kairo haven't officially called it quits, and Giselle is still in the picture.

It feels good to get this up off my chest. It's been a long time coming and that's something that I always wanted to say. It'll be the last time I'm in the hot seat, and exposing my feelings about how I feel about shit. I feel bare and I don't like putting myself out there.

***

I didn't sleep good at all last night. I tossed and turned all night. I couldn't stop thinking about what I told him. He was still asleep. I had to go to work, and meet his mother later for lunch. I snuck out of the bed brushed my teeth, washed my face, and threw on my clothes on, and hauled ass.

Going forward it'll be strictly co-parenting no chill shit. I was getting attached to soon, and I didn't like the hold that he had on me. It's too early for this shit. I refuse to fall victim to him this soon.

We're moving entirely too fast, just the other day we were laying hands on each other like we didn't even know each other. Now we are spending the night daily, taking baths and shit, next it'll be fucking, nope not me.

I booked me a room at the Marriott it wasn't far from my job so I could shower and get dressed. I couldn't be there when he woke up. I just couldn't I'm sure he'll be mad, but oh well, he'll get over it. If he calls me I'm not answering. It's easier for me not to talk to him, so I won't yearn for him.

I must protect me, and my heart. I'll consider my feelings before I consider anybody else's. I need to work on me. As soon as me and Juelz broke up. I was with Kairo, now me and Kairo are going through whatever, and Juelz is back on the scene. I need a break from men period. I need to focus on me and Jueleez. I'm about to get right with God and find me a nice church home.

I'm not repeating the same cycle. Khadijah asked me was I happy? No not really, I haven't been happy in a long time. Yes, I'm living out my dreams, and doing most shit that people can't, but there's still something missing.

I know my mother would be proud of me, but it's not her validation that I'm seeking. I missed my brother Khadir he'll be home from college this weekend. He normally calls me every morning, but he's late today. Let me call him and see what's up.

"Journee Leigh, what's up I was just about to call you," he said.

"You, I was wondering why you haven't called me."

"Khadijah said you were with Juelz, so I didn't want to interrupt you," he explained.

"I was, but that don't have shit to do with our daily routine. I need to know that you're good."

"I'm good I'll be home this weekend, what's up with you? I want you to be happy Journee and live your life. You raised me and Khadijah stop putting your life on hold. Focus on you and Jueleez, you deserve to not worry about anybody else other than yourself for once. Promise me that," he asked.

"Khadir, who's the oldest? I can't promise you that, because I'm set in my ways. When your accustomed to do something for so long, it's hard to just stop. It's embedded in me."

"You are, but stop it. I don't want you to miss living your life because your so consumed with working, and worrying about me and Khadijah we're grown. Please just live," he explained.

"I'll try I'll talk to you later if not I'll see you tomorrow."

I'm sick of Khadijah and Khadir already. Let me be great. I swore I was the oldest. I felt like he was my father chastising me. I didn't even want to get in details about what him and Khadijah were talking about. I can only imagine. I pulled up to the Marriott Hotel. I valet parked. I should've took my ass home instead of paying money to get dressed somewhere.

I could've went to Nikki's house, but Skeet said he didn't want to see me until his birthday. I'm sure he would've told Juelz I was over there. Juelz and Skeet or worse than me and Nikki. I wasn't going over Alexis's house I didn't like seeing Free and him asking me one hundred questions, the possibility of Kairo pulling up.

I could've went to Khadijah's, but I'm sure her hot ass is over Smoke's, or he's over her house. Everybody's laid up but me. Poor lil me. Looking for love in all the wrong places. I'm playing a dangerous game with my heart right now. Fuck what the heart wants.

Chapter 10-Simone Marie Thomas

Today was the day I was meeting little Ms. Journee with her trifling ass. It was something about her that Juelz liked or should I say loved. For that reason alone, I couldn't wait to meet her. I wanted to know what it was about her that had him on the edge about our conversation.

My son knows me, and he knows how I get down. I was raised to go hard or go home. I'm not taking it easy on her. As soon as me and her exchanged a few words this nigga was on my line checking me because I checked her.

I had to look at my phone to make sure it was my son talking to me crazy. I know it's more to the story, but no matter how you feel about person never pull no shit like that.

My son has never checked me behind any female. I slaughter Giselle every time I see her just because I know she's a snake, and I hate that he's with her. I can't wait to see Kassence, I have my own DNA kit to swab her mouth. I know she ain't his she doesn't look like us at all.

Journee had spunk and class she was holding her own. I could tell that she wasn't a push over. I'm not surprised because I love Khadijah she reminds me of myself.

I love little Ms. Jueleez Monroe, her name is beautiful and unique it's fits her. She's so smart Journee's is doing a great job with her. My face lights up when she calls me Glama. I love her to death. I can't keep her from my house, she has me and her grandfather wrapped around her finger.

She told me yesterday Glama don't be mean to my mommy. My daddy and mommy worked it out. Promise me she stated. I wanted to laugh because this little girl was too smart she knew me.

I arrived at the restaurant prepared to get this show on the road to see what little Ms. Journee was all about. Juelz said she wasn't a whore, but let me be the judge of that. I'm sure she was here already she said that she'll beat me there via text.

I had my strap in my purse, you never know when shit could ignorant real quick. I'm and ignorant chick and I don't mind clearing a fucking restaurant. I served five years in the FEDS because a bitch got ignorant with me behind my husband.

Valerie

See bitches better ask about me. Anytime a bitch sends for mine that's my age you best believe I'm the one that's coming. I'm at bitches a neck about mine. I don't give a fuck how grown Journee is I'm her Godmother, her keeper I wear that title proud. I'D be damn if anybody thinks it's ok to fuck with mine.

Approach me, because I'm the one that answers to grown bitches like you. I don't mind making house calls, and checking a bitch about her. I don't condone what she did, but she did it, so what move the fuck on. Juelz wasn't perfect, his mammy has another thing coming if she thinks that she's going talk to her like she's an average bitch because she ain't.

I didn't raise no average bitches. I breed bosses and Queens, and any nigga or bitch will treat them as such. Journee told me all about her popping slick at the mouth. I raised her to respect her elders, but as for me I'll disrespect anybody that shit doesn't apply to me. She doesn't need him or his family for shit.

I'm at the sit down right now with Journee and Simone, and if she has an ounce of attitude I'm snatching this bitch wig off and beating ass. I'm ready for Fulton County. I've never spared a hoe and I'm not about to now.

I've never been the type to ask any questions, it's always shoot first and ask questions later. I have my Glock 40 rested on my lap. I dare a bitch to try me. I don't even like the way this bitch looks. I can tell she's old bitter and messy and that's not a good combination in the presence of woman like me.

If a bitch even looks at me wrong I'm busting my guns or throwing hands. You have to come correct with me at all times. I don't let anybody tread lightly or give out passes. I raised Nikki, Journee, and Khadijah the same way. If you let a bitch try you once, they'll try you again let these hoes know off top what type of woman you are and what they're dealing with.

<u>Journee</u>

The tension in this room was thick. Everybody was on go mode. My Godmother Valerie was on the side of me, grilling the fuck out of Simone, and Juelz mother was in front of me. This meeting could go one or two ways.

We could be cordial for the sake of Jueleez and Juelz, or we could be at each other's head. It didn't matter to me. I love to get slick at the mouth, but I didn't have time to take that approach, and I didn't want my Godmother doing time for killing Juelz mother.

"Let me go ahead and break the ice. I'm Journee Leigh Armstrong. I'm Jueleez's mother and this is my Godmother Valerie." I reached out and extended my hand for her to shake.

"Hi, I'm Simone, Juelz's mother it's nice to finally put a face with the name," she stated and shook my hand, and Valerie's also.

"It's nice to meet you too."

We both sat down and I could tell that we both had to make sure we used the appropriate words before we responded to each other. I need this to go as pleasant as possible my life is already off the hook, and I don't want to beat ass today.

"Ok Journee I'm going to get straight to it. You can take this shit how you want too. You can take it as me getting smart, or you can take it as me being rude.

You were wrong as fuck for the shit you pulled it was trifling. I'm not going to go in on you because my son asked me not too. I don't know or even want to know why you did it at this point I don't even care.

He told me that he cheated, and I popped the shit out of him. You should've played the same game he played. You got him in the end. I love Jueleez and I just met her. I wish things would've played out a lot different for you and my son, but it is what is," she stated.

"I understand where you're coming from, and I'm listening. I'm not a cheater I'm not built like that. I just chose not to deal with Juelz. It wasn't so much of him cheating. Giselle came to my house, and I had to beat the shit out of her, excuse my language.

It wasn't about him she was out of line, and I'm going to demand my respect no matter what. It was another chick I wasn't about to deal with that my mother just passed."

"Ugh Giselle is another story for another day. I'm glad you beat the shit out of her. Every chance I get I slaughter her. It's something about her that I don't like. She's fake and sneaky. Respect is everything, I know exactly where you're coming from.

I did five years in the FEDS, because a bitch thought she could try me because she wanted my husband, and I stomped the fuck out of her in broad day light, and waited on the police to come. The state dropped my case and the FEDS picked it back up. I had to do time. I don't regret that shit one bit," she stated.

"You know exactly where I'm coming from."

"I do, the real question is what are you going to do to get your man back?" she asked.

"Nothing, I have a situation and he still has one too. She hasn't changed one bit, and I'm too old to be fighting over him because she's crazy."

"If you say so, Jueleez told me that her mother has been over her daddy's house two nights straight," she laughed.

"Hold up Journee you're keeping secrets and shit now. You didn't tell me shit about you spending the night already," My Godmother Valerie interrupted.

"Oops," I laughed.

"Yeah oops," they both laughed.

Juelz mother was cool. I could tell that we would get along just fine. She felt the same way I felt about Giselle. I couldn't wait to get Jueleez home, she needs to stop telling my business. We ate lunch and ordered a few drinks. Her and my godmother exchanged numbers.

Juelz

I called my mother at least a hundred times to make sure she didn't do anything crazy. Simone Marie Thomas is crazy as fuck and she wants everybody to know that shit too. She's hard-headed and she doesn't like to listen.

I had my father to go the restaurant also and follow her, because he knows that she acts crazy if somebody says the wrong thing to her. Journee hasn't called me to curse me out yet, so I'm praying everything goes good. Giselle already ruined us once I didn't need my mother doing it also.

My mother finally decided to call me back after I blew up her phone.

"Ma, how did it go."

"It went good Juelz, is that why you called me, and blew up my phone like you were my husband," she asked.

"Yes, ma because I know you. Journee isn't out to get me or what I have."

"I noticed that I like her, can you believe that? Why did you cheat," she asked?

"I can't believe that ma. She's the only woman that I ever loved. It's crazy because I never stopped loving her. I cheated because I thought I could get away with it. I figured if she ever found out we could work it out. She left my ass, and had no attentions of ever coming back. She took my princess too."

"You were dumb but young. You live and you learn she took your heart and you played with hers. For that reason, alone that's why you can't get over her. I like her she's real. She explained herself. She's not trash like Giselle," she argued.

"I know ma, I'll talk to you later. I love you."

"I love you too, and next time you don't have to send your father to check on me. I know how to act," she laughed and hung up the phone.

***

Chapter 11-Tyra Hussein

The game is to be sold and not told. Let me introduce myself I'm Tyra Hussein, I'm Kairo's wife not EX wife. I know y'all heard some foul shit about me. He could never divorce me, we have family ties that's bigger than mob ties. I'm a Queen and I refused to give any bitch my throne. We've all made mistakes yeah I fucked a few niggas before, and he caught me fucking a nigga in our home and killed him with his bare hands.

Sometimes we go through shit to get to where we are going, and you don't miss a good thing until it's gone. I'm tired of missing my good thang. I want my husband back. I've sat in the background for too long and watched him, and Journee do them with little Ms. Jueleez. Every woman has a breaking point and I'm at mine.

Don't get me wrong I fucked up, and dated a few niggas too but the shit that he has with Journee doesn't compare. I've learned my lesson and I'm ready to do right by him. He is in love with her. I refused to let my husband love another woman that's not me.

His mother told me that he wants out of the family business so he can legally divorce me and marry her. I be damn this nigga was ready to give up all his wealth for her.

If he gave up his wealth and divorced me I wouldn't have shit but this house and a few cars. Kairo has a bag that needs to be secured I'm his wife and I'll forever secure it.

I'm not saying I'm the baddest bitch, but I'm willing to go toe to toe, and fight Journee behind my husband. I have papers on him and a divorce is one thing that I refuse to give him. Yes, I've allowed them to be together for eight years, and Kairo only stayed married to me to obtain wealth and millions and my family connections and access to drugs more powerful than cocaine.

I've teamed up with Giselle, Free's baby mother. We've been friends for years. I'm Kassence Godmother and she's going to help me get my husband back. Giselle is my best friend and I love her to death and she's willing to help me.

Lately Kairo and me have been spending a lot of time together. Giselle and I have been double dating. I thought this was the beginning of us getting back on track. This nigga played me for a fool. I love him, and love will make you do some crazy shit.

Kairo left early this morning. He woke me up with dick for breakfast and in return he got morning head, then he left. He said he would be coming back later. He's been here for the past two weeks, so I didn't think anything of it.

I received a knock on my door. I rarely had company. Giselle didn't mention that she was coming by. I looked through my peep hole, and it was a white guy dressed casually. I instantly thought a salesman, and he said that he was looking for Tyra Hussein.

I opened the door so fast he said he had some papers for me to sign. I took the papers out of his hand, he said you've just got served. He was a process server. He served me with divorce papers.

Today was the motherfucking day, that all hell broke loose. Kairo served me with divorce papers. I've been too fucking nice. I agreed to play by his rules because I was getting a check every month.

All bets where off when Kairo decided to make my bed, and my pussy a permanent fixture for two weeks. My husband wined and dined me, it felt like the old us. I received nice gifts every day for the past two weeks he did this when we were happy and in love. Journee who?

He played me. He actually thought that he could fuck and finesse me, and it's not any consequences. Don't get me wrong I knew he wanted a divorce, but for you to sit here and fuck and suck on me week after week, and serve me with divorce papers the same day.

To make matters worse you had me sign some papers last week that I didn't pay attention too. I thought it was a for a new house, but it was the divorce papers. I called him and he changed his number.

Ok two can play that game. I'm telling it all today. I had to call Giselle it was time for a house call.

"Hey sis, what's up, what you are doing," she asked.

"I'm pissed Kairo served me with the final divorce papers today and changed his number. We're legally divorced." I cried.

"I'm confused you agreed to divorce him. I'm missing something," she asked.

"No, he tricked me. Come over here now, I'm going to his house to tell Journee everything. I need you with me. If we're divorced he's not the only one that's going to be single and miserable. He changed his number, he just left a few hours ago."

"I'm on my way, I have Kassence with me, let me throw on some comfortable clothes and I'm coming. I got your back he's wrong for that. I don't blame you for telling her. She can either hate it or respect it," she stated.

"It's not even about her. It's the principle on how he did things, and he led me on to believe that we could work out, hurry up I'm ready to get this over with."

"Ok I'm on my way," she stated.

Journee

My life went from perfect too crazy in a matter of weeks. I haven't heard from Kairo since the night he promised to come home, and that was two weeks ago. He never came home or showed his face. He's been sending me gifts by the restaurant, and I've been refusing every gift. You can't buy me. I don't give a fuck how much you cash out, I don't want nothing from you.

Each time he called my phone from different numbers attempting to talk, I never answered. I wanted him to tell me to my face what the fuck is going on. He's in town because Alexis told me that he came by the house with Free asking about me, and what I've been up too. He really wanted to know was Juelz in the picture and he wasn't.

None of that matters, where are you laying your head? That's the fucking question. I started to pack my shit up, and move out of our house. I'm not, I just changed the fucking locks and packed his shit up.

Today's Alexis's birthday and I'm having a small get together for her at my house. We didn't fool with many people, and I don't like everybody coming to my house. The guest consists of Khadijah and Nikki that's it. I made ranch, and lemon pepper wings, Rotel dip. **Mask Off** by **Future** was blaring through the speakers. We started dancing. I loved this song I had my own little mix to it.

Percocet molly Percocet

Percocet molly Percocet

Represent gotta, gotta represent

Chase a check, never chase a dick

Khadijah was the bar tender for tonight, and the frozen daiquiris was on the menu, we were tipsy as shit. Jueleez was with her father for the evening, she would be home later. We sat back relaxing and chilling talking about shit that girls talk about. Our conversation just started getting good Khadijah was telling us about Smoke. The doorbell rang, I wasn't expecting anyone.

"Khadijah get the door."

"Ok," my sister yelled.

We continued eating and sipping, Khadijah took longer than expected. I don't know who that was.

"Journee, you have company it's two bitches at the door asking for you and one looks familiar. I can't remember where I know her from," my sister yelled.

"Two bitches looking for me?"

"Yes, bitch I'm not lying. I swear this shit feels like Déjà vu," my sister stated.

My antennas were instantly up. I wasn't tipsy anymore. Nobody knew where I laid my head, so I was curious to see what the fuck was going on. I headed to the front door. Nikki and Alexis was right behind me. I stopped by the closet in the hallway and grabbed my AK.

One thing about it and two things for sure a bitch gone learn not to come to my house uninvited. I swung the door open and pointed the AK in these hoes face.

"What the fuck are you doing on my doorstep?"

"I had no clue, you're the hoe we were coming to visit," she argued.

I couldn't believe what my eyes landed on, it's this same silly bitch, and she brought company with her, and her daughter. That's a big no, I will body a bitch in front of her child and not give a fuck. Clearly your mother didn't give a fuck about you.

"I wasn't expecting you to do this bullshit again. You know better or did you fucking forget? Eight years later and you still knocking on female's doors about a nigga that don't want you, I beat your ass once, I'm grown now, I'll make a bitch eat bullets." I still had my AK trained in her face. I cocked that bitch back so she could know it was real.

"Let that bitch rip Journee," my sister yelled.

"Oh, I didn't even come here for you she did, I see your still a side bitch eight years later, just not to my nigga," she argued and laughed.

"I've never been a side bitch to nan nigga, you have me confused with yourself. It's funny you say that, because you're the same bitch that was having premonitions about me with your nigga correct me if I'm wrong."

"What the fuck did you just say," she asked.

"Tyra what the fuck are you doing here?" my best friend Alexis interrupted and asked.

"Tyra, why are you at my fucking house?"

"Are you sure that you want to know," she laughed.

"Look bitch you're not in the business to be playing games, because a bitch like me. I don't even ask questions.

I shoot first and you can explain to the police why you're trespassing," my best friend Nikki stated.

"I know I'm probably the last person y'all won't to hear from. I swear I didn't know you were Kairo's Journee. I didn't know this was your house Journee. I just came to support her," Juelz baby mammy Giselle said.

Nikki

I wasn't even going to come to Alexis party, because my daughter was sick, but my husband told me to go ahead he got it. I'm shooting the shit with my girls and stuff. We're tipsy and shit. Journee's doorbell rang and Khadijah said two bitches at the door asking for Journee. That statement alone just sobered me the fuck up.

A bitch didn't want no smoke. I already know what time it is. I'm on go, Alexis and Khadijah on go. Journee grabbed the AK out the closet and I grabbed my .9mm rugger out of my purse. Journee swung the door open its Giselle and Tyra Kairo's wife she pointed AK in Giselle's face. The two of them are suspect. Giselle popping slick at the mouth.

I didn't want to hear shit she had to say, she know she don't want none. I wanted to know what Tyra had to say she had a big smirk on her face. I couldn't wait to smash my gun in her face. If she even lets some slick shit roll off her tongue she gone wish Giselle didn't bring her over here. Don't let me start on Kairo if he played my sister with this duck ass bitch here, I'm beating his ass he gone feel me or he gone feel this .9mm pick one, I never liked his ass no way...

Why did Giselle bring Kassence with her? If I end up bodying this bitch. How am I supposed to explain this shit to Skeet and Juelz, that's my only concern? I'm catching a body just on the strength a bitch had the balls to pull up over here.

Anytime you come to a bitch's house about a nigga that you know don't want you, not once but twice, you deserve a fucking dirt nap courtesy of me. Let me call my husband, he's the only one that can calm me down besides Journee. I stepped back in the house to call him.

"Baby what you are doing?"

"Laying down waiting on your fine ass to get home a nigga miss you," he stated.

"Baby, call my momma to watch Nyla and Lil Skeet, I need you to come to Journee's house now. Giselle and Kairo ex's wife just popped up. Some shit is about to go down and I might fuck around and catch a body bring my bond money."

"Hold up Nikki, I'm on my way. Juelz just left here let me call him, so he can turn around I can ride with him I'll drop them off. Don't kill nobody I mean it, I know you.

Promise me you ain't gone make a mess, do you hear me,"
he asked.

I hung up in his face. I love my husband but I'm not
promising shit. It's self-defense. He called me back, I
didn't answer I cut my phone off. He already knew what
the deal was. If I say I'm going to do something I'm not
going to fucking hesitate to do it. These hoes are going to
get everything that's fucking coming to them.

If Journee didn't handle them I would. I don't
appreciate my buzz being blown because these bitches were
in their feelings about two niggas that ain't pressed for
them. Tyra is stupid if you ask me, she knew about Journee
all along if you're pulling up to her house. Me and Journee
couldn't point you out in a line up. To make matters worse
we don't even know where you laid your head for that
reason alone I know you've been investigating.

Kairo done something major to you today for you to
show your face and come out of hiding. I want to know
exactly what that was.

Chapter 12-Journee

"It's nice to see you too Alexis, since we're doing introductions. I'm Tyra Hussein, and I'm here to discuss you and my husband not EX. He's never divorced me I'm here today to let you know that your side bitch shit with Kairo stops today.

My husband and I are on one accord and your services are no longer needed. Oh, Alexis let me introduce you to Giselle and your stepdaughter Kassence," she laughed and stated.

"Side bitch, y'all hoes got the game wrong."

"I don't," she taunted me.

"Oh, so you're here because of your EX husband. I'm sure this bitch here told you about me and what I do to hoes popping up at my house. I don't take disrespect lightly, and I don't appreciate you coming to my home to confront me on some bullshit. Its levels to this shit, never confront the female confront the man.

I'm tired of hoes trying me about niggas. It's time I make an example out of one of you hoes. Schools in session so let me school you hoes. I always said if a bitch ever came to my house again about a nigga going forward,

I'm not sparing a hoe because she had the balls to bring her silly ass to where I lay my head."

"He's my husband, not my man, he never divorced me. I just allowed him to play school with you," she laughed.

"Oh, you think this shit is funny? Let me educate you really quick. Khadijah, grab my phone let me call Kairo really quick to clear some shit up."

"Ok, call him from my phone because I'm not busting a move from this porch. I'm ready to clear this bitch," my sister argued.

"Kairo, I had him on speaker phone so these bitches could hear.

"Hey baby, I love you, I miss you, and can I kiss you? What's up? You ready for daddy to come back home? You're not mad at me anymore," he asked.

"Umm uh cut that bull shit out, that's not why I called you. Do you have anything you need to tell me that could break our bond?"

"No Journee, why would you ask that? You know I would never hurt you. I love you too much. I want you to be my wife. Are you ready because I'm ready," he asked?

"Kairo, Tyra's at the house right now, with the same bitch whose ass I beat eight years ago on the same type of shit. Have you been fucking her recently? She said that she's still your wife, you never divorced her. Is that true?"

"Let me explain Journee," he argued but I cut him off.

"I don't want you to explain shit, answer my fucking question."

"Baby she's lying tell that bitch to show you." I hung up in his face I don't want to hear shit else he had to say.

"I told you," she laughed.

"You didn't tell me shit. The difference between me and you a nigga can't feed me no bullshit and dick. He fed you that, and it back fired that's why you're here. I don't give a fuck about excuses and explanations. I have a zero tolerance for that."

I don't know who was sillier her or Giselle. Kairo and his wife had to have something going on for her to come here. I'm not dumb, I don't know what it is but I don't give a fuck.

I'm tired, and I don't bother nobody, nor do I go looking for trouble. I wasn't even going to tap this bitches' ass, but it's the principle.

She had the sad face when this nigga was telling me how much he loved me, and he wanted to marry me, but as soon as that let me explain shit came out of his mouth she was laughing.

The jokes not on me it's on you now, because you're about to get your ass handed to you. She stood in front me with her arms folded smirking. Smirking and being petty is what's about to land you in a fucked-up situation, fucking with savage like me.

I don't play that shit, you came for me and I didn't send for you. I walked up on this bitch and smashed my AK in her fucking face. Her nose was fucking leaking It was show time. She wasn't even expecting it, she fell back I picked her up and slammed her on the pavement, she had her face covered.

"Stand up bitch and take this motherfucking ass whooping. I want you to laugh and smirk now hoe." She was taking her time getting up. She finally stood to her feet. I was ready to kick box her weak ass. I kicked that bitch in her stomach, she stumbled over. I picked that hoe up again, and slammed her ass on the fucking pavement again.

I grabbed her by that long as weave she had in her head. I had a mean grip on that shit too. I yanked it from her scalp. I punched her in both of her eyes and kicked her fucking teeth out. I blanked out I just started stomping her.

"Beat her motherfucking ass Journee, don't fucking ease up. Give her your best fucking work. Kill that bitch with your bare hands. The same way her husband did that nigga she got caught fucking. I'm waiting on Kairo to pull up we gone tag that motherfucka," my best friend Nikki yelled as she was pounding her fist in her hands.

"Let me go please I didn't come here to fight. I came here to expose him," she cried.

"Anytime you come a woman's house about any man, you're in the wrong be prepared to fight. Did you actually think that you were about to come here and talk shit and leave? You could've called me on the phone.

You still came to my house on some bullshit. Nikki, bring me my AK, so I can show this bitch how real this shit gets. Khadijah give me your knife so I can carve my name in this bitches' face."

"Journee, carve that bitch like you carving a fucking thanksgiving turkey," my sister yelled.

"Say no more. It's about to be some smoke in the fucking City. Juelz and Skeet on the way. You got about forty-five minutes to body Giselle too. Dispose the hoes before Gwinnett County comes. It self-defense and these bitches are trespassing," my best friend Nikki laughed.

"Please don't shoot me, I'm sorry," she cried.

"It's too late for that school's not in session anymore and you don't get a fucking pass. I don't give a fuck about your tears right now." Nikki handed me my AK. Khadijah gave me her knife. I wasn't going to kill Tyra. Kairo can keep this bitch. They deserve each other.

I shot her in the fucking face close range, I made sure my silencer was on so the neighbors couldn't hear. The same ugly ass face that she smirked, and taunted me with. It was a hole in her jaw, blood leaked all over her clothes. I carved my name in her face she'll never forget me, I'm the wrong bitch to fuck with. She should've asked about me.

"Giselle, do you want some too? Let's go bitch. You up next. You ain't learned a motherfucking thang. To make matters worse you bring your daughter with you."

"Nah Journee, I'll take it from here with Giselle. Get Free on the fucking phone now. I have a few questions to ask this bitch before I start tagging her and him too. What the fuck did Tyra mean your daughter was my step-daughter," my best friend Alexis argued.

"Alexis, don't ask her shit, the bitch looks like she's ready to tell a lie. Ask Free, him and Kairo just pulled up." I pointed to the driveway.

I can't believe all of this shit happened today. Why do I always run across a fuck nigga? My heart gets me in trouble. I always see the best in a motherfucka. When I should be looking for the worst, I always give a person a fair chance.

You have one time to cross me, and it's a wrap. Y'all wonder why I do the shit I do, and dip off on niggas. I don't have time for this extra shit, I can live without it. I'm not afraid to be by myself, I'm cool with that. Every time I give a nigga my heart or piece of me he breaks it.

I'll be alright. I'm just tired of going through all of this shit. It's always the hoes that get treated with royalty and loyalty. They get wifed up quicker before the good girls. If I was hoe I wouldn't even be going through this shit.

"Journee, its ok I got you let's fuck this nigga up though. I knew something was up with him. Old lying married ass nigga," my best friend Nikki stated.

"Journee, what the fuck did you do to her?" he asked and yelled.

"It's not about what she did to her, it's about what the fuck she's going to do about your lying married ass," my sister argued.

"Daddy, daddy, uncle Kairo, that girl beat up Auntie Tyra," Giselle's daughter cried and pointed at me.

Alexis got her conformation right there. I wasn't going to answer him, I wanted him to get close to me so, I could tag his ass a few times. I fucking hate him. I don't ask a nigga for much, but loyalty, respect, and honesty. Don't have me out here looking like a fucking fool.

If you wanted to be with your wife that's cool just don't drag me in your bullshit, and having a bitch come to my house. It's easy to just leave me the fuck alone. How does she even know where the fuck I live?

"Do you hear me fucking talking you?" he asked as he walked up behind me.

I turned around with the meanest scowl on my face, and hit him in his fucking eye. I jabbed him in his fucking jaw. I just started tagging him. He stood there and took that shit.

"Are you still married to her?"

"I was up until today Journee, divorcing her wasn't easy, but it's done now legally. I'm sorry," he stated.

"Lying to me was easy though, and keeping me in the background was easy for you? It's done legally now. You're going to regret lying to me, and fucking pursing me. You included me in your bullshit. I would've never fucked with you, and you know that."

My heart dropped when he revealed that. I punched him in his chest. I tried to knock the wind out of him. Nikki hit him in the back of his head with her gun. We beat his ass. We didn't ease up on that nigga either.

He fell to the ground and we stomped his ass out. I still had Khadijah's knife in my pocket. I wanted to cut his skin off of him. I can't even look at him. Khadijah was on standby waiting on Free to jump stupid, he couldn't because he had to explain his infidelities to Alexis.

I felt some strong arms get me up off of Kairo and pick me up. I turned around and it was Juelz and Jueleez. Ugh why did she have to see this shit? I'm going to kill that motherfucka for lying to me, and this bitch coming to my house, and my daughter has to see all of this shit.

Juelz

Skeet called me as soon as I was pulling up out of his subdivision. He said that Giselle and ole boy's wife, and my daughter was at Journee's house. He said, Nikki said that she was about to catch a body. We dropped Nyla and Lil Skeet off at Nikki's mother house.

I was headed that way to take Jueleez home anyway. I was pissed Giselle just wouldn't ease up. I got over there as fast I could. Me and Skeet pulled in the driveway. I hopped out the car with my daughter in tow. Journee and Nikki was beating some niggas ass. Skeet grabbed Nikki. I grabbed Journee because my daughter was crying. I picked Journee up.

"He ain't worth it, bring your ass on fighting in front of my daughter."

She turned around and looked at me, and she was embarrassed.

"Giselle, why do you have my daughter over here with you, and you're on some bullshit? Aye partner you can put my daughter down, let's go Kassence you are rolling with me because your mother is on some bullshit."

"No offense partner, but my daughter Kassence ain't going with you. Giselle tell this nigga that she's not his. I'm Kasson by the way," he stated.

"Daddy is she my sister," my daughter Jueleez asked.

"Wait a minute baby girl. Go stand with your mother for a minute. Daddy needs to handle some business." My daughter did as she was told.

"Giselle, what the fuck is this nigga talking about?"

"Let me explain," she cried and stated.

"Explain what let's go Kassence."

"You don't have to explain shit, I'm her father. I told her mother to tell you, years ago but she was too scared to speak the fuck up. My daughter is named after me Kassence Aliyah Hussein. I had a DNA test ran on her three weeks after she was born. I've been fucking Giselle for the past eight years," he stated proudly.

"Giselle Is this true? Please tell me this is a fucking lie. I told you what I would do to you, if you ever called yourself trying to play a nigga like me, and pen a baby one me. Is this nigga her father yes or no answer my fucking question?"

"Yes, I'm sorry Juelz. I didn't mean to hurt you," she cried.

"Nah you knew what the fuck you were doing. If she wasn't mine I would've been left you a long time ago. I knew you was fucking another nigga, your pussy was too loose. He can have you though. I would never wife or fall in love with trash, and a hoe like you anyway."

"What the fuck are you crying for Giselle, you want this nigga or something," he asked.

"I can't be mad, but I can be because I want too, but thank you for taking this duck as bitch off my hands. Giselle, I don't ever want to see you again. Everything that you have at my house. I'm boxing that shit up and sending it to your mother's house. I knew it was a reason that you didn't want to give a me a DNA because you knew she wasn't mine. You were selfish, but it's all good though.

Maybe he can love you, because I never loved you. I always saw you for what you were. I want you to meet somebody that you've been dying to meet. Jueleez Monroe, come here I want you to meet somebody."

"Who do you want me to meet daddy? Hi uncle Free," my daughter stated.

"I want you to meet Kassence and her mother Giselle."

"Hi Kassence! Hi Giselle! I'm Jueleez Monroe Thomas. It's nice to meet you," my daughter stated and mustered up the biggest smile.

I had to do it call me petty as nigga, but I knew her heart dropped when she saw Jueleez she looks exactly like me. Giselle fucked up playing with a nigga like me, and pinning her daughter on me. She's going to regret the day she ever laid eyes on me. I'm a heartless ass nigga and I'm going to hurt her.

Chapter 13-Alexis

My birthday really? I was in a fucking daze everything happened so fast. I had to process this shit. To actually look this child in the face, confirms Free has been cheating on me. She has to be at least seven years old. She looks exactly like him.

Free spoke so proudly about fucking with her for eight years knowing damn well we were still together. Free wasn't a real nigga, he wanted to be, but he wasn't. I asked him numerous of times did he want to see other people.

He never spoke up. I asked him because I didn't want him to feel like he was putting his life on hold for me. I wasn't selfish because I was fucking a few niggas too. In the Marines, I'm sure y'all heard of don't ask don't tell. Free never asked so I never said anything.

He didn't agree with me going to the Marines, but so what. I did what I had to do for me. I didn't want to be a drug dealer's wife. I didn't care about the money, cars, and clothes. I wanted to be somebody. The eight years that I was away I became the woman that I wanted to be.

I'm glad I didn't let this fuck nigga stop me. Did he forget that I was fucking out here? I had enough, and I've heard enough, he was about to feel me. I had to lay hands on Giselle because she played Juelz, and she's the same bitch that broke up Journee and him. She knew about me, I couldn't let this shit slide, she deserved a real a beat down.

"What's up Free, she's beautiful? In the past eight years, today was the day that you actually kept it real about what you've been up too? You didn't have to lie we're better than that. I knew it was somebody, but her. How can you be a side nigga to a bitch that already has nigga?" I approached him and Giselle, he put his daughter in the car, he knew I was on some fuck shit. My gun was tucked behind my waist.

"I'm sorry Alexis I never meant to hurt you," he stated he couldn't even look me in my eyes. Giselle had a big smile on her face.

"Nah nigga you ain't sorry, I don't want you to be. You can't even look me in my face right now. You're proud to be fucking with her, I heard you loud and clear. I always told you, I could always tell when you were lying by your tone. I thought we were better than that, I guess not. Congratulations."

"Thank you," she said.

"Excuse me bitch, but was I talking to you. Last I checked when I asked you was this his child you couldn't speak up."

"I'm glad that you finally know about us, we're engaged. We're getting married soon," she argued and sassed.

"Congratulations! I'm glad you finally cuffed a man that wants to be with you. Journee and Juelz can finally be a family together without a bitch like you interrupting. My niece is beautiful, isn't she? She looks exactly her father. Journee won, you were right about your premonition he was with her." I laughed.

"That's still leaves you single bitch," she laughed.

"See what goes around, comes around. I knew a long time ago that Free wasn't the man for me, and I was ok with that. Our relationship has run its course a long time ago. He's sampled some new pussy and I've sampled plenty of dick. I'm comfortable in my own skin, I'm natural, I'm self-made. A nigga can't make me or break me. I chase checks and not dick."

"I don't care I always had Free," she laughed.

Giselle has to be the dumbest bitch that I ever came across. She didn't know when to shut up. I was totally fine with that because I wasn't beating your ass for Free. I was beating your ass because of the shit you pulled between Juelz and Journee and you've been fucking this nigga the whole time. He can have you.

I walked up in Giselle's space and I spat in that bitches' face.

"You disgust me." She tried to push me. I punched her in her forehead. I wanted this bitch to fight me. I wanted her to walk it like she talks it. She stood up straight and ran up on me. I smashed her in the face with my fist, I punched her in nose.

It was leaking, her daughter was crying. She used her shirt to stop the blood from falling. I wasn't done with her yet. I picked her up and slammed her on the hood of Free's car. I pounced on this hoe.

"That's my motherfucking girl beat her ass," my best bae Nikki yelled, she was clapping her hands so loud.

"That's enough Alexis," he yelled and walked up on me.

I stepped back and looked at him and gave him the meanest scowl ever. I pulled my gun from behind my back and pointed at him.

"It's enough when I said it's enough."

"What are you going to do with that." he asked.

"I shoot first and ask questions later."

I shot Free twice in the chest. I told y'all if he ever played me and didn't say shit I would drop him right where he stands. I'm a woman of my word. I hate fuck niggas and he wasn't excluded. I don't give a fuck about our history.

"Bitch you shot me," he argued.

"Did you think I was pulling out this gun for fun, be glad it was just in the chest."

"Alexis, let's go fuck him and his whack as bitch," my best bae Journee stated.

"Die motherfucker, and ask your daddy how my pussy tastes? I rode his face on a numerous of occasions just off the strength, I knew you were cheating, I never like your mammy and the bitch never liked me."

"What the fuck did you say," he argued and attempted to walk up on me.

"You heard what the fuck I said."

"Bitch I'm going to kill you," he argued and yelled and attempted to walk up on me.

"Not if I kill you first. Tend to your family Free, you made your bed now lay in it. If you come any closer to me, you won't live to fuck that bitch tomorrow. I'm shooting you in your fucking head."

I can't believe him, It's a small world I knew he was doing something. I just didn't know what he was doing. Out of all people Free and Giselle. I heard about this bitch, but never knew she was fucking my man and had a baby by him.

"I'm sorry about your birthday," my girls said in unison.

"Don't be this is the best birthday I've had in a very long time."

"Girl, did you really fuck with Free daddy?" my girls asked.

"Hell yeah, y'all thought I was lying. I haven't fucked him, but he pays to eat this pussy on a regular. I only did it because I knew Free was on some fuck shit. I wanted to hit him where it hurts, I accomplished that. Look I took a picture of his daddy eating my pussy so I can show his mammy. Ah ha old bitch."

"Girl, you're the real MVP. I just can't believe he was fucking with Giselle and that's Kassence daddy. I'm glad you beat her ass she deserved that shit," my best bae Nikki stated.

"I had to beat her ass after she played Juelz like that. That's was wrong I started to shoot that bitch too, but her crying ass daughter was doing the most. It's all good though. The best is yet to come."

<u>Kairo</u>

Tyra gone make me kill her stupid ass. Yeah, I was still married to Tyra for the eight years that Journee and I were together, but today that bitch and I were legally divorced. You mad because I served you, and divorced you after I fucked you.

I know I was wrong. I gave Tyra everything that she asked for the whole eight years that we stayed married. She wanted dick, I gave her that shit. She wanted money, she kept a fucking bag. She wanted trips, I booked that shit. She wanted me, I couldn't give her that. Whatever she wanted I made sure she had. She couldn't have me, she lost me a long time ago.

I knew Tyra was gone trip when she finally got served, and realized that our divorce was final. I didn't think that she would take her dumb ass over to Journee's house with Giselle and Alexis was over there. I was surprised when Journee called me from Khadijah's phone I wasn't expecting her to hit me with question after question.

I knew I was fucked. I wasn't expecting to lose Journee behind this. I divorced Tyra, I just didn't do it when I said that I did. Despite what it may seems, and how

I did shit I love Journee, she got my heart, and I never wanted to hurt her.

Tyra knew that. I didn't come home because I wasn't comfortable lying in Journee's face about what was going on. I couldn't do that. As soon as Journee said that Tyra and Giselle was over her house. I knew I had to get over there before shit got sideways. Free and I drove in separate cars.

As soon as I pulled in my driveway. I witnessed Tyra laid out on the concrete with a hole in her face blood everywhere. I didn't know if she was still breathing or not. I panicked I didn't want her to die because she couldn't let go.

I approached Journee I knew she was mad, I let her punch me a few times. I stood there and took it because I deserved it. I didn't expect Nikki to pistol whip me and the two of them jumped me like I was a nigga on the street it's all good.

I don't hit women, but if I ever get tried like that again, I'm bodying a female. Beating my ass still ain't gone change shit. Skeet and Juelz pulled up. Skeet got Nikki up off me and Juelz got Journee up off me. I don't like the way that he touched her, his whole approach annoyed me.

Free got shot twice by Alexis, today was a mess. I called security to come and get Tyra's car. I had to take her to the hospital to make sure that she was ok. I owed her that much, Journee did a number on her. Khadijah and Nikki met me at my car with my stuff, I didn't even say shit because this wouldn't be the last time they saw me.

"Tell Journee that she can have everything, it's not what it seems." They just ignored me. Tyra still had a pulse. I love Journee and I'm sure we could work past this, she doesn't have a choice. I be damn if any nigga thinks they can come in between what we have.

Chapter 14-Journee

Alexis, Khadijah, and Nikki had already left for the evening. I fixed Jueleez some nachos a few wings, and a cup of juice. She was in the house eating, Juelz was inside with her. I came outside to clean my property. I poured bleach on the blood stains and sprayed it down with the pressure washer. I didn't want the blood to stain the concrete. I'm sure the neighbors got an earful.

I can't believe I just did all of this shit, I will always defend myself. I refuse to be played by anyone male or female. I demand my respect and I'll die behind that shit. I don't know how much Juelz and Jueleez saw but I was embarrassed and ashamed, because I know me and Nikki showed our whole ass. Let's not mention Alexis beat the brakes off of Giselle's maggot ass.

When she picked her up and slammed her I just knew she was dumping her ass through the windshield. I can't believe she lied about her daughter being Juelz and Free was her baby daddy ugh. I never really liked Free, it was something about him that always rubbed me the wrong way.

Maybe because he was smiling in my face and knew his brother was still married to his wife, and he was cheating with Giselle. Don't get me wrong Giselle is a beautiful girl with an ugly soul.

It took for Juelz to comeback in my life for all of this bullshit to start unfolding. If that's not a sign, I don't know what is. I feel so bad for him because he's considered her child as his own for seven years, and this bitch has been playing games the whole time.

As soon as morning came, I was calling my real estate agent to have this property listed for sale. I can't believe him, I'm glad I packed his shit. Everything he had here was gone, he wasn't leaving here without his stuff. I heard the front door open. I didn't pay it no mind.

"Married huh," he asked as he approached me.

"Yep."

"You good do you want to talk about it," he asked.

"Not really, do you want to talk about her child not being yours?"

"We can but I'm about to roll, are y'all coming with me or y'all staying here? I prefer y'all to come with me. You've been through enough today. Get you some stuff and let's roll," he said.

"I have to finish cleaning this blood and stuff up first."

"I'll take it from here, go get your stuff, so we can leave," he stated.

Sometimes Juelz is so perfect I swear he is. I would rather be alone to think about this crazy ass shit that just happened. I know I would have to explain to Jueleez what happened. I appreciate him more than he will ever know. I really hate that Alexis birthday party was ruined due to this bullshit. Everything you do in the dark comes to the light.

Juelz

Giselle played me, she played the shit out of me. I had a very strong feeling that Kassence wasn't mine, but I put that shit to the side, and gave Giselle the benefit of the doubt. I know I fucked her a few times raw. This bitch laid next to me a many of nights knowing damn well her child wasn't mine. This nigga has been in the picture the whole time. I don't even know how I didn't even see this shit. She was always sneaky and moving funny.

She's named after him that shit blows my fucking mind. It's all good I'm not fucked up about being there for her and her child. I'm the wrong fucking nigga to play. I know I wasn't the best nigga to Giselle in the past, but I haven't cheated on her in years.

I gave her anything she fucking wanted, she took my kindness for my weakness. I can't even lie I'm fucked up about that shit. I raised Kassence as my own for years, and to know that she's not mine hurts a niggas heart for real. Even these past few weeks with me and Journee, flirting and kicking it. I haven't over stepped my boundaries. I'm not cheater I don't cheat anymore.

It's all good though I didn't even lay hands on her today. For two reasons, both of my daughters were out there. I'll get up with Giselle soon, she's addicted to me. It won't be long before she comes running back. Especially since Journee's in the picture, but she'll set herself up. I'll catch her, he can have her I'm good on her. It makes sense where my daughter was the night her trifling ass pulled up at 5:00 am she was with him.

Now I know why she was heated about me asking for a DNA test, she knew Kassence wasn't mine. I knew I hurt her feelings when I introduced her to Jueleez. My daughter is my mini me, she so beautiful, she can't ever have a boyfriend. This is one conversation that I don't want to have with my mother.

Journee decided to take her precious time coming out. Jueleez and me, were sitting in the car waiting on her. She finally came out with a duffle bag. Who knows what she had inside of there. She slid in the car, and closed the door. I pulled off.

I purchased a condo not too far from her house. I planned on staying there when I didn't feel like driving home. I was tired as fuck. I really didn't feel like driving to the West Side fuck it. It was Saturday anyways and she was off on Sunday's and Monday's.

I can't lie this nigga did have her living good despite having a wife. This house looks like a fucking castle. I'll buy her and my daughter something better.

Jueleez was talking our heads off, she finally went to sleep. Journee stared out the window. I grabbed her hand and messaged it, I could tell she was stressed out. I knew she didn't want to talk about it. Holding it in isn't going to solve shit either. I know she was fucked behind that shit.

Journee was a good woman and great mother to my daughter. He fucked up royally. I remember the night I saw her for the first time, she bragged about him. I hated that shit, and this nigga was dogging her out the whole time, I knew him from somewhere. I used to see Free all the time in my hood. It makes sense now why the nigga was looking at me crazy he was still fucking with Giselle.

***

We finally made it to my house. Journee got her bag, and walked in the house. I carried Jueleez in her room, my baby girl was tired. I laid her in her bed, Journee undressed her, and put her pajamas on, and cleaned her face.

I don't know if Journee was ready to talk or not about what happened. I sat in my man cave and smoked a blunt to the head. Giselle was already calling my phone asking could we talk. She had eight years to talk, and she didn't say shit. She kept that shit playa and discreet.

I was tired so I went upstairs to my room to shower and go to bed. Journee was walking out of the shower, she didn't say shit to me. We walked right past each other. I cut my shower on high and just soaked up the warm water drenching my skin. I had ninety-nine problems and Giselle was the main fucking one.

I could take the high road and say fuck her. Nah, I can't let that bitch slide. For two reasons, she played me, not once but twice. The first time she broke me and Journee up knowing damn well I wasn't her nigga. The second time you knew your child wasn't mine, but you wasn't going to say shit, if that nigga didn't.

I'm heartless ass nigga and I refuse for a bitch to play me. I have to hurt you, so you can feel me. I apply pressure. I finished handling my hygiene. My mind was a little bit clearer now. I feel like I could sleep a little better since I don't have to worry about this nagging as bitch.

I dried off and threw my boxers on and made my way to my bedroom. Journee was sitting in the middle of the bed, braiding her hair in two French braids.

"What's up you good?"

"Not really, but I'll get over it," she stated.

"Did you know that he was cheating?"

"No, I knew he was doing something, one night his phone was off and he never cuts his phone off. That was the first red flag," she explained.

"You'll be alright. Fuck him and move on."

"What about you, did you know her child wasn't yours," she asked.

"I always had my doubts, but when I saw Jueleez for the first time. I knew she couldn't be mine. She never looked like me or my family. I'm real ass nigga so I took care of her, because I thought she was mine. I asked her for a DNA test the same day I caught up with you and my daughter. She had an attitude about it. Now I know why."

Journee and me we sat up, and talked for the rest of the night. She was still in her feelings. I had to cheer up. I told her she did that nigga dirty her and Nikki, and if they ever tried me like that. I'm killing them both I don't give a fuck. It was about 3:00 am we both got restless.

She thought she was going to lay beside me nope. On my chest is the only place she'll lay. I don't know what the fuck she thought. We could sleep peacefully tonight without any interruptions from Giselle and that fuck nigga. I started biting on her neck while she was sleep. I could feel the heat between her legs.

"I love you." I whispered in her ear.

"I love you too," she whispered.

"Why are you trying to act like you sleep?"

"Because I'm tired and my back is sore. Your dick keeps tapping my pussy," she whispered.

"He misses you."

"She misses him too, but we ain't ready to take it there," she whispered.

"Who's not ready?"

She ignored me. I know Khadijah ran her mouth to my mother, because she sent me a text telling me to come see her in the morning or she was coming to see me. My dad lets her do too fucking much. I got this trust me. If I don't get it she won't let me live it down. I'm going to handle my business no matter what.

<u>Chapter 15-Giselle</u>

I'm back like I never left. Yeah, I have a few scratches and bruises. Everything's out in the open now. I took that ass whooping that Alexis gave me like a straight G. She did entirely too much. My daughter was livid. Free's still recovering from the gunshot wounds to his chest. Alexis will have to see me it's not over. Don't ever come for me while I'm with my daughter.

Journee did Tyra so dirty she's still in the hospital from the severe impact on her body from being slammed in the pavement numerous of times. She needs plastic surgery on her face. I couldn't believe this is the bitch that had a child by him. It makes perfect sense now why I couldn't meet her daughter. His daughter is beautiful I can't deny that she looks exactly like her father.

I never knew this was the same fucking Journee. I swear to God that I didn't. Journee ain't no better than me. I've made some mistakes in my life. I don't regret any of the things that I've done. I hate Juelz found out about Kassence the way he did. I wanted to kill Free. I had two bags secured Juelz and his. I really do love Juelz despite what people may think.

Juelz can be with anybody, but Journee. I refuse to hand her over to him because it's a child involved. Don't get me wrong Tyra is my girl but she needs to get over her husband, and let him and Journee be together. I'm not handing Juelz over fuck that.

If Journee's thinks that she can come back eight years later, and stake claim to Juelz her, and her daughter. She's a motherfucking lie. I'm not the same nineteen-year-old girl whose tale she beat years ago, I'm shooting bitches now. I just purchased me a gun too, try me, I will run that bitch off a cliff. I tried calling Juelz he changed his number. I went by our house, and that bitch was up for sale.

He has to do more than sell our house to get away from me. I'll never give up on us. If I died today, I would haunt that nigga in his sleep, and any bitch that thinks they're going to lust or love him. If it's not Giselle it's no fucking body, I earned my place with him years ago. I'll nurse Free back to health, but after that I'm gone. I love Free but I'm not in love with him.

Juelz and I have both made mistakes, I think we can work out our differences. I'll accept his daughter, and he's already accepted Kassence. I think we've had enough time apart. Journee will just have to get over it. I'm not going anywhere.

Journee

Godmother Valerie was hosting ladies night, tonight at her house. This should be fun, she was into it with Uncle Nick. He went to New York for the weekend, and didn't take her. Mrs. Simone was invited also, me, Khadijah, and Alexis were coming too.

I'm looking forward to her getting drunk and telling us about ourselves. I hope she lays off me tonight I'm praying, that's too much like right. I'm sure she heard something about somebody. She and Khadijah sit up on the phone all day talking about people. Nikki had Nyla and Jueleez, they went to Disney on Ice earlier.

It's been a while since I was actually able to come over here and kick it like I wanted to without to having to look over my shoulders. My mom's house was vacant. I hardly ever come over this way, the lady that I rented the house to she wanted to buy it. I couldn't sale it my mother owned this home and I paid it off about three years ago. I wanted to keep it in the family.

Khadijah was thinking about moving in, Khadir said he wanted to move in also. It didn't matter to me. I wanted

Khadir to come back home and go to school. I missed him, Florida's not far but I wanted him close.

We were almost at Godmother Valerie's house Nikki called and said to stop by the store and bring some ice. They wanted Khadijah to make some daiquiris. Oh lord it's going to be a long night. Khadijah pulled up at the gas station on Northside Dr. It was a gang of niggas posted up. I'm hot in the ass and single too.

We all got out of her car. It was Friday night too. I planned to go home and relax unless my Godmother was babysitting. I had on some shorts and a tank top, and some sandals. My hair was brushed up in a messy bun.

It's like I was in beard heaven. The cat calls were hilarious, but I'm good on niggas for a while. My only focus is Jueleez. I swear I ran across some of the sexiest men ever, but I'm not looking for anything serious. I plan on being single for a while anyway. I have bad luck with men anyway.

Leave it to Khadijah and Alexis to be hot in the ass. I walked back to Khadijah's car and just posted up in front of it. I didn't want any parts of the fuckery. I'm standing in front of Khadijah's car. I look back toward the store. She and Alexis were talking to a few guys. I just shook my head. We're never going to make it ladies night. The ice is going to melt.

The sun was beating too, I put my big face Gucci shades on. This guy was approaching me, please don't come over here, and start talking to me. I don't have fucking time. Of course, he was coming over. Khadijah's car was locked so I couldn't get inside. I played it cool like I didn't see him. I started messing with my phone. It was easy turning down guys because I was in a relationship, but now I'm single so I don't have a reason too.

"Hey Ms. Lady how are you," he asked?

"Hi, I'm good and you?"

"I'm great now that my eyes have landed across you," he stated.

This nigga here swear he has some good game. Please get straight to the point so I can politely turn you down. He's cute but I'm not interested.

"What's your name? I'm Chase," he smiled as he extended his hand for me to shake.

"I'm Journee."

"Chase and Journee that's sounds good together, what do you think," he asked?

"It sounds ok." I laughed. This guy here was hilarious. I haven't laughed so hard in a while. I needed a good laugh. They say laughter is good for the soul.

"What's funny?" he asked.

"You."

"Why am I funny? What's wrong with me speaking how I feel? Oh, let me guess you're use to niggas that are afraid to express themselves. Not me if I want something, I don't hold back. I let that shit be known," he explained.

"Nothing is wrong with it." Lord please send this man on.

"Can I have your number," he asked?

"To be honest Chase I just got out of something serious last week, and I'm not looking for anything right now, not even conversation. I'm focused on me. I can't take your number because I wouldn't use it."

"I hear you Journee, every nigga isn't out to hurt you. You have to go through two fuck niggas to get the right nigga. Let me introduce myself my government name is Chase Mansell. I never had to chase a female before but it's something about you that wants me to start the chase.

In my twenty-eight years of living I have never been turned down by any female but you. Give me your phone. You don't have to call me, but I'll call you," he stated.

Chase was funny we sat in front of Khadijah's car and continued to talk. I like his conversation and he's easy on the eyes. Light brown complexion, pretty brown eyes. He's built nice, tattoos, waves, and a goatee that's trimmed to perfection.

Juelz

Me, Skeet, Smoke, and Alonzo just came from the car and bike show. We pulled up at the Texaco gas station on Northside Drive. It was packed to capacity because the car and bike show just let out. I needed something to drink, and Black a Mild and a cigar. Smoke was the first one that noticed Khadijah smiling all up in some niggas face. He was pissed. Alonzo wanted to know who Alexis was.

Skeet was looking for Nikki, but remembered she had Nyla and my daughter with her. I'm looking for Journee and I don't see her with them. I instantly thought she wasn't with them. Smoke and Khadijah started arguing.

I told him to come on. He got in the car. I pulled off. I passed by Khadijah's car on my way out. I see Journee and Chase chopping it up, she's smiling and shit. I'm heated instantly, I can't really get mad because we're not together. She knows what it is though. I couldn't let this shit slide. I threw my car in park and hopped out.

"Journee what's good?" I walked up on her. I didn't give a fuck about him smiling in her face she was mine and he needed to know that.

"What's up Juelz?" she smiled.

"You, let's go. Don't let Khadijah get you fucked up out here."

She did as she was told. I put Smoke and Alonzo out, they could ride with Khadijah and Alexis. Skeet got in the back, Journee got up front.

"Check mate Chase, she off limits." I yelled

We pulled off and Chase was looking sick. Nikki was keeping Jueleez tonight. Journee was scared as fuck too, she knew she was doing something she had no business doing. It's funny you want start popping back up in the hood posted up and shit being disrespectful.

Skeet jumped out of the car at Nikki's mother's house. We pulled off.

"Where are we going?" she asked

"Don't ask me any questions, sit back and ride."

"We had lady's night planned," she argued.

"How did you have lady's night planned and you smiling up in some niggas face?"

"I wasn't smiling up in his face. He was trying to spit some good game but I curved him," she argued.

"Yeah ok, that's not what the fuck it looked like. What are you trying to do?"

"I'm not trying to do nothing. I'm just chilling that's it," she pouted.

"Chilling."

Ok, since when did you start chilling in my hood? Last, I remember you left and never came back, but all of a sudden you posted up. You have these little as shorts on and a tank top with no bra. Yeah, you're chilling all right." I got something for her. I don't have times for the games and shit. If she wants to chill. I can find a few bitches to chill with. She can chill at home by herself too.

***

I drove to her house, and dropped her off, she was looking at me all sad; I don't care that sad face don't move me. You wanted to chill, so you can start chilling by yourself. True enough we both are single, and I've been curving ducks left and right. I wanted to be with Journee she can see it, but if you don't want what I want, then it's best for me to step aside and move on.

We can co-parent and I'll accept that. I would rather be with somebody who wants to be with me than somebody who doesn't. I'm tired of her confused ass she's stressing me the fuck out. My blood pressure is high fucking with her. I know she just got out of something so did I. Both of those relationships ended for a reason so we could be together with no strings attached, but she can't see that.

I ran across this bad little chick Mia she's my age. I knew her from around the way. She's been trying to get at me for the past two weeks, but I curved her each time because I've been trying to see what's up with Journee, and did she want to give us another shot, but I guess not.

I'll use her number now though, since Journee is chilling. I'm done though if it's not about Jueleez it's not about nothing.

Khadijah

Smoke had an attitude because he saw me talking to another guy. It was harmless flirting the guy already knew I was in a relationship. To make matters worse, he had girlfriend, he just said that I was cute.

Juelz had the nerve to put Smoke and Alonzo out of his car, and in the car with us. Whose too say I wanted this crazy as nigga to ride with me, while he's mad about some petty shit. Don't get me wrong I like Juelz he has always been a brother to me, but he does the most.

Journee sent me a text stating that he got mad because ole boy was in her face. Instead of her coming to lady's night. He took her home because he was pissed. Typical shit niggas do. Alexis got in the car with Alonzo they were going to get some drinks.

I took the bag of ice in My Godmother's house and came right back out, because Smoke wanted to argue about some shit that doesn't even mean anything to me. I started to send his drunk as mother out here to give him the business.

That's the thing about niggas they can dish out, but they can't take it. I saw the video he posted on Snapchat at the car and bike show, some chick was all up in his face.

He didn't curve her one time. I wasn't tripping because I didn't feel the need too.

I couldn't wait to get home so I can dig in his ass. He had the nerve to embarrass me in front of all those people. My daddy is KD not Smoke, and he don't even talk crazy to me. I don't know who he thought he was. Just because you slang dick good, and eat pussy like a pro don't mean shit too me.

My phone alerted me that I had a text. It was a group text from Nikki and Journee. Smoke snatched my phone I guess he thought it was some nigga. He better hoped like hell, they're not talking about him, and his bitter as brother because I'm sure it's some fuckery.

Journee was on a deep rant earlier, she was pissed Juelz took her home and she didn't ask to go home.

"KD, this is what y'all do all do is sit back and talk about us," he asked.

"Basically, you got a problem with it? Stop doing dumb shit, and we would have nothing to talk about."

Alexis

Damn we couldn't even have fun for just a minute. I knew Khadijah was in trouble when Smoke pulled up, and acted a damn fool. I didn't care I was single and could do what the fuck I wanted to do.

My eyes were trained on the nigga that got out with him. He was a fine chocolate specimen. Dreads adorned his head, milk chocolate covered his skin, and tatts covered his arms. I was intrigued, he had a set of lips that I would like in between my legs.

I saw Skeet and Juelz in the car laughing because Smoke was going in on Khadijah like he was her damn father. I looked toward the car, and I saw Journee smiling and laughing with a nigga.

I said quick a prayer hoping ole boy would leave. Juelz had to pass that way to leave. I knew he would spot Journee. How could you not? I left my phone in the car so I couldn't call her. Khadijah couldn't warn her either because Smoke would automatically tell Juelz.

Juelz caught that ass I watched it unfold he was a party pooper, and a cock blocker. He was actually calm, but he let that nigga know that she was his. Let my girl be great damn y'all are not official.

No lady's night for us tonight. Khadijah and Smoke argued the whole way. Alonzo asked me did I want to chill with him and get something to eat. Of course, I took him up on his offer. This is the same guy that Nikki was talking about that's back in town. Khadijah dropped him off to where his car was parked.

I got in and slid in the leather seats. He was gentlemen he opened up the door for me. He looked at me, and I looked at him.

"Once you get in the car with me, and ride passenger ma, it's no turning back," he stated.

"What's that supposed to mean? Enlighten me."

"You'll find out, what's your story," he asked?

"I don't have one worth telling."

"I don't care about you're ending. I'll help you create a new beginning," he smiled

***

Chapter 16- Journee

Man, these past few weeks have been crazy. If anybody would've told me that Kairo was cheating on me, I wouldn't have believed it. Y'all don't understand Juelz has always had my heart. I had to protect my heart. I couldn't shake him that's why I had to stay away from him. I was fighting temptation it was hard, but I fought that shit with everything in me.

Kairo came in and put me back together again. I loved him whole heartedly, you never divorced your wife. you've been living a lie. I would never pursue or date a married man and he's knows that. I've been with Kairo for eight years, I adored him.

When we first met he just came back from Africa. I didn't consider the Africa trips that he was cheating or fucking off with his wife. He was doing that before he met me. I just can't believe this bitch had the audacity to come to our home with Giselle in tow. You had better ask this hoe about me.

If you know your husband is cheating with somebody else. Why would you stay? A married man can't keep me period. I don't play that shit. Kairo forced that shit on me and lied to me, I tried to kill him. These past few weeks I have lost myself, my mother would not be proud of me.

I was blindsided by what Kairo was doing for me to pay attention to what was going on around me. I can't stop thinking about this shit, this nigga had the nerve to say you can have everything and I'm sorry.

I know I can have everything it's in my fucking name was any of this shit real? Giselle's daughter is Free's y'all some fuck niggas for real. I love Alexis she's a sweet girl and she doesn't deserve any of this shit. I don't either but I guess this is my karma for not telling Juelz. I've always played with the cards that I was dealt.

Somehow and some way I was going to get over this shit and move on. I'm good on Kairo but he still must pay. I'm selling that house and everything in that bitch. Too much stuff happened there for me to ever want to go back there. I must be a better parent Jueleez has seen too much stuff lately. I'm going to get back in church.

I'm tired and sleepy, I wish Juelz would hurry up and bring Jueleez home. She has school tomorrow she needs to eat and take a bath. I'm going to take my bath before she comes. The water was so relaxing and calming.

I lathered my loofa with Purple Lavender Caress body wash it smelled so good. Oh, shit I heard the doorbell ring. It must be Jueleez. I cut the shower off and attempted to dry off and wrap the towel around my body so I could open the door. I ran down the steps so I could open the door.

"Hi mommy," my daughter smiled.

"Hi come on so you can eat and take a bath."

"Daddy, can you put me to bed and eat with me," my daughter asked her father.

"Sure, is it enough for me," he asked.

"Yeah let me put my pajamas on and I'll fix you two a plate."

"I'll do it just show me the kitchen Jueleez," he stated.

"That's fine Jueleez give me a kiss. I'll see you in the morning. Lock my door when you leave ok." He nodded his head at me.

Juelz has had an attitude with me ever since he saw me up on Simpson and Hollywood Rd. I wasn't even doing anything. I was chilling with Khadijah and Alexis, and this guy Chase was all up in my face. He was cute I'm not going to lie.

I should've gave him my number, but I didn't because I didn't know if he knew Juelz or Skeet, and I didn't want my name buzzing about talking to him. I'm not even trying to entertain anybody. I don't have the time or the energy. I didn't even exchange numbers with him. Juelz was grilling the fuck out of me too.

This is the first time that Juelz has been to my house since the whole incident with Kairo and Giselle. Ugh, I can't stand his rude ass. I'm on to Jueleez she's using this against me, she's so damn bad and sneaky it doesn't make any sense.

She knows that he gets under my skin. Since he can make his own plate, he can lock up too when he leaves. I walked up to my room and put my pajamas on and closed my door and hoped sleep consumed me quick.

Juelz

Jueleez was my heart she had me wrapped around her finger. Anything she wanted she could get it. Journee and me co-parent pretty good. I wanted to spend more time with my daughter and take her to school.

Journee grilled salmon sautéed asparagus and loaded mashed potatoes and garlic bread. It was good she could still cook but I wouldn't tell her that. I fixed myself two plates, and I drunk all her Kool-Aid too just to piss her off.

What did she need all this food for anyway. Who was coming by Here, last I checked she was single and I don't want any niggas in my daughter's life but me. I've already missed too much.

I can't even talk to Journee without wanting to put my hands on her. I don't even acknowledge her. After we had the DNA test done and Jueleez was mine 99.999%. I signed her birth certificate and had her last name changed immediately. Her mother took care of everything else. I was trying to do some nice shit for her, to see if things could get back like they use too, we were cool for a few days.

I finally got her to open up, how she feels about me, and the moment I didn't tell her what she wanted to hear, she got in her feelings and left. I wasn't chasing her this time around. I refuse too. Me, Smoke, and Alonzo pulled up at the Shell gas station on Hollywood Rd. last week, Journee was posted up with some nigga all up in her face that shit pissed me off.

My first love gave me my first and only child what are the chances of that? After I caught Giselle and that nigga Free at Journee's house. I couldn't believe my daughter said that nigga was her father.

I was faithful to Giselle after she told me that she was pregnant with my child. I wanted to do right by her since I took her through a lot. I felt like I at least owed her that much.

I couldn't believe that bitch was still fucking him and he fathered our daughter. To make matters worse she was named after this nigga. Giselle was shaking when the nigga started telling her business. I assumed his girlfriend and Journee were cool.

His girlfriend almost killed Giselle and him too, they both deserved that shit. I had to break it up. I didn't want Giselle to get beat up in front of her daughter. Journee gave ole boys wife the business she fucked him up too and he stood there took that shit. He was begging too, Journee packed his shit and dumped it on his wife.

Ole boy Journee was fucking with was still married to his wife but you were mad at me behind an EX. I ate with my daughter and waited on her to take her bath. She finally came strolling out the bathroom in her pajamas. I put her in the bed read her a story and she was fast asleep. I tucked her in tight and kissed her on her forehead.

The devil was still on my back. Journee's room was two doors down from Jueleez. I told her every time that I saw her I would put my hands on her if the opportunity presented itself. I walked in her room she was asleep. She had on a see through white teddy her pussy was playing peek a boo. I wrapped my hands around her throat and cocked my gun back and pointed at her temple.

"Wake your motherfucking ass up and don't say shit." I yelled in her ear. She looked at me with a scowl on her face. I don't care about her having an attitude. We ain't good we'll never be good.

"Do what you have to do Juelz. I'm tired, tell Jueleez I love her," she whispered and licked her lips.

"You ain't worth a bullet. Next time I come over here don't ever answer the fucking door with a towel wrapped around you put some fucking clothes on. If it's you and my daughter here, you don't need to be lying in bed with this shit on. Don't have any niggas around my

daughter period. "

"Is that all Juelz? If so bye. If you decide to bring your daughter home after eight she can spend the night. I'm not dealing with you and your shit," she argued.

"Who in the fuck do you think you're talking to like that? My daughter is the only reason you're breathing."

"Good night Juelz lock my door when you leave and send me a text to let me know you made it home safe," she argued and turned her back against me.

Fuck that it's late anyway I'm spending the night. I took my clothes off and got in the bed with Journee.

"Scoot over."

"If you wanted to spend the night that's all you had to say. You can lose the attitude and stop being nasty mean to me. I'm sorry. It's a guest room right beside mine."

"I lay my head where I feel like it." She ignored me. I don't know what I was doing right now. I was tired and full and I didn't want to drive back to my house.

I was sleeping here I don't give a fuck how the person lying next to me may feel. Her phone rung and she didn't answer it. It rung again and she didn't answer it. Who was

calling her it's after 11:00pm? Her phone rang again.

I reached over her and answered it. I looked at the caller ID it said fuck nigga.
Journee crazy. I answered.

"What's up fuck nigga?"

"Who the fuck is this?" he yelled through the phone.

"Juelz."

"Put Journee on the phone," he yelled.

"Lower your fucking voice. Journee sleep shouldn't you be asleep with
your wife."

"Wake her up. Despite my ex-wife we still have business ties," he argued.

"It's after business hours call her tomorrow. In the future, any business ties, that y'all have sever that shit." I hung up in his face and cut her phone off. I don't have time to argue with a nigga about a bitch that's not his or mine.

"Wake up Journee I know you ain't sleep. What type of business do you and him have together? I need to know everything about him. I don't trust him." I knew she was awake. I grabbed her by her shoulder and made her face me. She was wide awake starring at the wall.

"We own three jewelry stores, real estate company, and a chain of car washes and we purchased some joint stock together, I'm cashing out on that. My attorney has already drawn up the paperwork to have my portion dissolved and he can buy me out. He's the plug and he smuggles diamonds," she stated.

"Why is he calling you this time of night?"

"He probably rode by and saw your car," she laughed.

"You're thinking about taking him back?"

"Hell, no he's married and he better be glad I haven't killed him. I don't fuck with liars. You got one time to play me and it's wrap. Anything else you want to know? "She argued.

"You love him?"

"Was I in love with him? No. Did I love him? Yes, how could I not, but my heart was taken a long time ago and I have never gotten it back. When we went through whatever. I was broken.

You broke me, that nigga put me back together again. He was there for me in so many ways, but I'll never fuck with him again on the strength that he lied to me, and we made a bond that we'll never hurt each other.

We met on the strength you cheated on me, and he

caught his wife fucking another nigga. We promised each other that we'll never cheat and he did more than that. Loyalty is priceless and that shit can't be bought," she explained.

"Loyalty is priceless and somehow you lost that trait after we parted ways."

"Juelz, I'm sorry and you may never forgive me for what I've done. I can't change the past at all, and now that I look back I regret that shit. I guess Kairo still being married to his wife is my karma but you know me. I always take the good with bad and move on. I don't have a choice. That's just how my life is setup. Good night," she cried and stated and turned her back toward me.

I wanted to console her but I just couldn't. She wasn't about to guilt trip me and she fucked me over. Nope I'm not putting her back together again, I'm not that nigga, I'm Juelz. She got up out the bed and started putting her clothes on.

"Journee were in the fuck do you think you're going this time of night?" I yelled and jumped out of the bed to stop her.

"Why does it matter Juelz? Go to sleep you can take Jueleez to school in the morning lock my door when you leave," she argued and sassed.

"Journee lose your attitude. I haven't done shit to you. I'm not about to pacify you either. That's what the fuck you get for trying to love another nigga that's not me. He was worse than me. Take your clothes off and get in the fucking bed take your ass to sleep. You'll be all right, you'll get over that fuck nigga.

Use the same tactics that used to force yourself to get over me. The only difference is now. I refused to let another man around my daughter. Get you a dildo or whatever because I don't want no man around Jueleez period.

"Juelz, last I checked my father was deceased. I've been raising myself for as long as I can remember. Jueleez is your child not me. What goes on in my personal life is my business. I'll respect your wishes," she argued.

Chapter 17-Journee

Juelz was the baby daddy from hell I swear. He knows how to get under my skin. I was perfectly fine. He had the nerve to sneak in my room and point his gun toward my head who in the fuck does that shit.

I said I was sorry what more does he want from me. Sleep finally consumed me, he went to sleep before me. My mind was in overdrive thinking about Kairo. I loved this man more than you would ever know.

He was there for me when I had no one, when I was pregnant with Jueleez. He was everything to me BUT Tyra held a title that I couldn't compare to. I don't do drama. I never thought he would fuck me over. I knew he rode by and saw Juelz car, but we would have to talk sooner than later.

I've been avoiding him because I can't look at him without killing him. We were building empire together. I wouldn't wish this feeling on nobody in the world. It hurts so bad. I keep myself busy with other thing so I won't focus on it too much.

I got up early took my shower to cook Jueleez and Juelz some breakfast. My restaurant was closed on Sunday's and Monday's.

Sausage, eggs, cheese grits and French toast and fresh fruit. I sat the table Jueleez would be dressed any minute now. She's already came in here once ready to eat. Juelz was already up he was sitting in the living room playing with his phone. I had my Beats headphones on listening to one of my Apple Music playlist.

After breakfast I was going to work out and pop up on Khadijah she has been avoiding me since Smoke caught her talking to a nigga too at the store. I didn't have anything to do with that. I'm single she knew better, but no she thought she was grown like me and Alexis.

"Mommy I'm hungry." my daughter yelled and wrapped her arms around my waist.

"I know Jueleez your food is ready I fixed your plate."

"Daddy come eat," my daughter yelled.

He did anything she said do. I looked at him and he smirked.

"What do you want to eat Juelz?"

"Everything," he stated.

"Alright Jueleez your bus comes at 8:00 am. Eat your food and brush your teeth when you finish and your dad can walk you to the bus stop."

"Ok mommy," she stated with her mouth full.

I walked back upstairs to my room and laid across my bed for a while. I would wait until Jueleez and Juelz are gone before I leave. I needed to clean my kitchen and things. I decided to call my bitch Nikki to see what she was up too. I know she was dropping the kids off. We rap every morning this morning would be no different. I called her.

"What's up Journee Leigh talk to me," she stated in her ghetto voice.

"What's up, what y'all up too? Where lil Skeet."

"Girl he gone already he was wondering why you didn't call him this morning. Skeet told him his uncle Juelz was over there," she laughed.

"Fuck y'all tell Skeet don't do me. It was nothing like that."

"Umm hum I called your phone last night and it went straight to voicemail. I said my bitch popping pussy for Juelz after two weeks," she laughed.

"You a damn lie, ain't no popping pussy over here. He's the baby daddy from hell bitch. I had to sleep with one eye open. He put his gun to my head while I was sleep talking shit. He's a fucking lunatic." I laughed.

"Journee, stop fucking lying. He's doing too much. I told you that nigga was crazy. He still wants you, y'all need to fuck and make up," she laughed.

"Bitch no he doesn't. He made it very clear that he doesn't want me and I disgust him. The feelings are mutual. I just thought I'd let you know if I come up missing make sure they know he did it, and you push his shit back fuck what Skeet talking about. I'm back on the prowl bitch
Journee Leigh is coming to hood near to bag a couple of niggas."

"I hear you bitch I'm here for it. It feels good not be hiding from a nigga huh. My bitch is free at last," she laughed.

"Hell yeah, you didn't know the summer is mine. Me and Alexis going on tour every weekend. Juelz and God momma Nikki babysitting too. Watch me work."

"Girl baby daddy from hell he's not about to let that fly. What are you going to do about Kairo I know he's still sniffing around," she asked.

"Fuck both niggas." I laughed.

"Fuck you too," he laughed.

"What's up baby daddy from hell?" My best-friend Nikki laughed
through the phone.

"Nikki, I came back to finish the job," he laughed.

"Juelz you a damn fool, let my girl live man and be great. I'm going to let y'all go hit me back Journee when your company leaves." She laughed and hung up the phone.

I looked at Juelz with a scowl on my face. I guess he was standing in the door the whole time. He needs to go home what does he want. He looked at me and licked his lips.

"What Juelz don't you need to go home? Jueleez is at school I got

moves to make."

"I heard you and Nikki's conversation I'm the baby daddy from hell," he snarled and licked his lips and walked closer to me.

"Yep."

"Back up don't get close to me. Don't you got moves to make?"

"I heard your little conversation with Nikki. The summer is yours huh? You got me fucked up. If you think you're about to be out here on some thot shit. I'm not babysitting for you to go on tour are whatever you call it," he yelled and pushed me on the bed and climbed on top of me and wrapped his hands around my neck.

"Get off me Juelz." I cried.

"What are you crying for now? You were just

laughing and bullshitting with Nikki talking about bagging a couple of niggas and fuck me. Tell me fuck me to my face Journee and watch what the fuck I do to you. I never thought you'll be the type to thot around you got me fucked up.

Don't bring your ass to my hood Bankhead no more trying to pull a nigga because I'm going to hurt your feelings and that niggas. Keep your ass over here where you been hiding from a nigga with your scared shaky ass," he threatened me and pressed his hands between my legs.

"Juelz, please just leave ok." I cried.

"Why are you crying Journee? I haven't done shit to you but what you've done to me. It doesn't feel good, does it?" he asked. He was still laying on top of my body looking me dead in my eyes.

"Juelz, have I physically hurt you? No, do I pull guns out on you when you're sleep? No. I fucked up I was young and naive and dumb as fuck. Jueleez knew that you were her father she has never called Kairo daddy. Give me credit for something. If I must go through this every time you come and see her. You can keep her at your house full-time and I'll see her on the weekends." I cried and argued.

"Journee you need to grow the fuck up. You're grown, but you haven't grown enough. Face what the fuck is going on around you and stop running from it. I don't care how you may feel. You did hurt me physically. I can't get over that shit. I didn't cheat on you on purpose shit just happened but that shit doesn't matter now.

The moment that you found out you were carrying something that belonged to me you should've reach out to me. I guess that's why I couldn't get over you. I'm so good on you and Giselle I fell for the wrong two. You had something that belonged to me that you failed to deliver to me. I missed the delivery of my first born. I missed birthday's. I missed a lot and your I'm sorry won't make up for that."

"Juelz, how dare you compare me to Giselle. I'm sorry that her daughter isn't yours but I have never cheated on you or lied to you. You can still have a relationship with her child. I've always kept it real with you why we were together but you can get off me right now comparing me to her. Move."

"Nope," he grinned and laughed at me.

I closed my eyes. Why me Lord why. Juelz started kissing on my neck and playing with my nipples and tugging at my shorts.

"No, we are not doing this." I moaned.

"Who is going to stop me?" he smiled and gritted his teeth. He pulled

my shirt over my head.

"Me. We can't Juelz it will complicate things and we're already complicated."

"Journee you owe me this pussy. It'll forever be mine. I was the first nigga to hit and this time around I'll be the last one to get it. If I should take it from you than that's what the fuck I'm going to do. You can do it my way, or you can learn the hard way." He threatened me.

"Juelz, we can't take it there. I'm not giving up any pussy now move I have to use the bathroom. Juelz wanted to fuck. Boy stop he was willing to take the pussy damn it's not that serious, is it?

Juelz was sexy as fuck, but I'll pass because if the dick was anything like I remember it was lethal. I couldn't get enough of it. I can't fuck him I just can't. When I do decide to fuck him, I'm going to fuck the shit out of him. I'm not the same seventeen-year-old that use to run from the dick. I've learned a few things. I got up and went to the bathroom. He followed right behind me.

"Damn can I use the bathroom in peace?"

"You lost your chances at having any peace weeks ago." He laughed. I just ignored him. I wish I had to shit, I bet he wouldn't be up here. I sat down to pee. I wiped myself and attempted to pull my shorts. He approached me and placed his shoe in between my shorts so I couldn't raise them up.

"Juelz, stop I need to wash my hands."

"You can wash your hands. I haven't stopped you from doing that." He snarled and gritted his teeth. I washed my hands and he was right on my trail. I turned around to face him and dried my hands off.

"What Juelz?"

He just stared at me. I attempted to walk off. He grabbed me from behind. I turned around and looked him.

"Don't say shit Journee just shut the fuck up and let me do me." He argued.

"Juelz." I pouted.

He snarled his face up at me and picked me up and sat me on the sink and pushed my legs apart.

"Juelz please don't."

"Did you hear what the fuck I said?" Shut up and don't tell me to stop," he stated.

"Do you have any condoms? The first time we ever had sex, you got me pregnant, I'm not trying to get pregnant Juelz."

"Journee, I told you to shut up and don't ask me shit. If you get pregnant again just deal with it."

My doorbell rang and someone was banging on the door like the damn police. Saved by the bell thank God. He stopped. I pulled my pants up and put my shirt on and rushed down the stairs to see who was at the door. He was right behind me. I looked through the peep hole and it was Kairo the last motherfucka that I wanted to see.

What the fuck does he want? He should not be here. I should've slammed the door in his face, but he walked right in like he owned the motherfucka.

Chapter 18-

Kairo

Man, I fucked up good. I know Tyra ain't shit. You know the saying how they say shit gets better with time. Well shit hasn't gotten better with time. I slipped up and fucked that bitch five times out of eight years only because she threatened to tell Journee.

The last time I fucked Tyra Journee pissed me off my partner Muscles told me he saw Journee at Kapture and had pictures of her and Juelz. Jueleez's father. I showed her the pictures and she was all nonchalant about the shit talking about he wanted to talk. At 2:00 am in the morning ain't no nigga talking about nothing with a female he used to fuck. I was pissed but Journee wasn't the type of female to do that type of shit. I knew her but I didn't like that nigga being in her presence.

We argued which is something that we never do. I left and refused to go back home. I called Tyra and told her to unlock the door I was dropping some money off. When I walked in her room she was playing her with pussy. She raped a nigga at the time I needed it and acted it on based off Journee and Juelz.

To make matters worse I guess the bitch got fed up and decided to tell Journee about us that was two weeks ago. Imagine my surprise when I decided to finally take my ass home. Tyra and Giselle were at my house and Journee was boxing this bitch out and Alexis was giving Giselle that work.

Me and Free both got caught up. Alexis found out that Free had a child on her. She tried to kill him. Journee tried to kill me too. To top it off Giselle boyfriend was Juelz he found out that Giselle's daughter wasn't his, this world was small.

I opened the door for Journee and Juelz to get back together. Tyra knew we wasn't shit our marriage was arranged based off our parents they were business partners.

I had to divorce Tyra and marry Journee because the FEDS have an indictment out for me. I could flee the states and never come back but I need my queen with me. I couldn't do those five years being married to Tyra because I would come back to nothing. Legally she was entitled to everything, but I refuse to give her anything that I put my blood on.

I called Journee last night because we needed to talk, two weeks was too long to be apart from each other. Imagine my surprise when Juelz answered the phone. I wanted ride over there and body that nigga.

I couldn't even sleep last night the thought of her fucking another nigga how she fucked me was forever etched in my mind. I parked down the street. I watched him put Jueleez on the bus but he didn't leave. He walked back in the house.

Fuck that he wasn't about to fuck her. I got out of my car and banged on the door like I was the gawd damn police. I was about to kick her fucking door open. Journee got a nigga going insane.

The door swung open Journee gave me a scowl. Juelz stood right behind her. I walked right in this bitch like I owned this motherfucka because I brought her this motherfucka.

"Journee I hate to interrupt you but we got some business to handle.
Go change your clothes and let's roll. Did you cook breakfast?" Juelz was grilling the fuck out of me. I don't owe that nigga shit and he don't owe me shit but he's not about to fuck my bitch, that's some pussy that'll I'll kill behind.

"Kairo, I'll meet you over there," she sassed.

"I got dropped off. You fucked my car up remember."

"You got plenty of cars."

"Journee you good? I'm about to get up out of here."
He asked and wrapped his arms around her waist and bit
her neck.

"What the fuck is this? Journee are you fucking him?"

"I'm good Juelz. Kairo you're not in the business to
be asking me who I'm fucking. I was fucking you for the
past eight years, BUT last I checked you were married and
guess what you ain't married to me so this pussy is back on
the market. I don't have papers on you. Don't
come in here questioning me about what the fuck I'm doing
because you created this," she argued.

"I'm sorry Journee let me explain some shit to you.
Hear me out that's all I ask? You got me fucked up. We are
not throwing away eight years for a few mistakes. I refuse
too."

"Why now Kairo?" she argued and cried.

"I couldn't divorce her due to family ties and our
family's business dealings."

"Ok and you should've told me that in the beginning.
We could've stayed friends but you didn't give me the
option to choose. You lied to me, you showed me divorce

papers. I would never fuck with a married man because I wouldn't want a woman to do that to me. We made a fucking bond that we would never cheat on each other because of what we went through, but you broke that shit on several occasions. You put me back together again only to break my heart. I can't do this with you right now." She cried.

"Baby don't cry I'm sorry."

"Kairo, I don't want to hear nothing that you have to say," she argued.
"Damn Journee you are making it real hard for me. I owe you an apology and
an explanation."

"Do you think that I want to hear you say that you've been married for eight years and why? I've been with you eight years too and you lied to me that you were divorced. No wonder we're not married. So, whatever you should explain doesn't fucking matter to me it's wrap. I thought you was a stand-up guy and would never make me cry," she argued and sassed.

"Do you think I wanted to be married to her? Fuck no. The only reason she said something is because I slipped up and fucked her two weeks ago because of you and that nigga, but I'm walking away from the business.

If I leave the family business she has nothing, this shit is about money and I have more than enough. Journee, we are not over. I'm not accepting that. Do you think that I would let you be with that nigga because he's Jueleez father and he's back in the picture?

I've been here for the past eight years and I'm not going anywhere. You got me fucked up. I fucked up and I'm man enough to admit that. It's not a nigga breathing that's going to take my family from me."

"Let's go Kairo," she sassed.

"Didn't I tell you to change clothes."

"I'm not changing clothes," she laughed.
"Do you actually think that I want to smell his fucking cologne on you?"
She walked toward the door ignoring what the fuck I said. I ran up on her and slammed the door shut.
"Go change clothes before I take that shit up off you."
"Whatever Kairo," she laughed and sucked her teeth.
"Ok come here," she approached me. I scratched my beard and snatched her shirt and shorts off her.

"Goodbye Kairo," she argued.

"I'm not going anywhere. I asked you nicely and you wanted to try me. Go change and let's go."

"Fuck you Kairo I'm not going anywhere with you, leave now before I call the police," she argued.

Juelz

Shit I forgot my phone at Journee's house. Ole boy was cock blocking? I was finally about to get up in that pussy. I had plans to bust straight in it. I had to turn around to go get my phone. I left my truck running because, I was going to be in and out. I approached the door and heard arguing at the door.

I was on go I opened the door Journee was naked and she was arguing with him

"Journee what's up why are you naked and crying?"

"He snatched my clothes off me because he didn't want to smell your cologne on me. I told him to leave and refuses too," she argued.

"Aye my nigga you are doing too much. He doesn't have to leave, but Journee get your shit and let's roll. You don't have to come back here. I'll buy you and my daughter a spot."

"I'll leave I don't want no problems," he gritted his teeth, and held his hands up.

"I don't want none either, but I refused to let any nigga disrespect her because they fucked up. Kairo left and

Journee packed her stuff up. I guess it was meant for me to turn around.

You could hear them arguing like crazy. He snatched her clothes off because he didn't want to smell my cologne on her. He was pussy whipped, I was too and it's been years since I had it. She was young then, but now she's grown.

I'll have to keep my eye out on him, he's up to some shit. I don't know what it is, but it's something. Journee isn't one to tell lies. I believed her when she said that she was dissolving everything. I don't want my daughter staying here if he's going to be popping up acting crazy.

I know she's been around him, but I don't trust him. His vibe screams snake and sneaky. Any nigga that has a wife for eight years and a girlfriend for the same amount of time can't be trusted. I need his full name so I can have my peoples to check him out.

We waited until Jueleez got out of school before we went back to my house.

Journee

Kairo had the nerve to come over here and show his ass. How dare you snatch my clothes off me, because I smelled like him. I didn't even have the energy to fight him. I couldn't even look at him. I loved this man. I thought he was the one. First of all, I didn't even invite you in.

Yes, we had some business to take care of, but all that went out the window, when you decided to get in your feelings. Nigga what about my fucking feelings? Do you know how I feel, when I think about sleeping with a married for seven years? I feel horrible

You're only worried about, if I'm fucking somebody that's not you. You admitted to fucking your wife to my face today, since you've been exposed, but two weeks ago you couldn't tell me shit. I haven't even fucked Juelz. Did I want too of course, I was about to before I was rudely interrupted.

Thank God for Juelz. I'm glad he came back, because Kairo wasn't leaving. I hate to leave my house, because of Kairo. I really didn't want to switch Jueleez's school again. I'm tired of running from shit. Moving isn't going to change anything. I tried to tell Juelz that, but he wouldn't listen. Jueleez finally got out of school. I packed some stuff to take to his house.

He said he was ok with taking Jueleez to school. He wanted me to ride with him, but I had to drive my car. I had to call Nikki, Khadijah and Alexis and tell them how crazy Kairo acted. I'm sure they could use a good laugh. I wasn't about to be cooped up in his house waiting on him to take me wherever. Kairo thinks that I sold my other house that I had when we first met. I think I'll stay there.

***

I finally made it to Juelz's house. He left me the key, he said he had to make a few runs and he'll be back later. I checked his refrigerator he didn't have shit in it. I had a taste for some Oxtails, rice, cabbage and baked macaroni and cheese. I needed to go to the grocery store.

Jueleez needed snacks and breakfast food. Juelz could stay gone all day for all I care.

Juelz

Journee and Jueleez got situated at my house. I had some moves to make. I couldn't stay at home and lay up. I did want to finish what we started earlier. Giselle was a crazy bitch she just couldn't let go. I changed my number, so she wouldn't have access to reach me. I had our house up for sale, and her mail forwarded to her mother's house.

My cousin works for AT&T she called me, and said that Giselle pretended to be my wife to get my phone number. Ok that was cool, I knew she couldn't stay away. I noticed she was following me. She followed me to Journee's house last night. I'm a calculated a nigga. I knew she was following me. I wanted to hurt her feelings before I fuck her up.

I knew she was waiting on me to leave last night. I peeped out the window and saw her car still sitting out there. I pulled my car in Journee's garage I didn't trust her. I wanted to walk up on her and handle her ass. I didn't want no heat where Journee and my daughter laid their head. I called my partner Bandz, and gave him Journee's address. I wanted him to follow Giselle to see where she laid her head at.

Bandz hit me with the info this morning. This bitch had another house in her name, and Free was on the deed. I swear I couldn't believe this shit. I had Bandz sitting out in front of her crib watching for movement. Free had left so Giselle was home alone. I'm a savage ass nigga and I'm bold. I knocked on her fucking door. I dared a motherfucka to call the police this bitch had stalked me and fucked me out of a shitload of bread. She opened the door. I could smell his dick on her breath.

"Juelz what are you doing here," she asked.

I could tell she was scared. I pushed her inside of the house.

"You want me here, you've been stalking me."

"I'm sorry Juelz. I love you," she cried.

I walked up on her, and smacked her. I choked the fuck

"Bitch you don't love me, stop saying that shit. You've had this house for seven years this niggas name is on the fucking deed. You had a whole family on me. I wish I never met you I swear I do."

"You don't mean that, I love you Juelz," she cried. I picked her up by her throat and slammed her in the wall.

"I should kill you, but you ain't worth it. Ma come and take care of this bitch," I spoke in the mic on my smart watch.

My mother walked in Giselle's house like she owned it.

"I told you from the beginning. If you ever played my son, and put a baby on him that wasn't his. I was going to beat your ass like I was your mother," my mother argued.

"I'm sorry," she cried.

"Nah bitch you're not sorry, you should've told the truth. My son can only rough you up because he's a man. I raised him not to hit women. I'm his mother and it's my job to beat the fuck out of you, for playing with my blood," my mother argued.

"Please Mrs. Simone fighting isn't going to resolve anything. I'm in love with Juelz I made a mistake and I'm sorry," she cried.

My mother didn't even respond. She picked Giselle up and slammed her into a glass coffee table in her living room. My mother walked over to Giselle, and slid her brass knuckles on and started pounding away at her chest and face. You could hear Giselle scream.

"Bitch shut the fuck up because I really want to shoot you dead," my mother argued.

My mother continued her assault on Giselle. She pulled her gun out.

"Ma, don't shoot her."

"Shut up and let me do me, you can leave," my mother argued. I raised my hands up and just shook my head. She was doing the most. She tore this fucking house up. She pistol whipped Giselle. She stuffed a dildo in her mouth and secured it with duct tape. I shook my head. My mother lost her fucking mind. Giselle laid there and took it I could tell she was unconscious. She kept her eyes trained on me. My mother was satisfied with her handy work.

Before we left I approached Giselle to check her pulse, she was still breathing. I hate that we had to come to this, but she should've left me alone a long time ago instead of using me and being sneaky. Every dog has it's say and today was hers.

I knelt down beneath her and whispered in her ear.

"Leave me the fuck alone. If I catch you stalking me or coming by house. I'm going to fucking kill you. It's over. You made your bed and family with this nigga keep it."

Tears ran down her face that shit didn't move me.

Journee

Juelz has been gone all day. I've cooked and cleaned. Jueleez and I ate already and we're full. She wanted to make some brownies and I let her. She also wanted her nails painted. She was getting on my nerves too asking when her daddy was coming back.

I swear she loved him like no other. She called and told him, he was late for dinner and he needed to get home. I hope he knew it was Jueleez saying that, and not me.

I combed her hair, and put her to bed. He hasn't made it home yet, and it's almost 11:00 pm. I put his food in the microwave. I called Mrs. Simone she didn't answer the phone, that's strange because she loves to gossip that's all she does.

I took a hot shower. I had to handle my hygiene before I went to bed. I guess I'll be petty for tonight, and not in sleep in Juelz room even though. I just showered and lathered my body with Jimmy Choo lotion and the smell alone lingered in the room. I walked to the guest room two doors down from his. I stripped naked. I cut my phone off because I didn't want to be bothered. I said a quick prayer before I went to sleep.

***

I was in a deep sleep. I felt Juelz biting and sucking on my neck. I started to stir in my sleep.

"You're hard headed, what are you doing in here you know better," he whispered.

I didn't answer him. He pulled the covers back."

"Oh, you naked," he yelled. I still tried to act like I was sleep. His beard tickled my neck.

He picked me and threw me over his shoulders. He started to finger fuck me.

"Stop Juelz." I moaned. We finally made it to his room.

He threw me on his bed and I bounced.

"I want you, can I have you," he asked.

"Nope we ain't ready." I licked my lips. He started undressing himself. He freed the monster that laid between his legs.

"Nah you ready, you're lying in bed but ass naked. I'll take it easy on you. You're twenty-five now. You're grown enough to take this dick and not run from it," he gritted his teeth and pulled my legs at the edge of the bed.

"Who's said that you were fucking me? If we fuck it's going to be me that's fucking you."

"Oh yeah, I want you to back that shit up," he smiled.

Juelz threw my legs over his shoulder and he started feasting on my pretty snatch. It's been a long time since he's been there. His beard tickled my snatch. He sucked the soul out of me. I tried to keep my composure.

He was licking and slurping real fast I wasn't ready to come just yet. I started riding his face to keep up with his tongue. I couldn't handle it, but I refused to tap out.

"Let that shit go," he yelled and slapped me on his ass.

I came not once but twice. I fed him. Juelz went in the bathroom to clean his face. He came out talking shit as always.

"I want you to back up everything you just said," he laughed.

Juelz thought this shit was a game. I always said if I ever had the chance to fuck him again. I was going to fuck the shit of him and leave his ass stuck. So that's exactly what I'm about to do.

"You ready for me to fuck you."

"I been ready, show daddy what that pussy can do," he laughed.

Juelz sat in the middle of the bed stroking himself. I crawled up to him smacked his hands. He bit his lip. I spit on his dick and wrapped my lips around it. I started licking and sucking his dick like, I was sucking a lollipop, he was moaning like a bitch. His moans alone gave me fuel to really go in.

You could hear the sounds echoing throughout the room. I could tell that he was about to bust. I eased up. He placed his hands on my head. He emptied his seeds down my throat.

"Round two." He nodded his head yes. He started stroking himself again. He motioned with his hands for me to come here. I pushed him down on the bed and started to mount him. I forgot how big he was.

It took me a minute to get used to his size. He grabbed my breast and started sucking each of them real foolish. I started to ride him. I started off slow to get a good feel of him, I picked up my pace, he tried to match my rhythm. I stood up and started squatting and riding him with no hands. I did a spilt on his dick he tried to grab me. I smacked his hands.

"No touching." I laughed.

I spun around and started riding him from the back. I made both of my ass cheeks clap. He smacked both cheeks. He raised up and grabbed me like incredible hulk. I sped up the pace and started bouncing on his dick real hard. He snatched me by hair and pulled me to chest. He hit me with that pound game.

"You know you done fucked up right," he yelled. I ignored him. I just wanted to fuck that's it with no strings attached.

"Whatever."

"This pussy belongs to me, in case you forgot. Let me remind you," he whispered in my ear. He started fucking the shit out of me.

We both had something to prove. It's been a long time since we've had sex. It started off as fucking then we made love.

Chapter 19-Journee

I've been sick these past few days. I couldn't even work like I wanted too. I couldn't keep anything down. I mustered up enough strength to get Jueleez ready for school and cook her breakfast. I walked her to the bus stop. It felt good to be out of the house. The morning air made me feel so much better.

"Mommy are you sick? I can call my father to come and take care of you," my daughter stated.

"I'm a little sick but I'll be fine. I will be ok by the time you get out of school."

"You promise mommy," she asked.

"Yes, baby I'll be fine. I love you go ahead and get on the bus and I'll see when you get home from school."

I couldn't go into work today feeling like this. I called my general manager and advised her that she would be running things today. I couldn't keep anything down. I just wanted to lay in bed all day. I had a fever too.

I would sweat it out. I haven't had this type of sickness in eight years. I swear if Juelz got me pregnant again. I'll go crazy. I didn't want any more kids. Jueleez was more than enough and she was spoiled as fuck. I finally made back in the house. The only time I felt relaxed was when I took a shower.

I jumped in the shower my breast where sore already my stomach felt fine. I know I'm pregnant. I'm just not ready to face the facts. I should've known better. History was repeating itself once again. Why I can't even just have casual sex with him and not get pregnant.

Kairo and I have had unprotected sex on a numerous of occasions and I have never gotten pregnant by him. Juelz has some magical dick, if he even breathes on me I'm pregnant. I swear I'm not ready. Why couldn't Nikki, Khadijah or Alexis get pregnant? I would be glad to be a Godmother to somebody's child.

Juelz

My daughter called me this morning while she was on the school bus, and stated that her mom was sick, and she wanted me to take care of her while she was at school. I know Journee's pregnant. I'm just wondering when is she going to have the balls to tell me.

I had plans to take Mia out for breakfast but I'll go check on Journee to see what she's up too. She owed me another child anyway. She was the only woman that would ever have the title of baring my children. I canceled my breakfast date with Mia, she was mad but oh well Journee and my children come before anybody the sooner she realizes that, the better will be.

Journee hard-headed as fuck. I already told her that she needs to move closer to me anyway. It takes me about forty-five minutes just to get to her house. I needed her closer to me in case something happened it wouldn't take me damn near an hour to get over house.

***

I finally made it to her house. I stopped by Target and grabbed three pregnancy tests for her. Panera bread was across the street. I got her some soup, sandwich, and some crackers and Fiji water. I made my way to Journee's house it was about twenty minutes from here. I had a key to her house for emergencies. I needed a key despite what she thinks. I need to know what's going on always.

I pulled in the garage, and headed toward the kitchen. I grabbed a bowl and poured her soup in a bowl and warmed it up. I didn't want to hear her mouth. If it was cold or room temperature, she likes her food cooked to serve.

I placed everything on her breakfast tray, and carried it to her room. She was laid on the bed naked. The ceiling fan was on high. It was cold as fuck in her room. I could tell she was sick her face was red, and she didn't have any cover on her. I placed my hand on her forehead she was burning up.

"Journee wake up."

"What are you doing here Juelz? I don't feel good," she stated.

"I know Jueleez told me."

"Juelz, you don't have to help me I'm good," she yawned and turned her back against me.

"Journee, stop playing with me. Why do you have to be so difficult? You're running a fever. I'm helping you because I want too. Get up so you can eat."

"Juelz, I don't feel good, I can't eat no food," she argued.

"Are you pregnant?"

"Probably so, did you pull out, or did you trap me again on purpose," she asked?

"You've always been a smart girl Journee. You owe me another child anyway so yeah, I knocked you up. Do you have problem with it? We're going to try having a baby again with me being in the picture out the gate."

"Why would you do that to me? You can't just be trapping me we ain't together, and I don't want any more kids," she argued.

"I can do what the fuck I want Journee, the sooner you understand that we'll be a lot better. When you decided to keep my daughter from me, did you think about what the fuck you were doing to me, and how I would feel? Nope you didn't give a fuck. I don't give a fuck about getting you pregnant. Take your ass in the bathroom and piss on these sticks." I was all up in her face. I didn't even care about her being sick right now.

"Damn can we move past this, every time we have an argument you throw that up," she argued.

"Just leave I'll piss on a stick when I feel like it. I'll let you know if I'm pregnant or not," she argued.

"Fuck that." I picked her up and carried her to the bathroom.

"Stop, I have to throw up now," she argued.

Journee was pregnant and didn't want me to know. She threw up in the toilet. I grabbed her hair out of her face. She was sick. She finished throwing up. She brushed her teeth and walked passed me. I handed her the pregnancy test so she could piss on the stick.

"Can you ease up," she argued.

"I will after you take this test, motherhood is a beautiful thing."

She went to the kitchen I was right on her heels, she grabbed a plastic cup and walked back toward her room. She snatched the pregnancy test off her bed and slammed the bathroom door and locked it.

"Open this fucking door before I kick this bitch open. Don't play with me." She opened the door and pushed passed me, and handed me all three-pregnancy test. I looked at the pregnancy test all three of them were positive.

"You can leave now," she argued.

"You don't tell me what the fuck to do. I don't have a problem with leaving. Listen to me Journee and listen good. I want a boy so make that shit happen. Take care of yourself. I want you to see my doctors I'll set you up an appointment.

Don't even think about trying to kill my seed, because if you do you'll be signing your own death certificate. I brought you some food you'll need to warm it again. I'm out. Make sure you tell my daughter I came over here to take of your ungrateful ass too."

"When your child comes be prepared to raise it too, since you want to trap me, leave my key. I don't know how you got one," she argued.

I wasn't even about to respond. I left I'm tired of kissing her ass and putting myself out there. If it's not about my kids it's not about shit. She's given me her ass to kiss the entire time, and I'm not doing that shit no more. I refuse too. It's to many women out here to be focused on her. It's not meant for us to be together and I've learned to accept that. She can do her and I'm going to do me.

Chapter 20-Journee

My life was perfect without Juelz in it. No bullshit or nothing. Why am I being punished. Our chemistry has been history a long time ago. Juelz and I are one in the same. He's an alpha male, and I'm an alpha female.

The only positive thing that came out of this situation was Jueleez meeting him and getting to know him. Kairo and Giselle, and Free getting exposed. I swear I'm sick of him. I'm not your child stop talking to me like I am. What man do you know goes around trapping a woman just because he wants too? I don't want to have his baby I can't deal with this man. He has some serious issues.

I appreciate him for coming by here to check on me, but I was good it's just morning sickness it'll pass. I should've never fucked him, but nope he wanted the pussy so bad he was willing to take it. I made sure I fucked his world up with one night and he trapped me.

I should call my girls on a conference call, I called Khadijah and Nikki. Nikki called Alexis.

"Hey y'all I have some good news and some bad news."

"Bad news first," they said in unison.

"I'm pregnant."

"We knew already," they said.

"How?"

"Your baby daddy telling everybody. I was wondering when you were going to call and tell us. He's so happy. Congratulations," my best friend Nikki stated.

"What's the good news," my sister Khadijah asked.

"I told him he has to keep the child since he trapped me again."

"Journee, I'm sick of the two of y'all. First y'all are falling for each other again, then y'all fuck and make up, now y'all at each other's necks. Can y'all two please get it together for the sake of y'all children," my best bae Alexis stated.

"All right I'll talk to y'all later." I hung up the phone on them, because I wasn't about to plead my case and make them see shit my way. It's not me this time it's him. I swear. I was a little salty when he came because I didn't give him a key.

Prior to that I've been cordial I accepted him and his little girlfriend. I didn't even trip on about her meeting

Jueleez and I should've. You had a heart attack when you thought somebody was giving me attention.

Chapter 21-Journee

Today was Skeet's birthday and Nikki was throwing him a Kickback party at their house. Now granted I have never been to Skeet's birthday party, because I didn't want to run into Juelz that was then, this is now.

Nikki called me, and said that Juelz told Skeet that he didn't want me to come because he was bringing Mia. I had to look at the phone I can't believe this nigga. What does that have to do with me? We're not together.

Don't get me wrong I felt some type of way it has nothing to do with Mia. If that what he wants, then he can he have her, it's all good. It's funny because if you even see a nigga breathing my way, you have an issue with that. You already let this chick meet Jueleez, and I haven't snapped yet.

To make matters worse, you got me pregnant again on purpose. I don't want any more kids, and not by him. I could be petty and play the same game that he's playing, but for what it's dangerous, and I'm to grown for that shit. I don't have fucking time for the bullshit. My life is already complicated.

I was going to the Kickback whether he liked or not. I wasn't going to step on any toes, but I'll break a few necks for sure. I was carrying my pregnancy well. I wasn't showing yet. I thumbed through my closet. I found this strapless tube top that covered my breast only. It was beautiful it represented the Jamaican flag.

I got this top in Jamaica last summer. I had the skirt to match. My faux locs were freshly done. I wanted to wear this outfit for the longest today was perfect. The skirt clung to hips and ass like a glove. I swear I'm tired of a motherfucka taking my kindness for my weakness. We can co-exist without any problems.

I told Nikki I was coming, but I wasn't on no bullshit, this isn't the first time that I saw Juelz with another woman and I'm sure it won't be the last. Me and Alexis were riding together. I'm pissed I can't have a drink.

Nikki

I swear I'm sick of Journee and Juelz either y'all or going to be or y'all not. Pick one it's that fucking simple. Today is my husband's birthday party, and I'm throwing him a Kickback party with all our closest friends and family.

Juelz is on his good bullshit for whatever reason. Everybody knew he was dating this Mia chick. I didn't have a problem with it, he didn't mind flaunting her in my face so I could tell Journee. You best believe I told her, but my girl is unbothered she didn't care.

Skeet had the nerve to tell me, Juelz said, he didn't want Journee at the party uninvite her. I looked at my husband like he was crazy. Juelz don't run shit here. Last, I checked I bussed down for everything. Journee catered the food.

If it's a problem with her being here, he can leave his bitch at home. I really don't want her at my house, it's something about that bitch that I don't like, she rubbed me the wrong way on a few occasions.

Of course, I gave Journee the heads up. I told her to bring her ass, all of it and make sure she's suited and booted. We laughed about the shit because Juelz is so funny. To make matters worse she's pregnant by him again. She pissed about it too.

I told her don't let that nigga get comfortable with trapping her with his children if he has no plans to marry her. She wanted to have an abortion I talked her out of it, Lord knows Juelz would kill her if she did, this maybe the son that she always wanted.

Journee

We finally made it to Skeet's party. Nikki had his party set up nice. I walked through the party like I owned that motherfucka because I did. I wasn't even going to show my ass, but I came to break a few necks.

As soon as I stepped through the door good, and made my way over to where everybody was kicking it. All eyes were on me. I saw Juelz and Mia was sitting on his lap. I smiled I thought it was cute. I wasn't bothered at all. I've seen worse. Leave it to Nikki and Khadijah to make a scene.

"Damn sis don't fucking hurt them, shit. Fuck it up," my sister laughed.

"Yaas Bitch you better work. That's my best friend. Journee Leigh brought that ass all of it," my best friend Nikki laughed, and we slapped hands with each other.

Nikki a fool she doesn't a give a fuck. I could feel the hate rolling off Juelz. It's all good though, he can keep his little duck on his lap, she can babysit him all night.

I'm not Giselle I don't have to chase nan nigga, but I will let you know how I feel. I knew I looked like Goddess tonight, but it was too much tension in this room.

Before I left and made my rounds I had to give Skeet his birthday gift, since he didn't want me to come. He was the main one that said he was staying out people's business. Juelz couldn't hurt my feelings, but I can damn sure hurt his.

I gave Skeet his birthday present. He looked at me like I was crazy. He knows Nikki wears the pants whatever she says goes.

"Don't look like that Skeet. I heard about you. I thought we was better than that. Here's your gift. You can thank me later."

I didn't have time to even rap with Skeet. I could feel Juelz starring a whole in me. I had to walk past him to get to the other side of the house. One of Skeet's cousins walked up on me and stopped me right in front of Juelz. Oh shit.

"Damn you fine, can a nigga get some of your time?" he asked.

"Thanks, you're not so bad yourself, my life is complicated and I can't involve you in my mess." I laughed.

"You got a man Shawty?" he asked.

"No, I don't."

"Your baby daddy he crazy?" he asked?

"Nah that nigga ain't crazy, he knows better. I'll get up with you later," I laughed.

I went to go find Nikki and Alexis and my Godmother Valerie. My phone alerted me that I had a text. I looked at my phone it was Juelz.

Babydaddyfromhell- You want me to hurt you huh?

I didn't even respond my read receipt was on. He could see that I read it. Why would you hurt me if we're not together? The text messages kept coming through. He needs to entertain his date, and not worry about what I'm doing. I finally found The Crew. Ms. Simone was here too. I thought my mother and my Godmother was a mess, but these two together. Oh my God it's tragic.

"Look at your hot ass. I heard you was pregnant again too. My son let you out the house looking like that? You must be trying to send him to jail for murder," Juelz's mom Ms. Simone said.

"Mrs. Simone, don't start with me and what I'm doing. Go meet your daughter in law and be nice too." I laughed.

Chapter 22-Simone Marie Thomas

"Journee, you and Juelz are playing a dangerous game, and I don't want any parts of it. I'm a little tipsy, but listen to me. I'm about to speak some real ass shit to you. All y'all take notes. I know he loves you and you love him too.

The games that y'all are playing isn't healthy. You're pregnant with his second child. How long are y'all going to keep this up? It's affecting Jueleez too. She wants her parents together, but y'all don't care how she feels.

The only thing that y'all care about is having one up on each other. Y'all two aren't kids anymore you're twenty-five and he's twenty-seven. For her sake grow up.

Stop fucking playing games. The whole time y'all were apart. It was killing the both of y'all. You are hiding babies, laying up with a married man. Pretending to be happy.

He's miserable with a bitch he knows he's not supposed to be with and taking care of child, he knew he had doubts about since day one. The moment y'all run into each other everything that was hidden from y'all comes out.

You act like you're scared to fight for him or give him a chance. I'm not defending him Journee, but damn you don't fight for anything that you want. Yeah, you'll beat a bitch ass quick, but if you love him embrace it and tell him how you feel. Your attitude is fuck it you don't even try. You'll carry the weight of the world on your shoulders before you admit to how you feel.

Y'all so blind y'all can't even recognize the signs and understand this shit. Trust me I've told him this same shit. He's not trying to hear it, and you're not trying to hear it. I guess something drastic should happen before y'all realize what the fuck is going on. I may not be here to see it, but if I am just know I told y'all so."

Journee

"Mrs. Simone, I do love him, but I'm not about to chase him and put myself out there. I've always had an old soul. Anything you tell me I take heed too. I'm paying attention. Y'all are on the outside looking in. Juelz is evil and mean. Maybe Juelz and I aren't meant to be together. It's so hard loving him.

We may be better off as friends, then lovers because we are toxic. When were good were good, and when we're bad we're bad. I know Jueleez would want us together, but we can't give her that right now. We're not ready, and I don't know if we'll ever be ready. At this point in my life, I'm willing to expect that."

"Journee, you have to much pride. Nobody can judge you. Stop worrying about what a person thinks about you, that's your fucking problem. You don't want to fight for shit. You haven't even tried. If you love him, damn at least fight for him. Give him the same fight that he's given you. You haven't even done that. If you try and it doesn't work than it is what it is, but you haven't done either. Try that's all I'm saying.

You know what your child told me the other day? She said, Glama can I stay with you. All my mommy and daddy due is argue when they see each other. They think I can't hear them, but I can. I just want them to get along, and my mommy cries when my daddy leaves," she stated.

"I'll do better."

"Do more that better, stop that shit. I smacked the fuck out of Juelz. She doesn't need to hear or see any of it," she argued.

Tears escaped my eyes. I'm speechless I can't believe Jueleez caught on too so much. I'm so embarrassed. It's not me this time, that's starting the arguments it's him.

Like right now he's texting me telling me to meet him in Nikki's guest room now. I'm not responding because he needs to worry about who he brought here. I'm ready to leave anyway I need to get my daughter and spend some time with her, before the new baby comes. I must get back to us. Journee and Jueleez.

Nikki

Don't get me wrong I love Mrs. Simone to death. Her and my mother have become close these pasts few weeks. She keeps it real no lie. I don't mind absorbing knowledge, but I felt she was being too hard on Journee because that's her son.

It's two sides to every story. We're on the outside looking in. Journee ain't no saint and Juelz for damn sure ain't one. Mrs. Simone was right about one thing Journee hasn't tried to make anything work with Juelz. The first time he cheated she was gone, she didn't want to hear it. Juelz has tried, I must give him that, but each time she pushed him away.

I understand where Journee's coming from, and why she has her guard up she's been hurt not once but twice. Every nigga isn't out to hurt you. I can instill that in her, but he should show her. Judging by his actions right now. She believes that he is. I don't think Juelz would do that again. I've been there play for play for every break up. I'm ready for the make ups. I just want my girl to be happy no matter what. What Kairo did was worse than what Juelz did.

I got my girls back no matter what right or wrong I'm riding. I'm rooting for Journee and Juelz to get there shit together for the sake of their children. You can love a person and not be with them I understand that.

Jueleez is Journee's weakness, she loves my niece so much. I know for fact that she wasn't arguing with Juelz in front her. It was her father and I can't wait to check him about his shit. I hate that Juelz got my girl crying behind his ass, and she's pregnant again. I knew he was mad about Journee coming, but guess what I don't give a fuck this is my house.

I don't care if it's Skeet's party or not. You'll never be comfortable in my house with a bitch I'm not feeling. You ain't never brought Giselle here, so what would make you think that you could bring her here. I knew Mia from around the way she's an ex stripper, she might still strip, but she was a well-known hoe.

"Come to my room with me Journee for a minute."

"Ok," she pouted.

We made it my room, Juelz was walking out of the guest room. He grabbed Journee and pushed her up against the wall.

"Move Juelz we're not doing that today." I pushed him off Journee, and she went in my room.

"Nikki I'm just trying to talk to her," he argued.

"That's not what it looked like to me, she'll talk to you later."

I'm sick of him he had better go on somewhere. I knew he couldn't wait to get ahold to Journee. I locked my door.

"Are you ok?"

"Yes, I'm good," she stated.

"I wanted to beat Juelz's momma's ass. You know I don't play about you."

"I already know. I watched your nose flare up a few times. I love Mrs. Simone but I felt she was being too hard on me," she stated.

"I agree."

"Fuck that shit, you look to cute to be mopping around about a nigga. Let's go party we're kid free for tonight."

We went back to the Kickback. Skeet was doing his thing, and we were doing ours. I decided to slow things up a little bit. It was a Kickback. I decided to play some R&B music from the 90's. It felt like old times. We started singing and reminiscing about how we use to be back in the day. I grabbed the mic.

Why I love you so much by **Monica** came on. Journee grabbed the microphone. She told me to start it over. Journee was a real song bird. She could blow. I'm here for it. I knew she was about to kill it. She loves this song. I watched Juelz he stood in the corner watching her like a hawk. Mia was all up in face, but his eyes were trained on Journee. I noticed Journee walking over toward him. Oh, shit I know she's not about to do what I think she's going to do.

She's about to do it. Damn she's bold tonight.

Chapter 23-Journee

Oh my God I love this song. I must kill it. I guess it was meant for me to hear today. When Juelz broke my heart many years ago. I would have this song on repeat. I always admit when I'm wrong. I haven't fought for him.

I'm going to put myself out there for the first time in my life. At the end of the day I have nothing to lose. I always finish last anyway. Nothing surprises me. I've always dealt with the cards that I was dealt. You only live once. I wanted Juelz to feel me, I didn't give a fuck about Mia being in the room or her being up in his face right now.

I walked over to where he was at and she was standing in face. I politely told her

"excuse me."

She had an attitude, a bitch will get popped today try me. I told Nikki to run it back. The music started playing. I was looking directly in his eyes. He was grilling the fuck out of me. I just smiled, and I started singing my heart out.

"Sang that shit Journee, get your baby daddy back, I schooled her," Juelz's mom yelled.

"You don't never say I'm too young, for you baby, I've been around enough, to know enough, to know just what I want. You don't move too fast or make rush," I sung the lyrics to Monica song to Juelz. I pointed my finger in his face. He was blushing

I was so nervous I attempted to walk back up front where Nikki and Khadijah were. Juelz grabbed me. I turned around and looked at him.

"That's how you feel," he asked.

"Yes."

He gave me hug, we just stared at each other. Until we were rudely interrupted.

"You got me fucked up, I can't stand a thirsty bitch, I got something for thirsty hoes" she argued, and threw a drink in my face.

"Oh, this bitch got me fucked up." Juelz wiped my face with his shirt.

"Let me go."

"Nah you're not about to fight her and you're pregnant with my child," he argued.

"Let her go, so I can tag her ass," she argued.

I tried to break free from his embrace, he had me in a tight bear hug. I couldn't move.

"Please Juelz let me go, your child will be just fine. Give me five minutes to beat her ass." I cried.

"Nope let's go. I don't want you fighting period you know I don't like that shit," he argued.

"I don't like being tried and I can't do nothing about it." I cried.

"It's ok I don't want you to ruin Skeet's party, let that shit go," he argued.

Khadijah

Fuck this shit. I don't give a fuck about this being Skeet's party. It's not a bitch walking that's going to be able to say they threw a drink my sister's face and we didn't do shit. I was sitting on Smoke's lap and watched the whole thing unfold.

As soon as the I saw the bitch approach Journee I was trying to get up. Smoke held me down with his arms. He knew I was ready to fuck it up.

"Let me go Smoke."

"Nah, KD you're not about to fuck Skeet's party up let it go."

"Fuck Skeet's party. A bitch gone respect my sister. I'll kill a bitch behind that one.

"Man, KD go on with that shit."

"Smoke if you don't let me tap this bitches' ass really quick you ain't getting no pussy or head for two weeks, I promise."

He let me go like I knew he would. I heard that bitch loud and clear. Let her go so I can tag her ass. I was coming from one direction and Alexis was coming from other. I made it first. Normally I wouldn't even get a bitch while her back was turned, but fuck that I was knocking her block off.

I cocked my fist back and swung a mean punch in the back of her head she turned around. I cocked my fist back again, swung and knocked her in her jaw. She swung back I ducked and upper cut her on her neckline.

Alexis yanked her long as weave, and she fell to the floor. It was on from there. Alexis and I took turns tagging that bitch. She was begging for us to stop. Fuck that bitch you need to know your fucking place.

Stay out of folk's business you already knew what it was when she approached him. You should've took the high road Journee didn't come at you out of line.

You made it an issue throwing a drink and cussing and calling my sister out of her name. For that reason alone. I had to tap your ass.

Smoke grabbed me, and Alonzo grabbed Alexis. Skeet looked at us, and shook his head. He already knew how we give it up. I don't know why he's surprised. Juelz picked ole girl up and carried her out the party. I hope he's sending that bitch home in an Uber.

"KD you wrong for that shit you, and Alexis," he argued.

"Whatever, if Kairo would've did that to Juelz you mean to tell me you and Skeet wouldn't have rocked that man to sleep?"

"Hell yeah, we would've," he argued.

"Ok so don't act like you don't understand where, I'm coming from."

Chapter 24-Alexis

Don't get me wrong I love Journee to death. Blood couldn't make us any closer. I just met Alonzo, and I wanted to get to know him some more, that shit was ruined before it started. I love Nikki too but she was messy ass fuck. I know this was Skeet's party or whatever but damn we just fought and fucked this bitch up.

As soon as we walked in the party all eyes were on us. You could feel the tension between Journee and Juelz as soon as they looked at each other. A knife couldn't cut it. I knew it was about to be some shit for one he didn't want her to come, and if he did I knew he wouldn't approve of that outfit she had on.

Every nigga in this motherfucka was lusting behind Journee and he was fucking sick. I watched him bite the insides of his jaw. Journee was so bold with the shit, she didn't give a fuck she was smiling and entertaining them letting be known that she was single as fuck.

He watched her like a hawk. He couldn't wait to catch her by herself. Skeet had to stop him on several occasions from running up on her and showing his ass. Khadijah and Nikki thought it was funny because he was tripping. I didn't find it funny, don't get me wrong I'm all for the good bullshit but I knew when to stop.

All bets were off when Nikki slowed the party down, and started playing her old school music (90's R&B) and gave the microphone to Journee. She started singing her heart out. Godmother Valerie and Ms. Simone were already drunk telling her to sang that shit. Get your man back. I knew she would get in her feelings, she does it every time, and tonight would be no different.

Nikki knew exactly what she was doing I prayed Jesus took the wheel. I fixed me a stiff drink, and kicked my shoes off, because I knew shit was about to get real. If Journee gets to feeling herself even more than she already is.

Kairo

I've been real patient with Journee these last few weeks. She's taking my kindness for my weakness. I knew she was still mad about my ex-wife, and I didn't want to force myself on her too much, but it is what it is. I know I haven't been the best man to her.

I would spend the rest of my life making it up to her, and putting her back together again. I knew I was living foul, but it took me to lose her to realize that none of this shit was worth it.

I knew Journee couldn't be bought. I wanted her to spend my money. I took FED chances for her. It's only right that she gets whatever she wants. I watched her and Juelz long enough. I know he wanted her. It's nothing wrong with wanting something that you can't have.

I fucked up, but I'm ready to right my wrongs. Journee can do it her way, or she can do it my way. The choice is hers, but I'm her only option. I tried to reach out to her on a numerous of occasions, she blocked my number.

Every house I purchased for her she tried to sale it. Anything that I've brought for her can't be sold. I don't give a fuck if it's listed or not. I've emailed her and got no response. I stopped by the restaurant and she had her employees turn me away. I sat in my car on a numerous of occasions and watched her have fun and smile.

Her smile alone burned me up, because I knew I wasn't the cause of that I've been in the states for the past month. I heard she was pregnant again by Juelz. I'm fucked up about it, because she was too quick to give him my pussy. I don't mind raising his children I been doing it. I deserve another chance. I'm not asking for another chance. I'm taking my chance.

Free

The game is to be sold and not told. I loved Alexis she always had my heart despite the double life I was living. I was ready to straighten up, and get my shit together. I wasn't ready to choose between Alexis and Giselle. I had a family with Giselle and I couldn't put Alexis before my daughter.

I was trying to figure shit out before things got too heated. Imagine my surprise when I pulled up to Kairo's and Journee's crib, and all my shit was aired out by Tyra. Giselle knew the deal she had a nigga and I had a fiancé.

Time wasn't on my side. I wanted to marry Giselle. Alexis and I were engaged to be married. My mother didn't like her for some reason, but I didn't care. I brushed that shit off and took it as my mom being over protective. Alexis cheated on me on a numerous of occasions. It's true what they say about a woman scorned and hurt. She'll tell it all.

Alexis broke me when she said my father ate her pussy. My chest tightened up and not because of the bullet wounds. She cheated on me with somebody close to home. I wanted to kill her just off the strength, she felt the need to get me back like that. To hear it hurt me, but too see the pictures with my own two eyes fucked me up.

Yeah, she was bold as fuck, she sent me the pictures so I could see the shit. I think the reason that I healed so fast is because I couldn't wait to fuck her up. I've been watching her for the past few weeks. She was living her life carefree. I noticed that she put on a few pounds colored her hair. She was different she had a nigga too.

The devil stayed on my back. I couldn't let her slide, and be happy with that nigga after she did all that shit to hurt me. I just couldn't let it slide, I had Giselle but that wasn't enough. I killed my father, I rocked his old ass to sleep once I found out that he fucked me over.

I sat up front at his funeral and pretended to cry and console my mother. Fuck him. Killing him wasn't enough I wasn't satisfied. I had to get at Alexis she thought that shit was funny. I'll have the last laugh. Just watch.

Chapter 25-Alexis

We had to blow Skeet's party and take our asses home. Nikki tried to act like she was mad and chastise us in front of Skeet. As soon as Skeet turned his head she was praising us for beating ass. Alonzo was pissed at me for cutting up the way I didn't I couldn't help it. I knew we shouldn't have jumped her, but oh well that's what the fuck she gets for making all that noise.

Journee was sitting on the passenger side in her feeling because Juelz took ole girl home instead of calling her an Uber. I had to tell her to cheer up because that nigga was coming home to her and Jueleez regardless. He forgot that bitch was in the room for a minute until she started bumping her gums.

Alonzo was so pissed at me we were supposed to leave together, and now I'm headed home with a hot and bothered pussy because Journee couldn't keep her feelings in check. That's my girl and I'm going to ride regardless. Hopefully Alonzo will get over it. I really lust him.

"I'm sorry Alexis for dragging you in my mess," she stated.

"It's cool I still had fun at least you got out of your feelings and told Juelz how you feel. I'm so proud of you.

My bitch is finally growing up and letting her stubborn ways go. I thought you were going to die alone."

"Yeah whatever," she laughed.

We started cruising down Hollywood Rd. I hit H.E. Holmes to hop on I-20E. I noticed a car was following us, but I didn't say shit too Journee. I didn't want her to get scared. I attempted to hop on the interstate real quick. The black SUV rammed us from the back twice.

My car flipped over.

"Alexis, what the fuck is going on," she asked.

"I don't know."

Journee attempted to kick the passenger side window out and climb out. A tall nigga dressed in all black with a Ski-mask, gloves and a gun yanked her out. He pointed a gun to her head and told her don't say shit. He pulled her of the car and slapped duct tape on her lips.

"What the fuck is going on?" I started panicking.

My back window was shattered. I heard a gun fire coming from each direction. It finally ceased. I grabbed my phone and called Nikki. She answered on the first ring.

"Nikki, get Juelz on the fucking phone now."

"What's wrong, he hasn't made it back yet from dropping Mia off," she asked.

"We've been ambushed, somebody just ran us off the road, my car flipped over and they kidnapped Journee. It's blood every fucking where. I think my arm is broke." I cried.

Somebody kicked the driver's window open and glass shattered in my face.

"Help."

"Yeah bitch, I didn't come to help you," he argued.

"Free."

"Did you think this shit was over? Tell me to my face, what the fuck you let my daddy do, repeat that shit. I kidnap bitches like you, and take them to Africa and kill them," he argued and laughed.

He yanked me out of my car by neck and threw me over his shoulder.

"Bitch you're not even worth a trip to Africa. Open your fucking mouth and eat this fucking lead," he argued.

"Please don't do this." I cried.

To Be
Continued

The

EVOLUTION
of an
ENTREPRENEUR

OTHER BOOKS BY JACK NADEL

Use What You Have to Get What You Want

My Enemy, My Friend

There's No Business Like Your Bu$iness

*How to Succeed in Business
Without Lying, Cheating or Stealing*

Cracking the Global Market

The

EVOLUTION
of an
ENTREPRENEUR

featuring

50 of My Best Tips for
Surviving and Thriving in Business

JACK NADEL

JNJ PUBLISHING LLC

JNJ Publishing LLC
Jack Nadel
2401 Main Street
Santa Monica, CA 90405
www.JackNadel.com

Publisher's Cataloguing-in-Publication Data

Nadel, Jack.
    The evolution of an entrepreneur : featuring 50 of my best tips for surviving and thriving in business / by Jack Nadel.
    p. cm.
    ISBN 978-0-9846282-2-3 (pbk.)
    ISBN 978-0-9846282-1-6 (e-book)

1. Nadel, Jack. 2. Businessmen --United States --Biography. 3. Entrepreneurship --Biography. 4. Success in business. I. The evolution of an entrepreneur : featuring fifty of my best tips for surviving and thriving in business. II. Title.

HC102.5.A2 N25 2013
338.092 --dc23   2012953330

To Julie,

My wife, partner, and best friend, whose positive attitude and constant care brought me through a life-threatening illness and who continues to provide encouragement and inspiration.

In 1978, newly divorced with two young daughters, Julie had to earn enough money to provide for herself and for the education of her children. With her love and talent for food preparation, her detail-oriented mind, and her outgoing personality, catering and event planning became her chosen field.

From high-profile celebrity weddings and Hollywood studio parties to the Super Bowl and the 1984 Olympics, Julie built her company, Parties Plus, into a well-recognized and respected organization that was sold to a public company in 1990.

Julie now devotes a great deal of her time to charity work, including some recent projects that will affect generations to come in our local community. Nothing could make me happier.

CONTENTS

HOW TO MAKE THIS BOOK WORK FOR YOU

W HEN YOU OPEN this book, I ask you to keep an open mind. The ideas presented are deliberately designed to engage your instincts rather than your analysis.

Next, assume these ideas will work. This sounds simple. But sadly, most people are skeptical, and some believe that nothing will work.

Your attitude is the one thing that you can change today that will transform the way you are perceived by everyone else immediately. An optimistic outlook instantly shifts thinking to the positive. It can and will work for you.

Give yourself the freedom to process what you have read. Some ideas will resonate with you immediately. These are the ideas to be closely examined and applied to your business plan.

The 50 tips in the last section of the book are not theoretical; they are distilled from 67 years of business success. Let them work for you.

INTRODUCTION

THREE FACTS ABOUT ME:

I don't have a college degree.

I can't use basic carpentry tools to save my life.

I've made a profit in business every year *for 67 years straight*
and have enjoyed a high standard of living.

WHEN I STARTED in business, we had no fancy equipment, office space, expense accounts, or board of directors. All we had was our instincts and primitive knowledge of how to get going—so that's just what we did. Off we went at full speed, hurdling obstacles, spotting opportunities, and connecting dots along the way. We relied on quick thinking and trusted our guts to lead us to profits where others had failed to find them. And with each new deal, my evolution as an entrepreneur continues.

Whether you are reading this book because you are unemployed or underemployed, you are no doubt tired of watching your expenses outpace your income and competing for higher-paying jobs that are very scarce. As you know all too well, your options are limited: reduce your standard of living, find a second job, or start a business and become your own boss. Choosing this third option was certainly a decision I've never regretted.

No matter how ambitious you are, you really don't have a business until you have someone on the other side of a deal. Too many start-ups fail because their owners think they must first invest in the latest technology, stylish office furniture, and impressive real estate. An entrepreneur should know that it all starts with a deal, and the successful completion of it paves the way for the next deal. This is what the beginning of an evolutionary journey looks like.

I have been a successful entrepreneur for many years and have created hundreds of new products, thousands of new jobs, and millions of dollars in profits. The thriving entrepreneur evolves in a clear progression of stages.

As I said, there is no deal until there are two parties involved. The process of becoming an entrepreneur starts with a simple concept for a deal. With each success, the entrepreneur climbs an evolutionary ladder. My decades of experience have given me, at the age of 89, the confidence to delineate for you the best methods to be prosperous. Use *The Evolution of an Entrepreneur* as a guide for your own climb up the ladder. My years in all facets of business have provided me with a great deal of satisfaction and a superb lifestyle. Throughout those years, and right up to the present, I have been making deals—helping to create new companies and products without ever losing any of the excitement and joy that come from success. My evolution enables me now to share this wisdom with you. I firmly believe that the solution to creating more jobs is to evolve more entrepreneurs. And how do you evolve entrepreneurs? Teach them targeted thinking.

Readers of my last book, *Use What You Have to Get What You Want*, responded enthusiastically to the book's 100 specific tips for business success. However, they also wanted to know more about my personal story and the context for the business vignettes presented in the book. *The Evolution of an Entrepreneur* is my answer to those many requests and provides insight about how you can take advantage of all *your* experiences.

In January 1946, I was discharged from the U.S. Army Air Corps and joined the world of business in earnest. My timing couldn't have been better. I entered a post-war commercial world filled with tremendous opportunities. I believe some of the same kinds of opportunities exist today. The key is, and has always been, to identify unmet needs in the marketplace. Most successful careers have begun when a real need was discovered and then addressed with the right solution, resulting in a profit.

I believe our problems can best be solved by our own efforts. You have greater capabilities than you think, and many of them can be translated into a steady cash flow. The suggestions in this book have been gleaned from thousands of real business transactions. For the last five to six years, our economy has been undergoing a major restructuring. Many of the jobs lost during the Great Recession are never coming back. Times are difficult, yes, but problems also point toward new opportunities. For example, the rise of cloud computing (the use of computing resources as services delivered over the Internet) has meant a steep decline in the sales of bulky desktop computers. Smaller devices are taking over, which has led to the building of many new data storage facilities and the addition of thousands of new jobs.

So as you plan your own entrepreneurial adventure, look for emerging needs. Don't pin your hopes on a sector that may soon become obsolete. Look out to the horizon and anticipate demands that you can fill. Your business life and your personal life revolve around this kind of problem solving.

Of course, even our best efforts can sometimes fail. These are the times to step back and take a broader view. I have always believed that we celebrate our successes without realizing how valuable our failures are. Mistakes are actually opportunities for learning, and we shouldn't waste them. A college degree constitutes only part of an education. I have just a high school diploma, but my ability to think and to find solutions has been honed by the mistakes I've made in the uncompromising realities of the marketplace. The trick is to be pragmatic and act on your errors quickly. Use them as building blocks for growth. This kind of positive attitude is one of the greatest assets a businessperson can have. However, don't overlook the importance of your gut instincts; they are the sum of all your experiences. Gut instincts come from our unconscious memories, and they often help us avoid serious missteps.

A good way to start down the entrepreneurial road is to take stock of your assets. Make a list of all your training, attributes, and meaningful experiences. Understand that each can contribute toward building a rewarding career. Armed with this list, give yourself a specified period—an hour, two hours, a half-hour (it doesn't matter how long; just define a time frame) and play the "What if?" game.

Essentially, the "What if?" game is a series of questions and answers based on your business possibilities and desired results. At all times, keep the outcome you want and your assets in mind. Each business action or option you select leads to a new decision point. In simple terms, what if I turn left instead of right? What new possibilities will result? Am I moving closer to my desired result or farther away? Use your imagination.

I once helped an accomplished individual who was a musician, orchestra conductor, producer, and theatrical director go through this exercise. He had spent 20 years in show business without achieving any personal financial stability. I showed him that given his combination of skills and background, he didn't have to learn anything new. What he needed to do was use his talents in a new way to provide a sustainable income.

First, he made a list of everything that he was trained to do and capable of doing. Thinking creatively and taking all of his skills into account, he discovered he was capable of training politicians and organizational CEOs to effectively communicate their messages through the media. This individual has become a huge success as a media trainer for the progressive movement in Washington DC.

Everybody agrees that the best answer to a depressed economy is to have more companies manufacturing more goods and providing more services. The rage among today's politicians is to claim that they are job creators. In reality, few of the groups that claim this capability understand how to increase the number of entrepreneurs in the marketplace. The answer has to come from someone who has actually done it...someone who has created jobs, products, services, and profits on a steady basis.

For the past six decades, I have founded, acquired, and operated more than a dozen profitable companies. It's time now for me to pass this legacy on because we need new entrepreneurs more than ever. The thought of helping launch others is what keeps me young and optimistic. Following the memoir section of this book (called "The Adventure Continues...") are 50 of my best tips for dramatically increasing your chances of achieving your goals. In life and in business, the three Rs apply: relationships, results, and rewards. Every deal starts with the forming of a relationship (the first R), which enables you to gain a fuller understanding of the deal you are proposing. Results (the second R) indicate the benefits to all parties by carrying out the deal. Attaining favorable results requires an intense attention to detail from concept to execution. Rewards (the third R) are the natural outcome of the first two Rs. You'll find tips like this in this book to help you.

We started this discussion with the fact that long-term success depends on doing something that you truly enjoy. Personally, as I have mentioned, I am all thumbs when it comes to a toolbox. But tell me about a need that exists in the market, and I will smile, find a way to fill it, and make a good profit in the process.

I realize that each stage of my career has helped me evolve into what and where I am today. There are very few success stories, if any, that start with a sudden inspiration or flash of universal understanding. Success comes as part of an evolutionary process. Each stage in my career prepared me for the next. I have turned my dreams into reality using past experiences as stepping stones.

I am very excited to now pass on my practical solutions for use in your career. In today's world, we are bombarded with new products, services, and circumstances. We must accustom ourselves to filtering incoming information to spot emerging needs. Since conditions are ever-shifting, and the content of what is thrown at us is unpredictable, there are no hard-and-fast rules for how to make a profit. The Nadel Method, outlined in the book's first section, offers tips to help you better sense opportunities and stay nimble in the face of rapid changes. My method simplifies the process of getting started in business and breaks down the many elements that may seem too difficult to conquer.

An entrepreneur's evolutionary process starts very early in life. My experiences during the Great Depression shaped me in particular ways that influenced me as an adult. Obviously, we all follow unique paths that lead to different arenas. Entrepreneurs come in a multitude of types, but we all make use of the raw material of our childhood.

When I was 10 years old, my family moved to the East Bronx (New York), a very rough neighborhood. My first day going to school, I walked through a gang-ruled area. I was stopped by a group of very tough kids who told me I would have to pay "protection money" to go through their territory. The price was 5 cents for one time, and 10 cents for a week. I shrugged my shoulders and said, "I don't have a nickel." They beat me up. I never paid protection money and never got beat up again. The solution: I simply walked a few extra blocks each day and avoided them completely. I learned that there were many ways to survive. The trick was to think of them all and choose the best one.

This experience prepared me for the next level of my entrepreneurial education: working at the age of 13 as a florist's delivery boy and truck driver's helper. I soon learned that opportunities during the Depression era often came unexpectedly, and I needed to be ready to take advantage of them. For example, I regularly brought flowers to a suite at the Waldorf Astoria hotel, where the butler had instructions to give a 25-cent tip whenever a delivery was made. After a few visits, I realized that if I had three boxes of flowers for that suite on the same day, I would come up three separate times—to collect a total of 75 cents.

The third stage in my evolution resulted from my service in the U.S. Army Air Corps in World War II. Flying 27 combat missions in a B-29 over Japan was an enormously important part of my development. During this time, I quickly learned what it meant to be part of a team and dependent on others for my survival. Overall, these three stages early in my life provided me with the tools I needed to begin an entrepreneurial career: an independent spirit, a pragmatic attitude, and confidence in the face of adversity.

When I embarked on my business career, the word *entrepreneur* was not commonly used. It certainly wasn't a term I was familiar with, yet that was precisely what I was intending to become. I started my company with a moderate bankroll, seeking no outside financing. I had saved up the money from my military pay. By starting small and working within my limited means, I was able to create a going business that produced a profit.

And now, after all these years of being immersed in the global marketplace, I believe I am well-equipped for the next stage of my evolution: to be a mentor to all those folks who yearn to strike off on their own. I am a serial entrepreneur who has prospered during many economic cycles and in a multitude of markets. From this experience, I have been able to refine my methods to pass them on to you. I cannot wish you anything better than an eventful and joyous journey.

The rookie entrepreneur who is wary of entering the global arena should keep in mind that 70 percent of the market for most products made in the United States is *outside* of the United States. This means there are enormous opportunities in emerging markets. Navigating the barbed wire of regulations should not intimidate you. There are fewer tariffs today than when I started. And expanding our country's foreign trade can be helpful diplomatically. Negotiating a good deal for both sides of the table can promote mutual respect and stability.

The core principles that make a business successful are the same as when I started, and they will continue to be. While new technology is always a factor, my basic method applies today as well as it did back when I began my entrepreneurial evolution in the global marketplace: find a need and fill it, and develop relationships based on mutual trust and delivered results. The rewards will follow without fail.

However, I have yet to mention one aspect of the well-rounded entrepreneur, and in many ways it is the most important one. For what use is wealth if you accumulate it unscrupulously or at the expense of others? Honesty and ethics are at the core of my philosophy. When I teach young people how to run a business, I always spend time on the importance of maintaining a high moral standard. One of my books, *How to Succeed in Business Without Lying, Cheating or Stealing*, came out just after the movie *Wall Street*, which featured Gordon Gekko's mantra, "Greed is good." In this era of computer stock trading, hedge funds, and derivatives, there is a tendency to substitute the question "Is it legal?" for "Is it right?" Don't be tempted by this short-sighted approach to business success. Associates often hear me say, "You make more money being honest than in any other way."

I have found this to be true over and over again. An added benefit is that I can sleep well at night knowing that I've played by the rules.

In my early years in business, I was told that it was important to separate my personal life from my professional life. The idea was that you could be warm and personal at home, but at the office, you should lose your humanity. In other words, you should lead two separate lives and have two distinct personalities. In all honesty, I don't think this can be done. I feel that morality and friendship should be applied to personal *and* business relationships. You are one person, with one basic way of treating people. When I planned my career, I wanted to do something I really loved. As a matter of fact, one of my great hobbies was my business, and it got my total attention because of my love for it. Many of my close business associates became close friends. Having an open mind is an enormous advantage in both the personal and business arenas.

When I was five years old, I noticed that my mother would cook two pots of soup at a time. I asked why she was making so much, as we could not possibly eat that quantity for dinner. Her answer was very simple, yet it made a profound impression on me: "The second pot of soup is for the Raboy family next door. You know, they are poorer than we." I have never forgotten the value of that lesson, and I'm sure it has subconsciously informed all of my business decisions—as well as inspired my desire to share with you the knowledge I have gained along my evolutionary journey.

THE NADEL METHOD

THE NADEL METHOD

S INCE THE BEGINNING of my career, I have been creating and refining what I call the "Nadel Method." After nearly 70 years of business experience, I am confident this method can be used by all entrepreneurs.

STEP ONE: *Identify a Business Idea You Love*

A few years back, I was teaching a business course at the University of California, Santa Barbara. One of the first questions I was asked was, "What is the right business today for me to be in?" My answer to this question is always, "What is it that you really love to do?" This is the first question you must answer; then you find a way to turn what you love to do into a business. When you make this choice about your career, however, you must clearly understand your strengths and weaknesses. There is a difference between a wish and a goal. A wish might be to play point guard for the Lakers. An achievable goal might be to work with an NBA team in their marketing or sales department or to become a supplier to an NBA venue or retail outlet.

STEP TWO: *Ask the Right Questions as You Research*

Okay, you have pinpointed a new business. Understand that if it is a good idea, the odds are that someone has thought of it before you. This fact should not necessarily discourage you, but it is imperative that you research what they did, how they did it, and how you can do it *better*. Before you spend a dollar or many hours of your time, you must use logical thinking to get answers to some very precise questions. First, is your business idea a product or a service? If it is a product, what other products in the marketplace are the same or similar? If it is a service, who else is performing this service, and is it being done successfully? How big is the market?

How fortunate we are that much of what we want to know is accessible right on our computers or even on our mobile devices. I remember one budding entrepreneur who came to me for advice on how to make his newly created business really work. I asked him if anybody was already putting his idea to use or attempting to develop it. He replied, "Absolutely no one has done it…isn't that amazing?" I immediately went to my computer; a number of different companies were doing everything he had talked about. Yet this person had spent a great deal of money on proposals and trying to raise capital. This is one of the first things you have to know. It is not easy to raise capital on an idea that you have not investigated thoroughly. Thousands of people come up with millions of ideas. But they have nothing until they have proven that an idea can work.

STEP THREE: *Plan a Deal and Focus on the Details*

At this point, you are ready for the first phase in structuring a deal and creating a business plan around it. (Note that the Nadel Method uses the term *business plan* to indicate the steps required to execute a particular deal. Also, the advice presented applies to any deal in the life of your business, not only to the first one.) Just as an athlete needs to condition his or her body to go into competition, you must likewise condition your mind to engage in business. The Nadel Method is based on the ability to think in terms of a particular situation and react to it in a specific time frame. An entrepreneur must learn to conceptualize in a highly focused way, with an emphasis on market demand and profit potential. Asking and answering questions is an ongoing part of this process. What tools are available to expedite your plan? How will you make the best use of them? How will you transition from proposing a deal to making a concrete business plan? Remember, the business plan has to tell you not only how to execute the deal, but how to do it profitably.

Visualize the steps you will have to go through to carry out the deal. I mean *really* go through them in your mind, step by step and meeting by meeting. Imagine that you are watching a video as you mentally go through the motions of completing a plan and making a deal happen. You write the script, and you are the star.

This process can take any amount of time. You should not put restrictions on it because it sets you on the right track and may save you from many mistakes. Take a totally optimistic view: Everything goes right, happening just as you had planned. In your mind, see the deal as it's made. Now sit back for a moment and ask yourself how you feel. Are you thrilled with the deal, or are you disappointed? I have gone through this visualization many times and occasionally felt at the end that I was really not happy with the results.

Remember, you went through this process as if everything transpired perfectly, which it never does. If you do not feel good about the deal, do not even start it. If you love where you are after the deal is completed successfully in your mind, you can go on to the next phase: putting your business plan on paper. Compare this process to a football team going up against a tough opponent (*the deal*). The coach must prepare a game plan that the team reviews many times before the opening kickoff (*the business plan*).

Now that the stage has been set mentally, you must be determined to start making good things happen. Every vocation requires a distinct mindset. A philosopher thinks in abstractions, while an engineer imagines the way things work. A comedian searches for humor in every situation, while an entrepreneur thinks in specifics with laser-like precision. Business details can be tiny, in the form of millimeters, pennies, or subtle shades of color. As an entrepreneur, you have to know that stress is guaranteed. You must have a genuine passion for success in order to manage the frustrations of the journey.

Here are examples of questions to keep in mind as you put together a deal and craft a business plan:

1. Have you determined your distribution channel?

2. How big an investment do you need in order to accomplish your goals? Will you require outside financing?

3. Is your time frame flexible enough to allow for unexpected delays?

4. Are you dealing with a patent or a brand name for your product, or are you just going to enter the marketplace and let the chips fall where they may?

5. What is it going to cost to make your product? What is the minimum you must produce and sell to ensure a profit?

6. What do you have to do to produce a superior product at a better price than your competitors?

7. Is your profit margin large enough to sustain steady growth?

STEP FOUR: *Fulfill Your Agreement and Then Some*

This is the all-important point where you execute the deal, and you must always be prepared to make course corrections along the way. It is almost impossible to anticipate all the problems and all the opportunities that will present themselves by virtue of your being in the marketplace. You must keep your ego out of it and make changes in accordance with the unanticipated conditions that present themselves. Never stop thinking of how you can improve your deal. In entering any new venture, always hope for the best but prepare for the worst.

Another rule of the Nadel Method is to document in writing every agreement or important conversation with suppliers and customers. You may think you have a deal, but the people with whom you are conducting business may not have the same understanding of what was said. You must get in the habit of confirming everything in writing. It's not that you expect problems or dishonesty, but you must protect yourself and your venture at all times by documenting your agreements.

STEP FIVE: *Review the Results for Next Time*

The final step of the Nadel Method is simple but vital. It involves reflection. As your business plan reaches its conclusion, it's time to take stock. Think about this entire experience, so that you can build on it to create your next deal. There are questions you need to consider. Have you achieved what you set out to do? Are you still excited about your role as an entrepreneur? Did you respond to unexpected modifications in a timely manner? How and where will you use this recent experience to structure an even bigger deal?

The Nadel Method stresses the importance of careful planning and great execution. The advantage of the veteran entrepreneur is that he or she is flexible enough to change course if necessary to make a business work. With the Nadel Method, you must *never* stop thinking creatively. Be prepared to add and subtract from your original plan. The more you evaluate through a critical lens, the more you will be able to spot the adjustments and corrections you need to make.

THE ADVENTURE
CONTINUES...

THE END OF WAR,
THE BEGINNING OF AN IDEA

I T WAS 9:00 P.M. on August 14, 1945. The night was unusually dark, probably another reason for my feeling of doom. The first reason was that I knew I was going back into combat as I checked into Hickam Field in Honolulu. I had already flown 27 intense and increasingly more dangerous missions in a B-29 over Japan, and I was not feeling lucky. My crew and I had used up our 10 days of R&R (rest and recuperation) leave. We were scheduled to report to Air Transport Command at 10:00 p.m. to return to our base in Saipan and resume bombing Japan in advance of a planned massive invasion. I was the navigator and radar-bombardier of this 11-man crew, which had survived without a scratch against all odds...so far.

I had spent the previous two days enjoying the beauty of Oahu with wine, song, and plenty of company. Still, it wasn't enough to ease the fear that was twisting my insides. I was returning to combat and knew I had little chance of survival. Of those who had started the tour eight months earlier, 75 percent had been killed in action.

As I started to walk across an open field to pick up my gear, my head was filled with memories. I recalled the good times with all of my buddies who were lost, as well as the pain of their loss. In just one hour, I would be on a plane heading back to the grim reality of Japanese antiaircraft fire and suicidal fighters, and the long trips over open water back to Saipan.

Within the space of a second, the entire airfield lit up around me. It was ablaze with light. I stopped walking and stood in the deafening silence. Then the PA system came to life, and a loud voice blared over dozens of speakers: "Attention! Attention, all personnel! World War II has just ended...all orders are frozen! Everybody stay where you are, and you will receive new orders."

I was unable to move; all of the air seemed to leave my body in one giant whoosh. I felt my face getting wet; when I put my hands to my cheeks, I realized that tears were streaming down. I was going to live! The war was over, and I had come through it unharmed. At 22, I was going to have a rebirth, a renaissance.

The next morning shone bright and clear. It was 10:00 a.m., and four of us were enjoying a pot of steaming black coffee. Many times we had trusted our lives to each other. For the past year, we had shared so much and been totally dependent on each other. Whether we were defending ourselves against Japanese fighter planes that swarmed at us from out of the sun, guns blazing, or we were nursing a wounded B-29 back to the base, it was the same task. Always the same. Do we bail out of our injured Superfortress, or do we tough it out? We knew that if each man did not perform perfectly, we were all dead.

There was Herb, the pilot, who was born to fly. Tall, lean, stoic, and from Mid-America, he was the quintessential leader. Robbie, the copilot, was a burly guy from the town of Big Stone Gap, Virginia. He spoke in a lazy drawl and had a wit with a fatalistic undertone. When his wife asked him in a letter if he would be home for Christmas, his response was, "I don't think they are going to drag the Pacific Ocean to find me and send me home." Then there was Ritchie, our short but stalwart bombardier. He was from Cleveland and, at 5-foot-4, could drink any of us under the table.

Herb started our first serious conversation that had nothing to do with planning or executing a mission. "We should be going home pretty soon, and I'll have to make a decision about being discharged or reenlisting. Flying is in my blood. I have to keep on flying. Maybe I can get a job with an airline, or do some crop-dusting. I don't know, but I'll talk it over with my wife, Betty Jo. I can't wait to see her," he added wistfully.

Robbie scratched his head and then said, in a slow drawl, "I reckon I'll be home long before Christmas, and nobody has to scrape the ocean for me. I need to see my wife and kids. I don't want to leave the Old Homestead. Maybe I can find a few more acres and settle in." There was a pause. "Hey, guys, we're way too sober to talk about such serious stuff."

"Cleveland is looking mighty good to me right now," Ritchie said with a laugh. He reached into his pocket and pulled out a flask, from which he took a long pull. "I'm feeling better already." He shot me a quizzical glance. "Are you ready for the Big City again?"

Staring at my crewmates, I said, "I'm ready to be a civilian right now! I can't even imagine how great the freedom to make my own decisions about what to eat, to wear...and what is off-limits is gonna be. I have a crazy desire to start my own business, make my own decisions, and be my own boss. There is a whole new world out there, and there is going to be a big demand for civilian merchandise. I am going to get into that arena, and work all over the world. What a great opportunity to see new places without being shot at." I mused, "I spent a weekend in Los Angeles before shipping out overseas. New York is fine, but I am ready to move to the West Coast, where everything is warm and fresh."

My throat tightened as I gazed at the guys with whom I had spent the last year. "We have been one hell of a team...without you, I could not have survived." There was a catch in my throat as I spoke. "I want to thank each of you for your friendship and for always being there. I think we should join Ritchie and toast each other."

Looking back, I realize it was at that very moment that I started my career as an entrepreneur.

I have no idea why I survived combat against such overwhelming odds. I do know, though, that the situation was made tolerable by having a positive outlook. The power of the mind was never more succinctly proven in my life, because even under those adverse conditions, there were many laughs and good feelings. My natural inclination was to look on the bright side, even though the other side was a disaster. It was then that I learned to hope for the best and be prepared for the worst.

I was honorably discharged as Captain, U.S. Army Air Force, having flown 27 combat missions and served as a navigator and radar officer. I was decorated with the Distinguished Flying Cross and the Air Medal with three oak leaf clusters.

FINDING AND FILLING NEEDS IN THE POST-WAR WORLD

L IFE IN THE United States in 1946 was different than when I left in 1942 for the U.S. Army Air Corps. There was a feeling of economic optimism in the air—ironically because much of the world had been devastated by the war. The industrial centers of Europe and Japan were all but destroyed. Because consumer goods had not been produced during the war, there was a huge demand for them after.

When the Japanese bombed Pearl Harbor in December 1941, my brother Saul was stationed there as a marine. The day the war ended in August 1945 found me there, too. It seemed as though the Nadel brothers had bracketed the war. Now we were joining forces to enter the post-war world.

I was 23 and he was 26, and we were ready to take advantage of international demand…to find as many needs as we could and fill them. We each had a high school education, very little money, and unbelievable energy and ambition. What we lacked in formal education we made up for in street smarts developed during our childhood in New York City. There was no doubt in our minds that we would be successful.

We moved to Los Angeles because of a feeling that the West Coast offered the greatest opportunity. New York was full of established businesses, but in Los Angeles, almost everybody was just getting started. Our first stop was the Los Angeles Chamber of Commerce, which had a very active foreign trade section. The chamber published a weekly bulletin of inquiries received from around the world for all kinds of merchandise. Everything was in short supply. It was very much a seller's market—if only you had a good source of supply.

One of the first inquiries came from China, for navy blue woolen material. Nobody had navy blue woolen material. We were aware, however, that there was a huge amount of army olive drab on sale at war surplus stores. We figured out that we could buy the surplus army olive drab, dye it navy, and sell it to the Chinese. That is exactly what we did. And it worked! We did not know until much later that the material was used to make uniforms for the then Chinese Army of Chiang Kai-Shek.

With no money, no connections, and no education, we sold a huge quantity of navy blue woolen material to the Chinese. We learned on the job, with our feet to the fire and the need to produce. In the course of the deal, we figured out how to buy, how to sell, and how to finance a transaction. The key to financing was to establish a relationship with a good commercial bank that specialized in international trade. The manager of international banking at Union Bank and Trust Company was able to help us establish a schedule whereby we could swing the deal and get a letter of credit from the Chinese to use as security for payment of the material and the dye-works. (Dye-works is a facility where dyeing is done.)

We formed a company named Trans Pacific Traders, and there followed a whole series of deals in which we exported "hard to get" merchandise. The experience resulted in one of my fundamental insights for a successful business: Find a need and fill it.

Harry Truman was president of the United States, and General George C. Marshall was secretary of state. Truman had been vice president and assumed the presidency when FDR died in 1945. Filling Roosevelt's shoes was next to impossible. Truman had been a senator before he became Roosevelt's vice president. Before that, he was a haberdasher from Missouri. General Marshall had been the commander in chief of the armed forces. Together, Truman and Marshall created the Marshall Plan, which extended American help to the devastated countries of Europe and Asia. It enabled their recovery with much-needed equipment and raw materials from the United States. We were a united country during the war and immediately after. The great American auto, steel, and oil corporations were at the height of their power, but at the same time, the small and medium-sized companies built by American entrepreneurs became increasingly more important.

Trans Pacific Traders generated a continuing business with industrial chemicals. Caustic soda, a substance used in the manufacture of soap, was in short supply all over the world, including in the United States. In order for us to export it, the importer needed a special import license; these licenses were hard to obtain and involved an extra step in the process. (At the time, most products sent overseas did not need export or import licenses; but some foreign governments required them for a few products.) Our customer in India had obtained an import license and so was able to place an order for caustic soda. In normal times, producers sold caustic soda to soap manufacturers for 4 cents a pound. In 1946 and 1947, we were able to pick up various quantities at 8 to 10 cents per pound and sell them on the export market for 16 to 18 cents per pound. (Do the math and you will see what a nice profit we made!)

We did a good business in small quantities, but one day we received an inquiry from India for 2,000 tons of the product. We did not think there was a chance of finding such a large quantity but could not resist the temptation to go after it. It was then that we learned something so important in any deal: Personally do the research. Of course, in those days, there was no Internet. Today, you would immediately know why there was a shortage of caustic soda. However, when this deal took place, intense research and the ability to investigate were required in order to find the source of the problem.

Through our research, we discovered an amazing fact...there was no shortage of caustic soda, but there was a shortage of steel to make the drums that held the product. If we could supply a caustic soda factory in Texas with steel drums, they would sell the caustic soda to us at mill price.

We went to work...buying steel in Pittsburgh at a high price and selling steel drums (produced by the steel mill) to the caustic soda factory at a price low enough to get caustic soda at mill price. The result was that we were able to export 2,000 tons at a good net profit. Everybody was happy...the steel supplier, the caustic soda maker, the importer in India, and most of all Trans Pacific Traders. We were able to celebrate the biggest sale for this product in history.

THE START OF
JACK NADEL INTERNATIONAL:
"IDEAS THAT MEAN BUSINESS"

I N JANUARY 1953, I had spent the last three years working as an independent contractor with an advertising specialty company in Los Angeles. I was doing very well in what was the narrowly defined field of calendars, business gifts, and advertising novelties. In my mind, there was great potential in expanding the scope of the business. After several intense meetings with the owners of the company, I realized we were in total disagreement about how the business could develop. They were happy to provide a salesperson with a short line of samples to sell wherever he or she had current buyers. (A short line of samples indicated a starting line; as a salesperson increased sales, he or she would be able to get additional samples. As an example, the samples I received when I started were a line of calendars and painter's caps.) Therefore, most salespeople would be able to sell to those they already knew, and there was no effort or training put into developing new accounts.

There was no control over or guidance for our sales force. A salesperson could take orders for whomever he or she pleased, receiving no training, no monetary advances, and very little direction. Most salespeople could not sustain themselves financially and therefore would drop out of the business. The decision to advance commissions, in select cases, gave the salesperson infinitely more staying power.

I believed the sales promotion business held limitless opportunities, but the company had to establish itself as a brand. My idea was to train a sales force that would work for us exclusively. At that time, the salesperson was an independent contractor; he or she could decide to work for several different distributors at the same time. Our policy from the outset was that salespeople could take orders only for our company. In return, their accounts would be protected.

By age 29, I was married to Elly, a bright, ambitious lady of 26. She was a fashion model who loved to manage showrooms. She could also type and take dictation at an amazing speed. After a great deal of soul searching, we realized that there was no way to change the company I was working for. To accomplish our goals, we would have to take the plunge and start our own business, becoming entrepreneurs. I severed my connection with the old company after sharing all the information I had on my pending deals.

I had been personal friends with the owners of the business, and I did not think it was necessary to break off the friendship. Unfortunately, they tried to make things as difficult as possible for both customers and me. They applied pressure to suppliers, telling them they would lose their accounts if they did business with me. Today, this conduct is illegal. It was just another obstacle. Elly and I started our new company in a tiny, 12-by-12 office in the business section of Beverly Hills, California.

We had spent endless hours creating a business plan, in the traditional sense of a long-range plan establishing the strategy for achieving a business's objectives. As part of the plan, we decided to invest all of the money we had worked hard to save...$10,000. In 1953, that was a lot of money. On an unsuspecting world, we launched Jack Nadel International with the slogan "Ideas That Mean Business." Our plan was not to restrict ourselves to what had been previously considered the advertising specialty and business gift arena. We wanted to get into total marketing and compete for the advertising and marketing dollar. It was very ambitious. If a potential account asked if we were in the same business as the leading company at the time, Brown & Bigelow, my answer was, "Not really...they manufacture calendars and remembrance advertising. We have ideas that can go to work for you right now to build traffic and help establish your brand."

Nineteen fifty-three was a remarkable year. General Dwight D. Eisenhower was inaugurated as president of the United States. He had campaigned with the promise to end the Korean War, and end it he did. Despite a general feeling of optimism, many people complained about a recession they were experiencing. Nevertheless, Jack Nadel International moved ahead with its plans. Our thinking was that there was never a better time for American products and American ingenuity. There was never a better time for manufacturing new products and taking advantage of new technology. There was never a better time for us to export our products around the world. We printed badges that said, "Business Is Great Because We Promote It," and promote it we did.

We started to fill bigger orders for products and services that had never existed in our business. We also attracted great sales personalities who helped to build the brand of our company. I trained the salespeople one at a time, in the field and in the office. I stopped calling them salespeople, and they became "account executives." When I realized I knew of no female account executives in the specialty sales business, I hired one. It is hard to believe how much criticism I took from my friends in the industry for daring to bring women into what had been an all-male business. Today, half of our sales and profits come from our female account executives. With this team of highly motivated account executives, we created a never-ending stream of new products and new promotions. Every advance was based on fresh ideas that had not been used before. Our accounts became our clients.

When a local brewery won the Pan American Gold Medal Award, we persuaded it to have us make hundreds of thousands of gold medal replicas out of brass. Liquor stores gave away this very inexpensive collectible as a gift with each purchase. It served as a permanent piece of advertising and a topic of conversation. We received an unanticipated bonus, and the brewery got a huge amount of publicity, when it was discovered that our replicas fit into the dollar slot machines in Las Vegas. The brewery had to stop distribution, but one million coins were already in circulation, and the publicity was priceless.

During this time, we also created a totally unique product called "Sun Lashes" for a major women's bathing suit manufacturer. Sun Lashes were coated paper that went over the eyelids and shielded the eyes from the sun without the need to wear sunglasses. We produced them in the shape of matchbooks, and each pack carried three pairs of Sun Lashes.

Retailers distributed huge quantities. They put their advertising on one side of the matchbook and the brand name of the bathing suit on the other. Our client was able to get this huge piece of advertising practically without cost, as the retailers paid for the units they distributed with their own imprint. We had also created an expanded source of business that came to be known as co-op programs. A co-op was an arrangement in which the manufacturer and the distributor/retailer shared the costs and advertising, so the manufacturer's logo was on one side of the item, and the retailer's name, address, and phone number were on the other.

When banks used premiums to open new accounts, we created a program that took all of the guesswork out of the promotion. The banks hated handling merchandise. They felt it cheapened their image. These were the days when banks had much greater prestige. JNI was in the merchandise business and was able to solve the bank's needs without any problem. We would provide the gifts for opening accounts and charge the banks only for the merchandise used. That worked for them. They were able to open much-needed accounts without being in the "general merchandise" business. We gave the banks what they wanted...new accounts. We gave the public what they wanted...free gifts. And we came away with the lion's share of the business.

A great deal of our business emerged from our ability to create new products and promotions. The ballpoint pen was a relatively new product in 1953. For the next several years, we were able to make distribution deals for advertising with several brand-name pen manufacturers, like Sheaffer and Paper Mate. After that, the deals changed. Initially, we would make a deal with a manufacturer to sell pens with advertising copy exclusively in a specified geographical area. As the business grew, the manufacturer removed the exclusive deal to take full advantage of the expanded market. Now exclusivity had almost been eliminated.

The specifications for our pens without a big brand name were superb quality and a distinctive and expensive-looking outside barrel. On these specially designed writing instruments, we promoted our brand by printing "NADEL" on the clip. When we were able to sell large quantities of exclusive products, we had reached profit heaven. Writing instruments became a staple of our industry, and we sold them to almost every client. I would have to believe that over the years, I was responsible for more advertising pen sales than anybody else in the world.

RETURNING TO JAPAN ON AN
AIRLINER INSTEAD OF A BOMBER

I N 1957, AFTER just four years in operation, Jack Nadel International had already developed a reputation as a very creative, aggressive company selling "Ideas That Mean Business." We had positioned ourselves squarely as the company to call to solve advertising and marketing problems. We were also a prime example of a company that achieved measurable results. In the advertising world of 1957, television was coming into its own, and advertising agencies were searching for the largest audience for getting out the client's message. Our goal was to give our clients what they wanted most, business-building ideas and brand proliferation. One of our major clients at the time, Vons Grocery Company, which then had 26 supermarkets, gave us a project: Provide Vons with a traffic-building advertising premium with universal appeal that we could sell at a door-busting price.

One of our best-selling executive gifts was sets of stainless-steel place settings that were imported from Denmark. We sent a sample to our agent in Japan to find a factory that could make the product for a price lower than we were getting from Denmark. At the time, Japan was the low-wage, low-price source. Our agent advised us that the project was doable. It would not be at the very cheap Japanese prices, but it would be far below what we would have to pay with Denmark.

I went to the Vons executive offices with a sample of my Danish flatware. I told the buyer that our goal was to bring in a five-piece stainless flatware set of equal quality that the market could sell for under a dollar. He started to laugh. "There is no way you could provide this quality for under a dollar."

With a big smile, I told him he could hold the sample, and I would provide him the same quality from Japan for a firm order of 100,000 sets. I told him that immediately upon receiving his order, I would personally go to Japan and make sure he got what he wanted. If I succeeded, he would have the hottest self-liquidating premium in the supermarket business. "If I do not succeed, it will cost you nothing." I had become quite friendly with this buyer, also a World War II veteran. He looked at me with a quizzical smile and said, "Didn't you tell me that you flew more than 25 missions in a B-29 over Japan?"

I replied, "You have a good memory. I can't wait to tell you what Japan is like today and how you and I scooped the industry by importing the first quality flatware from Japan." We made the deal.

I raced back to the office, where my wife and co-founder looked up at me with a smile; she knew I was coming from Vons. "Pack your kimono," I said excitedly, "we are going to Japan!"

She jumped up from the desk. "Sayonara...when do we leave?"

It was hard to believe. Here it was just 12 years after the end of the Second World War, and I was actually flying back to Japan on Japan Airlines with my wife by my side. We chose an all-Japanese meal with lots of sake. As we flew through the quiet skies, I gazed out the window at thousands of miles of Pacific Ocean. In a place between slumber and consciousness, my memories flooded back. I was in a B-29 reading the white caps on the waves to get the direction and speed of the wind. As our bomber approached the Japanese coast, I began to sweat. When we flew alongside Mount Suribachi, I could see the fighter planes dashing in and out, firing wildly to break up the formation as it approached the bomb run, antiaircraft fire exploding everywhere. Suddenly I realized someone was rubbing my shoulders. Elly was pleading with me to wake up, because I was visibly having a nightmare. Shaking my head to clear it, I realized we were flying peacefully alongside Mount Suribachi. It was 1957, and we were going to Tokyo to do business with my former enemies. From that point on, I wiped away the horrors of war and concentrated on the pleasures of doing business in a new market and learning the culture of the Japanese people.

My association with a very capable and experienced agent headquartered in Tokyo was an asset. Previously, we had worked together importing Japanese cigarette lighters, which were duplicates of the Ronson and Zippo brands. In preparation for my arrival in Japan, the agent set up appointments at a dozen factories that manufactured stainless-steel flatware and that he felt were capable of filling my order for Vons. Going through the same preparation for each meeting was a remarkable experience. At the factory, we would remove our shoes and walk into a reception area that featured several Japanese-style tables, where we were served various teas as we became acquainted with the owner and foreman of the factory.

We spent two weeks doing preliminary work before we chose the factory we felt had the combination of equipment and personnel that could produce superior quality. Our order was for 100,000 place settings (500,000 individual pieces). After a number of questions and answers, we were able to negotiate a satisfactory price. Then I totally blew their minds by saying, "Now, I must have absolutely perfect pieces as good as or better than the sample from Denmark that I am leaving with you. For this I will give you a 10 percent bonus over and above the price we just agreed to. There is one more detail. I am going to hire an independent inspection agency to examine the merchandise on the factory floor before it is packed for shipment." I don't believe that any American importer had ever voluntarily offered more money. There was a constant push to drive the price down.

The result was fantastic. We delivered 100,000 perfect sets. Vons was happy, as the entire amount was sold within six weeks; they repeated the order, for a total of 200,000 sets. The promotion created a great deal of customer traffic and even generated a profit for all parties. The Japanese manufacturer was delighted, as he had produced a quality of which he could be very proud at a good profit. It was thrilling because it opened up new opportunities for us.

What wasn't obvious at the time was that I had a tremendous opportunity to expand the business and make a lot more money. The problem we solved at the time was how to produce quality merchandise in Japan. A great promotion had been developed for supermarkets. My next step should have been to sell the entire package to other markets across the United States. Instead, a combination of youth and elation led me to buy my first luxury car (a Cadillac) and then go on to new ideas.

I learned from that missed opportunity but never regretted my mistake. In fact, I learned to use my mistakes as cautionary tales for new projects, so I didn't make the same errors again. Regret is a wasted emotion; mistakes serve a purpose.

EVOLVING AWAY FROM YOUR EGO

D URING THESE EARLY years, I felt like an explorer. It was very flattering to be described as a creator of new ideas and new products. However, a better explanation for my success would have been that I was an opportunist. Instinctively, my mind always went to the opportunity of the moment and the immediate future. Baseball offers an analogy. If you are at bat, you must keep swinging. The swing becomes almost automatic. You are going to get a lot more hits this way and even a few home runs. You will also strike out a number of times. Babe Ruth is one of the greatest home run record-holders in baseball. However, most people do not know that "the Bambino" also held the record during his era for the most strikeouts.

Some of the best things happen by accident, but I always try to keep an open mind when opportunity arises. It has become axiomatic never to let your ego get in the way, and you must never think you are automatically right just because you have had some success.

In the early 1960s, an opportunity came along that ultimately resulted in a great profit. A sales representative brought me a product called the "Watch Band Calendar." It was a simple strip of aluminum imprinted with a monthly calendar, with prongs that enabled you to attach the calendar to the band of your wristwatch so that the date, as well as the time, was immediately available. This was in the days before watches were manufactured with a built-in calendar. I really did not like the product, as I felt that very few people would put this cheap piece of aluminum on an expensive watch. However, as a favor to the sales rep, who was an old friend, I gave 15 account executives a sample without a pitch or a presentation. The next day I had a dozen orders, which was really amazing. Every day thereafter, the number of orders increased and proved how wrong I was.

Several months after my sales rep friend presented the product to me, I received a frantic call from him. He told me that the Watch Band Calendar manufacturer was about to go bankrupt. He just did not understand how to handle a dated item, such as a calendar. By that time, I was convinced we had a product of great potential coming from an incompetent supplier. "No problem," I said. "Call me back tomorrow and I will have a solution."

Previously, I had hired a special manufacturing executive who had a history of success with new products. As I suspected, the cost of manufacturing was very low in relation to the selling price. That day I worked on several programs to sell Watch Band Calendars as promotions for different businesses. My friend gratefully provided me with a complete list of all his customers on my promise that I would fill all their orders at the same or a lower price.

It was magic...that year we sold 22 million Watch Band Calendars.

THE MIDDLE YEARS:
MIXING BUSINESS WITH POLITICS

THE DECADE FROM 1960 to 1970 represented 10 of the most action-packed years in American history and in my life. In 1960, we elected John F. Kennedy as president of the United States. John and Jackie Kennedy projected an image of optimism, youth, and new ideas. John Kennedy inspired the nation in his inaugural address when he proclaimed, "Ask not what your country can do for you. Ask what you can do for your country." This made a great deal of sense to me. It inspired me, along with millions of other Americans, to get involved in politics and community activity. The nation enjoyed a powerful resurgence of confidence and energy.

There was a civil war going on in Vietnam. The United States sent military advisors to South Vietnam. In November 1963, John F. Kennedy was assassinated in Dallas. This tragic event was followed by a period of violence and revolutionary activity. The Civil Rights Act had been passed and met enormous resistance. Lyndon B. Johnson was elected president in 1964, after serving out the remainder of Kennedy's first term. He had run a successful campaign against Republican senator Barry Goldwater of Arizona, who seemed to be advocating for deeper American involvement in the war in Vietnam. Yet Johnson himself took an aggressive stance when U.S. Navy vessels were apparently attacked by North Vietnamese PT boats in the Gulf of Tonkin, an arm of the South China Sea off the coast of Vietnam. A few months later it was revealed that we really were not fired at, but by then the conflict had already been greatly expanded, and Congress had passed what was known as the Gulf of Tonkin Resolution. This resolution offered an excuse to enter a war based on an event that never happened.

At the same time, Johnson boldly enforced civil rights, meeting stiff opposition in the South. Meanwhile, the military draft was expanded. Demonstrations in the streets exploded into riots. Civil rights leader Dr. Martin Luther King Jr. was assassinated in 1968, and shortly after that, Robert F. Kennedy was shot and killed in the middle of his campaign for the presidency, immediately after winning the all-important Democratic primary in California.

With these whirlwind events unfolding so rapidly, I was faced with a personal dilemma. As a combat veteran of World War II, I found all of the pro-war propaganda and the reasons we were given for risking American lives and capital to be bogus. Revolutionary groups like the Black Panthers, as well as progressive groups, were in the vanguard of the peace movement. Students were being drafted, and they felt not only that they were in danger but that their entire future was being threatened. I had always felt that business and politics did not mix. However, I changed my mind after studying all that had been written and said about the Vietnam War. I came to the conclusion that I agreed with former president Dwight D. Eisenhower that it was the wrong war in the wrong place at the wrong time. Whether I moved to one side or another politically was not a calculated decision but an act of emotion. I could not stand idly by and take only an academic interest. I had invested almost all of my energy into creating and growing my business, but now I was ready to contribute my time and money to the antiwar movement.

Elly felt even more strongly about this. We had military-age children, and she became a member of an organization called Another

Mother for Peace. She felt that our lives depended on peace. A Catholic nun had created the slogan, "War is not healthy for children and other living things." I made jewelry products (bracelets, key chains, and lockets) engraved with this slogan, which were used for fundraising. Elly joined Paul Newman, Joanne Woodward, and four other involved people on an expedition to Congress proposing that we withdraw from the war and that a cabinet position be created called "secretary of peace."

I joined a very active group called Business Executives Against the Vietnam War. I felt that the war, in addition to being counter to our interests and our values as a nation, was really bad for business. I gave speeches to business and veterans' groups. When I was accused of being a Communist, I responded with the statement, "I am a card-carrying capitalist." As a decorated war veteran, I had some pretty good credentials. There were a number of people who inspired me, particularly Senator Wayne Morse, a Republican from Washington. He said to me, "Jack, this is the biggest damn fool thing we have ever done in our country. Everybody must get involved, and we have to rethink our foreign policy."

Despite my political involvement, Jack Nadel International continued to prosper. By 1966, the company had moved and expanded five times. I decided then that it would be a good idea to buy our own building, in Culver City, California. My younger brother, Marty, had joined the company in 1959, fresh out of UCLA. Although nepotism was considered a bad thing by the establishment, I had absolutely no problem with it. Marty soon became the company's most powerful account executive and spokesperson. He partnered with me in the purchase of the building. I decided that in the future, wherever we had a sizable operation, we would try to buy the real estate. This turned into an excellent investment strategy. Our property was 50,000 square feet, which included 20,000 square feet of offices and warehouse. It was a strong bet on our future, and it paid off. Since then, we have expanded in many different ways and many different directions, but this great building that we bought in 1966 became our headquarters until 2012. It was the location of many wonderful stories over 46 years.

Living in the 1960s was like existing on multiple screens. So much was going on that it was almost impossible to stay on any one track. It was like a huge opera that started with very beautiful, romantic music and evolved into a crescendo of sound. John F. Kennedy's appearance on the world stage was remarkable, starting with his vow of going to the moon and ending with the terrible day in Dallas when he was assassinated. I was immersed in my experience with international trade, and I could feel the increase in American prestige. Business with Hong Kong and Taiwan kept growing, and we were starting to investigate the new European Common Market. In 1965, Elly and I were invited to and attended President Johnson's inauguration. It was a magical time in our lives. We flew to Washington on a chartered jet, and the passengers included many movie stars. While there was political turmoil, it was a time of remarkable optimism. We attended a number of glamorous events and rubbed elbows with cabinet officers and politicians.

I was particularly interested in and became personally involved in the Peace Corps. I sought an audience with Sargent Shriver, who was married to a Kennedy sister and was the driving force behind the Peace Corps and special domestic projects. I had written up a proposal that would involve business organizations in special programs to train and hire unemployed people from the inner cities. It was not an altruistic gesture. I projected big trouble ahead if we did not solve the problem of high unemployment, which was in double digits. To me, much of the problem was a lack of training and motivation.

For a variety of reasons, neither the U.S. government nor the private sector economy seemed ready to address unemployment by creating adequate numbers of jobs with good incomes and secure futures. There was a sense of frustration coming from the poor areas, while the middle class and the rich seemed to be doing just fine. This sounds amazingly like what we are facing today, 48 years later, save that the fortunes of the middle class have also dropped dramatically. Unfortunately, the more things change, the more they remain the same. It is up to us to make the changes that make sense for most people.

We were able to arrange a special meeting with Sargent Shriver and his staff, which included a long discussion on the feasibility of inaugurating a program to identify, train, and employ large numbers of people from the inner city who had local businesses that needed help in sales promotion. One of the main objections was that there was no budget to accomplish this task. I had prepared for this. "The financing will be done by business associations," I said. "I have had some talks with several groups, and there is definite interest and desire to do the job."

The question was immediately asked, "Why would businesses spend money on this?"

I replied, "Because I believe it is in everybody's enlightened self-interest, and there are quite a few people who agree with me."

Everybody walked away from this meeting with a positive feeling. Shriver and his staff even asked if I would head the new office at a salary of $1 per year. I said I would be happy to do so. I sensed that there would be intense dissatisfaction and possibly even riots if we didn't do something. It was a terrible feeling when I was advised the next week that they decided it really could not be done. When I questioned the decision, I was told confidentially that unnamed people in the bureaucracy felt that I would be taking over their jobs. It was the first time I realized how difficult it is to get something positive done in government if it in any way steps on somebody's toes. I decided I did not have the time, patience, or money to pursue this matter any further. It was not long after this event that the Watts Riots broke out, along with many other civil disturbances across the country. I returned to my business full-time. We still had to operate our businesses and our lives within the framework of the events that were exploding all around us.

• • •

Nineteen sixty-eight was a year of enormous change for Jack Nadel International, the little company we had started 15 years earlier. We had grown into a strong sales promotion company with a major presence on the West Coast. The building we had bought two years earlier was a perfect headquarters. From it, we expanded our operations both in services rendered and territory served. We were making bigger and better deals with companies headquartered in California.

In April 1968, one of our account executives made an appointment for me to meet a top executive of Republic Corporation. I was aware that this company had been the most active stock on the New York Stock Exchange in 1967. The company was originally Republic Pictures, a major studio known for cowboy films and B movies. Such great personalities as John Wayne, Gene Autry, and Roy Rogers rode the range at Republic Pictures. Republic was sold to an investment and management group that changed the name to Republic Corporation. Republic sold the real estate that they occupied in Burbank and also sold their film library to television. With a huge amount of cash, they started to buy many diversified companies, and their stock climbed from $5 to $40 per share. Their program was to buy growing companies with a profitable history. Most of their purchases were on a "tax-free exchange of stock." With a great public relations program and a very creative financial staff, Republic was able to grow and make a profit just by including the profits of the acquired companies. This era of conglomeration on the stock market had also produced such giants as Gulf and Western and Litton Industries. I was therefore not surprised when shortly after being introduced to me, the CEO asked if I was interested in selling Jack Nadel International to Republic Corporation.

"Our company is not for sale, but I have no problem discussing it," I said. The executive from the public company started to tell me about the advantages, the big one being the opportunity to convert all of our hard work to real value. I responded that my main interest was to continue to build the company and provide greater opportunities for all of the people involved. At the same time, I certainly was not against increasing my personal wealth. This was the start of intense negotiations, and within 30 days, we made a deal.

WHEN PRIVATE GOES PUBLIC: AN ENTIRELY DIFFERENT BALLGAME

THE DEAL MERGING Jack Nadel International into Republic Corporation was transacted as a tax-free exchange of stock. On the official date the deal was consummated, we noted the price of Republic Corporation on the New York Stock Exchange. Then we negotiated the current value of Jack Nadel International, with the help of a private appraisal firm that considered many different factors when reaching a number. It included everything from the book value, which is the net worth carried on the books of the company; to the goodwill, variance, present, and anticipated future values; to the market value as compared to other companies in the same business. In April 1968, that worth was appraised at approximately $2 million. Republic stock on the same day was selling for $40 per share. The number of shares I was to receive was subject to the estimated worth of the company acceptable to buyer and seller. We agreed to 50,000 shares of Republic Corporation in exchange for all of the stock of Jack Nadel International. Then they renegotiated an incentive for future performance that would increase the value of the Republic stock that would be issued to me.

We did perform very well, and the price of Republic stock kept increasing. By December 1968, we owned 100,000 shares of Republic stock, and it was now selling for $90 per share. It was an amazing roller-coaster ride; on paper, the value of the transaction was $9 million. There was one hitch, however; the Republic stock was lettered, and it could not be sold until Republic removed the lettering—or two years passed, at which time the stock was free to sell. (Letter stock, also known as restricted stock or restricted securities, refers to stock that is not fully transferable until certain conditions have been met.)

During its two-year acquisition binge, Republic Corporation acquired 85 disparate private companies. In most cases, the former owner remained with the company and became that division's general manager. A group of us had a meeting with the president of Republic with the goal of persuading him to remove the lettering on all or part of the stock given to owners of the purchased companies. His smile exuded confidence. "It's too soon," he said. "We have more room to grow before releasing this substantial amount of stock for sale. It will reduce the overall price."

There followed a very heated discussion, which escalated into a true confrontation. After an hour of rising tempers, the president of Republic finally said, "Okay, I will promise to remove the lettering on part of your stock as soon as it hits $100 per share. This is not an arbitrary number on my part. I say it will happen within three weeks. Then we will see what the market is doing and what percentage of your stock I will be able to clear."

I was not happy with that decision, but the majority decided to accept it as a reasonable compromise.

The stock never hit $100 per share. Everybody was unhappy, but nobody complained publicly, as this would have had a devastating effect on the stock price—though it could not have been much worse than what actually happened.

• • •

Over the next year, Republic stock kept dropping and eventually plummeted from $90 to $2 per share. I was able to save a great deal after taking a very strong position on the next lap of what turned into a four-year experience. Most of the other people who had sold their companies to Republic were hit pretty hard, so their personal fortunes diminished considerably. This entire adventure in the public marketplace was full of new experiences. The big lesson I learned was that running a public company is an entirely different ballgame than running a private company. In all my past experience, my greatest concern had been to build our capability and reputation and to provide an atmosphere that promised a good future for our employees.

The private sector has to be concerned equally with short-term and long-term growth. We did not worry about outside interests other than our clients, suppliers, and employees. Public companies, on the other hand, have an intense concentration on short-term earnings, which increase the value of their stock on the public market. They use every device in operations and bookkeeping to show the highest earnings per share. "Long-term" to them is usually the next quarter. It is pretty cold-blooded. An indicator is the terminology they use that strips away the human element. For example, in bookkeeping terms, employees are "headcount."

I almost went into shock at what the chief financial officer said at a meeting about new financial regulations. He rose to his feet, surveyed the room, and declared, "I don't care what new regulations the government issues. I will find a way to beat them."

Nobody seemed to bat an eye. Here was a brazen challenge by the chief financial officer of a public company that he was prepared to defy the spirit of any ruling put out by the government. I was naïve enough to say, "That is not right."

He responded with a gleam in his eye. "But it is legal."

I recalled how the same attitude of immorality was evident in the last phase of my negotiation for the merger of my company into this big New York Stock Exchange corporation. One of the issues, after everything else had been agreed to, was the fact that I owned the property, and Jack Nadel International, the corporation, leased it from me. I suggested that we simply give the same lease to Republic. They felt this would represent a conflict of interest and wanted to buy the building as well as the company. They offered to get a current appraisal, and they would issue more stock for the amount that we agreed to. I rejected this offer with the statement, "I am okay with the exchange of stock for stock. But if you insist that you must own the building, I will only accept cash for the property." After trying to persuade me that I would be better off with stock, Republic conceded to paying cash.

Everything was finally agreed to, and I was asked to come to the corporate office to sign the deal and have it properly witnessed and notarized. I have an innate habit of reading everything before I sign it. When I sat down to read the document, I felt a surge of resentment. I looked up at the vice president in charge of acquisitions and said, "This is not the deal we made. The way this is written, the property is assessed at $90,000, and you will issue $90,000 worth of stock at the same $40 per share. Our agreement was perfectly clear that you would pay cash."

The vice president's face flushed as he said, "We did agree to it, but Republic has since decided that everybody's best interest would be served by paying for the property with stock."

Impatiently, I said, "I came here to sign the deal that we had agreed to, not to renegotiate the deal."

Incredulous, he said, "You mean you would blow this deal just for that?"

I looked him squarely in the eye and quietly said, "As of 30 seconds from now, there is no deal." I zipped up my bag.

"Wait a minute," he said. "Don't do something you'll regret."

In the same quiet and neutral tone, I asserted, "I never do anything that I regret later. No harm, no foul, no deal. I am perfectly happy to keep the property and charge you the same rent as my company has been paying, but this is my final word."

The VP sighed and said, "Okay, the deal stands, and you keep ownership of the property."

This situation is an affirmation of one of my tips: Never negotiate in fear, and always be prepared to walk away from a bad deal.

Four years later, we bought back our company along with five other divisions, in what would eventually be known as a leveraged buyout. Up to that moment, I had never heard that term, but it later became a recognized strategy. I never lost a single month's rent.

Jack Nadel International had grown steadily and needed more space. We wanted to move to new quarters. The property had increased dramatically in value so that when we sold the property in 2012 to a real estate developer, it was for many times the original value. This fantastic story came about not because I was smart but because I was tough, and I always kept my word.

TAKING MEASUREMENTS: GROWING INTO YOUR SUIT

THE FOUR YEARS as we transitioned from the late 1960s to the early 1970s was an enormous learning experience for me. Operating as a division of a publicly held conglomerate created a lot of problems. Republic concentrated on keeping up a good appearance and continually enhancing the value of the stock. Their skill was in bookkeeping more than in operations. I was concerned with growing the business. Throughout this time, I was able to keep control of the company. More than ever, I realized how important it was to stay in command. It was a time of great strain, but I was able to maintain my cool. It was like having a cranky parent who did not have a clue as to your activities. Fortunately, the ultimate goal of both parties was to have a company that operated well and made a profit.

I felt I was drowning in a sea of mediocrity and an endless stream of corporate rules and restrictions, which I realized were rarely enforced or followed up on. I filed the memos from division heads in a particular drawer in my desk and rarely responded to or executed their directions. I realized more and more that the public corporation was more concerned with the price of the stock every month than with the long-range practical execution of a business plan.

As I said in the previous chapter, in 1969, the price of Republic stock kept slipping. Despite the fact that Republic claimed increased earnings every quarter, the cash position never kept up with the profits on paper. This was called "creative bookkeeping." Republic would buy a private company with an exchange of stock. If Republic was selling for 30 times earnings, they tried to buy companies at less than 15 times earnings. So if a company was acquired on this basis, its value would double just through bookkeeping. For example, if an acquired division's net worth was $2 million, its net worth on the new books became $4 million. Republic was able to project a profit of $2 million. The strategy was so well-known that there was a humorous phrase in financial circles describing it as "creative math." However, after 85 acquisitions, with no new companies being purchased, the overvaluing of stock and the increase in earnings slowed down or stopped. As mentioned previously, over the period of one year the stock went from $90 to $2 per share. Then it was acquired by another company at the price of $2 or less per share.

During this process, Republic tried to maneuver their position into a more realistic arena. In 1969, the chairman of the board called me in for a special meeting.

We met at the very elaborate corporate offices. The top brass of the company was there. With a big smile, the chairman said, "Here's the deal, Jack. You are, of course, aware of the fact that the stock has been dropping. The company is great and has a big future, but the analysts just do not understand how we do it with so many different divisions all in different businesses. They should understand that if you know how to run a company, it doesn't matter what business you're in, the principles will still work." He paused for a moment. "Jack Nadel International has done very well since it was acquired. As a matter of fact, you have run this company better than almost anybody else in the corporation. Since you have a well-defined business—advertising and marketing—we would like to move all of the advertising and marketing companies into a separate corporation. It will stop being a division of Republic operations, and it will be an independently operated subsidiary. We would like to take five of our divisions and merge them into Jack Nadel International. Within one year of that date, we would like to sell the new company on the public market. After we go through an understanding of how we will operate, we would like to appoint you as the president and chief executive officer of the new company." He paused again to let it sink in. "How do you feel about that?"

I thought for a moment, and in an even tone that belied the excitement I was feeling, I said, "I would be interested, but as part of the deal, I would like to get the lettering removed from my stock so that I can gain some liquidity. Having to fulfill your promise to remove the lettering once the stock hit $100 per share seems to be negated by the fact that the stock has dropped from $90 a share to about $60 today, and every forecast says it is going to continue to go down."

The chairman took a minute before he replied. "I think we could work something out. I can't clear all of your stock, but let's talk about what's doable."

After some discussion, I agreed to an immediate removal of the lettering on 25 percent of my stock. I would go to work on a business plan and submit it to the chairman within one week. We agreed that time was of the essence. I asked him what companies he would include in the new subsidiary. I suggested that when this was pinned down, I would like to take a trip to visit each of the offices to make sure I understood the market and what the company was doing. I stated that I simply did not have the kind of ego to assume I could operate any business in any area. It was all very exciting.

At the end of the week, I submitted my business plan. We agreed how we would operate and to whom I would report. We set up a time line for how to proceed and decided what personnel I would need for the new subdivision. My new company, Measured Marketing Services, Inc., was taking shape.

At first, the chairman did not like the name, saying, "It will never fly."

I explained to him that we would be the only company in the world that was ready to offer measurable results. Everybody else promised audience share, which did not necessarily produce the desired business. The objective in business should be profit. The way we operated, the client would have a goal to sell a certain amount of product. With the promotions we created, the client knew exactly how much was invested and exactly what was sold. We offered a simple way of measuring results.

By 1970, the new company, Measured Marketing Services, was ready to roll. We were an advertising and marketing conglomerate. Each division of Measured Marketing Services had a separate identity and had been in business for quite some time as a privately held company before being acquired by Republic Corporation.

Jack Nadel International was in the advertising specialty and sales promotion business. Krupp-Taylor was in the direct-mail business, while Art Mold Products manufactured sales promotion products. Everlast Pen Company was a manufacturer of writing instruments, and Impact Merchandise was an importer of sales promotion products. I was the president and CEO of the parent company, and we remained a totally owned subsidiary of Republic Corporation.

• • •

The second two quarters of 1969 had not been kind to Republic stock. The price kept falling, and the need for a cash infusion became greater. There had been calls for Measured Marketing Services to do well and become a tremendous source of income for the parent company. The ultimate objective was to make a separate public issue for Measured Marketing Services, and be able to transfer the entire stock price in the form of cash to Republic. While I set about expanding the business and improving our position in the marketplace, Republic was exploring the public sale of Measured Marketing Services with their bankers. The public marketplace was going through a tough cycle, and very few IPOs were successfully launched. For me, it was hard work but an unbelievable amount of fun running five separate companies simultaneously.

Each of these companies had its own president, who worked closely with me to build the business. This arrangement was testimony to my rule that everything starts with a relationship. I had great relationships with the presidents of all the divisions of Measured Marketing Services. I acknowledged, rewarded, and respected their abilities; in turn, they accepted my suggestions for improvements. Although they operated their divisions like separately held companies, they knew they were responsible to the parent company, Measured Marketing Services. Their loyalty to me and our solid relationship really paid off; we had to present a solid front to Republic Corporation in backing up our leveraged buyout.

Our direct-mail company grew very fast as we picked up great new clients. We started to do the frequent flyer program for United Airlines. Within several years, a very young and technically remarkable company named Apple had us find new customers through direct mail. Later on, Jack Nadel International also created a program for the police that sponsored an anti-drug campaign called DARE. We struck a royalty agreement by which we sold DARE's merchandise through school districts and police departments around the country, and we paid DARE a royalty of 10 percent on all sales. At the program's peak, we were actually able to contribute $1 million per year to DARE.

We were all young, loaded with ambition, and charged with creativity. Operationally, Measured Marketing Services was on a roll but having technical problems with the parent company—which kept dipping into our capital for their cash needs. I felt a lot of pressure to do something very creative that would solve this problem and allow us to gain our independence.

The public market was very tight, so our investment bankers were trying to strike a deal to sell Measured Marketing Services. One of the major deals that looked like it would go through was to merge us into the largest company in the specialty advertising business, Brown & Bigelow (B&B). Standard Packaging, in New York, was B&B's parent company; its main business was paper products. They worked out a deal to merge Measured Marketing Services into Brown & Bigelow on the condition that I would be the president and chief executive officer of the surviving company. I met with the principals, and there was an immediate feeling of compatibility. They presented their offer, and they had a feeling that I would jump at it because of the prestige and the possibilities for expansion.

In our discussion, it was pointed out to me that Brown & Bigelow's headquarters were in St. Paul, Minnesota, and that I would have to move there. My gut reaction was that I would not be happy relocating from the West Coast to the Midwest. However, it made sense to discuss this possibility with my wife and two children, who were 12 and 10 at the time. All three objected strongly to the thought of moving to an extreme climate and leaving their friends and family. I totally agreed with them. I was deeply involved both politically and socially in Los Angeles, as was Elly. The thought of uprooting our family did not appeal to either of us.

I returned to corporate the next day. "I am deeply flattered and feel very challenged with your job offer. However, I am not prepared to move to St. Paul."

I suggested that I would take an apartment in St. Paul and spend whatever time was necessary there, but I really could not move my family. They received my comment without emotion, exchanged meaningful glances, and said they would like to have a private meeting to discuss my proposition.

They returned to the meeting table in an hour and said that they had thought it through thoroughly, but they were old-fashioned and felt that the boss's foot had to cross the threshold every day in order to be effective. That was it. We would not move from our respective positions. Republic was very unhappy with the results of this conversation and would have fired me and replaced me with somebody more reasonable, except for the fact that the management of Brown & Bigelow would settle for nobody else.

A couple of weeks later, the position of chairman and president at Republic went through some changes. The net result was that the company brought in a new chief executive officer rumored to be the choice of the bankers, who now felt they had to find a way to ensure they would collect some part of the $40 million that Republic owed them. The new CEO was a well-known attorney who had an impressive reputation for running large, publicly traded companies.

I was quite pleased with the change because I had had several confrontations with the former president. However, the new CEO soon became very angry with me when he was told that I had been talking to some investment bankers in New York. He set up a very early appointment to see me the day after he made the discovery. His voice was bristling with anger. His conversation came in short bursts.

"Okay," I said calmly, "eight o'clock a.m. is not the best time of day for me, but I will be there."

The minute I walked in the door, the president of the company shook his index finger at me and said, "You have no goddamn loyalty! I know you are on Wall Street and talking about making a deal for Measured Marketing Services. Let me remind you that we own 100 percent of that company, and you are not authorized to make any deals."

"Loyalty to whom and why?" I said firmly. "You have only been with this company a couple of months. I have been here for two years, and I sold my company, which took 15 years to build a brick at a time. The last time I looked, I owned 100,000 shares, so I have a big stake in this. The best thing you could do for me is to fire me, which would nullify my contract not to compete. I do have to make a living. So are you saying we settle down, have an intelligent conversation, and come to some kind of a deal that would be good for both of us? We are both interested in the same thing, to make Republic stock more valuable by concentrating on the operational business."

The new CEO and I were able to get to a civil level where we could talk about operations and how best to accomplish both goals (making Republic stock more valuable and improving operations). At that moment, we would only reach a temporary solution. I would have to come up with an idea that could make the situation good for everybody.

After my meeting with the new president and CEO of Republic Corporation, my optimism soared. We were on the same page. Here was a guy I could talk to, reason with, and generate some workable ideas with. We had a mutual respect and a real understanding of the fiscal condition of the company.

In a meeting of the presidents of the five divisions of Measured Marketing Services, we examined each company as a separate entity but working closely in conjunction with the others. At the end of the meeting, we were convinced that we had the makings of a great independent company; but it would take the best effort of each of us to achieve our goal of severing ties with Republic.

We arranged a meeting for me and the president of Republic. I prepared for this important negotiation using a technique I had developed. I envisioned the scene and visualized the discussion so that when the time came, I was ready.

The negotiation was to buy the advertising and marketing divisions of Republic. Their goal was to get the maximum amount of cash. My goals were to execute the deal in such a manner that no time was lost in operations and to find the financing to provide the cash for the transaction.

NEGOTIATION: MAKING A DEAL
THAT IS MUTUALLY ADVANTAGEOUS

W E MET IN the very luxurious offices of Republic Corporation. It was 3:00 p.m. I had arrived 15 minutes earlier and brought my secretary with me. My plan was to have her wait for me in the reception area, and when the deal was made, she would be prepared to type up the agreement in a letter format that called for both my and Republic's signatures. I had previously participated in meetings in which something was agreed to, but when it came time to draw up the agreement, it was different than what had been verbally decided on. Sometimes, buyer's remorse or just the passage of time killed the deal. My experience at the close of the sale of Jack Nadel International to Republic Corporation was a perfect example, when they changed our verbal agreement in the written documents.

From behind his massive desk, the president of Republic motioned for me to sit down facing him. He immediately came to the point. "You said you have a proposition to make. Let's get right to it."

I gave him an approving smile. "I like that," I said. "We don't need any preliminaries. You are planning to sell Measured Marketing

Services." We talked about a public offering and the fact that the market was down and it was not a good time for an IPO. At the same time, he was aware that I had tried to make a private sale to bring in much-needed cash for Republic. "I'm really sorry," I said, "that we could not go along with the Brown & Bigelow offer. However, I think I have a better approach that could make everyone happy." I paused as that sank in. "I would like to join with three of my associates, buy the company, and take it private."

He calmly replied, "Okay, what are you prepared to pay, and how will you handle the financing?"

"You tell me," I said. "Let's be realistic on what it would take. What's your price?"

He snapped back, "We will take six million, cash."

"Six million," I repeated slowly, letting the tension build. He nearly jumped out of his seat when I said, "Okay, we have a deal. I agree to the figure, but it is the way we propose to pay for it that is unique. We would like to call this our 'option to buy,' with that right to be activated at any time within this calendar year. Since Republic currently owns us, we will pass on to Republic every dollar in profit we make from the day the deal is signed. However, this money will be deducted from the six million. For example, if we give you one million during the year, it will be deducted from the six million, so that at the time we are ready to exercise our option, we will owe you five million, which we will pay in cash. In other words, it will be real money."

There followed a long conversation in which we discussed many different possibilities. He insisted, for example, that until the deal was consummated in its entirety, Republic would have total oversight, and if there was a disagreement, they would have the option of rescinding the deal.

There were a number of other details that we had to discuss. There was a conversation about the current operations and how I would change them. We also had to talk about our relationship with Republic and with all the other divisions within the Republic family. Finally, he opened the box of cigars on his desk and offered one to me.

I said, "Looks like we have a deal."

He smiled. "I will draw up the agreement and have it ready for you to sign within a few days."

I paused. "Why don't we draw up and sign the agreement now?"

He leveled his gaze at me. "In addition to other obligations, I would have to get the approval of the board, and it's almost 9:00 p.m. There's nobody here to type the agreement."

I took a puff of my cigar. "I have my secretary, who is an excellent typist, sitting in the reception room waiting just in case we were able to make a deal."

He laughed, rose from his chair, and walked around the desk. As I swiveled to face him, he stuck out his hand. "If you can make a profit and pay the balance in cash, we have a deal. Call her in and let's do it." We shook hands.

STARTING OVER: THE FREEDOM
OF TAKING BACK CONTROL

I N 1972, WE made the deal with Republic Corporation. I was now the president and chairman of the board of Measured Marketing Services, Inc., and our corporate office was established in Santa Monica, California. We were on the top floor of a six-story office building owned by Lawrence Welk, the very popular bandleader. As a fun sidelight, I had lunch with him and was impressed by the common sense hidden behind the façade of an unsophisticated Midwestern musician. His television show opened with a bubble machine, which actually produced the sound of bubbles. In the office he leased to me, there was another bubble machine.

I was now 48 years old, and it seemed that I was starting my business life all over again when we bought Measured Marketing Services. Before we sold Jack Nadel International to Republic, I had settled into a very comfortable groove. JNI had established itself as the gold standard in the sales promotion business in California. We had offices dotting the West Coast, from San Diego to Portland. Before JNI became a public company, I was not only able to run the business, but I managed to play golf a few times a week. I was enjoying all that life had to offer.

Although I did put in the hours that were needed, one of my ambitions was to go from being a pretty fair golfer to being an excellent one. Elly and I were involved in several charities and put most of our leisure time into helping to end the Vietnam War.

When we sold the company to Republic, life changed dramatically. I now had a corporate boss who set the rules. I was in the office every morning at eight and did not leave until five. Our lunches were served in the corporate dining room. Despite all this, I ran the company as if I was the acting sole proprietor. I met the corporate challenge and was able to produce predictable monthly earnings, so Republic mostly left me to my own devices.

Every so often, the executives above me would create some harebrained scheme that would theoretically increase earnings. For the most part, they were out of touch with reality. This was the most frustrating part of working for somebody who did not understand my business. One day, the executives called a meeting in which they informed me that they had been doing a study and were convinced they could dramatically increase our profits. I sat there amazed when one of the executives brought out a portfolio of facts and figures proving that they could make more money by decreasing the percentage of commission earned by the account executives. They asked what I thought. I answered, "I think it's the dumbest thing I've heard. Don't you realize that we live in a competitive market, and I cannot pay a lower commission than my competitors? If I did, I would lose all my salespeople. Whose time did you waste in putting together this study?"

An argument followed in which I made my point, but I was completely frustrated by the waste of time and the obvious ignorance of my bosses.

I realized I was never happier than the day I took back control of my own company. I had created my own rules and regulations, founded on experience. The reality is that if you put yourself in a position where you can be screwed, someone will find a way to do it.

The freedom to make my own decisions and be responsible for their execution was a major ingredient in business heaven for me. I realized then and to this very day that no rules fit every situation. Each person has his or her own personality, hang-ups, ambitions, and talents. I know I can get along with people and that if I put my mind to it, I am capable of taking orders. I discovered that as a soldier and even more so as a businessman. Many people need a structure to work from and lots of rules and regulations. I am happiest as an entrepreneur and opportunist. Having freedom in my business life is as important to me as being an American citizen. Now, in 1972, I was ready to embark on the next stage of my career.

A SECRET WEAPON, A SECRET ESCAPE

I HAD STARTED JNI locally, but I was thinking globally. In 1972, I traveled to Milan, Italy, to check out the latest and greatest marketing and specialty items at the Italian Trade Fair. At the time, it could well have been the largest such event in the world. It was designed like a little city, with everything from tractors to small novelties displayed. I was looking for a product line that would supplement the pens that we manufactured in New York. The pen business in the United States was very competitive, and I had seen a number of novelty pens at the trade fair that we could sell in large quantities if I could arrange exclusive distribution. We had been importing different products from Asia, as well as some higher-priced gift items from Europe. We had built a good business in the United States for the pens that we manufactured in New York, but now the operation needed an injection of something unique that would be exclusive to us. The value of the American dollar was falling. I had long before discovered the truth about export and import: When the dollar is strong, we should be importing to the United States from other countries; when the dollar is weak, the best opportunity, by virtue of the exchange, is to export. A cheap dollar made our merchandise cheaper in the foreign marketplace.

The Italian Trade Fair was so large that there were different sections designated for different kinds of merchandise. In fact, there was an

55

entire building dedicated to writing instruments. I entered one of the bigger display rooms and was immediately attended to by a man who seemed to have a British accent. "Can I help you?" he asked as we stood in front of a display of very interesting novelty pens. Each one had a different top over a barrel containing a standard ballpoint pen refill. The caps were in various shapes, such as a nail, a hammer, a wrench, a screwdriver, and other tools.

We started to explore the possibilities of importing these writing instruments and offering them for sale on the American market. The gentleman who was taking care of me was the export manager for a big Italian pen company. I explained that we manufactured writing instruments in the United States and would like to sell these pens alongside our regular merchandise. "Would you show me a sample of your product?" he asked. I was carrying some samples of our most popular product. I knew there was nothing quite like it in Europe. This pen looked like jewelry, as it had an antique Florentine finish. Actually, it was brass that had been manufactured to look like gold jewelry.

"Very handsome," he said. "How much is it?"

"Our lowest price for this pen is 15 cents each."

He nodded approvingly. "That's not bad for 50 cents."

"No, you did not understand. I said 15 cents, not 50 cents."

He jumped to his feet excitedly. "I would love to sell your pen in the European market."

At the end of the conversation, we had a deal. The Italian pen company would export the novelty line that they made in Italy to Everlast Pen Company, USA. And we would export the Everlast line to distributors all over Europe, with the man I was talking to representing us and collecting a commission. He claimed he could sell millions of our gold Florentine pens in Europe. Amazingly, both ends of our deal were very successful, opening up a new avenue of business. As it is today in the United States, the export business was almost a secret weapon. The dollar was cheap then, and it is cheap now. All of my experiences since 1946 came into play in 1972, and for many years thereafter. I have always found that when you explore new avenues of business, the door is opened so that you can go in many different directions.

This is one of the many experiences that show me we are living in a global marketplace. There are many well-meaning attempts to shrink our capabilities when we restrict our purchases to only merchandise that is "Made in America." We are constantly opening up new markets for American products. It would be the wrong way to go for us to force foreign merchants to only buy merchandise that is made in their own country. Everybody's best interest is served when we buy the best product at the best price. At the same time, American manufacturers should stop playing games with where they hold their money and beat American taxes. It would be great if, at the same time we are putting out good products, we showed corporate responsibility. As time goes on, millions more Americans will depend on the foreign marketplace to make their businesses grow. Perhaps it is an oversimplification, but people who trade with each other do not go to war with each other. We all welcome the ability to keep the playing field level. There are many possibilities if we can just explore them with an open mind. We should all be involved with seizing opportunities and solving problems that benefit our pocketbooks and our great country's economy.

• • •

Our export program worked great. We actually did more business in Europe that year than we did in the United States. This business made our pen factory much more profitable, and it opened up a whole range of new activity. We had established distributors in every major market of the newly formed European Common Market. A year after we started our export business to Europe, the Italian pen distributor approached us with a proposition. He said we could greatly expand our business in Europe if we assembled the products in Italy. He offered us an opportunity to form an Italian partnership with him as a minor shareholder in the European corporation. The offer made sense. By importing parts instead of completed product into Italy, we were able to take advantage of a much lower import duty. We could offer immediate delivery from Italy instead of the minimum 60 days that we needed in order to ship from the United States. They would also set up a silk-screen printing facility that would allow us to imprint the advertising copy at a lower cost. The advantages were a better product, quicker delivery, and greater profit. A new company was formed, which we called Measured Marketing Services International (MMS International).

Everything seemed right on the surface, but in practice, the move was a mistake. Financing by the bank in Italy was totally unreliable, and the interest rate was much higher. It was a period of great unrest in Italy, and one strike or another was always hampering our business. Even when there wasn't a strike, many of our employees would simply take time off without regard for the needs of the company. Our plight was brought graphically to us when I received a call from an Italian official.

It was a rainy day in April, and I was in the office in Turin feeling cold, shivery, and overall pretty miserable. I answered the phone to hear the official tell me that we were breaking the law. I was in a foul mood and responded sarcastically, "I did not know that it was against the law to lose money."

"No, signore," he said, "the law states that your workforce should consist of a minimum of 20 percent who are handicapped or are veterans."

Hiring disabled workers and veterans was not the real issue. It was the constant government interference that proved to be the last straw for me. It was time for us to move out of Italy and into more business-friendly headquarters. It was not simple. We discovered that we were not the only ones faced with an impossible interest rate and labor issues. Singer Sewing Company had a factory down the road and endured similar problems.

Singer had decided to move their factory and did not keep it a secret. Their employees had a sit-down strike in which they occupied the factory and defied the company to move anything. It did not help when one of the major post offices in Turin burned down, and a version of one of the great lies came into common usage: "Your check was in the mail that burned in the Turin post office." Since the Italian prime rate was now 20 percent, we started to face serious financial problems.

We decided to steal our own factory, and we plotted the evacuation with the precision of a military operation. Two weeks before the day, we sent our most expensive and intricate machinery to Switzerland for repairs. Then we hired 10 French longshoremen and rented 10 trucks. The operation began on Christmas Eve, and all the forms were presented at the very last minute, when Italian officials were stamping everything in sight in order to get home early for the holidays.

At 6:00 p.m., the move started. The packing was efficient and fast... at 1:00 a.m., Italian police arrived, guns drawn, thinking a theft was in progress. We explained that it was our own factory and we would simply be moving to another location. We neglected to tell the police that it was not a local move. We were actually on our way to the south of France. Our excuse was that we were very busy and had to start moving immediately after Christmas in order to fill our orders. Somehow, the exchange went well. I did not understand what was being said, since the conversation was totally in Italian.

Apparently, it was the most covert operation ever conducted in the history of American-Italian business. The next day, local newspaper headlines shouted that an American capitalist had stolen his factory. It was not a popular move, but it saved our business. It really did no damage, since the factory would have closed in time, with a big loss.

ARRIVEDERCI, ITALY
...BONJOUR, FRANCE

U PON REFLECTION, I should have been able to predict my experience in Italy. In the interest of learning from my mistakes, I asked
myself what I did to make the venture go bad. All the indications
were there; I just did not do my research. Launching a business in a
foreign country is fraught with obstacles, some of them formidable. I
should have taken a closer look at the economic and political conditions
in Italy. If the move made sense, then I should have investigated the
different locales that could work before making a decision. The Italian
distributors were the ones who expressed urgency. Of course, they
wanted me to choose Italy; but in fact, I could have picked any country
in Europe. In hindsight, I realize that most of the other possibilities
would have been better.

Before we made the decision to go to the south of France, we thoroughly investigated conditions in that region. The French were eagerly
seeking foreign companies to invest in France and hire French workers.
At the time, the situation was very similar to what we find in the
United States today. The most important word in the language was,
and is, *jobs*. We discovered that the French were actually paying

foreign companies to provide jobs in France. One of the incentives we received was $200,000 in cash for hiring about 150 people to work in our factory. At the same time, French banks were very aggressive and offered excellent terms for both loans and the financing of export shipments. Furthermore, there was a definite tax benefit to companies that exported French merchandise.

We know that we cannot change the past, but we certainly can learn from it. When making the move from Italy, we had already purchased an empty factory in the south of France, near the city of Grasse. We knew this was a good area in which to work because we had spoken to a number of people who were successful there in the perfume business. (In other words, a pool of labor and business were already established in the area by virtue of the perfume business.) Without missing a step, we closed the Italian corporation and founded a French corporation. We were not, however, ready to resume operations.

Our new business plan called for creating or finding some new products. We had already established a group of distributors in every country in the European Common Market. American pens had been well-received and were selling briskly throughout the European Common Market. However, there are no secrets in business. Our standard line had to meet the competition from new American companies that were ready to cash in on our discovery. When a product or process is successful, many imitators soon follow. Now I realized that we had to have a recognized brand that we could control. While my associates organized the factory, I returned to the United States. I felt the need to make a deal with a well-known brand that had achieved strong distribution in the retail market. We were strictly in the advertising business and sold very few writing instruments to retail stores for resale.

Jack Nadel International had established a solid relationship with Sheaffer Pen Company. We were already successfully selling one of its products, called the "No Nonsense" pen, in the United States. In checking the European market, we found practically no pens in this category—virtually a guarantee of success. The European distributors were selling the prestige line of Sheaffer pens that featured a white dot on the clip. Most of the distributors had not heard of the No Nonsense pen. In many cases, they did not even know that Sheaffer had a lower-priced line to sell.

The opening was clear to me. I should make a deal with Sheaffer to distribute imprinted No Nonsense pens in the European Common Market. Because of our previous business, we had no problem getting right to the top. "Here's the deal," I said. "I would like to work out a deal with you for our European company to get exclusive distribution of imprinted No Nonsense pens. We will import the parts and do all the assembly and printing at our plant in the south of France. We will not upset any of your current business with your regular distributors, because they are not selling the low-price line anyway, and I am talking about moving big quantities."

When they said that they really had no setup for export companies, I replied, "No problem. I will pick up the merchandise at your various plants and will be happy to pay on regular terms. This is all part of our corporation, and you do not have to make an adjustment on the books or worry about the credit." They agreed, and the deal got even better, as they were able to give me a low price that made me very competitive; at the same time, the deal introduced a popular line of Sheaffer writing instruments into the European market. We negotiated a three-year contract starting immediately. It was all plus business for them (that is, business they had never had before), and we had a quality, name-brand product on an exclusive basis.

I had to give Sheaffer a minimum commitment, which turned out to be way below the potential. It was like discovering a goldmine. We were able to sell millions of No Nonsense pens, which were a quality product at a low price. Everything flowed smoothly until Sheaffer started to receive a lot of inquiries at their factory in England for the No Nonsense pen. The British office was really miffed to discover that they had to buy their own pens back from our European company.

MMS International continued to get stronger and stronger as we added dynamic new products. We held educational seminars, where we were able to teach the distributor's salespeople how to sell the Measured

Marketing Services products. With great new merchandise and spectacular service, we had been able to establish ourselves as the gold standard for suppliers in the promotional business throughout the European Common Market.

After the fiasco in Italy and the move to France, I had resolved to take my time and more carefully prepare for each step of our expansion. The No Nonsense pen gave us a strong foothold. Before returning to the United States, I met with everybody involved in the new operation in Grasse. At the start, they would be doing printing and assembly work on the pens. Meanwhile, I was researching French business and labor laws as we were establishing our French corporation. Everybody in this area was most friendly and helpful. Again, the operative word was *jobs*, and we were prepared to bring new employment and new potential to that region. The physical setup was much more comfortable, starting with the legendary weather in the south of France. Our factory offered a panoramic view of the Mediterranean. I also realized that the only way I could make the business work was to come back to France for at least three months. Elly and I decided to rent a villa and settle in. We always enjoyed France. I guess we could even be called Francophiles.

I found a beautiful home for lease in the city of Mougins. The area was astounding in its physical and historical beauty. Literally surrounded by great French restaurants, it had been the home of many famous artists. It was the area where Picasso lived and worked and where reproductions of signature pieces were available on the street for sale. If I was to choose a picturesque village in the south of France that epitomized the Provence lifestyle, this would be it. And it was just a 20-minute drive to the factory.

On the business side, I made some interesting discoveries that were at odds with my experiences with American corporate life. For example, we had to form a board of directors, one member of which would be known as the commissar of accounts. He was actually an accountant similar to our certified accountants. This individual had to have a seat on the board and represented the employees. Like rules all over the world, some are good and some are bad, but I had no way of knowing which was which until I had lived with them for a while. I also made it clear to my associates that when I returned, in any dispute, I was the chairman and had the right of veto. I did not make a final decision to return to France until I had thoroughly examined the conditions and how much of a commitment I had to make personally.

I spent the next month in the United States working on all the other aspects of our business and did not go back to France to concentrate on the company until it was really up and running. One of the necessary conditions for operating in France, I felt, was that I be able to speak French. That way, I could communicate directly with the people in the factory and the office. In order to accomplish this, I hired a French teacher to speak to me and Elly in conversational French for three hours a day until we departed. It was amazing how well it all worked...until it didn't.

Unfortunately, the Sheaffer Corporation advised us "regretfully" that they would not renew the contract at the end of the three years. They were very gracious. They thanked us profoundly for opening the door, but at the end of our contract, Sheaffer UK, their factory in Great Britain, would handle this business. The termination came despite our record-breaking sales during the three-year contract. The problem was due as much to ego as to business principles. While the European market had never sold the popularly priced Sheaffer line, now they were turned on to it. Sheaffer's factory in Great Britain insisted on becoming the exclusive European source for a pen they had never sold before we came on the scene. Although they offered to supply us from their own factory in England, the economics of a non-exclusive agreement killed the deal, as our needs could not be satisfied.

When he heard the news, our general manager in France phoned me with panic in his voice. "How can they do this after we did such a huge job with that product?"

Our factory in Grasse would soon need new projects to remain productive. My response to the general manager was simple and direct: "We just need to find a new pen that is as good or better both in quality and prestige. We need a brand."

There was a moment of silence on the line between Grasse and Los Angeles. I said, "Let's establish our own brand that we totally control, but we cannot just make up a name. We need a name that is recognized for quality and style. We are a French company. Why not make a licensing deal with a French designer? There are several great names. Two leap to mind that are totally French...Christian Dior and Pierre Cardin."

"What a great idea!" he exclaimed, almost jumping through the phone.

"Okay," I said, "start making the contacts right away, and as soon as we can, get a meeting with the principals. We will try to negotiate a licensing agreement. I can't think of anything better than having a French designer of great repute design a special line of merchandise for us, starting with a knockout writing instrument."

It took six months to get to the right people and make the deal. We had a licensing agreement pending with Pierre Cardin, which would include rights for the entire world with the exception of the United States, where a licensing agreement was in effect for another year. It was with a jewelry company, but it also covered writing instruments. We had a date to sign the agreement, which I insisted be written in both French and English, so there would be no misunderstandings.

• • •

The date had arrived, and I was in Paris at the headquarters of Pierre Cardin ready to sign the agreement. As I read it, I found a clause that would kill the whole deal. The contract stated that no name other than Pierre Cardin could appear on the product. This was not possible. Our entire distribution was based on advertising specialties that featured the advertiser's name imprinted on each pen. Pierre Cardin's name would appear on the clip of the pen as the brand name. I explained it was the name of the company and/ or its products that would be advertised on the pens. "For example, what would that be?" I was asked.

I said, "It could be the Banque Nationale de Paris, or it could even be the local butcher."

"No, no, monsieur, the butcher...impossible!"

I could see six months of negotiation going down the toilet. I also could see that I would not be able to dissuade this individual. "Is Pierre Cardin in the building?" I asked. "If so, I would like to see him immediately." We got lucky, as he was, in fact, in his office.

I listened patiently as the licensing executive explained to Cardin the horror of allowing a butcher to advertise on his pen. Cardin turned to me and said, "Mr. Nadel, how many pens would you sell this way?"

"I am sure I would sell many millions," I said.

He thought for a moment and said, "Okay...it's a deal."

This great designer was able to look beyond his ego and recognize the potential. We signed the deal without that provision. Within 30 days, I had a great model of a pen designed by Pierre Cardin. In this way, we started a relationship that lasts to this day. It was so successful for all concerned that two years later, we made a deal to buy the name for stationery products covering the entire world. The opportunity presented itself, and we actually made a lot of money on sublicensing the name to other manufacturers.

EUROPEAN MARKET SUCCESS: OPPORTUNITY AND INNOVATION

O UR EFFORTS IN Europe were groundbreaking. As we prepared for a new product promotion, we would often hear about all the reasons it could not be done. We started with the premise that people in business are most comfortable selling and buying brand names. When I speak about brands, I do not refer only to the great trademarks that everybody recognizes, such as Coca-Cola, Apple, and Wrigley. Specialized brand names have been created in every business. Today, for example, Jack Nadel International is a name that businesspeople around the world associate with "Ideas That Mean Business." The brand has built a history of success, advancing new products and new processes.

The operation we started in Europe was innovative and unique. We adapted the most successful ideas that we used in the United States to the new European Common Market. To me, it was like betting on a horse race after the race had already been run. We just had to make the changes necessary to run on a different track, always thinking of what would work best for our clients. We became aware of the cultural differences between the countries in Europe, although one of the most important accomplishments of the European Common Market was to minimize these differences. It helped our business enormously that one of the reasons for the European Common Market was to eliminate tariffs between countries.

Many years ago, I found myself saying, "Nobody argues with his or her own pocketbook." In the business arena, there are differences between countries, as there are between individuals. Furthermore, conditions change, and what makes sense today may not make sense tomorrow. Still, the incentive to make a profit remains the same.

When we started our operation in Europe, the climate was excellent for an American presence. There are many people around the world who have a quarrel with the American lifestyle, but everybody would like to live like an American in an economic sense. When I make a statement like that, I automatically exclude fanatics in every area of life. In general, we were welcome wherever we went—because my experience tells me that the biggest brand of all is the United States of America. Everybody goes to movies, watches television, and reads newspapers, thereby glimpsing the way of life in the United States. In addition to that, today we have the Internet, which did not exist in the 1970s.

In the modest operation we started in France, we were able to introduce the American system of promotional advertising, tempered by what we learned about the culture of our new customers. The results were that we were able to teach them to use our products and ideas, and we enjoyed learning from them and understanding the character of each area in which we worked. The friendships built over the next 15 years were greatly rewarding to me and added substantially to my quality of life. I was also having a ball. This is one of the ideas that I'd like to pass on…you must be having fun with what you are doing. The trip to the goal has to be as rewarding as the arrival. Another concept I found very gratifying was that by visiting the locations of some of our customers, viewing the art there, and listening to the music, everything became three-dimensional. The whole deal became much more than the sum of its parts.

• • •

Those initial years in Europe were exciting and financially rewarding. They also had a positive effect on our operation in the United States. Ideas are never a one-way street. I saw new products being introduced in the European Common Market that had not appeared in the United States. In most cases, they were easily adaptable for American promotion.

In Germany, at a specialty advertising trade show, I found a collapsible travel bag. This case folded in such a way that it took up little space in a regular suitcase. It then expanded to a full-sized travel bag to accommodate items you had acquired on your trip. The quality was terrific. I had a meeting with the head of the company after he introduced it at the Düsseldorf trade show. He told me he was having great success with the bag, which was made in Hong Kong. "I am sure," I said, "that there will be more bags just like it on the market because it looks to me as though it would be very easy to knock off in China. I would like to bring this collapsible bag into the United States, which would not interfere with anything you are doing here. The most economical way to do this is for me to import the bag from your supplier in Hong Kong. If you introduce him to me, I will probably get the advantage of the same price that you are paying. This will take no commitment or follow-up on your part, and I will pay you a small brokerage on my purchases."

We made the deal. Jack Nadel International introduced the product in the United States and had some great sales. It had taken little research on my part, with no development cost. We sold a huge quantity in the United States before other importers knocked us off and made the market more competitive.

That same year, we found a great new product at a different trade show. It was a note pad with 500 pages, compressed so tightly that advertising copy was screened on all four sides. This was not a good candidate for import because every order had to be customized, and the freight would be prohibitive. When I returned to the United States, I brought some samples back with me and looked for a silk-screen operation that could replicate the product. No one had seen it in the United States. In order to move fast, I made a deal with a

California silk-screening company. I knew it would be a great product for a while, but there was nothing to keep other silk-screeners from copying it. In order to get into the business, I bought a half-interest in the silk-screening company and went into production immediately.

Once more, we did a great job at a high profit. A couple of years later, as the price became more competitive, we sold back our interest in the silk-screening plant and became just a customer. Everybody benefited. My friend in the silk-screening business made a nice profit, Jack Nadel International had an exclusive item at a big profit, and our customers had the advantage of a new promotional item that everybody wanted. This example illustrates how good things can happen when you keep your eyes open and welcome new products. It also helps to know just how to translate a promotion to provide a good return on investment in time and money.

After selling to distributors throughout the European Common Market, we had made a great impression on that market. With the Sheaffer No Nonsense pen leading a complete line of proven products with the United States behind it, we had become the go-to company for promotional products in Europe. Our factory was running well, and we received great cooperation from the banks in France.

CONDITIONS ARE NEVER PERFECT

T WO OF THE direct-mail companies that I ran at Republic were Krupp Corporation in Los Angeles and Taylor Company in Portland, Oregon. Krupp was a well-established family company when Republic bought it, about six months before Jack Nadel International was purchased. I was very familiar with the company and its operations. After Krupp and Taylor had operated as separate companies for a year, I decided it would be much more efficient if we merged them.

We established Krupp-Taylor in Los Angeles and closed the printing plant in Portland. We brought necessary equipment and inventory to Los Angeles, and converted Portland into a sales office. That year, we were able to sign up United Airlines' frequent traveler program and Sprint; later we added a young but very aggressive company competing with IBM, called Apple. Our business was to promote the brands of our clients, to sell the merchandise directly in some cases, and to produce business-to-business promotions.

In the early 1960s, lists of customer addresses were kept on addressograph plates. One of the reasons that clients were reluctant to move from one company to another was that the plates were so bulky and heavy to transport that it just didn't pay to make the change.

During these years, we became pioneers in computer programs. The old addressograph plates disappeared as we entered the computer era. One million names and addresses used to take up thousands of square feet, but now the same million names were on tape and could be carried away under your arm. This technology dramatically streamlined the direct-mail business.

In Los Angeles, we were operating in three separate locations, and it became imperative to find a single building that could house our new computer-centered operation. After several months of searching, we found the perfect building. It was 100,000 square feet on 11 acres in the Marina area of Los Angeles. This was expensive property owned by The Broadway Department Stores, which were closing their direct-selling business. We also had the problem of very high interest rates. The prime rate at the time was 18 percent. After taking a giant gulp, and still with a dry throat, I told the real estate broker that we would go to $12 million. My research told me that it would be one hell of a buy at that price. The offer was accepted.

The direct-mail business was booming, and every indication was that we were about to hit a home run. A wise man once said, "Be careful what you ask for...you may just get it." After redecorating, relocating our equipment from the two factories, and adding a special press for a mere $1.5 million, we were all set. This decision represented a huge investment. Looking back on it now, I realize how gutsy it was. We did have a steady flow of work and a wide range of clients. Now we had a well-equipped factory that could accommodate between two and three times as much business.

For a while, it seemed as though we had given up a manageable overhead for a much more expensive situation that would be very difficult to maintain. In fact, six months later our accounting department gave us the bad news. We were losing $100,000 per month. And although the rest of the operations were doing very well, this was a big nut to carry.

I called an all-day meeting with the president and general manager of the direct-mail operations. After a long discussion, we decided that we just were not doing enough business to support this huge factory. When our production had been limited, we were very choosy about the jobs we took. In the new factory, we had a great deal of room for more business, particularly if we could book enough to put on another shift. It was at that point we made a big decision: to handle a lot more volume at considerably lower margins. Like some huge monster, the new plant had to be continually fed with work.

Our meeting to correct and reorganize the newly expanded direct-mail division was very successful. We looked at all angles of the business and pinpointed our capabilities and the needs of the marketplace. With one hundred thousand square feet of space, and more automatic machinery and equipment (particularly the high-speed multicolored presses), we were ready to compete for the heavy-volume clients.

We put this new policy into effect immediately. It's an amazing fact that when you have a full load of work, the factory actually functions more efficiently. Within three months, we had two complete shifts and were considering starting another so that we would be operating 24 hours a day. We also put in place a cost-efficiency program that went even further in reducing our costs of operation. As part of the program, we dramatically improved the productivity of our employees.

It worked. A few months later, we were no longer losing money but making a profit. One of our huge expenses was mortgage payments. You will recall that our original mortgage was at an insane 18 percent. With a $10 million mortgage, we had to pay almost $2 million a year in interest and principal. However, our printers were operating at full blast, and we were doing a fantastic job for our clients. It was very exciting—and profitable.

At the same time, we realized that the ground rules had changed. We had to look forward; in order to maintain our position, we would have to keep up with technology. This was challenging for a private company, because every time you had to install new equipment, the commitment was in the millions of dollars. It was like going from a friendly neighborhood poker game to a major no-limit table. Supporting an operation like this was very difficult with only operating profits.

The situation called for a significant bankroll or a public company behind us. The decision was made that we should look for a large company that was ready to make a capital investment. We had to either go public ourselves or sell the direct-mail division to someone for whom it would be a strategic acquisition.

I should have followed this strategic tip: Scale your business plan to fit your ability to finance it. If funds are limited, take the implementation of your business plan in stages.

THE CLICKETY-CLACK OF THE PRESSES

W HEN WE MADE the decision to increase volume, our sales force of 10 highly skilled and creative account executives went out with a new mission. We not only had to sell clients that we could fill their needs, we had very expensive equipment that had to be continually in use. I remember when we closed that meeting, I made a simple statement: "Whenever I walk through this plant, I've got to hear the clickety-clack of all the presses."

It was amazing how quickly the increase in business reduced overhead and turned losses into profits, as mentioned earlier. We came up with a slogan that really applied: "We provide a one-stop shop from concept to the mailbag." We were even able to get a branch of the post office to establish a station directly in our factory. It was a quick trip from the press to the post. Our volume with big clients kept increasing as we achieved more measurable results. In addition to our growing business and client list, we became the experts at soliciting and acquiring new savings accounts for banks around the country.

As volume increased, the need for more capital equipment was constant. From automatic, high-tech multicolor presses to special inserting equipment, we were suffering from an overdose of prosperity.

Although continuously investing in expensive new machinery was not part of the original plan, we realized that the timing was just right for a move that brought us into the financial arena of venture capital as well as mergers and acquisitions. The market was open and filled with opportunity.

A major advertising agency with worldwide billings of over $6 billion was very interested in acquiring us so that they would have the advantages of vertical integration—total control of two profit-making entities under one roof. They would be able to benefit from the profit of the advertising agency as well as the profit of production. They could plan and produce almost any direct-mail program.

The advertising agency was well-aware of the fact that we were able to achieve measurable results, a very tough thing to pin down in the advertising business in those days. Very creative ads that people talk about do not necessarily result in sales.

• • •

There are several types of deals in the field of mergers and acquisitions. One is that the acquiring company will advance a large amount of money, feeling that they can grow their investment at a rapid rate. However, the deal that really works best is the strategic acquisition.

In our direct-marketing efforts, we were able to do the all-important task of measuring the results. The goal of one promotion was to achieve more bank depositors. If a bank wanted to acquire a large number of deposits, it could advertise through a mailing that would offer an incentive (premium) for customers opening new accounts of a certain size. The bank could then directly relate the amount of money it spent on advertising to the amount of cash it was able to generate in new deposits. In today's market, billions of dollars are generated on the Internet, where the advertising message goes only to a pre-determined demographic.

As I mentioned before, the advertising agency that was talking to us had $6 billion in international billings. The standard advertising agency commission was 15 percent on the amount spent for newspaper space and radio or television time. Our direct-marketing (direct-mail) company would be able to do the actual printing and mailing that was generated by the advertising agency. Therefore, the agency could not only make their regular 15 percent commission but could profit on the production.

We already had two shifts going, and if we had enough business, a third shift would be enormously profitable. Since we would be using the same facility as in our regular business, it would cost no extra for the equipment and the rent. The only additional cost would be the paper, ink, and labor to do the jobs. We projected that by putting $20 million a year worth of work into our plant, under these conditions, we could actually generate an additional profit of $10 million.

The negotiations opened on a very high note. We were talking to a fast-growing international advertising agency. The idea of acquiring a company that could give them vertical integration was very appealing. They found it hard to understand the concept of a manufacturer's profit. As stated earlier, traditionally, an advertising agency makes its entire income as a commission from the newspaper, radio station, or television station that is broadcasting the message. Again, this comes to 15 percent of the billing amount. Therefore, if an agency arranges for $1 million worth of advertising on a television network, its gross profit is $150,000. It also charges creative fees to craft the message and design the campaign. A great deal of promotion in advertising calls for printing, and the printing costs are marked up by 15 percent, as well. By buying our direct-mail company, the agency would own the printing press and would therefore be capable of making a manufacturer's profit. We were already grossing about $50 million per year, and it was a profitable business. By adding another $20 million to the manufacturing side, most of the overhead would be paid for, and the profit would be much greater.

There seemed to be a terrific synergy in this package. Our initial conversations went very well, and in time they developed into negotiations. My suggestion was to take everything we presented as fact and make a deal based on that. After we decided on the practical aspects of the acquisition, there would be an amount of time for the acquirer to do due diligence and check that the actual numbers agreed with what we had presented. The sale involved all of our direct-mail operations, and the agency wanted to keep the management team, which had already performed so successfully, in place. As part of the package, they would give the president of Krupp-Taylor a five-year contract, and he would have to sign a covenant not to compete during that period. Finally, we arrived at a figure. They were a public company, so they would pay $20 million…$10 million in cash, and $10 million in company stock. I would have nothing further to do with the operation of the acquired company. However, they suggested that as part of the deal, I would be a member of the advertising agency's board. I felt I was ready to accept that challenge. I was flattered that the chairman felt that I could be an important addition to the board of this huge company.

The deal was scheduled to close in September 1988. Since the agency's fiscal year was the same as the calendar year, they were anxious that the months between October and December prove very profitable and increase the value of the acquisition. They arranged for me to meet with some senior members of the board to make sure we would be compatible. The board had one opening, and this looked like a perfect fit. We agreed on everything, including a cash bonus to be added to the price of the company based on a very profitable last quarter.

Two weeks after we made the deal in principle, I received a call from the chairman. "Everybody just loves you and the idea that you're coming on the board. However, we are in the process of making another deal that would make us even stronger, as we are about to acquire an advertising agency in Japan. This would give us an important worldwide position. Part of the deal is that the president of the Japanese company wants a seat on the board. This is really important, and I wonder if we can delay appointing you to the board for a year, when another vacancy will be available."

This looked to be a very important acquisition for them, one that would be crucial to their strategic position and their image in the world marketplace. I responded that this would be perfectly okay with me, but since I would no longer have the option of being on the board of directors, I would prefer to convert the deal from 50 percent cash and 50 percent stock to all cash. I knew they were flush with cash and would readily agree to the change.

By the end of the year, our direct-mail company had made enough additional profit to qualify for the acquisition bonus. When the final deal was signed, it was for $20 million cash. The incentive for performance during the period from October to December was an additional $4 million. Everything went through, and the deal was signed. The agency performed its due diligence, and we collected $24 million in cash. I thought that was pretty good for a company that just two years earlier had been losing money at the rate of $100,000 per month. In the leveraged buyout, we had paid $4.5 million dollars for Measured Marketing Services; we now sold a part of the company for $24 million. In addition, Measured Marketing Services continued with three terrific profit-making divisions: MMS International in Europe; Art Mold Products in Providence, Rhode Island; and Jack Nadel International, headquartered in Los Angeles. By 1991, we had sold off MMS International and Art Mold Products. This left our core business, Jack Nadel International—our total business today—with 19 offices around the world.

Now it was time to come up with a new business plan.

A PRESIDENTIAL MISSION TO JAPAN

I N THE LATER 1980s, the United States faced a huge trade imbalance with Japan. Imports from Japan were much greater than American exports to Japan. The real problem was that there was not enough American merchandise being sold in Japan. My business success had evolved to the point where, in 1988, I was delightfully surprised when the Office of the President of the United States contacted me.

At that time, many people were complaining about a recession in the United States. Japan was leading the way in business and was a dominant manufacturing power. At the same time, the U.S. economy was becoming more and more service-based. Even the mighty American automobile industry had fallen significantly behind the Japanese. Overall, our imports far exceeded our exports, particularly in our relationship with Japan.

President Ronald Reagan and key members of Congress recognized the danger of this trade imbalance, so a presidential trade mission was created. Its members would travel to Japan to study how more American merchandise could be sold in the Japanese market. I swelled with pride when I was asked to become part of this trade mission.

The group consisted of nine American entrepreneurs who had success-fully exported to Japan and other parts of the world. The invitation came as a great surprise to me, as I was not a registered Republican. In putting the mission together, the White House worked with people who had considerable experience and paid little attention to their political affiliation.

I happily accepted the invitation, and we embarked with Secretary of Commerce William Verity from Travis Air Force Base in Washington DC on a version of Air Force One. Mr. Verity lost no time in getting acquainted with the other members of his mission. It was an interesting flight, particularly when I noticed that for security reasons, there were no windows on the plane. A section was set aside as Secretary Verity's office. En route, we had a most stimulating conversation. He told me he would seek my advice because of my extensive export-import background, particularly in negotiating with Japan.

We had receptions and meetings with the most important people in Japanese industry, including the presidents of Mitsubishi, Toyota, and Sony. There followed a week of constant, well-organized meet-ings, as well as tours of a number of factories. Everything was very impressive, indeed.

The message that the Japanese hammered home to us was that our mission could be quite successful, but almost everything was built on respecting Japan's traditions and distribution system. With discount stores and mass marketing rising in the United States, the Japanese insisted on the control of pricing and distribution. They really wanted us to make sure that we fit into their system, which called for first selling goods to an importer or trading company. These entities worked in close cooperation with the banks and the government. Each importer had a group of small retailers that carried very little inven-tory. The retailers were totally dependent on the trading companies to back them up with the needed inventory. Usually, they had little more than the merchandise that was on display. To understand how we were out of step with this system, one of our goals was for the Japanese to allow us to open mass-merchandise stores like Toys "Я" Us, Walmart, and other chains. Cameras made in Japan were a good example of the differences between the two systems. The prices for the same Japanese cameras in the United States were much lower than they were in Japan.

I remember how much I enjoyed having lunch with Akio Morita, the president and founder of Sony. He said something very wise. "The problem we have with America is that you come over here and want to make a deal. We meet you and want to form a relationship from which we can make many deals. Most importantly and the basis of everything is that we have a relationship where we honor and trust each other." This became one of my most important rules.

• • •

During these memorable meetings in Japan, I realized once again how the key to good business is understanding the problems of our customers and then trying to solve them. One day I was driving down a Japanese road with the president of Winnebago, with whom I had become very friendly. He told me that he had been frustrated by the company's inability to do as much business in Japan as he thought possible. Looking at the road we were traveling along, I said half-jokingly, "In order for the Japanese to buy Winnebagos, either they would have to make their roads wider or you make the Winnebago narrower."

He laughed but agreed. "I remember the Japanese exporters saying when they came to the United States that they did not try to sell what they had but instead inquired about what adjustments they had to make to increase sales in the United States." We agreed that it was important for Americans to adjust their thinking in order to adapt to foreign customers.

The Japanese hospitality was unbelievably great. Each reception outdid the other in the quality of the food. The equipment that the Japanese set up for meetings was remarkable. I was particularly impressed by a huge, round table where we sat at one particular meeting. There was a button at each position which, when pressed, produced a television screen in front of you. Their computerization was advanced far beyond that of the United States, and they had many methods of keeping a positive balance of trade. The discussions were brutally honest. The

Japanese insisted that they could make any product that we invented cheaper and better. They urged us, instead of increasing any conflict, to cooperate as much as possible with the understanding that, in reality, we were great at producing software, and they were great at producing hardware.

It was a wonderful week. I learned so much, as did the rest of the people on the mission. The secretary of commerce came away with a better understanding of Japan and its potential. We were able to make a deal for more and better distribution. Most importantly, we came away with a better understanding of each other's needs. We were able to realize an immediate increase in business because the Japanese allowed us the opportunity to create a retail presence for Toys "Я" Us and other retailers.

My feeling was that Japan's old distribution system was in jeopardy because it was becoming outdated, and you cannot hold up progress. By allowing free trade, Japan had a major adjustment to make over the next decade.

On a personal note, my respect and friendship for the Japanese and their industry grew immeasurably.

SETTING A NEW AGENDA

B Y 1993, JACK NADEL INTERNATIONAL had been in business for 40 years, and I was ready to celebrate my 70th birthday. I was still full of energy and thoroughly enjoying all the facets of the business. My personal life was beyond great. Elly and I had been married for 45 years and were both in good health, traveling to all parts of the world for both business and pleasure. We felt it was now time to sit down and seriously discuss my retirement and how we would spend the rest of our lives. Elly was a co-founder of the business and spent the first 10 years as a very active participant. Then we had decided that she would devote much of her time to raising our two children and to her various philanthropies. She was a fine pianist and was very active in musical education as well as charities.

We had two homes, one on the beach in Santa Monica and the other in a beautiful area of Santa Barbara. I guess you would say that we were fully living the American Dream. I had started to write some books and was enjoying the process. In my business, I had seen and done so much, and I felt it was important to share my experiences and lessons. I have always felt there is no such thing as an unselfish act because invariably, a benefit bounces back. As one grows older, pleasure comes as a reflection of the influence you may have had on others. Neither Elly nor I was interested in simply dangling our feet in the pond. We planned on having an active retirement, complete with new experiences and the expansion of our friendships. The decision was made.

As I approached my 70th birthday, I retired from active management of the company, but I would remain on the board of directors of Jack Nadel International. The major goal was that Elly and I be able to spend more time together and enjoy whatever activities we chose. We did not really feel any pressure to slow down, but we wanted to do everything on our own schedule and in our own way.

The old concept of retirement was that it should be planned and defined. In today's world, not everybody can retire without financial hardship. I remember when I was in my 30s, a good friend said to me, "You work seven days a week—I would never work that hard. Why do you do it?"

My answer was very simple. "I love the work I do, and I want to make as much money as I can today so that I don't have to worry about it when I reach an age where I cannot realize this kind of income. I work this hard so that I will never have to lower my standard of living."

The question and the answer were unusually prophetic. This friend of mine lived his philosophy. As the years passed, he became incapacitated physically, and he had to cut back on the time he spent in his business. By the time he reached 65, he could no longer work and had no financial resources to fall back on. I remember listening to him complain bitterly that the golden years were pure crap. From that point on, he had very few happy days and always struggled financially.

I feel very strongly that we must all prepare for retirement. I hear more and more about pensions being reduced if not disappearing entirely, so I try to help individuals plan for these years. Many people feel they have been victimized by the general economy, politicians, unions, or any other source from which they may have received a false sense of security. I am continually discovering that there is no easy answer. Every one of us is an individual and must determine up front what our specific needs are going to be and how to address them.

I know many people who are financially secure but still miserable. In many cases, the misery is illness brought on by living longer. But there are other people enjoying good health and good finances who just do not know what to do with their time. We go to school for many reasons, but there are very few lessons in how to survive and even enjoy old age.

My life since 1993 has been filled with the adventures of writing, exploring new places, and mentoring young people in their careers. It has also been very important for me to remain on the board of directors of Jack Nadel International and help to determine its future. In the 60 years of its existence, the business has been helmed by three Nadels. My brother Marty became president of JNI when I formed Measured Marketing Services in 1972. He passed away five years ago, and his son, Craig, took over as president. I remain chairman of the board. What a pleasure it has been switching from a set schedule to the freedom of enjoying my own agenda.

In 1996, I launched a weekly television show called *Out of the Box with Jack Nadel*, which aired on the local ABC affiliate station and ran until 2001. The show addressed current issues and featured inspirational and legendary guests, including Karl Malden, Elmer Bernstein, Hugh O'Brian, Marilyn Horne, Rob Reiner, Julia Child, Hal David, Barnaby Conrad, Barbara Marx Hubbard, Riane Eisler, and Jack Canfield among the many I had the pleasure of interviewing.

I was asked to take on the role of adjunct professor at the University of California, Santa Barbara, and taught a course in world economics from an experienced entrepreneur's point of view.

In 2002, our happy and active retirement was interrupted by tragedy. Elly, my wife and lifelong business partner, died of lung cancer. Everyone handles these personal tragedies in his or her own way. I spent three months in relative seclusion and the frustration of experiencing memories that I knew would not be repeated.

Yet I was enjoying good health and many close friends and was in the process of being regenerated. The lesson became clear to me that the world continued and life should go on—and most importantly, I would never value my present and future against the past. Like anything important, a new attitude does not immediately spring to life, but it evolves at its own pace.

Suddenly, at 79, I felt ready to start a new chapter by going out on dates and being social again. When I was introduced to Julie, the dynamics changed. I'd met someone that I wanted to see a second and a third time and then for the rest of my life. I never compared Julie to Elly in the many ways they were similar and the many ways they were miles apart. Julie had a fantastic background as an event planner and caterer. Twenty-two years my junior, she was divorced with two children and three granddaughters. We spoke a common language because she had been an entrepreneur and possessed a wonderful sense of humor. Julie was very attractive and had an effervescent personality that I just loved to be around. We found that we had much in common, and our lives came together in almost perfect harmony.

Over the last nine years, we have produced an Off-Broadway musical, traveled extensively, and settled down to a lovely life in Santa Barbara, being involved in several philanthropic and community activities.

My life seemed again complete, but there was something that kept nagging at me. I realized that there were millions of people who were struggling to make ends meet. The world had gone through dramatic changes, and along with the numerous advances, many people suffered distressing reverses. The tragedy of lost jobs was not going away easily. I had not heard viable solutions from our politicians, industrialists, or unions. We needed to face the universal truth that productivity had improved dramatically through the use of new technology, and fewer people were needed to do the same jobs.

It is my feeling that the majority of business courses do not meet the needs of 2013 and beyond. After 67 years of experience in marketplaces around the world, I know that success comes when proven methods are applied in flexible ways that meet unique circumstances. Situations change so rapidly today that *pragmatism* and *adaptation* are key words for entrepreneurs to keep in mind at all times. The most important asset we can have as individuals is the ability to think, just as a scientist must know the basics before he or she can create and test new theories.

We live in an era in which we are all individuals. One size does not fit all. Each problem has its own genesis and its own solution. In my opinion, the health of our economy depends on the success of small and medium-sized businesses. There are many theories on how to create jobs, but the reality is that the number of available jobs is a response to the demands of the marketplace. The concept of supply and demand works in the job sector as well as in every other economic arena. New industries create a demand for more workers, and unemployed people become the supply.

My goal is to use my experience to help spread knowledge to as many people as possible and to help prepare entrepreneurs for success. When entrepreneurs succeed, the number of jobs rises organically, and prosperity follows.

Now that I have retired, my success in filling business needs has been replaced by a desire to fill needs in my community. My experiences in business have fueled my eagerness to help less fortunate people and improve conditions. In Santa Barbara, Julie and I are financial and hands-on philanthropists with Sansum Clinic and Visiting Nurse & Hospice Care. We have recently provided support to brick-and-mortar developments for Sansum, including improvements for a major lobby at the Pueblo facility as well as renovations to the OB-GYN facility to help improve the quality of medical care. We have also developed and executed a music therapy program being implemented in hospice, which has become a benchmark for the organization. When I reflect on all of my life experiences, it becomes clear that when you help others, you are actually helping yourself. The material assistance you give your neighbors and associates will be repaid in many unexpected and fulfilling ways.

USING MY TIPS IN TODAY'S WORLD

I READ IN the newspaper and hear on television every day that the solution to our economic problems is tied directly to the success of entrepreneurs who run small and medium-sized businesses. The very foundation of our economy depends upon the success of these business owners…the folks with ideas, products, and services who need a plan and some financing to get their businesses off the ground.

Politicians, unions, and corporate executives understand the importance of small and medium-sized businesses, but no one, to my knowledge, has yet come up with an effective plan to encourage and guide new entrepreneurs nationwide and help those already in business to achieve maximum success. New and ever-changing technology dominates the world economy, and to fully participate today, I believe entrepreneurs must first adopt a methodology that will work under all conditions. The Nadel Method provides a proven foundation for success.

A number of people I know have carved out new directions for themselves, working within their capabilities, and stretching beyond their expectations—and I believe you can do the same. Your education might be limited (remember, I have only a high school diploma), but your ability to think and to resolve problems is the greatest asset you have. Please know that regardless of the pressure, every step along the way for me has been filled with fun and excitement. The money that I have earned has afforded me the great luxury of making choices and having opportunities.

As I have mentioned, there's no substitute for the power of critical thought. Today's world provides enormous opportunities and great technological tools, but technology must be preceded by the ability to think, act, and adjust as each deal develops. We must understand that entrepreneurs come in all shapes and sizes, from the individual who starts a small local business to geniuses like Steve Jobs, who grew a project created in his garage into the largest business in the world.

Becoming an entrepreneur starts with critical thinking, which develops into gut instinct. You must be determined that good things *will* happen. Success begins with your attitude and in your mind. Do not fear failure on your journey—learn from it. When you make a choice in your career, think it through and then use all of your senses to make it work. The more you exercise your mind, the more you will be able to trust your gut.

Making deals came to me very early in life. Becoming an author and mentor came much later, after gaining the insight that experience has given me for so many subjects. As a result, I have the good fortune of being able to reach into my own life with very little need for theory.

Creating businesses, products, and distribution networks is best explained by example. The 50 tips that follow are illustrated by their use in real-world contexts under all kinds of conditions. Through these ideas and methods, you can create your own path to success and financial freedom.

I hope that learning more about the challenges and successes of my personal journey encourages you to move forward with your own entrepreneurial intentions. It's an evolutionary process for everyone. Begin a new path, or continue down the road you started, with the knowledge that success ensues when you follow your passion.

After all these years of following my passion, I can still be pleasantly reminded about the impact I've had. A funny story...Julie and I were at a trade show in Las Vegas recently, and we introduced ourselves to a young sales rep from a luggage line. Her mouth fell open, and she asked if I was "The Real Jack Nadel" of Jack Nadel International. That is how long I have been around. In fact, she did not even think there really was a Jack Nadel! In January 2013, JNI celebrated its 60th anniversary, with offices in 19 cities around the world.

WHAT'S MY NEXT STEP?

B EFORE YOU DIVE into my 50 tips for entrepreneurial success, let's briefly review the five steps of the Nadel Method.

Keep in mind that an entrepreneur must conceptualize this method in a highly focused way. Attention to detail is paramount for success. Lack of attention is a recipe for failure.

1. Identify a business idea you love. Start with your aspirations. Articulate your dreams in writing and then realistically assess your strengths and weaknesses. Modify your goals as necessary.

2. Ask the right questions as you research. Identify unmet or underserved needs in the marketplace. Find a product or service that suits you. Thoroughly investigate your competitors.

3. Plan a deal and focus on the details. Structure an equitable deal and create a custom business plan. Visualize your deal proposal step by step, and keep your focus on specific details. Ask and answer lots of questions. Consult professionals and mentors as necessary.

4. Fulfill your agreement and then some. Execute the deal as promised, but be prepared to make adjustments for unplanned contingencies. Protect your assets with written guarantees from suppliers and customers.

5. Review the results for next time. As the deal reaches its conclusion, take time to reflect on the entire experience. Build on this experience as you seek your next deal.

50 OF MY BEST TIPS

*for Surviving and
Thriving in Business*

TIP 1

Self-motivation is the key to success and will achieve powerful results.

In business, there is no safety net. Successful businesspeople don't rely on manipulating markets or government regulations—they have to find their own internal motivation and use it to propel themselves forward, whether to create financial prosperity for a family or community, support a cause they're passionate about, or bring an innovative idea to the world. Self-motivation helps entrepreneurs ignite the drive needed to push through challenges when the going gets tough.

FROM THE JACK NADEL ARCHIVES

In my role as a mentor, I have given strong advice to an individual that, if carried out, would have produced a successful deal. In some cases, however, that individual did not have sufficient self-motivation to take the steps I recommended. I learned that many people lack the strength of their convictions, which leads to failure. No one can teach self-motivation...either you have it or you don't.

HOW DOES THIS TIP APPLY TODAY?

Imagine being fired from your job as a magazine editor because you "lack imagination" and "have no original ideas." The last thing you would likely do is start an entertainment company, but that's exactly what Walt Disney did. This entertainment company soon went bankrupt, forcing Disney to partner with his brother Roy in starting the company that would become the Walt Disney Company. At almost every stage of its early life, the Walt Disney Company was discounted. It had trouble with financing, and distributors literally laughed at the idea of animated cartoons with sound. But Walt Disney could not be dissuaded from his goal of creating a movie and entertainment company. Luckily for families everywhere, Disney's passionate pursuit of his vision resulted in the creation of one of the world's most well-known and beloved brands.[1]

TIP 2

Find a need and fill it.

In my nearly 70 years as a successful businessperson, this **basic** idea has been the reason I started every deal. The greater the need, the greater the potential.

FROM THE JACK NADEL ARCHIVES

As I outlined earlier, in "The Adventure Continues…," the very first deal I made was with the Chinese Trading Company, which had a clear need: navy blue woolen material to make uniforms. There was none available, but olive drab was for sale in large quantities at war surplus stores. I bought the army olive drab, had it dyed navy, and sold it to the Chinese. We were able to supply exactly what was needed through a "value added" factor, completing a fantastic and profitable transaction.

HOW DOES THIS TIP APPLY TODAY?

MP3 players had been around for a few years when Apple CEO Steve Jobs introduced the iPod in 2001. But the iPod was something different—up until then, the most common way to get digital music was to copy it from CDs or use an illegal peer-to-peer sharing network. Jobs had a new idea: He would create an online store where people could buy and download their favorite music, one song at a time—instantly and legally. The effect was revolutionary—the music industry would never be the same, and by 2010, the iTunes store had sold 10 billion song downloads. Not only did Jobs find a need and fill it, he brought innovation to an entire industry and revitalized music sales.[2]

TIP 3

Understand your strengths and weaknesses.

Even the most successful businesses are vulnerable to trends, fads, and pet projects. Yet problems can arise when businesses move away from their core strengths to pursue new ventures in business segments they know little about. When you're considering something new, it's best to do a careful analysis of your strengths and weaknesses, and then look at the market's opportunities and threats. This is called a SWOT (strengths, weaknesses, opportunities, and threats) analysis. Don't be afraid to seek out advice from others who have gone before. In today's connected world, it's easier than ever to find experienced mentors.

FROM THE JACK NADEL ARCHIVES

When starting out in business, I had limited time and limited funds. My selling skills were great, but my detail skills were—and still are—terrible. So I decided to spend money hiring competent people to do the detail work. I wound up with more efficiency and greater profit by devoting the major part of my time to selling. As another example of understanding strengths and weaknesses in business, the product for one of our clients was trademark jewelry. We found a plant that was doing beautiful die casting, the technique required to manufacture the jewelry...they were able to do everything we needed with the equipment and staff they already had. I didn't have to get into the particulars of manufacturing the product myself.

HOW DOES THIS TIP APPLY TODAY?

If you have pets—and most of us do—you're probably familiar with Iams®, a premium brand of pet food and products. But did you know Iams® also offers pet insurance? The company's move into pet insurance is a perfect example of identifying strengths, researching a new market, and finding the right partners to expand into a new business. Iams® executives knew their company already had excellent relationships with veterinarians, and they knew that, even by 2003, less than 1 percent of the U.S. pet-owning population had pet insurance. Their approach to this new market was to partner with Veterinary Pet Insurance Company and add IAMS®/VPI pet insurance to the new puppy and kitten packets it already distributed to vets' offices. Early results were promising: Some vet clinics experienced a buy-in rate for pet insurance that was 14 times the national average.[3]

TIP 4

In providing a service or product, remember you *are the service or product.*

Here's an old truth: People don't buy services, they buy people. Think about it. When you last hired a house painter, did you choose him because his colors were better than those of other painters? The last time you hired a caterer, was it because her knives were sharper? Of course not. In any kind of service industry, *you* are the main product. You and your reputation are your own best advertisement. It's up to you to identify a market for your skills and talents—and pursue it. From the moment your prospective customers meet you until they sign on the dotted line, every action you take is part of the sale.

FROM THE JACK NADEL ARCHIVES

I had a client with different groups of distributor salespeople...I offered the service of conducting a sales meeting to show them how best to take advantage of the merchandise we had to offer. In addition to having the right products, the promotion was a success due to my personal presentation.

HOW DOES THIS TIP APPLY TODAY?

There have been TV chefs since the advent of television, but it's probably fair to say that the mold for the modern TV chef was created by Emeril Lagasse. The one-time Food Network chef, whose trademark "Bam!" kicked things up a notch all the way to international success, understood instinctively that the food—as good as it was—wasn't really enough to draw people to watch his show. So he added a live band and a live studio audience, and brought his own magnetic personality. Then he looked for ways to turn his personal brand into a thriving business. Today, Lagasse sells kitchenware, knives, cooks' clothing, and cookbooks, and he even has his own spice collection—an empire built largely on the strength of his personality.[4]

TIP 5

All business is personal.

Regardless of the scale of an establishment, from a huge corporation to a mom 'n' pop store, customers like to do business with people they respect and trust. Success in business isn't about numbers; it's about people, and meeting their needs and wants. Buying and selling are as much instinct as science, and if you want to get ahead, you'll need to develop your own instincts for dealing with people—and be the kind of person who inspires confidence.

FROM THE JACK NADEL ARCHIVES

Very early in my career, I was offered a role in a deal based on the Mexican government's subsidizing of the use of silver in Mexican products. In 1950, the silver content of a Mexican silver tray was worth more than the cost of making the tray. I was told that by simply melting down the tray and extracting the silver, the precious metal could be sold on the commodities market for a handsome profit. My gut told me this was a bad deal because melting the tray served no purpose other than to take advantage of a misuse of the subsidy. The Mexican government withdrew the subsidy when it realized its mistake. Those who had invested in the deal suffered a great loss.

HOW DOES THIS TIP APPLY TODAY?

If you watch late-night TV, you have probably heard of P90X®, the hot workout craze that has swept the nation. P90X® was created in 2006 by Tony Horton, a personal trainer who blended the newest findings in nutrition and exercise into a powerful program. So what made this program such a success? It was the combination of Horton's charismatic personality and the powerful first-person accounts of people who transformed their lives with P90X®. There is no better way to inspire people than to show them someone else who has already succeeded. At the end of the day, Horton may or may not be the best trainer in the world, but he certainly understands one thing: All business is personal, even when your product grosses half a billion dollars in sales before it is even 10 years old.[5]

TIP 6

Do your own research.

Trust is essential in running a successful business, but it's important to remember that everybody has an agenda— one that may not match yours. This applies to people you ask to research your major decisions. When you're thinking of making any major business decision, it always pays to do your own research to get the real facts. There's never any danger of being *too* informed.

FROM THE JACK NADEL ARCHIVES

One of my division managers strongly recommended that we go into the business of producing trade shows. He gave me statistics that turned out to be false. I did my own research and decided that the chances of success were very small in an overcrowded and expensive field; I turned the deal down. He resigned, bankrolled his own trade show company, and lost his entire investment shortly thereafter.

HOW DOES THIS TIP APPLY TODAY?

Aviva Weiss and her privately held company, Fun and Function, had reached a turning point by 2011. The company, which specialized in selling therapy tools and items for children with special needs, had done well, growing sevenfold from 2007 to 2011. Weiss and her co-founder (her husband, Haskel) had achieved this success by targeting their products to the home market and parents, who accounted for more than 60 percent of sales. However, in doing so, the company left behind the institutional market, including schools and clinics, which really drives growth in the industry. To address this other important market, they hired a new company president, who pushed them to overhaul the catalog to feature more classrooms, doctors' offices, and clinical product descriptions. Weiss wasn't so sure. She knew she wanted more sales, but her company had been founded on a colorful, family-oriented image. Finally, after Weiss spent months studying where sales came from and the size of the institutional market, she agreed to meet her new president halfway: The catalog would feature both classrooms and its usual home scenes. By doing her own research and keeping an open mind, Weiss was able to stay true to her founding principles while providing her company a route for future growth.[6]

TIP 7

Truly understanding the problem is halfway to the solution.

Really understanding a problem can be complicated and difficult. It often involves talking to multiple people and digging into the numbers. This kind of deep understanding is crucial to solving issues: You can't design a solution for something you don't understand. Sometimes the central issue will be related to people, including people in your own organization. Once you figure this out, you can design an effective (but not always easy) solution.

FROM THE JACK NADEL ARCHIVES

We acquired an advertising agency headquartered in New York City, which was part of a leveraged buyout. One of the reasons it was losing money was its executive expense accounts. The executives' lunch meetings started with three martinis. I spent several hours with the company president explaining how essential it was to reduce the limits on the expense accounts. Then my chief financial officer created a plan of checks and balances. Nothing worked, and it finally dawned on us that the culture and character were almost impossible to change. Reluctantly, we had to close down the operation.

HOW DOES THIS TIP APPLY TODAY?

Lorenzo Thione didn't start out to become the "Netflix of the art world." It happened by accident. The entrepreneur was on a trip to Mexico City to visit an artist friend when he first saw how the art world worked—and he didn't like what he saw. The more he researched the problem, the more he realized that many of the people who purchased art were buying it for all the wrong reasons. He learned that they were approaching art like an investment, instead of looking for pieces they enjoyed. Most of these investors lost money and ended up with art they didn't feel strongly about. Once he understood the problem, he teamed up with a partner to start Artify It, an online subscription service that "rented" fine art pieces to people who loved art but weren't investors. Thione's venture quickly attracted almost $1 million in venture capital funds, thanks to his new spin on an old problem.[7]

TIP 8

The three Rs of business success are Relationships, Results, and Rewards.

The three Rs in education are reading, writing, and arithmetic. Without these basic skills, learning becomes almost impossible. In a similar way, business starts with a relationship. You are then judged by the results. Rewards spring from the results.

FROM THE JACK NADEL ARCHIVES

When President Reagan asked me to join a trade mission to Japan, the objective was to help sell more American products overseas and correct an imbalance in trade. When we met with noted Japanese industrialists, it was clear that building relationships together was the first step in forming any deal. These meetings were highlighted by a luncheon where the president of Sony, Akio Morita, shared a powerful statement with me: "The problem we have with America is that you come over here and want to make a deal. We meet you and want to form a relationship from which we can make many deals." These meetings helped forge closer relationships with our Japanese counterparts, resulting in increased business and greater understanding. Results and rewards were the dividends of forming those relationships.

HOW DOES THIS TIP APPLY TODAY?

Luke Beatty knew he had a good idea: unleash the power of the Internet by letting thousands of "citizen journalists" report and analyze the news. He wasn't so sure how to make it happen—at least until his old roommate urged him to turn his dream into a reality in 2005. His roommate? Tim Armstrong, chairman of AOL. According to Beatty, "When I was scratching out plans to create Associated Content, I also needed to convince myself to quit my job. He was the first person to endorse the idea." You never know which relationship will turn out to be the critical one that leads to results and future rewards. Associated Content was sold to Yahoo! in 2010 for $100 million.[8]

TIP 9

Silence is golden.
Listen, learn, and prosper.

You'll learn much more about a deal with your ears than with your mouth. During a negotiation, really listen to what the other side wants, and then try to deliver it. People will almost always tell you the truth about what they desire; you just have to learn how to recognize it and act on it. In business, your simple mantra should be, "Listen. Think positive. Project energy." Say this at least three times before an important negotiation.

FROM THE JACK NADEL ARCHIVES

One of my better clients was a good-sized manufacturer. As part of my sales presentation, on the first call, I asked him what his biggest problem was. Usually, the answer to this question from that kind of company was "sales" or "I need to develop new products." He looked me in the eye and said, "My biggest problem is safety. We have too many accidents, our insurance costs have gone through the roof, and I personally agonize when one of our workers is severely injured." I presented this customer with a complete safety program that included incentives and special awards for injury-free performance. I was able to help solve his problem. I would never have been successful with this account had I not asked for, and listened to, the client's real problem.

HOW DOES THIS TIP APPLY TODAY?

Today, Dell is known as a powerhouse of social media, but the company took the hard way to get there. In 2005, Dell was the unfortunate subject of an ongoing series of posts by an influential blogger describing his troubles with his Dell computer. Around the same time, a photo of a Dell laptop catching fire went viral. It didn't take long for returning CEO Michael Dell to announce that Dell was jumping into social media with both feet. In just a few short years, Dell launched a number of social media initiatives that turned "ranters" into "ravers," including a social outreach services group that monitors and responds to complaints made via social media. By becoming an active listener, Dell learned how to truly understand customer issues and turn them into valuable profits.[9]

TIP 10

More deals die from sloppy execution than from bad concepts.

Never judge a deal by what people hope or say they'll do—the only thing that really matters is what's in writing. Sloppy execution can lead to misunderstandings and lawsuits, even among close friends and associates. Successful deals happen when everybody knows exactly what to expect and all parties have thought through the details.

FROM THE JACK NADEL ARCHIVES

I once made a deal to manufacture ballpoint pens in China. The factory was slow and late in delivery. Our warehouse was not properly set up to handle this merchandise, even if it had arrived on time. The concept was great but the execution was poor, and the deal died.

HOW DOES THIS TIP APPLY TODAY?

Successful execution isn't everything...it's the *only* thing. The best ideas can easily founder on the rocks of poor execution, bad management, competition, and inflexibility. Think about Microsoft's Zune, an MP3 player introduced in 2006 as a competitor to the iPod. The Zune had features the iPod lacked, like the ability to share music between players. Product developers at Microsoft had overlooked one powerful feature: a captive music store. The Zune wasn't compatible with iTunes, the music store that really drove the iPod's success. In business, you have to plan for the unexpected, prepare for the worst, and hope for the best. As Wharton School of Business professor Lawrence G. Hrebiniak said, "Only recently have people begun to realize that effective execution is a competitive business advantage."[10]

TIP 11

Always confirm your agreements in writing and *quickly.*

There's a saying in business: Invest in haste and lose your money in leisure. Once you've finished a negotiation or a deal, and you're happy with the results, immediately get it in writing. It's also a good idea to preserve notes from conversations and meeting transcripts, and to follow up phone calls with an email confirming what was discussed. Too often, people forget what they've said or agreed to. Keeping a written record protects you and makes sure everybody is on the same page. Having a written agreement can save everyone time, aggravation, and money.

FROM THE JACK NADEL ARCHIVES

We were attempting to buy a large piece of property for our direct-mail plant. When we went to sign the contract, we ran into a conflict. The owner's lawyer tried to renegotiate. I was not interested in renegotiating but had nothing in writing to confirm the terms of the offer. Because I had not immediately confirmed the agreement in writing and received a written confirmation in return, the deal fell apart.

HOW DOES THIS TIP APPLY TODAY?

Young companies are notorious for so-called "gentleman's agreements" and verbal contracts. At the outset of a new company or organization, it's common for partners to think that nothing bad will ever happen. Further, because their young company has no assets anyway, what is there to worry about? So they don't bother with a detailed partnership agreement. What they don't realize is that success can be the bee in a company's bonnet, and can actually undermine the whole arrangement. History is riddled with examples of partnerships that started out great and went sour once a company began making money. Think about Facebook, Microsoft, and too many other "small" businesses to name.

TIP 12

Scale your business plan to fit your ability to finance it. If funds are limited, carry out your plan in stages.

Most small businesses have one overwhelming need: cash to grow. It's better by far to work with what you've got than to bite off more than you can chew. Plan your growth in stages, to match your cash reserves. Slow and steady often wins the race. As you develop a proven track record, it is easier to raise additional funds—making each successive phase of your business plan easier to finance.

FROM THE JACK NADEL ARCHIVES

Most of our catalog sales in direct mail were based on a picture of a single sample of a given product. We did not inventory the merchandise until the sale was made. We simply ordered it after we received orders through the catalog and made sure the delivery time was within the promised window. That way, we never depleted our cash reserves, and we never had an inventory problem.

HOW DOES THIS TIP APPLY TODAY?

The restaurant business is one of the toughest in the world, especially in New York City. Therefore, it is especially important to pay attention to your costs and keep an eye on the road to profit. To see this at work, look no further than the war of two meat vendors in Manhattan. In 2011 and 2012 respectively, Currywurst Bros. and Meatball Obsession opened within blocks of each other. Currywurst Bros. sold currywurst, a German fried pork sausage dish, from a high-priced storefront. Meatball Obsession sold meatballs in a cup from a stall right near a train entrance. Not surprisingly, Currywurst Bros., which had a monthly rent of $16,000, didn't even make it a year before it had to close its doors due to cash-flow problems. Meatball Obsession, meanwhile, was still going strong months after opening—and if sales continue, who knows? The business might just expand to a nearby empty storefront.[11]

TIP 13

Your business should be market driven— not product driven.

Few things can be more frustrating than having a great product that doesn't sell, yet it happens all the time. Plan your business around the market there is, instead of the market you wish existed. If you're not sure about the market, there are plenty of ways to find out. Conduct market research, pay attention to social media, put together a focus group, conduct an online survey, or study your competitors. Great products are not great products if there is no demand for them. Find out what the market needs, and then design a product to meet that need.

FROM THE JACK NADEL ARCHIVES

There was a tremendous demand for ballpoint pens, but most of the instruments were unreliable in the way they wrote or in that a person's signature could be easily transferred to another document. (That is, you could roll your thumb over the original signature and then transfer it to another document.) We were able to partner with Paper Mate on the first reliable pen that bankers officially approved. We got the distribution for the industrial marketplace, where we put the advertiser's copy on the barrel of the pen. When we were able to distribute a reliable product, the demand became huge; thus, we had fantastic sales.

HOW DOES THIS TIP APPLY TODAY?

The owners of Del Mar Racetrack faced a problem, like any horse racing facility in the United States. Their business was dwindling away, steadily losing patrons to other casino options and forms of entertainment. It wasn't the product that had changed but the world around it. According to Craig Dado, who handles marketing for Del Mar Racetrack, the owners decided to do some serious market research. What they found was that older men, racing's traditional audience, weren't as interested in betting on horses anymore, and younger people, especially younger women, had never really been interested in it. So, letting the market drive its business, Del Mar Racetrack launched a major new campaign. They adjusted prices, downplayed the gaming and racing aspects, and launched a new social media campaign. The race club also started featuring younger, hipper bands; microbrews; and gourmet food carts. The market responded. Within a few years, attendance shot up at Del Mar Racetrack, despite a general decline throughout the industry.[12]

TIP 14

A great product is one that sells.

There is no such thing as an artistic success in the world of products. There is only one test. If a product sells and makes a strong return on investment (in both time and money), it is a good one. If it creates a great profit over an extended period, it is a *super* product. The best way to tell if you have a potentially super product is to make a few prototypes and see if you can sell them. Don't set up your whole factory to produce 10,000 units a day without knowing if people will buy them. If you're selling a service, offer it in a small test market—and don't forget to collect feedback whenever possible. Only ramp up production and advertising if the market responds. This will save you money and time and allow you to make adjustments to your offering.

FROM THE JACK NADEL ARCHIVES

There was a need for a flexible measuring tape to measure the inside diameter of oil pipes. I asked a manufacturer of metal measuring tapes to design one that oil workers could use easily in the field. We sold hundreds of thousands of these special tapes to an oil tool manufacturer, imprinted with the company's logo. We turned something ordinary, a tape measure, into a great product with a special application for a unique industry.

HOW DOES THIS TIP APPLY TODAY?

It might have seemed like the last thing the world needed was another brand of bottled water, but thankfully, J. Darius Bikoff disagreed. Bikoff founded Energy Brands in the mid-1990s to produce a line of "enhanced" bottled water called smartwater®. Originally, it was only distributed locally, in health food shops in the New York City area, to test the market. Initial returns were positive, so in the early 2000s, the company expanded its product line to include the now familiar vitaminwater®. In a market overrun with bottled water brands, vitaminwater® was a hit: By 2006, the company was selling $350 million in water annually, and by 2011, it had expanded into overseas markets and become a privately owned subsidiary of the Coca-Cola Company. It just goes to show, there's always room for a great product, even in a crowded marketplace.[13]

TIP 15

If you can't explain your product or service in 30 seconds, you probably can't sell it.

It's called the elevator pitch: If you can describe your idea in the time it takes for an elevator trip, you're halfway to a sale. The best ideas are the simplest to understand, the ones that *any* member of your team can easily explain. They're the kind that make people say, "Oh yeah, of course!" Think of your sales pitch as a text message, not a formal letter. But simplicity is only part of the equation. The idea also has to meet an existing need. So if your new business idea is to sell horse blankets for the mass horse blanket market (which doesn't actually exist), even if you have the best horse blankets, your idea will fail.

FROM THE JACK NADEL ARCHIVES

Make every word count. We were very successful in selling custom jewelry—tie bars, money clips, and key chains—made in the shape of the customer's trademark. It took a lot of time to quote the cost of the stamping dies; however, they averaged $200. We vastly increased the value of the sale by not making this an issue. We charged $200 for every die regardless of its complexity and could sell the idea without the complicated conversation about the cost of the die.

HOW DOES THIS TIP APPLY TODAY?

Robin Chase calls it the "elevator pitch I've given probably close to a thousand times." It goes something like this: Her company, Zipcar, parks cars throughout dense metropolitan areas and university towns. Buyers make an online reservation for a car at a certain place, and the reservation is confirmed wirelessly. When the buyer reaches the car, he or she holds a membership card up to the windshield, and the car automatically unlocks, ready to drive. As Chase says, "It's simple, it's elegant"—and it's the foundation of her start-up company. Does her pitch work? Next time you spot a Zipcar, see if her simple pitch doesn't hop right back to mind.[14]

TIP 16

It's better to sell smart than to sell hard.

Sometimes, there's no alternative to experience. When it comes to sales, the best kind of experience is practical; you just have to get out there and sell. You have to learn who your customer is, because there is no business without a customer. Over time, you'll discover how to recognize the difference between good and bad leads, and you'll be able to talk intelligently about your potential client and their needs. Selling smarter, not harder, works.

FROM THE JACK NADEL ARCHIVES

When banks were using free products as promotional items, customers responded in huge numbers by putting their savings accounts where they could get the best premiums. Our bank customers were amazed that we knew more about their industry regulations than they did. We invested the time to research the regulations so that banks could do business with us and have full confidence that our work conformed to the banking industry's rules. At that time, banks offered a specific gift with the opening of an account of $1,000 or more. But those gifts had to cost the bank less than $2.50 each. We sold them gifts that conformed to banking regulations and opened the most accounts.

HOW DOES THIS TIP APPLY TODAY?

Here's a good problem: There's too much premium wine in the world. It turns out that the world's finest vineyards regularly produce too many grapes and end up with "extra" top-shelf fruit. What to do with this surplus? Enter Cameron Hughes and his wife, Jessica Kogan, owners of Cameron Hughes Wine. Instead of growing their own grapes and trying to compete with established vineyards in a crowded market, they had a novel idea. They would buy the leftover grapes from some of the world's best vineyards and sell the final product as private-label wine. To protect their sources, they agreed not to blend the wines or identify where the grapes came from. Instead, their wines would be labeled only with a lot number and region. It's up to wine drinkers to decide if they hit it lucky with a world-famous wine or not. By selling a little smarter, Hughes and Kogan have really squeezed the most from their business: They sold a reported 400,000 cases in 2011.[15]

TIP 17

Perceived value is what sells.
Real value is what repeats.

You may have heard the expression, "Sell the sizzle, not the steak." With all due respect to old sales wisdom, you'd be better off selling the sizzle *and* the steak. Solid, long-term businesses are built on great products and services, as well as repeat customers. Be careful not to oversell your product or service—let people know how your offering will really meet their needs, and then make sure it delivers. This is how you'll create customers for a lifetime.

FROM THE JACK NADEL ARCHIVES

As mentioned previously, for years we manufactured ballpoint pens. The outside look of the pen was what caught the customer's attention and made the sale. But when we developed the best refill in the world, with the greatest writing quality, the reorders came pouring in. Your product may look good, but it has to work great.

HOW DOES THIS TIP APPLY TODAY?

Imagine the throaty growl of a motorcycle on the highway. If you're like many people, chances are you just conjured up the sound of a Harley-Davidson, a uniquely American motorcycle with such a distinctive sound that company officials once tried to trademark it. (They dropped the effort in 2000.) Besides its motorcycles, Harley-Davidson is known for one of the great turnarounds in American business. Throughout the 1990s and the first decade of the 2000s, Harley-Davidson went from a company on the rocks to a branding icon—all while spending a fraction of its annual budget on advertising. How? By selling a distinctive product with a great reputation and cultivating long-term relationships with its die-hard fans.[16]

TIP 18

Don't let your ego get in the way.

There's nothing quite as exciting as a new idea—especially when you're convinced the idea is worth a million bucks (or more). But watch out! Great ideas are rarely born fully formed, and a new idea is like a two-year-old. It's loud, it's self-centered, and it's completely without perspective. Good business means stepping back and letting the ego naturally deflate out of your million-dollar idea until you can see it for what it really is, with its strengths *and* weaknesses. In fact, learn to watch out for ego in all its forms. Good business leaders are guided by reality and actual profit, not empty volume, slick campaigns, and their own brilliance. Bounce your idea off trusted advisors who will give you the straight story.

FROM THE JACK NADEL ARCHIVES

Before the advent of digital watches, we were presented with the Watch Band Calendar, an aluminum tab with a calendar of the month that wrapped around the wristband. I really didn't like the product but, because of my relationship with the person selling it, I sent it to my salespeople. I was shocked by the orders we received, and ultimately, this product, which I did not originally like, was one of the most profitable products we ever sold. Twenty-two million Watch Band Calendars later, I learned to love this super product!

HOW DOES THIS TIP APPLY TODAY?

Michael J. Fox made the DeLorean famous in *Back to the Future*, but this sports car is famous among businesspeople for another reason. The DeLorean was created by John DeLorean, a renegade auto exec who reportedly walked away from a huge salary to create his signature automobile. It featured a stainless-steel body, Italian styling, and gull-wing doors. If the news reports are true, DeLorean made one very basic error: He fell in love with his idea at the expense of his business. Plagued by production problems and runaway expenses, he refused to change course (a classic ego-driven mistake). The DeLorean Motor Company crashed and burned, relegating the famous sports car to the could-have pile of great ideas that just didn't work.[17]

TIP 19

Subcontracting is the cheapest form of manufacturing.

If you don't already own a factory, now is *not* the time to build one. The truth is, someone, somewhere, already has just the right plant to manufacture your product. Even if you don't sell products, there are companies that contract out business support services like secretarial, invoicing, fulfillment, and warehousing. All you have to do is find your suppliers and let *them* be the experts in their area, so you can concentrate on *your* area. In the end, most consumers won't care where your product is made or who is handling your invoicing. Traditionally, customers value quality and price above all else. While it may be politically correct to manufacture locally, for the majority of businesses operating today, doing so is usually a better marketing practice than business decision.

FROM THE JACK NADEL ARCHIVES

For every product, we sought a company with the right equipment to turn out what we needed. When we decided to develop metal-barrel ballpoint pens that looked like jewelry, we discovered that lipstick manufacturers could make this item for us with the equipment and personnel they already had. As Sherlock Holmes would say, "It's elementary." Look at a ballpoint pen and ask who would make something similar; the answer is a lipstick manufacturer.

HOW DOES THIS TIP APPLY TODAY?

It might sound like a comedy routine, but sometimes it pays to outsource your lawyer. At least this is what David Galbenski, founder of Contract Counsel, hoped. Contract Counsel specialized in providing temporary lawyer services to individuals and firms who needed legal help on a contract basis. By the middle of the first decade of the 2000s, revenue was flattening, and Galbenski and his partners were worried. That's when the idea hit him: He could outsource the grunt work—discoveries, managing documents—to service firms in India. His partners were skeptical at first. What about the language difficulties? How would lawyers in other countries know U.S. law? But Galbenski and Contract Counsel forged ahead, and within a few years, Contract Counsel had morphed into Lumen Legal, with offices in 19 U.S. markets and two locations in India.[18]

TIP 20

Build a better mousetrap, and the world will beat a path to your door...as long as you have a good marketing plan.

If you don't believe marketing and branding work, think quickly: What company uses the slogan "I'm lovin' it"? Quality is essential, execution is critical, and positive word-of-mouth can work wonders, but don't neglect your marketing budget (even if you can only afford a few targeted Internet ads). Nobody will buy your wonderful product if they haven't heard about it, and advertising is one of the oldest and most effective ways to get the word out. As a final note, don't advertise just for the sake of it. Meet your customers where they live, meaning target your marketing and advertising efforts carefully, and make sure to track leads so that every marketing dollar is spent wisely. (P.S. The company is McDonald's...odds are, you've heard of them.)

FROM THE JACK NADEL ARCHIVES

We created a great employee-incentive program for a client. In order for the program to be successful, the client needed to continually publicize it to its employees. The client said, "The program is so good it cannot fail." But the client failed to "sell" the program, by not properly explaining its benefits. The program did not have a chance because it was not properly marketed, and nobody understood it.

When I retired in 1993 from day-to-day management of the company, I wanted all of our employees to put out a super effort in their daily routine. I felt that stock ownership would motivate them, and I sold two-thirds of my stock as an ESOP, employee stock ownership program, at a ridiculously low price. As time went on, I felt the company was not publicizing this program enough. We were actually giving people stock at no cost to motivate them and improve the value of the stock. When

I realized this was not really incentivizing the employees, the company bought back the stock that the employees had received at no cost. Most of the employees were stunned to get a payment far greater than they thought the stock was worth. This was a communication failure; our employees had not realized the strength, security, and potential of owning the stock, because the company had not properly communicated these benefits.

HOW DOES THIS TIP APPLY TODAY?

In 2009, the international hairdressing company TONI&GUY had an opportunity to gain some visibility for its brand: Company co-founder and CEO Toni Mascolo was getting ready to accept the Officer of the Order of the British Empire (OBE) honor for his contribution to the hairdressing industry in Great Britain. While the award was nice, the company set its sights on bigger fish, namely raising the company's international profile as a successful English company that had gone global. To accomplish this, TONI&GUY enlisted all the instruments in the modern marketer's toolbox, including targeting specific journalists with story ideas and news items, publishing media releases, and implementing a social media campaign that pushed the key message. The result? Broad coverage by newspapers, magazines, and television stations around the world for both Toni Mascolo and the company he runs. The message? Look for opportunities to promote yourself, and don't hesitate to think big.[19]

TIP 21

Ask not how many people your advertising reaches, ask how many people it sells.

The first rule of advertising is to know who your customers are. The second rule is to reach them. There's no question that advertising can be effective, but the business world is awash with options. Print? Broadcast? Internet? Which is the best for your company? One of the smartest ways to design your ad campaign is to first create a "perfect customer" profile. Then request media kits from potential advertising outlets. Media kits vary from channel to channel, but they all serve the same purpose—to educate potential advertisers about the reach of the medium and the general demographics of the audience. This powerful information can mean the difference between a successful advertising campaign and a flop.

FROM THE JACK NADEL ARCHIVES

This is more than just a single story. Our entire business was built on the premise of selective advertising—reaching only people who were genuine prospects for what our clients had to sell. If you consider the entire world of advertising, with its various channels reaching a wide range of demographics, the only products that really pay for themselves are those that everybody needs, such as food, soap, toothpaste, etc.

One of the best campaigns we ever ran was soliciting sales for the Apple computer in Apple's very early days (the early 1980s). We were able to target a particular demographic and send out a direct-mail offer within a two-mile radius of every Apple retail dealer. The results were phenomenal. Apple's target was to sell 10,000 computers, and they sold more than 100,000! The cost of the campaign was very low, as the percentage of sales was high due to the specific targeting of potential buyers.

HOW DOES THIS TIP APPLY TODAY?

Today's media landscape is more fragmented than ever—which makes doing good research that much more important. When Microsoft rolled out its Internet search engine, Bing, it knew it needed a gold-plated ad campaign that cut across many types of media. Yet before it placed any ads, the tech giant went deep with its customer research. It first identified the "ideal user" who would switch to Bing from the rival search engine, Google. In the United States, about 80 percent of all Web searches are conducted by 20 percent of surfers. These were the people Microsoft wanted. So the company conducted TV and Internet research to find out where these heavy users "lived," and then designed an ad campaign that targeted those media outlets and programs—whether they were online, print, or broadcast. In the end, Microsoft increased the effectiveness of its ad buy by about 25 percent by focusing on the consumer it wanted to reach instead of on the marketing channel.[20]

TIP 22

The marketing program that worked in the past may not fly today.

Marketing used to be a fairly simple proposition...you developed a great product and then made the media buy from the newspaper, magazine, radio station, or television show in your targeted demographic. Today, however, the world of marketing has exploded. Traditional advertising venues have been augmented by specialty advertising, multichannel marketing, Internet marketing, guerilla marketing, conferences and online webinars, and even mobile marketing on tablets and smartphones. But knowing that these outlets are available and designing the right campaign are two different things. So don't fall for the latest marketing trend. Instead, if you focus on knowing your customers and figuring out how to reach them, you can't go wrong.

FROM THE JACK NADEL ARCHIVES

In 1953, the largest company in the sales promotion business featured exclusive calendars. Promotional calendars included everything from Norman Rockwell pictures to special information about specific dates. Today there is no need to hang a calendar on a wall and, in most cases, no wall space on which to hang it. The computer makes the old-fashioned calendar obsolete. Jack Nadel International never depended on a particular item. Ideas that mean business never go out of style.

HOW DOES THIS TIP APPLY TODAY?

No matter how your company approaches marketing, keep this fundamental rule in mind: Word of mouth works. In fact, word of mouth may be the single most powerful form of endorsement your product or service can earn. This is one area where the Internet shines. According to Nielsen's Global Trust in Advertising study, up to 70 percent of consumers trust online opinions—that's more than trust the newspaper! This is exactly what the famed entertainment company Cirque du Soleil was hoping to tap into with its pre-release campaign for *LOVE*, its show featuring the music of the Beatles. The company hoped to spark word of mouth by harnessing a traditional PR campaign—featuring enthusiastic customers—to modern social media. Happy customers soon flooded carefully chosen forums like message boards and chat rooms. Amazingly, later analysis showed that 42 percent of the people encountered in this word-of-mouth campaign said they were interested in purchasing tickets.[21]

TIP 23

A good deal is only good if it is good for everybody.

Shifty dealing may make for good television and movies, but in real life, good deals are good for everybody, and bad deals—in the long run—are often bad for everybody. There's nothing wrong with a tough negotiation. At the end of the day, if both parties feel that they are walking away winning something, it will create the opportunity for future deals and future business. Business is not a zero-sum game. Have you heard the expression, "A rising tide lifts all boats"? It's true in business also—successful relationships beget more success.

FROM THE JACK NADEL ARCHIVES

As you read in "The Adventure Continues…," I made a licensing deal with Pierre Cardin in 1979. I needed a glamorous brand name for ballpoint pens that we were manufacturing in France. After we negotiated the license agreement with Cardin, he designed the pens carrying his name. He benefited by gaining a completely new and reliable income stream from a royalty on every pen sold, and we were able to manufacture and advertise a quality, designer-name product. Our distributors had an exciting new pen to sell that marked the first volume entry of a designer brand into the advertising pen business. The deal was good for everybody.

HOW DOES THIS TIP APPLY TODAY?

Yahoo! was an Internet pioneer, but in 2008, its CEO, Jerry Yang, made what some say was one of the worst business decisions ever. He turned down a 44.6-billion-dollar buyout offer from Microsoft. Yahoo! shareholders have been regretting this ever since. Why did Yang turn down the offer? In part because he believed he could negotiate a slightly better offer than what was on the table. A year later, shares were selling at a third of their former value. Sometimes you can drive a deal right off a cliff.[22]

TIP 24

Find ways to agree as early as you can in a negotiation.

Too often, negotiations are described in the same terms as warfare. Good negotiations are not battles; there are no hostages or innocent victims. Instead, the best negotiations start from a positive space, with both parties looking to conclude a piece of business in terms that are favorable to both of them. A negotiation should end on a positive note, as well. It's almost impossible to underestimate the power of a simple gesture or small gift at the conclusion of a successful negotiation. It creates enormous goodwill, and it's a classy move to show your appreciation at the end of a business deal.

FROM THE JACK NADEL ARCHIVES

Offering an extra incentive can often seal the deal. In 1957, when Japanese manufacturing had a reputation for poor quality, we made a deal with a Japanese manufacturer to produce a large quantity of high-quality stainless-steel flatware. After negotiating the best deal we could, I offered the Japanese manufacturer a 10 percent bonus if he delivered on his promise of a high-quality product. He was amazed, as no one had ever offered him a premium for quality. Traditionally, negotiations for merchandise in Japan were like combat. At that time, Japan was the go-to low-cost producer, and every customer fought for the lowest price possible. By offering the manufacturer a bonus for quality, I gave him a way to deliver that quality and still make money. I am convinced that by giving the Japanese something extra, we were able to produce a better product and even generate a little extra profit for the manufacturer, which is the best incentive in the world.

HOW DOES THIS TIP APPLY TODAY?

Talk about a negotiation that seemed like a potential win/lose situation: Sarah Talley, only 19 years old, entered into negotiations to sell her family farm's produce (pumpkins and melons) to Walmart, one of the biggest corporations in the world and a famously tough negotiator. But Talley had one powerful advantage—her attitude. Instead of viewing the negotiation as an opportunity to get pushed around by Walmart, she looked for ways to successfully partner with the much larger company. She showed the Walmart team how her company had cut costs by using old school buses instead of tractors to deliver product and how Frey Farms would be willing to manage inventory levels and sales in exchange for a highly coveted co-management agreement. In the end, the negotiation was a win all the way around, for Frey Farms, Walmart, and even Walmart's customers.[23]

TIP 25

An agreement is only as good as the people involved.

We talk about the importance of contracts—and they are important—but there's something else behind contracts that matters even more. People. If you sign a contract with a person of good character, problems are much less likely. Because when you get down to it, there's no such thing as an ironclad contract. There will always be a skilled lawyer who can shred the best one. So deal with good people, and don't be afraid to investigate their business record and character (for example, by conducting a background check or simply paying attention to their reputation). If you find out that your negotiating partner makes deals in bad faith, or if you feel like you're being swindled in a contract negotiation, don't be afraid to walk away. You can't regret a mistake you didn't make.

FROM THE JACK NADEL ARCHIVES

I was introduced to a pen manufacturer who had a shady reputation but gave me a very low price on a large quantity of pens. The specifications called for metal refills—plastic refills were available at a lower price. The pens were drop-shipped to our customers. One day, someone gave me one of those pens and, lo and behold, it had a plastic refill. That was the manufacturer's last order from us. When an individual has a shady reputation, he or she has usually earned it. This became an opportunity for a lesson learned…the net result of the transaction was that I was able to negotiate the same price with a reputable manufacturer because I could guarantee a huge quantity. I also confirmed the new manufacturer's veracity by spot-checking the merchandise sent to my customers.

HOW DOES THIS TIP APPLY TODAY?

Unfortunately, we live in a time of rapidly deteriorating trust in public and private institutions. The Business Roundtable, a leading association of CEOs and corporations, said in a 2009 report that widespread public distrust in business was hurting companies throughout the entire U.S. economy. Although it might not seem like one business can do much to change this perception, in fact, it can. First, you can always approach business from a place of integrity yourself. Second, you can hold your business partners to a high standard. Don't be afraid to check references and then make your decisions.[24]

TIP 26

Confront problems squarely.
They won't just go away.

Nobody ever succeeded in business by sticking his or her head in the sand and pretending a problem didn't exist. Conversely, plenty of businesses have gotten into hot water or even failed completely by ignoring a problem until it's too late to fix it. No one knows your business as well as you do, so if your gut is telling you that something just isn't right, listen to it. Dig into the problem, and take action to fix it, even if it means asking for help. Just like the little boy with his finger in the dike, you can hold back a catastrophe for only so long—unless you're willing to start over and even build a new dam.

FROM THE JACK NADEL ARCHIVES

A major issue at a meeting of our board of directors was the salaries of company officers and how they related to each other. There were easier issues on the agenda, but I started the meeting with the statement that the salary problem had to be resolved before anything else was discussed. It wasn't easy, but it was finalized at the beginning of the meeting, and we were able to proceed with other items.

HOW DOES THIS TIP APPLY TODAY?

The "Our Pizza Sucks" campaign launched by Domino's illustrates how truthfulness and transparency can triumph. In 2011, Domino's CEO Patrick Doyle perceived widespread customer dissatisfaction through complaints posted via social media channels like Facebook, so he decided to solicit criticism online and in person. Words like "flavorless," "cardboard crusts," and "processed cheese" were frequently mentioned. In response, Domino's ran a series of national ads that admitted its pizzas were inferior and explained how dozens of cheeses, sauces, and crust seasonings were being tested in various combinations to find a superior-tasting product. Doyle closed his ads with a pledge: "We're going to learn; we're going to get better. I guarantee it." And that's exactly what they did. By getting out ahead of the problem and fixing it sooner rather than later, Domino's introduced higher-quality pizzas, store sales increased, and quarterly profits doubled.[25]

TIP 27

A mistake made once is human.
A mistake made twice is stupid.

You've probably heard Albert Einstein's famous definition of insanity: doing the same thing over and over and expecting different results. In business, this means that making a mistake once is normal—all part of the risk of enterprise—but making the same mistake again signals a deeper problem. There are two main issues when it comes to mistakes. The first is companies that don't allow them, because this stifles the risk-taking behavior that business thrives on. The second is companies that refuse to see mistakes as teaching moments and instead double down on failed strategies and policies. Rest assured, those companies won't be making the same mistakes for long...they'll be out of business.

FROM THE JACK NADEL ARCHIVES

We started a profit-sharing program with our employees in the early days of Jack Nadel International. The idea was to invest the money to bring the greatest return while protecting the investment. Our chief financial officer one day boasted to me that we were getting a ridiculously high return of 15 percent on our investment. I wanted to know what investment was bringing such a high return. He said with a big smile that we were buying Mexican treasury bonds. I turned pale as I ordered him to get out of them immediately, since I did not trust that specific economy or government. He claimed that no one had ever lost any money on those bonds and asserted that since he was the CFO, it was his responsibility. One month later, the Mexican government devalued the peso, which resulted in an immediate loss of 40 percent of our investment. I should have fired him on the spot, but he remained in the position for years. When he was finally terminated, I was faced with an unlawful termination suit. The moral here is don't make the same mistake twice—trust your gut.

In retrospect, I realize why I responded so dramatically to the loss of employees' money on what I considered to be a speculative investment. I had anticipated the problem when I found out the investment was made. My instincts were correct, and the unfortunate loss was totally unnecessary. The reality is that bad news is usually not an orphan—it has a lot of company. You cannot expect a person who exhibits poor judgment and a lack of responsibility to change.

HOW DOES THIS TIP APPLY TODAY?

There was no question that Ben Cohen was already a successful businessman when he decided to launch a new company called Community Products, Inc., in the mid-1990s. You'd probably recognize Cohen as the "Ben" in Ben & Jerry's. But Community Products was a different kind of enterprise—it was designed as a socially aware company first, and a business concern second. According to Cohen's vision, Community Products would pour more than half of its profits into worthy causes, pay above-market rates for environmentally safe products, and otherwise be a good corporate citizen. This all sounded fine on paper and attracted gobs of great press. The reality was something different, however. From the first months, there were problems with pricing and with suppliers, some of whom made shipments of "rainforest safe" nuts with spent shell casings and cigarette butts in them. Instead of learning from the company's mistakes, Cohen and his management team dug in and stuck to their original idea long after it was apparent it was no longer working—right up until the company folded after just a few years.[26]

TIP 28

Is it urgent, or is it an emergency?

In medicine, an emergency is something that must be taken care of now, immediately, before it kills you. Urgent, on the other hand, describes what you might feel if you were very thirsty or needed to use the bathroom. See the difference? The same distinction applies in business: An emergency threatens the lifeblood of your business, while an urgent issue must be resolved but will not drive you into bankruptcy. The mistake many managers and entrepreneurs make is treating everything like an emergency. There's no better way to burn out your staff (and even yourself) than by responding to every issue that arises as if your entire enterprise depends on it. Learn to recognize the real severity of an issue and respond accordingly. You might just be saving your company's life.

FROM THE JACK NADEL ARCHIVES

The largest order I received in 1954 was from a major swimsuit manufacturer. We had helped them to develop a promotional product for women, which (as you may remember) we called Sun Lashes. Sun Lashes shielded the user's eyes from the sun without the need to wear sunglasses. I closed the sale by convincing management that there was nothing in the product that could be patented, and the word was out to enough people that any company could copy it. Therefore, it became urgent that the product get to the marketplace as quickly as possible. After giving me a huge purchase order (PO), the president of the company looked me in the eye and said, "You received this order now because you had a tremendous sense of urgency without saying that it was an emergency."

HOW DOES THIS TIP APPLY TODAY?

If you offer a product, here's a great idea to help your customers decide whether their need is an emergency or merely urgent: Provide the option of a rush fee for faster delivery. Companies like Amazon already do this successfully, by making overnight delivery available. The idea is that money talks volumes about urgency. If people are willing to plunk down the extra dollars to receive their item the next day, clearly they are dealing with a high-priority situation. By giving your customers control over their own priorities, you're offering them a valuable service—and in the case of a true emergency, maybe even helping them save their business.

TIP 29

A good accountant is not just a scorekeeper.

Accountants sometimes get a bad rap as boring number-crunchers, but nothing could be further from the truth. Your accountant can be one of your most powerful allies. As your business grows and becomes more complex, your accountant can help you track costs; produce the necessary statements and returns for creditors, the IRS, and banks; and even save you money by streamlining your business. So find a good accountant early and take advantage of his or her expertise. Also remember: Accountants, just like lawyers, are paid by the hour, so when you visit yours, have your questions written down and keep the exchange focused on the matters at hand. After all, you're paying for it, and that's something your accountant will surely understand!

FROM THE JACK NADEL ARCHIVES

When I interviewed my present accountant about income taxes, he said that overly aggressive accountants may save clients a lot of money in the beginning but may cost them much more through accounting practices that do not follow the letter of the law. I told him that I was willing to pay whatever taxes were due and did not want to take questionable deductions. The good news is that I have not had a tax conflict of any kind.

HOW DOES THIS TIP APPLY TODAY?

You don't need to look very far to find examples of why accountants matter. In late 2008, the global financial industry was rocked by the news that Lehman Brothers, Inc., one of the world's largest investment houses, was going bankrupt. No doubt, every business owner remembers this event: It signaled the beginning of the global financial meltdown that consumed the next two years. When the whole story was told, it turned out that the collapse of Lehman Brothers wasn't due just to bad investments but also to bad accounting. Investigators

realized that Lehman had been using accounting tricks to hide trou-
bled assets, and the firm's accountant, Ernst & Young, had knowingly
certified false financial reports. The accounting company ended up
in multiple lawsuits. Of course, very few of us will ever be as large
as Lehman Brothers, but the lesson is the same: Good accounting is
good business.[27]

TIP 30

The three Ps: Process and Policy lead to Profit.

In some ways, running a successful business is a bit like coaching a football team. The fundamentals of football are blocking and tackling. The fundamentals of a business are its governing policies and processes. To carry out the metaphor, touchdowns are profits. The best business idea in the world cannot survive bad execution. So when you sit down to develop your workflow, internal policies, and business structure, be merciless, probe for weaknesses, and assume that the worst will happen. It probably won't, but you'll never regret being prepared. At this time, you might develop an employee handbook, define salary policies and spending authority, and even establish how management of the company will be structured and fostered.

FROM THE JACK NADEL ARCHIVES

When we purchased a pen factory in New York City in 1970, it took a lot of analysis because our biggest-volume product was writing instruments. We knew that by manufacturing the pens, we could make the manufacturer's profit in addition to the distributor's profit for all of the business that we controlled. The process (the first P) was to closely examine all of the factors and, through calculation and understanding, assess the risk as well as the reward. Our goals were to determine how much additional profit we could make and to expand our own capacity to serve by controlling manufacturing. The product was the ballpoint pen and all its permutations; I had the idea to add a highlighter to the opposite end of the pen, etc. The policy (the second P) was to establish this division under a totally separate name, the Everlast Pen Company, so that it had its own character and the pens could be sold to other distributors, as well. The profit (the third P), of course, was realized by doing all of these steps successfully.

HOW DOES THIS TIP APPLY TODAY?

Zingerman's Delicatessen is an Ann Arbor, Michigan, tradition, but it has attracted attention for more than just its corned beef on rye. The legendary deli has one of the most interesting employee handbooks to be found anywhere. Employee handbooks are notoriously dull, which is a problem because they are where you spell out your company's procedures and policies. If employees don't read your handbook, you can hardly expect them to support the policies you worked so hard to create. So Zingerman's applied some of its marketing principles to its handbook—which is one that employees actually read and refer to according to Maggie Bayless, who handles training for the deli. It features cartoons, funny anecdotes, and the trademark Zingerman's wit, all while effectively communicating the company's vision, philosophy, and operating principles.[28]

TIP 31

The meeting doesn't end when the meeting ends.

Ask a group of office workers about the biggest productivity killers, and they're likely to mention endless meetings. This is because many businesspeople—even some very successful ones—don't use meetings correctly. A good meeting is a focused, efficient, and streamlined opportunity to get things in motion. The best meetings are beginning points—the real progress is made *after* the meeting. Increase your company's productivity and communication by using your meeting time well: Set a clear agenda ahead of time, chart progress, keep meeting notes, send a meeting synopsis to attendees, and make sure everybody involved clearly understands what is expected of them as a result of the meeting. Without follow-through, a to-do list is simply a list.

FROM THE JACK NADEL ARCHIVES

It seems that there are no simple deals anymore. After any business meeting, particularly when a deal has been discussed, it is important to document the conclusions. One of the most important deals I ever made was for the leveraged buyout of my former company and several other companies in the same division of the public company I was working for. Our negotiations did not end until 9:00 p.m.

I had anticipated that this might happen and kept my secretary waiting in the reception area so we could document the deal as soon as it was made. Memory has a habit of distorting the facts, so urgency is important in these situations.

HOW DOES THIS TIP APPLY TODAY?

Remote meetings can be very effective. Today's videoconferencing technology makes it possible to conduct face-to-face meetings across the country or even the globe just as easily as placing a phone call. Whether it's a remote sales call or a gathering of partners in different cities, a remote meeting can be recorded, and attendees can plug their computers into the meeting interface for presentations. So the next time you're contemplating a conference call, it might pay to research remote meeting software and take advantage of the incredible power of modern communications. It's a good bet that your competitors have added this layer of efficiency to their operations.

TIP 32

Try to settle all disputes out of court.

You do not want to end up in court. It's that simple. For the vast majority of businesses, time spent on lawsuits and in court is time lost for production, sales, marketing, and all the things that make a business successful. This means you should keep your lawyer informed about everything that's going on in your business. If you have any reason to suspect that you are vulnerable to a lawsuit, tell your lawyer everything (you needn't worry about "leaking" damaging information—lawyer/client privilege will protect you). An informed lawyer can help you make decisions that will keep you out of court and in the office or factory, where you belong.

FROM THE JACK NADEL ARCHIVES

We caught a warehouse foreman stealing from the company. Confronted with the proof, he admitted his guilt. We fired him but did not bring any charges. Six months later, he sued us for unlawful termination. We turned to our insurance company, which promptly settled with him, paying him $10,000 to withdraw his lawsuit. When we questioned the insurance company's payout, we were told that while the former employee was guilty, it would have cost $30,000 to defend the lawsuit.

HOW DOES THIS TIP APPLY TODAY?

For a large, deep-pocketed corporation, a lawsuit can be a very expensive nuisance. For a small business, a lawsuit can be an existential threat, whether it's for negligence, labor issues, or patent protection—like what happened to football helmet and pad maker Schutt Sports, which was repeatedly sued for patent infringement until it finally closed its doors. There is no way to completely protect your company against lawsuits, including frivolous ones from people looking to cash in. That doesn't mean you shouldn't take every precaution. An ounce of legal protection is worth a pound of lawsuits.[29]

TIP 33

Taking a partner is like getting married.

The decision to take on a partner has to be made with great care. It is a *business* marriage, and separating from a business partner can be just as costly and painful as a real divorce. You may not love, honor, and cherish your business partner, but you better make sure that you trust and respect him or her, and that he or she is serving an irreplaceable function in the company. The best partnerships are calculated risks that bring greater rewards than both partners could achieve alone.

FROM THE JACK NADEL ARCHIVES

When I created a new but very important company, I included the financial officer as a partner, thinking it would be better for the company. I have since learned that professional people, accountants, and lawyers are very happy if you pay them a generous salary; you do not have to make them partners. As it turned out, the inevitable separation was painful, and like most divorces, a good deal of money was spent on lawyers. In addition to the cost, there was a great deal of aggravation.

HOW DOES THIS TIP APPLY TODAY?

It might be hard to imagine now, but the company that would become one of the largest medical device manufacturers in the world started as an odd-couple partnership. In its early days, Boston Scientific, maker of minimally invasive medical technologies, was run by John Abele, a technology visionary who clearly saw the potential in minimally invasive medicine but wasn't plugged into the world of finance. Before long, Abele brought in Peter Nicholas, who was every bit the corporate-chieftain-in-waiting that Abele was not. Nicholas understood finance and the tools used to capitalize and grow a business. With Abele scouting and developing products, and Nicholas arranging financing and acquisitions, the pair eventually built their basement company into a global leader in the medical business, with almost $8 billion in revenue in 2011.[30]

TIP 34

Good planning often beats out hard work.

You've probably heard the age-old expression, "Work smarter, not harder." In today's complex working world, there are more opportunities for chaos than ever before. There's nothing wrong with hard work—most entrepreneurs are used to working hard—but you should always look for ways to simplify your efforts and take the straightest path from point A to point B.

FROM THE JACK NADEL ARCHIVES

A simple process, like thoughtfully planning in-person sales calls, can save a great deal of time and increase efficiency. A salesman once complained to me that he was working too hard. I reviewed the sales calls he was making and found that he was driving great distances between them. By simply planning better around geography, he increased his sales by over 100 percent.

HOW DOES THIS TIP APPLY TODAY?

Perhaps the most famous example of successful planning in recent history comes out of Detroit, where U.S. manufacturers faced an existential threat in the 1980s. Long used to unrivaled supremacy in the automobile business, the "Big Three" of Chrysler, Ford, and General Motors were blindsided when Japanese manufacturers came in with cars that were not only cheaper but of much higher quality. American consumers flocked to the new imports, triggering serious soul-searching in Detroit. It turned out the Japanese had enthusiastically adopted the management techniques pioneered by manufacturing guru W. Edwards Deming, who laid the groundwork for just in time (JIT) production and total quality management (TQM). Over the next 20 years, U.S. car companies redesigned and retooled their factories, and by the 2000s, they were once again producing cars that were competitive in both quality and price.[31]

TIP 35

Stay loose and be able to pivot on a dime.

The only constant in business is change. If you don't believe it, ask a manufacturer of buggy whips. Business today is moving at whiplash speed. Technologies are always evolving. Regulations are forever changing. The competitive landscape is global, so a good idea can rocket into your market from Brazil, India, or South Korea and change everything in the blink of an eye. The only way to survive the onslaught of change is to learn how to roll with it. Remember that a blade of grass is much more likely to survive a hurricane unscathed than the biggest and toughest of old trees.

FROM THE JACK NADEL ARCHIVES

I once sold 10,000 small screwdrivers to an electrical supply company with its name imprinted on them. The name, Associated Wholesale Electric Company, was too long to fit on the miniature screwdriver, so we condensed it. Immediately after delivery, I received a phone call from the customer, who was outraged. "Did you see that imprint?" he demanded. Upon pulling out the sample, there it was: "Ass. Whole Electric Co." I laughed out loud at the shorthand used for the company's name. "What a break!" I told him. "Everyone will notice that imprint instead of ignore it. You are buying advertising." The customer began with a demand that I take the screwdrivers back...instead he kept them and followed up with two more orders specifying that exact imprint.

HOW DOES THIS TIP APPLY TODAY?

January 2012 marked a cautionary milestone in business history. That was the month Eastman Kodak Company filed for bankruptcy. For more than a century, Kodak had been one of the most storied names in American industry. The company had pioneered instamatic cameras and, at one time, completely dominated the photography industry. In an ironic twist of fate, it was one of Kodak's own inventions that eventually drove the company to its knees: the digital camera. Kodak invented the modern digital camera, but because the device didn't use film—and Kodak made so much money selling film—the company neglected its own invention and never worked to build its digital camera product. Other companies were happy to take up the slack, and within a decade, digital cameras had overtaken the consumer photography market. Kodak, which was too slow to recognize this tectonic shift and unable to adapt to changing circumstances in time, was forced to close its doors.[32]

TIP 36

Do not resist change. Moving forward is always better than moving backward.

Businesses don't stay flat for long. They either grow or decline, adapt or die. While it's important to develop sound processes and programs, it's equally vital to constantly review your business, looking for signs of complacency, inefficiency, or a potentially dangerous status quo. Then, once you've identified where your business is stagnating, you can look for ways to update and streamline your products, procedures, or services. Businesses that change with the times are the ones that last.

FROM THE JACK NADEL ARCHIVES

Our bookkeeper could never get her work done within the eight-hour workday. So I asked her, "What is your most time-consuming operation?" She answered, "Checking credit. For every new order, I check the purchaser's bank and two trade references by phone." I asked how many accounts she had rejected for bad credit in the past year. She answered, "None." "Okay," I said, "from now on, do not check credit for orders under $500. Just automatically approve them without examination." The result: We suffered no credit loss, and the bookkeeper was able to complete all of her work without overtime.

HOW DOES THIS TIP APPLY TODAY?

When he worked at Hallmark, Gordon MacKenzie probably had the strangest business cards in corporate America. They read, "Creative Paradox." You might not think of the greeting card business as fast-moving and full of breathless innovation, but MacKenzie would have disagreed. In the 1990s, instead of joining senior management, MacKenzie convinced his bosses at Hallmark to let him open a new department under his control. He outfitted the department with roll-top desks and retro stained glass, and he called it the Humor Workshop. His department's job was simple: come up with better greeting cards outside of the corporate bureaucracy. And they did—launching greeting card lines that would help propel Hallmark into the 2000s. It just goes to show, no matter what business you're in, flexibility is always important.[33]

TIP 37

The harder I work, the luckier I get.

With all due respect to lottery winners, good luck is sometimes described as the intersection of opportunity and effort. The idea here is simple: People are often "lucky" because they work hard to put themselves in the right place at the right time and then take advantage of the opportunities that show up. If it seems like good luck comes from the outside, that's only coincidence—in reality, it's usually more about persevering, keeping your eyes open for good opportunities, and planning carefully. Good reputations aren't created by magic; they are earned. This isn't to say some people aren't really lucky, but even a lottery winner has to buy a ticket.

FROM THE JACK NADEL ARCHIVES

When I merged my company into Republic Corp., a New York Stock Exchange company, we became a division of the parent company and, as you read, I was kept on as the general manager of that division. During the next four years, I worked diligently and propelled the company to be one of the best-earning divisions. We measured our percentage of profit on sales and ROI (return on investment).

When Republic needed to create more cash flow, they decided to spin off Jack Nadel International by combining it with five other divisions into a subsidiary. When the public offering failed to happen because of a bad market, I proposed a plan to buy back the company plus the other five divisions in what was later known as a leveraged buyout.

The key was to convince the bank to lend the money to my new company in order to make the deal. Their confidence was in me and my reputation.

HOW DOES THIS TIP APPLY TODAY?

One of the greatest examples of "luck" in business surely has to be the story of NutraSweet. The now common artificial sweetener was discovered by a G.D. Searle & Company researcher named James Schlatter, who was part of a team diligently working on developing amino acids to help treat ulcers. In the midst of his work, he licked his finger to help turn a sheet of paper and was surprised to find that his finger was sweet. Instead of discarding the new substance, he realized the potential in artificial sweeteners and started to develop aspartame. The timing couldn't have been better, as the country was in the midst of an uproar over the potential health dangers associated with saccharin. The market was primed for a new artificial sweetener. Knowing a good thing when they tasted it, management at G.D. Searle translated one lucky find into FDA approval in 1974 and thus launched one of the market's most successful artificial sweeteners. Oftentimes in business, success is a matter of translating "luck" into hard results.[34]

TIP 38

Confidence breeds success, and success breeds confidence.

Inexperienced businesspeople in movies are sometimes told, "Fake it until you make it." While this makes for witty dialogue, there's also an element of truth to it. Customers, employees, and colleagues are attracted to confidence. The trick, of course, is to deliver on your confidence, which will in turn inspire more confidence in you. This is exactly the kind of positive, self-reinforcing cycle that good businesses depend on for growth.

FROM THE JACK NADEL ARCHIVES

The first steps in business are scary. It gets easier as you grow. My method of growing Jack Nadel International was to proceed from one arena to another. It's like advancing the pieces on a chess set: The more you move, the better you are equipped for the next move. Expanding my business from Los Angeles to San Francisco was a major move that taught me a great deal. That success made it easier to go across the country and then the globe. Being successful at one stage of business equips you mentally and financially to make the next leap.

HOW DOES THIS TIP APPLY TODAY?

Raising money for a start-up company is the ultimate act of confidence— especially when your company plans to compete in a 60-billion-dollar market against some of the world's best-known brands. But that's exactly what Tamar Yaniv set out to do in 2012 for her company, Preen.Me. According to Yaniv, Preen.Me was founded to give women "objective recommendations" about beauty products and help them buy the products best matched to them. As with any new venture, she needed funding. "As for securing funding, I honestly don't think there's any magic formula behind it," she said. "So much of it is the ability to keep going back day after day, pound the pavement, and continue to have confidence in what you're doing." This confidence certainly paid off for Preen.Me, which raised $800,000 in seed funding from major venture capital firms and was able to successfully launch.[35]

TIP 39

Money attracts good people,
but pride makes them great.

The professional incentive industry is devoted to discovering ways to inspire and motivate employees to perform better, whether they're in sales, engineering, or even management. Over the years, incentive experts have conducted dozens of studies on how to best motivate people, and they have made an interesting discovery: Money does not top the list of motivators. Instead, the single most motivating factor for most people is public recognition of their work. Never underestimate the power of instilling pride in your employees—they will work harder, smarter, and better.

FROM THE JACK NADEL ARCHIVES

Forty years ago, we created a sales incentive program for our account executives in which those who achieved certain goals came to be called Golden Tigers. Earning the status of Golden Tiger became very desirable because it included extra bonuses and a special trip for all the Golden Tigers over a long weekend. Winners were not only proud of themselves but took enormous pride in the accomplishments of their peers.

HOW DOES THIS TIP APPLY TODAY?

Jon Katzenbach thinks he knows why Southwest Airlines is able to consistently rank at the top of its industry in both profitability and customer satisfaction—and it's not because of the company's snazzy paint jobs. According to Katzenbach, author of *Why Pride Matters More Than Money*, Southwest Airlines cultivates an aura of achievement and success throughout the company, from baggage handlers to the executive suite. The company publicly rewards high-performers, allowing them to express themselves naturally (which is why flight attendants have been known to sing safety instructions), and generously awards free airline travel to employees. The result is a company that has been able to outgrow and outperform almost every other airline in the heavily unionized airline industry, in which pay scales are fixed for most of the workforce.[36]

TIP 40

Competition breeds innovation and is usually good for everyone.

The term *creative destruction* is often used to describe a free-market economy. It's a simple and quite beautiful idea: The free market unleashes creative entrepreneurial potential that constantly seeks better, cheaper, and more attractive ways to do things. Creative destruction can be wrenching, especially when companies and industries are caught by surprise and plowed under by competitors. If you can learn how to harness the incredible power of an economy that is free to continually reinvent itself, you will succeed in business. Competition sharpens companies and makes them better.

FROM THE JACK NADEL ARCHIVES

For years, IBM towered above all competition in the computer business. When Apple, Dell, and Hewlett-Packard challenged the giant with new and innovative products and services, the market expanded for everybody. When the consumer has many choices, the whole world benefits. Open competition forces all companies to do better.

HOW DOES THIS TIP APPLY TODAY?

Several companies offer sun-blocking clothing lines. Columbia Sportswear is one of the largest. However, there is only one that carries approval from the Food and Drug Administration (FDA): Solumbra. Shaun Hughes, the founder of Sun Precautions, survived melanoma and vowed to create a fabric that would shield users from dangerous exposure to UVA rays. Existing fabrics could provide only partial protection, of SPF 30 to 50. Hughes's Solumbra line of outdoor wear provides sun blocking of SPF 100. His personal health crisis motivated him to improve a very competitive market and set the bar higher. No matter your business, it always pays to watch the competition closely and look for ways to gain an advantage.[37]

TIP 41

The inability to make decisions can destroy a company.

Our modern business climate is clogged with information. In fact, a new term has sprung up to describe it: *big data*. Big data refers to the avalanche of information that flows over businesses every day, driven by cheap computing power and the seemingly limitless reach of the Internet. Unfortunately, big data and information overload can get in the way of effective decision making. It's tempting to spend too much time poring over data and trying to interpret what it all means without considering the human element. Good managers gather as much information as they need (and not more), consult experienced mentors, and then make a definite decision. Afterward, they track the results of their decision so they'll be informed the next time a similar situation crops up.

FROM THE JACK NADEL ARCHIVES

I mentioned that while working in Europe, I discovered that a huge number of expandable carry-on travel bags were being sold. Investigation told us that the bags were actually made in Hong Kong. We found the manufacturer and seized the opportunity to import a large quantity. As noted earlier, we became the first to import this expandable carry-on bag, before anybody had seen it in the United States. By introducing it, we got the bulk of the market share for this business. The timing was perfect, as the following year the bag dropped in price. As more importers entered the market, we moved out.

Experience tells you that a remarkable new product that is not patented or branded will definitely be "knocked off." Because this kind of merchandise has a narrow window of opportunity, an immediate decision is required; if you move fast enough, you can get the majority of the business. Likewise, it is critical to time your exit from the market, before you're stuck with a lot of inventory that's losing profit and collecting dust.

HOW DOES THIS TIP APPLY TODAY?

Alexa von Tobel had a lot of things going for her when she started her business, including a powerful group of mentors. In 2009, von Tobel launched LearnVest, an online resource to help young women navigate the world of finance and investing. When she started her business, von Tobel did two of the smartest things any entrepreneur can do: She wrote a business plan, and she recruited A-list advisors like Betsy Morgan, former CEO of Huffington Post; and Catherine Levene, former COO of DailyCandy. Her mentors not only helped her attract financing and gave her tips to help manage the company, they even advised her about site content and brand messaging. The result? The young entrepreneur made *Inc.* magazine's prestigious 30 Under 30 list of up-and-coming entrepreneurs in 2010.[38]

TIP 42

Think global, start *local.*

Nobody conquers the world in a day. Even the most promising, borderless Internet businesses typically take months—sometimes years—to grow past their original markets. If you've got a good idea or a successful small business, concentrate first on your local market (even if that market is a niche audience online). *Learn* everything you can about your product or service, including how to sell it, and then expand slowly and deliberately. The odds are almost certain that there is a market for your business somewhere in the world, but reckless growth can be much more damaging than staying local.

FROM THE JACK NADEL ARCHIVES

I am often asked if I envisioned our international company when I started Jack Nadel International in 1953. The truth is that I put no limits on how big we would grow and never set a specific destination or time line. In the back of my mind was the idea of a global company, but on a practical basis, I knew that it would happen only one step at a time as we acquired the knowledge and resources to expand successfully.

JNI's success has a great connection with the philosophy of thinking globally, starting locally. We began as a Los Angeles company operating locally. We knew our ideas were universal and would work as well in other parts of the country and the world. At that time, the investment to expand beyond our local market would have been far too great and the chance of major mistakes very probable due to a lack of knowledge about the real conditions in various markets. By taking it a step at a time—expanding first in California, and then to the Western states, the entire United States, and the world—we now have 19 profitable offices around the globe. Our growth was financed by the cash flow that was generated as time went on. We proved that a sound business with a good business plan prevails wherever it is initiated.

HOW DOES THIS TIP APPLY TODAY?

What's more all-American than taking your hamburger joint global? If you ask Fatburger, a California burger chain with a cult-like following, nothing. In late 2012, Fatburger made waves when it signed a partnership deal to bring its famous burgers to China. By the end of the year, analysts expected that half of the restaurant's locations would be overseas, mostly in Asia. This is quite a step for a company that was first made famous by rappers such as Ice Cube and Tupac Shakur, who mentioned the restaurant in their songs. But that's part of Fatburger's success: It conquered its local market and gained a following among tastemakers before launching overseas. No matter your business, this is always a recipe for success.[39]

TIP 43

Age and senility do not go hand in hand.

In our never-ending rush forward, there is sometimes the tendency to think that technological innovation can replace experience and wisdom. But this just isn't true. Computers, smart phones, the Internet…these are all tools. And just like a carpenter's hammer, they can be used wisely or foolishly. So don't discount the advice and experience of people who have "been there and done that." Sometimes a simple conversation with an experienced mentor can prevent you from making a serious mistake.

FROM THE JACK NADEL ARCHIVES

Throughout my long career, I have witnessed the effects of aging and of changing conditions. In our modern society, we don't give enough credibility to experience. Sometimes we discount the wisdom of older people because they do not seem to be accepting of new ideas and technology. For this reason, a younger executive might dismiss the powerful advice of an experienced pro—with potentially serious consequences.

I encourage older people to embrace new methods. The principles of good business are constant; the tools that are used are constantly changing. Regardless of age, we must always reinvent ourselves to meet changing conditions. I can no longer travel around the world for personal meetings, but the Internet has made it possible and practical to conduct business with anybody from the comfort of my own home.

HOW DOES THIS TIP APPLY TODAY?

It might be hard to believe, but one of America's most recognizable brands was conceived by a retiree who lived on Social Security and had been forced into retirement when the government decided to build a highway right through his restaurant. Of course we're talking about Harland Sanders, better known as Colonel Sanders, of Kentucky Fried Chicken fame. Sanders didn't even start trying to franchise his famous fried chicken recipe until he was 65 years old—and then it wasn't easy. He drove all over the South, cooking fried chicken and trying to get restaurants to carry his signature dish. According to legend, Sanders received more than one thousand rejections before he finally found a restaurant willing to sell his branded chicken. And the rest, as they say, is history. Within 20 years, he had six hundred franchises, and today KFC is one of the largest fast-food franchises in the world.[40]

TIP 44

The world judges me on results and not on how hard I work.

There is no award in life for "most hours at the office," but there are plenty of rewards for people who work consistently. Don't fall into the trap of giving your life over to your work—some of history's best innovators, artists, and businesspeople received their inspiration when they were completely occupied with something else. Live a rich, full life, and your business will reap the rewards.

FROM THE JACK NADEL ARCHIVES

I previously told the story of how we discovered the Watch Band Calendar—one of the most profitable items we ever made. But a great deal of hard work went into making it the product it eventually became.

When we decided to manufacture the Watch Band Calendar, we spent hundreds of hours designing presentation packages. The original product came to us with the 12 monthly calendars packaged in a clear plastic case. We designed packages by the month, quarter, and year, tailored to different industries. We had packages for pharmaceutical manufacturers, automobile dealers, insurance companies, and banks, as well as subscription services. The scorecard of success is how much money you invest and how much money you make. Nobody cares about how hard you worked or how many hours went into development; they care about the end product or service you're selling and whether it suits their needs.

HOW DOES THIS TIP APPLY TODAY?

Silicon Valley is famous for its hard-charging, 80-hour-workweek culture, so it's only logical to assume that Google—the equivalent of Silicon Valley royalty—would take pride in working its engineers nearly to death. Nothing could be further from the truth. Google recognizes the power of working smarter and of harnessing creative talent, so the company gives its engineers one day a week to work on anything they want. The results include amazing new ideas, such as Google's self-driving car, which ultimately benefit the company by stimulating innovation—even though not every new brainstorm turns into a marketable product.[41]

TIP 45

Keep it simple.

This simple tip is incredibly powerful. Don't complicate your business by adding unnecessary and redundant bureaucracy. Don't give more information than you need to. (Your secretary, for example, should never tell a client you're out golfing—even if you are!) And don't embellish your products with bells and whistles that add nothing but cost to the consumer's experience. There is beauty in simplicity, in doing something well. Some of history's most successful entrepreneurs made their money by figuring out how to deliver a simple, cost-effective solution to an everyday need.

FROM THE JACK NADEL ARCHIVES

A new supplier, in presenting his products to our sales force, spent a great deal of time talking about the factory: where it was located and the kind of superior equipment it had. I interrupted the meeting and explained that we were not interested in their statistics, just how their product compared to others in both utility and price. If someone asks you what time it is, do not tell them how to make a watch.

HOW DOES THIS TIP APPLY TODAY?

Maxine Clark is an entrepreneur who succeeded by keeping it simple. When she took a 10-year-old shopping 15 years ago, they weren't able to find a stuffed toy the child liked. She wondered why she couldn't just make one. As a result, Clark came up with the Build-a-Bear Workshop. Today, stores worldwide have helped children create more than 100 million furry friends through a simple selection process that kids love.[42]

TIP 46

Honesty is not only the best policy; it's the most profitable one.

Every successful business relationship relies on trust. Being honest begets long-lasting bonds and creates better opportunities. Legendary baseball coach Leo Durocher said, "Nice guys finish last." But if you examine the records, he didn't finish first too often himself. Respecting the dignity of others has never been a deterrent to success. You can prosper in business without lying or cheating. Truthfulness and transparency are strategies for the long run.

FROM THE JACK NADEL ARCHIVES

When I hired my kid brother, Marty, as a salesman, I was aware of the fact that he was the nicest guy I knew. I also knew that he was totally honest and wouldn't resort to shortcuts. This "nice guy" broke all sales records and eventually replaced me as president of Jack Nadel International. Despite the belief that nice guys finish last, this one finished first. Being open and trustworthy is an especially vital asset in highly competitive markets.

HOW DOES THIS TIP APPLY TODAY?

It is said that the cover-up is often worse than the crime. That can definitely be true in the high-stakes world of business. Think of some of the business scandals that have made headlines in recent years, from Merck's cover-up of the medical problems associated with its blockbuster painkiller, Vioxx, to the off-the-books debt that eventually brought down Enron. These prominent cases became symbols of a business culture run amok, but they offer lessons for businesses of any size. When something goes wrong, it's always better to be open about it and quickly move to fix it. If you don't, the consequences can be devastating.

TIP 47

Deals are like buses. There is always another one behind the one you just missed.

Don't despair when you lose a deal that you really thought you wanted. It will probably be followed by another proposition that is even better. If something doesn't feel right, take note. The rapid pace of change today ensures that new or improved processes and products are appearing all the time. In other words, opportunities are abundant.

FROM THE JACK NADEL ARCHIVES

In the closing round of negotiations for the purchase of the building we had hoped would house our direct-mail company, there was a series of misunderstandings. I felt sad that the other side was inflexible and the deal collapsed. The very next day, I received an offer from another broker for a property that was actually superior, and we bought it. Everything about the deal that we consummated was better than the deal that we lost.

HOW DOES THIS TIP APPLY TODAY?

History is littered with famous examples of people who missed the "big deal." For example, did you know that there was a third co-founder of Apple, Inc., in addition to Steve Jobs and Steve Wozniak? His name was Ronald Wayne, and he wrote the original partnership agreement for the company as well as the manual for Apple's first personal computer. He even designed the famous Apple logo. Two weeks after helping found the company, however, Wayne sold his share to his partners for $800 and thus begged off a personal fortune that would likely have been in the billions. When asked about it later, Wayne had no regrets. "I was going to wind up the richest man in the cemetery," he said. Instead, he took a job with an electronics company and later wrote a book, *Adventures of an Apple Founder*. Looking back on missed opportunities and missed deals is a waste of time and energy. Instead of thinking about the past, keep focused on the future and what's around the next bend.[43]

TIP 48

Time is your most productive asset, and it cannot be recovered.

If there is one word that sums up today's business world, it's probably *busy*. Everybody is busy. Between the 100 emails you might get daily, the texts and tweets you have to pay attention to, and the phone calls, it's possible to spend a whole day very occupied but completely unproductive. Aggressive time management is the solution. Guard your work time like a lion protects her cubs. Some managers check email only once an hour. Others rely on sophisticated time management software to plan their schedule and track where their time goes. Whatever your strategy, make sure you control your day, not the other way around.

FROM THE JACK NADEL ARCHIVES

When I first took on the job of running six companies at the same time for Republic Corporation, I had to depend on a monthly report from each division president. The reports contained too much detail, so I created a new rule: All reports had to be no longer than one page. When challenged by one of the division presidents that there was too much information for one page, I took out his last report and showed him how much unnecessary detail was in it. Then we made a list of the facts that were required in these reports; if I wanted further details, I would ask for them. I told him the problem with the long report was that he had to take the time to write it, and I had to take the time to read it. The division's efficiency improved dramatically.

Part of the task of running a business is to determine whether you are operating at top efficiency. When you are monitoring a process, the first thing to do is determine if that process can be eliminated or minimized.

When I started to run a factory in France, the original design allowed for workers to be in different cubbyholes, where no one could see what they were doing. To create efficiency, I had all the walls removed and situated various operations where I could easily see what was going on from my office. I did not have to monitor the activity of the employees... the fact that I could *was strong enough to enforce the discipline needed.*

HOW DOES THIS TIP APPLY TODAY?

The figures are sobering: According to IT Business Edge, U.S. organizations lose $1,250 annually per computer user due to lost productivity. Most of this time is spent dealing with spam, unnecessary email from coworkers, and poorly written communications. At the same time, the average working adult gets less sleep than recommended and, according to *Bloomberg Businessweek*, 60 percent of all meals are rushed. The truth is, we are a harried nation of people with too much to do in too little time. That's where time management comes in. Before you burn out, think hard about your schedule and even invest in time management software to help track where your efforts are spent. A balanced life is good for business.[44]

TIP 49

The trip to success should be as much fun as arriving at the destination.

No one ever said success was easy. Often, the road to monetary success is stressful and difficult, with frequent setbacks and obstacles. That's why it's especially important to enjoy every minute of the journey, particularly your achievements and accomplishments, no matter how small. Enjoy the fruits of your labor and look for positive lessons in the challenges you encounter. None of us knows how long we have in the game of life, so if you aren't enjoying the process of earning your success, you might be on the wrong path. Never postpone enjoyment in your life by working for the promise of success.

FROM THE JACK NADEL ARCHIVES

I can honestly say that I have never spent a boring day in pursuing my career. More importantly, I have even enjoyed those hours of uncertainty between creating and executing a deal. One of the secrets to enjoying what you do is to recognize the humor in every situation. And true enrichment comes from the friendships that are formed.

When I once had a problem in Europe, I mentioned it to a client from Belgium. He told me he would fly to meet me the next day to help in any way he could. When he wasn't able to get a flight, he drove from Antwerp, Belgium, to Cannes, France, just to help me. His actions reinforce my basic idea that all business is personal.

On our honeymoon in 2005, my wife, Julie, and I traveled to many foreign countries, where we were welcomed by old friends with whom I had done business for decades. The cultural benefits of traveling abroad were greatly enhanced by these personal relationships. Many of these business friends are still in the promotional marketing industry and have grown with the times along with Jack Nadel International. We share a common bond, one that has no language barrier or time limitation: the enjoyment of success.

HOW DOES THIS TIP APPLY TODAY?

Richard Branson never seems like he's having a dull moment, despite amassing a fortune of $3 billion and building such companies as Virgin Airlines. For Branson, it has never been about the money—instead, one of his major rules in business is to have fun. This helps explain his unique approach to business attire (no suits or ties), publicity (jumping from airplanes), and even media appearances (where he laughs at his own image and compares himself to Peter Pan). We don't all have to be as eccentric as Branson, but there is still wisdom in his example. If you're not having fun in your business, you're probably in the wrong line of work.[45]

TIP 50

Pass on your secrets to the next generation.

One of the great fallacies in the business world is that success is limited, that there is a finite amount of it. In fact, some of the most successful people are also the most generous with their contacts, knowledge, and expertise. A rising tide truly does lift all boats, and your knowledge and experience might just help someone dramatically improve his or her life and business. You'll never lose anything by sharing your ideas and secrets for excellence—you'll only deepen your relationships and give back to the world in important ways.

FROM THE JACK NADEL ARCHIVES

My motive in writing this book is to pass on what I have learned to as many people as possible who can benefit from my experience. They say, "You can't take it with you." This applies even more to ideas than to money. One of my greatest joys is when I witness the success of people whom I have mentored.

The main thought I would like to leave people with is that we are blessed with the ability to think. Even at the age of 89, I find that I am constantly rethinking problems that have not yet been resolved. I realize that one of the greatest issues we have is dealing with the rapid changes in today's world. What worked only a few years ago does not necessarily work today, so the ability to make adjustments and even change course has to be part of our skill set. Although the principles remain the same, the ingredients keep changing. In the modern world, one size does not fit all. Human beings are all different, and we face different problems. Compassion, intelligence, and understanding have to be part of the overall solution. When I was a child, my mother, poor as we were, taught us to share what we had, to spread good ideas, and to feel a sense of responsibility to others. Those principles still work today and are needed now more than ever, in this globalized world.

HOW DOES THIS TIP APPLY TODAY?

Oprah Winfrey isn't just one of the most successful entrepreneurs and entertainers in America, she's one of the most famous and public of mentors. Oprah has long believed in mentoring. She has said her own personal mentor is Maya Angelou, and she has given back in spectacular fashion. The list of people Oprah has helped includes Dr. Mehmet Oz, Dr. Phil, and untold girls and women, including the hundreds of girls who attend her Oprah Winfrey Leadership Academy for Girls in South Africa. "A mentor is someone who allows you to see the hope inside yourself," Oprah says. In 2012, some of that hope became real when the Oprah Winfrey Leadership Academy graduated its first class of 72 girls. So after you've achieved your success, don't be afraid to give back and help the next generation. You'll never regret it.[46]

Special Thanks

*...to all the people at Jack Nadel International
who have perpetuated and extended
the entrepreneurial spirit for the past 60 years.*

NOTES

1. "The Walt Disney Company History," *Funding Universe*, http://www. fundinguniverse.com/company-histories/the-walt-disney-company-history/.

2. Peter Pachal, "Remembering Steve Jobs: His Best Keynote Moments," *PC*, October 8, 2011, http://www.pcmag.com/article2/0,2817,2394358,00.asp.

3. "Iams Buys a Stake in VPI," *dvm360*, http://veterinarynews.dvm360.com/ dvm/article/articleDetail.jsp?id=46993. Kelly Roper, "Iams Pet Insurance," *LoveToKnow*, http://dogs.lovetoknow.com/wiki/Iams_Pet_Insurance.

4. "Emeril Lagasse," *Biography*, http://www.biography.com/people/ emeril-lagasse-9542380.

5. "P90X History, How It All Started...," *Extreme Body Workout* (blog), July 1, 2008, http://www.extremebodyworkout.com/blog/2008/07/01/p90x-history-how-it-all-started/. "P90X," *Wikipedia*, http://en.wikipedia.org/wiki/P90X.

6. Adam Bluestein, "Case Study: Targeting the Right Market," *Inc.*, October 2011, http://www.inc.com/magazine/201110/case-study-targeting-the-right-market.html.

7. Mary Catherine O'Connor, "Q&A: Lorenzo Thione, Cofounder of Artify It," *SmartPlanet* (blog), May 29, 2012, http://www.smartplanet.com/blog/ design-architecture/q-a-lorenzo-thione-cofounder-of-artify-it/6545.

8. Peter Wolf, Hakeem Jeffries, Luis A. Ubiñas, and Luke Beatty, "College Roommates, Rich and Famous," *The New York Times*, July 23, 2010, http:// www.nytimes.com/2010/07/25/education/edlife/25famousroommate-t.html.

9. Jennifer Rooney, "In Dell Social-Media Journey, Lessons for Marketers About the Power of Listening," *Forbes*, September 25, 2012, http://www. forbes.com/sites/jenniferrooney/2012/09/25in-dell-social-media-journey-lessons-for-marketers-about-the-power-of-listening/.

10. "Got a Good Strategy? Now Try to Implement It," *Knowledge@Wharton*, April 6, 2005, http://knowledge.wharton.upenn.edu/article.cfm?articleid=1173. Zac Frank and Tania Khadder, "The 20 Worst Product Failures," *SalesHQ*, http://saleshq.monster.com/news/articles/2655-the-20-worst-product-failures.

11. Jon Burgstone and Bill Murphy Jr., "Sausage vs. Meatballs: A Study in Start-ups," *Inc.*, April 3, 2012, http://www.inc.com/jon-burgstone/the-epicurious-case-of-currywurst-bros.html?nav=next.

12. Casey Hibbard, "How Social Media Drew 27,000 More People to the Races," *Social Media Examiner*, February 3, 2011, http://www.socialmediaexaminer.com/how-social-media-drew-27000-more-people-to-the-races/.

13. "Energy Brands," *Wikipedia*, http://en.wikipedia.org/wiki/Energy_Brands.

14. Jon Burgstone and Bill Murphy Jr., "How to Build a Brilliant New Venture," *Inc.*, July 31, 2012, http://www.inc.com/jon-burgstone/how-to-build-a-brilliant-new-venture.html.

15. Jon Burgstone and Bill Murphy Jr., "Squeeze More Juice out of Your Business Model," *Inc.*, April 24, 2012, http://www.inc.com/jon-burgstone/cameron-hughes-wine-innovative-business-model.html.

16. Glenn Rifkin, "How Harley Davidson Revs Its Brand," *strategy+business*, October 1, 1997, http://www.mbadepot.com/external_link.php?ID=7697. (Requires free registration.)

17. "Nerves of Stainless Steel: Auto Maverick John DeLorean," *The Selvedge Yard* (blog), May 29, 2009, http://theselvedgeyard.wordpress.com/ 2009/05/29/nerves-of-stainless-steel-auto-maverick-john-delorean/.

18. "General Counsel and Law Industry Insiders Chronicle Rapidly Changing Legal Services Industry in 'Unbound,'" *PRWeb*, April 3, 2009, http://www.prweb.com/releases/Unbound/David_Galbenski/prweb2295104.htm. Darren Dahl, "Case Study: Was Outsourcing to India the Right Move?," *Inc.*, January 1, 2006, http://www.inc.com/magazine/20060101/handson-casestudy.html.

19. "Our Story," *TONI&GUY*, http://www.toniandguy.com/pages/category/about-us/our-story.

20. "Microsoft Case Study: Optimizing Cross Platform Ad Effectiveness," *Nielsen Wire* (blog), June 22, 2011, http://blog.nielsen.com/nielsenwire/online_mobile/optimizing-cross-platform-ad-effectiveness/.

21. Paul Chaney, "Word of Mouth Still Most Trusted Resource Says Nielsen; Implications for Social Commerce," *Social Commerce Today*, April 16, 2012, http://socialcommercetoday.com/word-of-mouth-still-most-trusted-resource-says-nielsen-implications-for-social-commerce/. "Why Cirque Du Soleil LOVES Word of Mouth for Pre-Show Awareness," *WOMMA*, http://www.womma.org/casestudy/examples/preproduct-launch-marketing/why-cirque-du-soleil-loves-wor/.

22. Frank Watson, "Yahoo Rejects Microsoft: Worst Decision Ever?," *Search Engine Watch*, May 9, 2008, http://searchenginewatch.com/article/2066473/ Yahoo-Rejects-Microsoft-Worst-Decision-Ever. Jay Yarow, "Yahoo Is So Cheap Right Now, It's Basically a Free Takeover Target," *Business Insider*, August 9, 2011, http://articles.businessinsider.com/2011-08-09/ tech/30019666_1_carol-bartz-yahoo-share.

23. "Negotiating with Wal-Mart," *The Negotiation Experts*, http:// www.negotiations.com/case/negotiating-wal-mart/.

24. "Public Trust in Business," *Business Roundtable*, http://www.corporate-ethics.org/initiatives/public-trust-in-business/.

25. Hamilton Nolan, "Domino's Strikes Gold with 'Our Pizza Sucks' Campaign," *Gawker*, January 13, 2010, http://gawker.com/5447282/dominos-strikes-gold-with-our-pizza-sucks-campaign. Charlene Li, "The Art of Admitting Failure," *HBR Blog Network* (blog), March 28, 2011, http://blogs.hbr.org/cs/2011/03/ the_art_of_admitting_failure.html.

26. Edward O. Welles, "Ben's Big Flop," *Inc.*, September 1, 1998, http://www.inc.com/magazine/19980901/995.html.

27. "Lehman Brothers Holdings Inc.," *The New York Times*, April 4, 2012, http://topics.nytimes.com/top/news/business/companies/lehman_brothers_ holdings_inc/index.html.

28. Carole Matthews, "The World's Best Employee Manual," *Inc.*, January 24, 2003, http://www.inc.com/articles/2003/01/25083.html.

29. Mike Masnick, "Football Helmet Maker Drives Competitor into Bankruptcy with Patent Lawsuits," *Techdirt*, September 24, 2010, http://www.techdirt. com/articles/20100914/12133511006/football-helmet-maker-drives-competitor-into-bankruptcy-with-patent-lawsuits.shtml.

30. "Our History," *Boston Scientific*, http://www.bostonscientific.com/ templatedata/imports/HTML/AboutUs/History/history.html.

31. "W. Edwards Deming," *Wikipedia*, http://en.wikipedia.org/wiki/ W._Edwards_Deming#Key_principles.

32. Dawn McCarty and Beth Jinks, "Kodak Files for Bankruptcy as Digital Era Spells End to Film," *Bloomberg Businessweek*, January 25, 2012, http:// www.businessweek.com/news/2012-01-25/kodak-files-for-bankruptcy-as-digital-era-spells-end-to-film.html.

33. Eric Barton, "Hallmark's Hairball: A Former Artist Told How He Didn't Get Sucked Down Its Drain," *The Pitch*, May 21, 2008, http://www.pitch. com/plog/archives/2008/05/21/hallmarks-hairball-a-former-artist-told-how-he-didnt-get-sucked-down-its-drain.

34. Ned Smith, "Good Luck in Business Is Hard Work," *BusinessNewsDaily*, May 29, 2012, http://www.businessnewsdaily.com/2592-luck-role-business-success.html.

35. Angie Chang, "Interview with CEO Tamar Yaniv, Co-Founder of Preen. Me, After Raising $800K Funding for Her Beauty Startup," *Women 2.0*, October 10, 2012, http://www.women2.com/interview-with-ceo-tamar-yaniv-co-founder-of-preen-me-after-raising-800k-funding-for-her-beauty-startup/.

36. "Why Pride Matters More Than Money," *Random House, Inc.*, http://www. randomhouse.com/book/90136/why-pride-matters-more-than-money-by-jon-r-katzenbach. Donald J. McNerney, "Creating a Motivated Workforce," *HR Focus*, August 1996, http://faculty.washington.edu/janegf/motivatedworkforce. html.

37. Mary Elizabeth Cronin, "Sun Precautions: Skin Cancer Inspires Protective Clothing Line," *The Seattle Times*, May 24, 1995, community.seattletimes. nwsource.com/archive/?date=19950524&slug=2122726. *Sun Precautions*, www.sunprecautions.com.

38. April Joyner, "Alexa von Tobel, Founder of LearnVest," *Inc.*, July 19, 2010, http://www.inc.com/30under30/2010/profile-alexa-von-tobel-learnvest.html.

39. "Fatburger to Expand Internationally with Hundreds of New Locations," *The Huffington Post*, September 18, 2012, http://www.huffingtonpost. com/2012/09/18/fatburger-international-expansion_n_1893891.html.

40. Deepak Nair, "Business Biography: Colonel Sanders," *Helium*, April 13, 2007, http://www.helium.com/items/149073-Business-Issues.

41. Joseph Walker, "The Google Way of Learning," *The Wall Street Journal*, July 5, 2012, http://online.wsj.com/article/SBB0001424052702303918204577448500101101414.html.

42. *Build-A-Bear Workshop*, http://www.buildabear.com/.

43. Brian Reed, "5 Costly Missed Business Opportunities," *Investigating Answers*, April 26, 2012, http://www.investinganswers.com/personal-finance/rich-famous/5-costly-missed-business-opportunities-4244.

44. "Time Management Statistics," *Key Organization Systems*, http://www.keyorganization.com/time-management-statistics.php.

45. "Lesson #5: Have Fun," *Evan Carmichael*, http://www.evancarmichael.com/Famous-Entrepreneurs/592/Lesson-5-Have-Fun.html.

46. "Thank Your Mentor Day: Bill Clinton, Oprah and Others Recall Their Mentor," *The Huffington Post*, November 17, 2011, http://www.huffingtonpost.com/2009/01/22/thank-your-mentor-day-bil_n_160083.html.

ABOUT THE AUTHOR

J ACK NADEL has been an international entrepreneur for nearly seven decades—and has made a healthy profit every one of those years. He has founded, acquired, and operated more than a dozen companies that have produced hundreds of new products, thousands of jobs, and millions of dollars in profits. Each of his transactions has been an adventure he loved.

From his broad and solid experience, Nadel has authored a number of popular books, including *Cracking the Global Market*, *There's No Business Like Your Bu$iness*, and *How to Succeed in Business Without Lying, Cheating or Stealing*. All were written with the purpose of helping others attain greater success with their endeavors. He has also penned one novel, *My Enemy, My Friend*, set in the intriguing environment of international trade.

In addition to pursuing his commercial enterprises and writing career, Nadel has lectured at colleges and universities, and for several years hosted his own television show, *Out of the Box with Jack Nadel*. Though insisting that he has retired, at age 89, Nadel—a decorated World War II veteran—continues to share his expertise and wisdom by mentoring future business leaders.

Jack Nadel is a happy man who leads a robust life, savoring every moment. He resides with his wife, Julie, in Santa Barbara, California, and enjoys actively supporting their ongoing philanthropic efforts through the Nadel Foundation and involvement in the local community.

CPSIA information can be obtained at www.ICGtesting.com
Printed in the USA
BVOW011905180113

310890BV00004B/6/P